IRREVOCABLE

SKYE CALLAHAN

VINCI
BOOKS

By Skye Callahan

Sins of Ashville

Irrevocable

Unbreakable

Insurmountable

She-Devil

Redline

Ignition

Torque

Brake

Exhaust

Clutch

Vinci Books

vinci-books.com

Published by Vinci Books Ltd in 2025

1

A CIP catalogue record for this book is available from the British Library.
Paperback ISBN: 9781036701796

Printed and bound in Great Britain by Clays Ltd, Elcograf S.p.A.

Chapter One

TAKEN

THROUGH THE HAZE OF SLEEP, I felt hands on me. Cold and rough. I thought for a fleeting moment that it might have been Kyle.

Then, I remembered our break up.

It had happened weeks ago, but maybe that part was the dream. My memory was fucked, and I couldn't latch onto a thought long enough to ride it out of the fog.

"Did you make a decision?" Kyle asked.

I rolled over and pulled the comforter up to my neck. I had decided that I didn't want to make a decision—mostly that I didn't appreciate him trying to force me into a decision when I had told him time after time that I didn't want him moving into my apartment even after six months together.

"You can barely afford the place anyway since your sister moved out. I don't get why it's such a big deal unless you don't want to be together."

I did, and yet, the threat of him leaving seemed like a relief….

Hands groped and pulled—rough against my skin and digging into muscle and bone. Too many hands. The bits of

1

memory faded as I tried to retreat from the onslaught. My back pressed into a hard surface beneath me, and my nostrils filled with the smell of musk and damp stale air.

I had no idea where I was, or how I'd gotten there.

I kicked and gasped, trying to get back to the surface where reality lurked. It shimmered in the distance, just out of reach, like the sun on the surface of the water during a dive.

A hand latched onto my hair and held my head back. My eyelids were finally freed from the sticky muck that held me in semi-consciousness, and I opened them to find myself staring up into unfamiliar eyes.

I only held his gaze for a few seconds—if that—but it seemed like it lasted for hours as my brain fought to categorize the details. Its useless attempt to understand what was going on.

The man clutching my hair had vivid green eyes, but they may as well have been black given the emotionless void they displayed. His hair was shaggy, brown with a mix of grey, the same colors that stood out in his unkempt stubble.

As if he needed any help looking rough.

He exhaled, and his breath settled over my face, reeking of booze and cigarettes. The smell made me queasy, but I didn't have time to dwell on that, as another set of hands tugged at my jeans.

My gaze traveled around the room, taking in the small crowd. At least half a dozen men surrounded the table where they had me spread out like a holiday feast. All dressed differently, from ragged tank tops to well-fitting dark button-down shirts, they all projected an air of unchecked danger. Necks marked with tattoos, hands covered in callouses and scars. Scruffy faces accented their sneers and

2

smirks, as they stood above me staring down with eyes starved of humanity and full of lust.

Apparently, they didn't expect me to put up a fight, because aside from the hand tangled in my hair, no one seemed concerned with keeping a tight grip on me. Probably because they outnumbered me, and I assumed they would have no problem beating the crap out of me if I struggled.

They'd downright enjoy it.

Unfortunately, I didn't fully consider how that scenario would play out. I bucked and managed to knee the one pulling on my waistband in the face. He grunted, but I can't imagine I inflicted as much pain as did his retaliatory blow to my ribs. I sucked in air and rolled, curling around the injury and gasping for each painful breath as the sickening throb exacerbated my confusion.

This couldn't be happening. All I wanted to do was curl into a ball and protect my body, but their hands kept me splayed. Helpless. I jerked, pulled, and squirmed with every bit of strength I had, but a five-and-a-half-foot girl against a circle of rabid men was a hopeless battle.

And, with my defense, I had broken the dam on their violence. Seven pairs of hands turned on me, spreading me across the table. Bony hands squeezed my arms and legs, and adrenaline took over my judgment.

I screamed, and a hand clamped down over my mouth, half-covering my nose as well. Every time someone moved the wrong way, his hand slid up, cutting off my air completely. I clamped my mouth closed, not letting another sound escape in hopes that he'd get bored of holding my mouth closed.

Where ever I had ended up, all I knew was that I didn't want to die in some dank concrete room at the hand of a group of ruffians. I'd just started living my life. I made it out of the small town to find a place where I wasn't constantly answering to someone about every decision I made. At sixteen, I had dyed my hair blue and our minister told me I was going to hell.

Well, I had found it, but I doubted this was what he'd had in mind.

Threats, insults, and random profanity echoed against the cinder block walls of the room and roared in my head propelling my struggle.

One of my shoes slipped off, giving me an opening. As that attacker attempted to readjust his grip, I straightened my leg quickly, hitting him square in the chest. He grunted and took a step back, then slammed my flailing leg against the table. The impact sent a bolt of pain up my body and for a brief moment I stilled, letting the pain radiate through me and then pushing it to the back of my awareness.

I sunk back into my mind, trying to distance myself from the pain. I couldn't believe it was real. How quickly I had gone from planning to have dinner with my friends to being groped in some dank basement by a group of disgusting bastards.

They must have thought that my pause meant I was giving up, because the one holding my arm loosened his grip and I slipped free again, this time, planting a punch to the nose of another attacker. It took him a second to shake it off, but I was instantly restrained again by yet another. The man I'd punch snarled and ripped open my shirt, then pulled a knife from his pocket and flipped it open.

The room went quiet, and I froze, watching the silver tip of the blade move closer to my sternum.

Then, a single voice rose from the back of the room. "What the hell breed of trouble are you lot causing?"

The knife jerked away, slipping below the edge of the table and out of sight. I twisted my neck to figure out who they'd all stopped to stare at. Another man dressed in dark jeans and a black tank top stood above us at the top of a metal stairway that connected to a catwalk running along the top of the back wall.

I almost regretted the interruption as it allowed the pain from every injury to rise to the surface and penetrate my body. Each breath became a struggle between managing the sharp stab of pain every time my chest expanded, and my need for air. All I wanted to do was close my eyes. It had to be a dream—the most fucked up dream I could ever imagine, but as long as I could wake up, everything would be fine.

Another man appeared on the catwalk, stopping just short of the stairs. He was also wearing black, but unlike the other men, he looked like he was groomed for a formal occasion in his tailored suit.

"The customers will hear the racket," the man wearing the suit grumbled, straightening his tie.

The racket? I thought. They were holding down a girl in ripped clothes, for goodness' sake, and he was concerned with the noise. My hope that the two new men were part of some rescue party eroded and turned into a useless lump in my gut.

"As if they aren't used to it," Green Eyes replied with a snort of laughter. "Besides, everyone is at least two levels up right now."

"You never answered Kirk's question," Suit said, leaning against the railing in a pose that resembled some kind of power shot you'd see of an executive in a Fortune 500 magazine.

I squeaked as Green Eyes gripped my hair harder. "We

5

need new meat, and conveniently, the butcher dropped this one off."

Suit shook his head and looked to the man he'd referred to as Kirk. "Take care of this."

Kirk rolled his neck and started down the stairs. "We didn't order new meat, and I don't trust unscheduled deliveries."

One of the other men leaned against the table, pressing his weight into my wrist, and I gasped, waiting for it to snap. He kept his body casual, as if he had no idea what he was doing, but then he looked down at me and winked. "It's been months since we've had any fun breaking a new girl," the man leaning on my wrist said. "So, Gabe picked her up."

Green Eyes scowled across me at the other man, while taking out his frustration on my scalp. I assumed that he was Gabe, and he didn't appreciate the other man calling him out for the transgression.

My vision clouded, leaving me lightheaded and nauseous. I closed my eyes for a second—not daring to let the monsters out of my sight longer than that.

Everyone except Gabe loosened their holds and stepped away from the table. But the threat of pain hadn't diminished from their eyes.

Pain sliced through my chest as I tried to inhale, and I silently pleaded for the new man to save me, even though he seemed concerned with everything except my well-being. At least with him in the room, the attack had ceased, but at any moment, he could leave or, even worse, simply join in and I'd stand no chance.

They all watched me, taking in my every flinch. Drinking in my pain and fear.

Kirk stood over the head of the table, leaning against it to look me in the eyes until I dropped my gaze away.

"There's a reason it has been a while." Kirk's words were smooth and calm. "You all are sloppy and when you break the rules, we end up with women that are of no use to us." He closed his hand around Gabe's arm, and the hand in my hair jerked, then released. I looked up again, catching another glimpse of Kirk's blue-grey eyes.

"We can't release her," Gabe growled. "So just go back upstairs to your work and let us have our fun."

Can't release her? The air caught in my chest, hardened, and refused to move. There was a good chance I wasn't making it out of this basement. The craziest thing I'd ever done was ride some insane roller coaster at Cedar Point—and now that seemed like no big deal. I'd never been out of the country. Never played with my unborn niece.

Never made amends with my parents and sister since our continued fighting began almost eight months earlier.

"You're right," Kirk said, his voice low and calm for someone who had just agreed that I could never be set free. There wasn't a hint of acknowledgment that he'd just sealed my fate with two simple words. Life would go on for him—business as usual. "Why the hell should you be rewarded for breaking the rules? Remember how things work. You make a mess, I have to clean it up—I'd rather start now than wait for the mess to get bigger."

"How things work…." Gabe chuckled and looked around at his crew. "Seven against one is how things currently work, or are you counting on two for your side? She is feisty."

The group of men followed Gabe's lead, many of them crossing their arms, or raising their hands in preparation for a fight, but before they could make a serious move, Kirk grabbed one by the neck. "You're right, Gabe, she is feisty. She managed to inflict at least one bloody nose, and I imagine a few other injuries. So what makes you think I'm scared of a crew who can't even manage to wrangle a single girl?"

The man in Kirk's grasp, stuttered. "We were... having... fun."

"Game's over." With one shove, Kirk sent the man stumbling backward. "And if you do want to try me, remember that even if you win, I'll be counting on the boss' gun to your head afterward. I believe you all are supposed to be working tonight, yet you smell wasted, and you're down here causing trouble. Either find a productive way to use the rest of your day or I'll send you to the dregs."

They all took a step away, watching Gabe for their next move. He shook his head and started toward the stairs until Kirk caught him by the shoulder. "You and I will have a long discussion later, Gabe."

Gabe shook him off and the men emptied out of the room, leaving me barely covered and laying on a table under Kirk's gaze. The coldness of the room hit me for the first time, clawing against my sweat-moistened skin, and causing me to shiver.

"Sit up," Kirk said. His voice was even colder than the air.

I hugged my shirt to my chest as I obeyed, then I quickly angled myself so he was no longer behind me. He was tall and sculpted with hard muscles, but from where I sat, he didn't look any less scary than the rest of them. His face had a hint of stubble around his chin, but he looked far more groomed than the clods he'd just run off. Tattoos ran down both of his arms, but my attention fell to the tribal snake that wrapped around his right forearm.

"Please," I whispered without looking up. Despite his agreement with Gabe that I couldn't be released, I hoped that he would take pity since the other men were gone. Holding on to a hopeless desire was far better than concentrating on the other images that hammered through my brain—all the other things he could do now that he had me to himself.

He walked around the table without acknowledging the request and picked up my discarded shoe. Then, he slid off my other shoe—tossing both effortlessly into a trash can in the corner.

My heart sank, and I searched his eyes for something I could latch onto, some shred of compassion, a hint of hope. His face didn't hold the brutality of the others', but it had its own carved sternness. The anger burning inside of him was almost palpable, and now that the direct cause of that anger was gone, I was left to fill in.

He took me by the arm. "You can walk?"

I wasn't sure it was a question, but I nodded, and he guided me off the table without loosening his iron grip on my arm. When we reached the stairs, I noticed the others hadn't fully dispersed; a few loitered on the end of the catwalk near a side entrance. But with one look from Kirk, they scowled and disappeared into the next room.

If he could scare off the lot of them, I wasn't sure that meant I was in better hands. Although he hadn't assaulted me... yet.

My legs shook as we climbed the iron stairs, and Kirk pulling at my arm faster than I could move didn't help. As the adrenaline wore off, my extremities felt heavier and heavier, so each step took its toll on my waning strength. I grabbed the railing to keep my balance and help pull myself up.

At the top of the stairs, Kirk jerked me in the opposite direction of the door the men had used. I heard voices, and soon, we were walking through what looked like the lobby of a five-star hotel. There were a few people sitting in corners chatting while drinking coffee, but even though my clothes were ripped and barely hanging on, none of them gave me more than a passing glance—if they even looked up to acknowledge our presence in the first place.

My mind raced too fast for me to keep up, apparently trying to make up for the time it has lost while I was unconscious. Where were we? Why was everyone okay with this?

At one point, I even wondered if we were still in the real world.

Kirk shoved me into an elevator and pressed a button for the tenth floor. The building was huge, and no matter where we were, it couldn't have been inconspicuous. The place could easily accommodate a couple hundred people, so I reasoned that there had to be people coming and going all the time. How could it not stand out? Especially with that motley crew who drastically clashed with the lush business the decor reflected.

My head ached, and I slumped against the wall, rubbing my temple. Between the pain and swelling in my body and the fog threatening to reclaim my mind, each breath and thought became more and more of a struggle.

"Do you remember what happened?" Kirk asked, keeping his voice low—almost calmingly low. A misleading façade to hide whatever beast he locked inside.

I shook my head, unwilling to give into his mock concern.

The elevator halted, and my stomach slammed into the lungs, adding to my nausea. I feared I'd lose its contents for a moment, but I managed to swallow as Kirk dragged me out of the elevator and down a hall.

"What is this place?"

"Quiet," he hissed, wrenching my arm.

"Please, just—"

He hauled me around to face him, lifting me by my upper arms. "Not listening is a good way to get yourself killed here, which is exactly what would have happened if I hadn't come downstairs to see what trouble our resident dipshits had dragged in. You have yet to be ripped to pieces or to be removed of your ability to speak. If you want to keep it that way, I suggest that you learn to obey simple commands. *Shut up.*"

I clenched my jaw. I didn't want to admit the truth in what he said, but with every breath I took, my ribs sent a sharp reminder of what *could* happen. Regardless of that warning, my brain didn't stop screaming. All I wanted to do was go home, where neither of us would have to worry about my body parts being ripped off. But, I nodded, and he pulled me forward so quickly I tripped over my own feet and wouldn't have stayed upright if not for his grasp.

He pushed open a door and shoved me into a large office where the same man in the suit who'd left Kirk in charge downstairs reclined in an oversized black leather seat behind an enormous cherry desk. Behind him a window looked out over trees and rolling hills.

What happened to the city?

Suit jerked forward, and I noticed the top of a head, covered in deep red hair. I gasped and pulled back from Kirk, but he seemed unfazed.

"Don't tell me you decided to keep their toy." Suit pushed the girl away with his foot, then stood and fastened his pants. I turned away as the scantily clad girl crawled across the floor and sat next to the desk.

How much did I have to drink? I wondered. *And where the fuck was I drinking?* I barely remembered leaving the house, let alone ending up anywhere I'd get so shit-faced that I couldn't remember the last several hours—at least. I had no idea how much time I'd lost, but it was obviously enough to get abducted and dragged out to who-knows-where.

Kirk shoved me a few steps further. "Faulted though their tactics may be, she might be a nice addition."

Suit pressed his lips together and folded his arms. He looked less than impressed and far from convinced. "She looked like a handful. She certainly managed to keep Gabe's crew busy long enough for you to intervene. Seems like the kind that's easier to break than bend, which makes her no use to us."

Suit moved toward us. I had the insuppressible urge to back away as he approached, but Kirk's solid grasp made that impossible. Everything about him read power, from his smooth linen suit to the posh office. And unfortunately for me, it was dirty power. I figured on one level I should be appreciative of that power, since it was that power that had saved me thus far—that and Kirk's undeterrable attitude. But on the other hand, I had a feeling that, like the girl knelt next to his desk, I was about to become a cog in whatever business provided him with the expensive clothes and furniture.

"We all need a challenge from time to time," Kirk said as he released my arm and stepped away, leaving me feeling even more vulnerable. I wanted to curl up into a protective ball and hope that neither of them felt like smashing it to pieces.

"So, is a challenge what you're interested in? I was

beginning to think nothing could get you riled." Suit looked me over, walking in a small circle and touching exposed flesh as he passed. I felt my skin crawl everywhere he touched, and I couldn't help but cringe. His hand reached for my hair, and I had to strain to keep from smacking it away or jerking my head back.

Then, the words slipped from his mouth that made my chest want to collapse and fold into itself.

"Take off your clothes."

I stood there blinking at him. Hoping that somehow my muddled brain had misinterpreted what he'd said. As if it hadn't been bad enough when they were ripping my clothes off, now they expected me to willfully strip without an objection.

With a single swift motion, Suit grabbed me by the throat and lifted me to my toes. "She has skewed sense of self preservation."

I struggled for air as he leaned his face closer to mine. "Is your modesty worth death?"

He released me, and I stumbled back, panting for air. He simply pointed at my shirt and held his hand out.

I slid the ripped shirt off my shoulders and threw it at his feet. He smirked, but it wasn't amusement that I saw in his eyes. Lifting an eyebrow, he waved at the rest of my clothes.

I took a breath, closed my eyes and—as slow as I dared to move—I dropped my jeans, underwear, socks, and bra to the floor. I straightened but didn't dare meet his gaze. Being naked didn't really bother me. I knew I didn't have a cheer-leader body, but I was comfortable with it. Seeing a naked woman's body was nothing to them either. Kirk hadn't even reacted to walking in on his boss getting a blow job.

The problem was in the men's sneering gazes that

reduced me to nothing more than an object to be ogled, and the vulnerability of standing in front of them with nothing to protect me from their grimy desires.

To my surprise, Suit didn't touch me again, just stared at me for a few long minutes while pacing back and forth and rubbing his hand over his chin. "Her chest is a little small, but she's not bad to look at. If you want to keep her, she's yours to train. But she better be worth it. And I'm not giving you forever to accomplish that."

Yours? My heart thudded. *She's yours*. Somewhere along the line, I'd not only lost my freedom, but also my human identity. Maybe death was better—but the fear of that finality overpowered my sensibilities.

For better or worse, I was attached to being alive.

"Have Clarence look at her and get her prepped." Suit said, walking past his desk toward the window. He ran his fingers through the other girl's hair as he passed, and she grinned up at him, licked her lips, and scowled in my direction.

A shiver coursed through my body and I wondered if it was possible to get hypothermia simply from shock. My tongue felt like it was sealed to the roof of my mouth, dehydration making it almost impossible to swallow.

"If you really want to prove her worth," Suit said slowly, not even glancing back at us. "Bring her to the Outlook *tonight*."

Chapter Two

TAKE MY NAME AWAY

I COULD BARELY HEAR anything over the pulse pounding in my ears by the time Kirk took my arm and pulled me back toward the door. I wasn't sure which part to fear more, getting "prepped" or whatever the "Outlook" was. I bent to gather my clothes, but Kirk tugged harder.

"You won't need those, and you may as well get used to that now."

My skin burned with embarrassment as he led me down the hallway completely naked. There was no one around, but the air felt foreign, intrusive, as if even it saw my indecency and took an extra effort to remind me of my vulnerability.

I kept my mouth shut, and my eyes on the floor as Kirk led me to another room. It was stark, white walls and a white tile floor. Most of the walls were covered in cabinets, and through some of the clear doors, I recognized medical equipment. I got the feeling this building was like some self-sustaining hive of iniquity.

Kirk pointed to an exam table and, still in shock and

feeling shaky, I climbed up and sat down. He placed his hands on either side of my thighs. "I don't care what your name is, and neither will anyone else."

There it was. I knew what was coming. They were going to give me a number, brand me, strip me of my identity, and I'd be just what Suit had called me—a new toy.

Kirk stepped back, but his gaze still bore into me. "I suck at naming pets, so I'll give you one chance. Make it good."

"Silver," I said. I didn't know where it came from; it was the only word that came to mind.

He lifted my hand to display my chipping silver nail polish that I had put on while I was making arrangements with my friends to have dinner. Why couldn't I remember the rest of the day? I couldn't even pinpoint the last thing I remembered. It all seemed choppy and malformed.

"Silver," he repeated, dropping my hand. "I can live with that."

I wanted to ask if he usually did this—or for him to clarify what this was, but I wasn't sure I was ready for his answers.

I especially wasn't ready for another death threat, so I stared down, wringing my hands in my lap. It was the only activity that could keep me slightly occupied and out of trouble. I couldn't imagine never seeing outside of these walls again. What had I done that had been so stupid or terrible that I woke up here?

The door clicked, and footsteps approached. I balled my hands into fists and curled my toes into the base of the table. Too afraid to physically turn and look, I watched the newcomer out of the corner of my eye. He was an older man with graying sandy hair, probably in his mid-forties. He wore an outdated Hawaiian shirt over black golf shorts, looking more like a misplaced tourist than a doctor, but he opened the cabinet and laid out his supplies on a nearby tray table. As, he pushed the table closer to the exam table, Kirk stepped to my side to allow the doctor access.

At least, I assumed he was a doctor and not just some guy they picked up off the streets.

I stiffened, but he didn't make an immediate move to touch me, instead, he crossed his arms and leaned back against the counter in front of me. "Gabe isn't going to be pleased to find you not only ruined his fun but claimed the girl as your own slave."

I kept my head lowered, watching my auburn hair shudder with every thump of my heart. I tried to follow their conversation, reminding myself that as long as they were chatting with each other, they weren't groping me, but at the same time, their casual rapport made me feel even more broken. I was the foreign element. They were set on keeping me, but I didn't matter.

"Glad Ross filled you in so thoroughly," Kirk said. "Gabe is a hot head who doesn't plan. What else are we going to do with her?"

"I get your reasoning, but I've seen his crew's work and I'd rather just avoid it all around. They have a tendency to blow off steam in destructive ways, especially when *you* feel the need to remind them who the boss' right-hand man is."

Squeezing my eyes closed, I pulled in a deep breath through my nose.

Kirk made a sound in his throat, and I heard feet shuffling. "That's how I got the job."

I opened my eyes as they both closed in on me. My back straightened and the hair on my neck rose, every instinct telling me to back away. Fighting would make the pain worse, but at least I'd be doing *something*, yet my body refused to move.

"And that's all there is to it?" The sandy-haired man smirked, continuing the casual conversation as if having a terrified woman sitting in front him was just another day at the office. "You're lucky I was here today, and you won't even have to wait."

"I doubt I got *that* lucky. It's a Saturday, where else would you be?"

"And you dragged me away from my morning with a lovely doll." I heard the old man grunt, as he moved to stand next to me and put on a pair of rubber gloves.

My eyes widened, and my body finally broke out of its frozen condition. "I—uh—"

"He won't hurt you"—Kirk squinted at the doctor and scoffed—"much."

The old man extended his hand toward my ribs.

I jerked back as Kirk moved to hold me in place. "I'm allergic," I blurted.

"Latex allergy?" The doctor stepped back and narrowed his eyes.

I nodded, waiting on the threats or violence to punish me for speaking out of turn, but as soon as I stilled, Kirk also stepped away. His eyebrows were drawn together, the first real hint of emotion I'd seen him display.

The rubber gloves snapped, slicing through my thoughts. Clarence dug around in a drawer, then returned a few seconds later with bright purple gloves. This time, he took no delay in prodding me—paying particular attention to my sore ribs. With every poke, I felt more off center. I wasn't sure if it was my brain trying to escape from the pain and the situation or the effects of whatever had screwed with my head.

By the time he was done, I was convinced that he especially liked watching me squirm and jump in pain. I wouldn't put that against anyone within these walls.

"You've never taken much of an interest in the girls," Clarence said, elbowing Kirk as he moved around me, checking everything from my throat and ears to my reflexes. "*That's* what has paid off for you. While the others play, you get ahead. Although, I'd say it's about time you learn to balance them both. Why live in a place like this if you can't indulge sometimes?"

"I indulge plenty; I just don't make a public offering of it."

"Mmh hmm, well, we'll sit back and take bets on who kills who first."

The doctor dropped a tray onto the bed next to me with empty tubes, a tourniquet, alcohol pads, and a hypodermic needle.

"What?" escaped before I could stop it. All I got was a glare, and I was thankful for that small reprieve.

I kept my mouth clenched as the doctor drew blood three vials of blood and set them aside. "Birth control?" he asked.

I nodded. "Shot five weeks ago." As soon as I handed over that piece of information I wondered if I really wanted them to know that, but it was probably inevitable since I didn't want doped up on double doses.

"Sexual partners?"

"Uh." *Answer their questions and stay alive long enough to figure something else out.* "Three."

He pulled the stirrups out of the end of the bed and my eyes widened.

"Feet up. Lay back."

"No, no…," I whispered, my body froze in shock again.

Kirk put his hand to my chest, inches below my neck and pushed me back. "You may want to hold still."

Hold still? Right. Assaulted in the basement, stripped in the boss' office, and now laid out in front of a doctor who looked like he belonged on a tropical golf course and he just wanted me to hold still.

The doctor started to lift my foot into a stirrup, but I jerked both legs up and rolled off the side of the bed. I barely managed to land on my feet, but as soon as they hit the floor, I sprinted toward the door.

Just as I grabbed the handle and pulled it open, Kirk's weight slammed into me pushing it closed again.

"We're on the tenth floor, where the hell do you think you're going?" He twisted me around pressing my back into the door with his forearm against my throat.

Fight, I screamed, but the room tilted, and it was everything I could do to keep down the rise of nausea.

Kirk grabbed a handful of hair, using it to drag me back to the table, then he lifted me up and dropped me into place. This time, he kept his hand pressed into my chest and the other on my hip as the doctor lifted my legs into place.

I squeezed my eyes closed as the doctor prodded. I was too tense to relax, but even if I could, he seemed intentionally rough and intrusive.

It felt as if his exam would never end, and I fisted my hands at my sides, trying to stay in control. *Just a little longer.* I tried to push my mind to a different place—to an escape plan.

He removed the speculum and fingers slipped inside of me, stretching until my breath squeaked out. I thought for a second he was trying to rip me open, but he pulled his hand out and I breathed in relief, until he coated his fingers in more lube and went for another hole.

20

My foot kicked up out of the stirrup, but Kirk pressed me into the bed, glowering down at me.

I returned his dark gaze until a finger slid into my asshole, and I clenched my eyes closed. Within an hour of waking up here, they were sequentially taking away everything I could possibly keep to myself.

Maybe I should have been happy that they didn't want my name to tarnish, but taking it away was just going to be another reminder of their power.

"She looks clear, but I'll let you know when the tests come back. You know the drill until then."

Kirk rested his fists on the edge of the bed next to me and leaned over. "Anything we should know—keeping in mind that we'll find out if you're lying?"

"Not unless I caught a skin disease from your dickheads downstairs." I tried to keep the words from spilling out, but my frustration was outweighing my filter.

"Want to try that answer one more time?" Kirk pulled me to a sitting position, and the room swayed and went dark. He caught me and held me by the shoulders—that was the only thing that prevented me from landing face-first on the floor.

I could hear him and the doctor talking to me, but they sounded muffled. Too far away to make out the words. I couldn't get my body to do anything; my entire existence was stuck in the muck again.

My brain panicked, making it even harder to breathe. My eyes grew heavier, and I was certain I was going to die.

I felt a blood pressure cuff fasten around my arm and tighten. My tongue was dry and sticky, but I managed one word. "Thirsty."

The doctor deflated the cuff but left it around my arm and walked to the sink. I struggled to keep my eyes open, while Kirk held me upright. The doctor handed a small glass of water to him, and Kirk pressed it to my lips, letting me sip slowly.

Slowly the volume of their voices increased again, and the darkness that had been looming around the edge of my vision faded.

"I'll test for drugs, too," the doctor said.

"I'm not on drugs," I said, as loud and insistent as I could manage, but I sounded drunk at best.

"How'd you get here?" Kirk asked.

I shook my head and managed to raise a hand to my face to rub my temple. "I have a pounding headache."

"You'll need to get her hydrated and let everything flush from her system, but if she gets worse, call me directly."

Kirk pulled me off the table and set me on my feet, keeping an arm around my waist to stabilize me. On one hand, I was grateful he wasn't letting me fall face first against the tile floor, but it also meant my naked body was pressed against his. I felt his heat rolling into me, another unwelcome intruder on my personal space.

The doctor dropped a black bag on the bed next to me. "Ross also had me grab this on my way up. Should be everything you need for a bit."

Clarence then packed up and disappeared through a side door.

Kirk paused a moment, giving me enough time to recover from the dizzy spell.

"I just want to go home," I said.

"If you're well enough to complain, you're well enough to walk." He kept his pace noticeably slower as he led me, still naked, down the hall and back to the elevator.

Oh god, I thought, hoping he wasn't planning on parading me through the lobby again. If I didn't get dizzy again, I'd probably pass out from embarrassment—possibly a combination of the two.

He pressed "9" and my chest relaxed a little. *Small victories*, I told myself. If I concentrated on that, at least I'd have something positive to hold onto.

After we exited the elevator, he led me to another door —this time, he used a key to unlock it, and pushed me in first.

An apartment, small, but without a doubt, luxurious. A leather sectional couch filled the center of the room, facing a large TV screen. A desk with a small laptop faced the wall behind the couch, and beyond that, was a kitchenette, and a large pane window that faced out over the same view as Ross' office above.

"How do you feel?" he asked.

"Still lightheaded and a little queasy."

"I'll get you some water, and I think I have some crackers. I'd tell you not to think about running, but I have a feeling that even if you did, you'd collapse before you got very far."

I nodded, allowing him to lead me to the couch where I crumpled up into a ball and closed my eyes, hoping that would help the headache. But the pounding in my forehead didn't ease. I heard a bag rustle in the kitchen, and cupboards and drawers closing. Every sound twisted in my head, seeming far louder and more annoying than normal.

Kirk returned and used his shin to push the coffee table closer to the couch. Then, he laid out a napkin with crackers and a bottle of water.

"I'll put something more substantive together for you in a while if you can hold down the crackers."

I nodded and reached for the bottle of water. "Pain medicine?"

"What hurts?" he asked draping a blanket over my body.

I wanted to glare back at him and repeat his stupid question. "My head is pounding. Ribs sore. Ankle. Wrists." I could have continued the long inventory, but when Kirk stepped away, I figured he either got the picture or didn't care.

He returned after a few seconds and dropped two red capsules in my hand. In any other situation, I'd think I was out of my mind for accepting some unknown drug from a criminal, but I popped them in my mouth and swallowed them down.

"Thanks," I said, on the verge of passing out.

I was afraid to let my eyes close. I had already woken in the middle of a nightmare once, and I feared that as soon as I closed my eyes, I'd be dropped into something even worse. Or something even more confusing than having my captor care for me and wait on me.

"Get some sleep," Kirk whispered. "You'll be safe."

"I'm lying naked in some criminal headquarters with a strange man caring for me," I mumbled. "What's safe?"

———

I DRIFTED in and out of sleep, managing to eat a few crackers and finish off the bottle of water during my inter-mittent moments of consciousness. I rolled onto my back and draped my arm over my forehead, the pain meds had lessened the pain, but it still felt like someone had smacked me in the face with the back of a shovel.

"It's not a breach." I heard Kirk say.

I opened my eyes and peeked over the couch, but he wasn't in the same room, so I dropped my head to the pillow and pulled my knees to my chest, tucking the blanket under my chin. I strained to hear the rest of the conversation, latching on to his mumbled words as they floated through the room.

"It was minor, and she's definitely not a threat, but I'll be keeping my eye on her anyway…. Milo doesn't have to worry about it…."

Me? I wondered how I could possibly be considered a threat to this place. Especially since they definitely weren't letting me go anywhere. I reached for the bottle of water, and remembered that I had already finished it, so I closed my eyes again, hoping that sleep would give me a few more moments of peace. But the bedroom door swung open, and I started at the sound of something landing on the desk behind me.

The following silence lasted a few seconds before I heard him approaching. I wanted to tense up, but I tried to keep my body lucid enough to appear to be sleeping and hoped he hadn't seen me flinch. He didn't stop, picking up my water bottle on the way toward the kitchen. A few minutes later, he replaced it with a new bottle and walked to the desk behind me.

"Thank you," I whispered, knowing that as soon as I reached for the bottle, he'd know I was awake anyway. I wanted to keep him on my good side.

"How long have you been eavesdropping?"

I took a long swig of water to wet my throat and give myself a moment to consider my answer. "I heard the door open." It wasn't quite a lie, but I hoped he wouldn't press it.

"How do you feel?"

"My head is still pounding, but it's better…" My voice trailed off again, the darkness coming for me again, but I had a bigger problem. My bladder felt like it was about to explode from all the water—and yet I was still dying of thirst. And I had been putting off the bathroom issue for as long as possible. "I have to—" *Just spit it out, he's already seen you naked and felt up by a sadistic doctor.* "I need to use the bathroom."

"First door," he said.

That was easier than I had expected. I rolled to my feet, but my knees gave way, and I caught myself on the couch arm. Kirk moved toward me, but I willed my legs to work before he got close enough to touch me.

"Leave the door open," he called after me.

"Right because where am I going to go?"

He raised an eyebrow.

I flipped on the bathroom light—it wasn't as if there were even any windows for me to escape through, so I wasn't sure what the hell he didn't want me doing in here behind closed doors.

Not in any particular hurry to get back to the living room when I was done, I stood in front of the mirror, taking in the bruises that circled my wrists and shoulders, and the massive purple spot that covered my right side.

I turned on the sink and scrubbed my hands, digging out all the grime from under my fingernails. It was the most of their filth I could get rid of at the moment.

I cupped my hands and splashed the water over my face, then reached blindly for the hand towel.

I jumped when it landed on my shoulder.

"I take it I'm not allowed to wash my face without your permission either."

Kirk grabbed my chin, yanking my head back. "Washing your face is fine, but your smug taunts are only going to lead to pain."

He released me, and I rubbed the towel over my face

before catching the stray droplets that had run down my neck and chest. I wished he'd stop looking at me. Even with my face covered, I could feel his eyes on me. I'd been alone with him and naked for—I didn't even know how long.

My stomach grumbled, and I dropped the towel to stare down at the traitor. I had much higher priorities than food. Not to mention I still felt a little nauseous.

"Do you think you can eat?" Kirk asked.

I rubbed my eyes and shrugged. I did, but I wasn't telling him that, and I wasn't going to ask him for food.

He walked me back to the couch, apparently suspicious that I'd somehow disappear through the floor or a wall and left me there as he went into the kitchen. I leaned against the arm of the couch, listening to the sound of his footsteps as he moved around. Now that he and I were alone, the odds had evened out.

Aside from the fact that he was still bigger, stronger, and even if I managed to get away from him, there were eight floors and who knows how many people between me and freedom, unless I could find a fire escape.

And clothes.

I squinted at the door—it had a double cylinder deadbolt, so it required a key to get in and *out*. Yet another inconvenience that didn't bode well for me.

Kirk handed me two more pills and sat down a new bottle of water and a sandwich wrapped in a napkin. Either he didn't do dishes, or he didn't trust me with a plate. As he leaned over, I noticed the keys dangling from his belt loop. All I had to do was manage to get them off and figure out which one opened the door without him noticing.

He returned to his desk, giving me a few minutes to eat in silence, but my mind was so busy trying to process everything else. I could have been eating cardboard on rye. And the pounding in my head wasn't making anything easier. I left the empty napkin on the table and nestled back under the blanket. "You think Gabe drugged me?"

I heard the squeak of his chair move then the couch shifted as he leaned his arm against it. "I'd guarantee it. Unless you make a habit of taking drugs that make you pass out."

"I've never even smoked pot." I met his eyes, barely managing to keep my own open. Whatever I had been given was a stubborn enemy, and now that my stomach was full, it threatened to pull me back into the darkness.

"Do you remember anything from last night?" he asked.

I shook my head. Every time I got close to a memory, the thoughts seemed to pull away. "I remember having lunch at a coffee shop to check my email," I mumbled. I realized the words were coming out, but I wasn't sure why I was saying them out loud and I couldn't stop myself. "I think I went home. I had plans to meet some friends for dinner, but I don't remember if I even made it there. I can remember being on a sidewalk...." Some things were becoming clearer, so I hoped that by the time the drugs wore off I'd at least remember something helpful.

Although helpful to what effect, I wasn't sure. Figuring out how I got here probably wasn't going to get me out.

"It was dark, and a car came around the corner with bright lights. I put my hand up to block the light. And I think that's the last thing I remember." My words started to run together. Whether or not I had anything else to say, my tongue was giving up the battle. I curled against the arm of the couch and felt the blanket brush gently against my skin as Kirk covered my bare shoulders.

The movement a contrast to the chaos I felt inside, but still a reminder that nothing I knew mattered anymore. Fear was supposed to be completely set apart from anything gentle and comfortable, but here I was lying on a soft couch wrapped in a warm blanket. My brain couldn't comprehend why, after I'd been kidnapped, and not a single person had shown an ounce of compassion for my well-being, I was currently being treated with gentleness.

Deep inside my gut, I knew it didn't bode well, and I still had no idea how to escape the dark fate that threatened to suffocate me within these walls.

Chapter Three

BAIT AND TRAP

I OPENED my eyes then jerked up to look around the room. It took my brain a few seconds to recognize the surroundings, before my shock melted into disappointment. "It wasn't a dream...."

"Sorry," Kirk said.

My heart thumped in my chest, and I twisted to see him sitting at the desk behind me.

"You're feeling better?"

The fog and nausea had definitely lifted, but I wasn't sure that made anything better. "I think it wore off, but I still have a headache."

I looked around trying to find a clock. I had no idea how long I'd been here, or how long I'd been sleeping.

"It's only been about three hours since I gave you the last pain pills, so you'll have to wait a bit." He said, as if recognizing the questions in my head. "It's almost seven o'clock and I have to go take care of a few things before we head up to the Outlook tonight."

The Outlook. How vague could anyone possibly be? "You

wouldn't happen to be willing to tell me what going to the 'Outlook' entails?"

"Dinner." His quick and simple answer didn't seem contrived, but it wasn't comforting either. I hoped he meant real food and wasn't using it as a vulgar euphemism.

"And what's for dinner?"

He gave me a sideways glare. "I have no idea, probably steak, maybe chicken. That's what they normally serve during business dinners."

I exhaled and relaxed a little. At least I wasn't going to be the main course, and hopefully a business dinner meant there would be more talk than paying attention to me.

Unless I was the business they were attending to. God, I begged my brain to shut up. So far, all of its ideas and conclusions had simply landed me in more trouble.

"What? You thought on top of everything else that we're going to cook *you* for dinner?"

"No." I scoffed. "I thought you were just using it as a sexual metaphor."

He pressed his lips together. "You haven't even been cleared yet. You just have to sit, *silently*, and look pretty. You'll kneel on your knees at my feet, keep your hands in your lap, and your eyes on the floor in front of you."

Now that I was breaking free of whatever had polluted my system, the full reality of the situation set in, tightening in my chest. I pictured myself, at some fancy dinner where everyone at the table wore suits and I sat naked on the floor next to Kirk's feet. "I can't do this."

"If you want to say alive you will." His tone was even, as if my begging didn't faze him in the least.

I jumped off the couch and backed away from him. "What you want me to do isn't living."

He took a quick step toward me, I stumbled trying to

keep my distance, but it was too late as his fingers knotted in my hair, yanking me back and slamming me into the opposite wall. With little effort, he pinned me there with only one arm and his bodyweight. "Make your choice."

I kneed him in the groin, and as he stooped backward, I jumped toward the door, remembering too late that I needed a key to open it.

I spun around, but as soon as I did, my back hit the wall beside the front door. He pressed against my body, so I couldn't leverage another attack and pulled the keys off his belt. "You want out?"

I bit my tongue, tasting blood. I knew it was a trick question. There was no right answer and even if I did answer, he already seemed set on his path. He slid the key into the lock. I heard every pin slide and click into place, and then it squealed as the bolt released.

He jerked open the door and shoved me out into the hallway. I stumbled and before I caught my balance the door closed behind me.

Oh, fucking hell. I looked up and down the hallway. *You got the escape you wanted.*

But I knew it couldn't be that easy. I started for the elevator, waiting for one of the other apartment doors to open. I was already in the fucking cage. No redemption here.

I would have sworn that anyone on the floor could hear the thumping in my chest as my bare feet slid across the carpeted hallway. I didn't dare break into a run, because I was just as scared of what was ahead of me as what was behind me.

The more I thought about it—the more I thought about Gabe—what was ahead of me was far more terrifying. Running for the door was the stupidest idea yet.

The elevator dinged, and I pressed myself against the wall. It wasn't going to help anything, but at least I didn't feel exposed on all sides. My useless limbs trembled, and my throat tightened as the elevator doors opened and a huge man with chestnut skin stepped off the elevator. He smirked when he saw me.

"Disobedient slave looking for a home?"

God, no. I shook my head and slid against the wall, back toward Kirk's room. I bumped against a man's chest and jumped away. I hadn't even realized Kirk had opened the door, let alone stepped out into the hallway.

The dark-skinned man reached for me and I ducked backward managing to make it past Kirk, but then I heard the deadbolt of the door next to me release.

Not another. I dashed back toward Kirk. *The enemy you know....* The phrase flashed through my mind. I didn't know whether it had any weight, but in the current situation I'd take the one who let me sleep relatively unharmed on his couch and gave me food and water instead of trapping me on a table in the dank basement.

Even if I had just pissed him off.

As I stumbled away from the opening door, the dark-skinned man caught me and shoved me into the wall.

"She is a nice addition to the collection."

"Please," I cried, knowing it was useless that anyone around here would care about my requests. I had nothing to bargain with that they wouldn't take by force either way. Large hands pawed at me, effortlessly blocking all my attempts at fighting back. His forearms were so big I wasn't sure my fingers could even wrap half way around.

His large forearm pressed against my neck, threatening to cut off my airway if he pressed just a bit harder, his hip immobilized my body, and he twisted so that one bent knee

33

rested across my legs, preventing me from kneeing or kicking him.

He'd obviously done this before. And the position left his other hand free to grope my naked body. I tried to shove his bulky hand away, and he pressed harder against my throat.

My body bucked and jerked, craving more oxygen than it could get through my pinched throat.

"Behave," he growled.

I pushed my strength into the wall, forcing my body to stop fighting him, and he released my throat.

"I'll have a turn," said the blond man from the other side of the hall. He leaned casually against the wall, watching my attack.

One hallway and I was already up against three men.

There was no way in hell I'd ever make it nine floors down and out of the lobby. I had to bide my time. Find a back way or some path that wouldn't cross with half a dozen men on the way out.

That depended on my ability to survive long enough. *Survival*, I thought. If I had anything on my side it was obstinacy—sometimes blind obstinacy that got me in deeper, but I didn't go out without a fight. The problem was that here, the fighting, kicking, and screaming that I wanted to do was going to get me killed.

Or worse.

The third man took another step toward us, and my chest shook until I had to close my eyes and remind myself how to breathe. I was pinned and struggling only made me more exhausted.

"Want to play?" The dark-skinned man pulled me from the wall, moving me to stand in the middle of the group. He held me against his body with his arm around my neck, while his other hand trailed down my naked sternum, over my bellybutton—

My hands were free but tightened into useless fists at my sides. I was more afraid of what would happen if I fought. Tears burned at my eyes as my body shivered. No matter what I did—if I fought, if I gave in—the pain was going to come.

His hand moved between my legs, and he smacked my inner thigh, forcing them apart. I bit back a scream and pulled my lower lip between my teeth to keep my mouth closed.

"Go ahead and scream," Kirk said. His arms were crossed over his chest. This was my punishment, he'd let whoever showed up do whatever they wanted to me. "Maybe you can get the attention of all the other men on this floor."

"And the one below," the one holding me said and chuckled.

The third man who had been mostly silent rubbed at his own growing erection through his pants.

My vision darkened, but I held on to one last hope. Maybe I could at least delay the inevitable. As the grasp around my neck loosened, I grabbed at my last chance, throwing myself at Kirk's feet.

"Please, I'll do what you want." The operative word being 'you'. One man I could possibly handle. Three would leave me ripped apart—body and soul.

I expected the other two men to grab me. To drag me back into the middle of the hallway and have their way, but everyone went still.

Horrifyingly still.

I kept my head down, my fingers wrapped in the hem of his dark jeans. I waited for the order. Waited for him to tell them to haul me off and give them the go ahead to rip me apart.

But he crouched in front of me, snapping my head back with a fistful of my hair. "You wanted out."

"No. I was stupid. I shouldn't have." *The only way you survive is if he keeps you.* It wasn't a guarantee, but it was better than the alternative. One quiet piranha was better than an entire lake full.

He yanked and twisted me before releasing my hair, and I toppled to the floor on my side. My arm and hip burned from rubbing against the carpet, but my attention to the pain was quickly replaced, by the images flashing through my mind. Laying sprawled on the floor with three men glaring down at me was too similar to waking up in the basement.

There were fewer men, but now I was completely naked. Exposed for them to do as they pleased. A new wave of nausea pounded at my gut and it took some effort to swallow it down. Pulling myself back to my knees, I grasped at Kirk's leg.

Just take me back in the apartment. Please. My mind begged —shouting the words that wouldn't break free from my mouth.

A foot against my ass knocked me forward into Kirk's legs.

They snickered and jeered as I tried to regain my balance.

I was nothing to them.

Just a toy, like Suit said. And they were like a bunch of bratty rich kids who knew that every toy was replaceable.

My sobs vibrated through my chest but not a single tear came. My gaze fluttered up to meet Kirk's.

"Please," I whispered through my tight throat.

As I pulled myself to my knees, the muscular arm of the man behind me tightened around my throat again, pulling me backwards as he lowered his mouth to my ear. "I think you'll have to do better than that if you want your *Master* to keep you. But if you like, we can find you different accommodations."

He pinched my nipple, then rubbed his palm over it and gave my breast a hard squeeze. The blond who'd been waiting for a turn cleared his throat, and Kirk shot him a scowling glance waiving him off.

It was my first bit of hope. Maybe Kirk wouldn't throw me to any of the others.

"I am sorry." My voice cracked.

The arm tightened around my neck, then released again. It couldn't have been a coincidence that the man holding me had stepped off the elevator while I was in the hallway and proceeded to play into Kirk's interest.

"I'm sorry, M-Master." I was on my knees begging the man who saved me from the kidnappers to *keep* me captive. My brain tried futilely to come up with another solution, weighing how many people in this building could be like Kirk, against how many could be like Gabe. "Please, let me stay with you, Master."

Kirk flipped his hand at the man behind me, and I was released. Not even my pulse pounding through my veins was enough to make me feel alive. I was a pile of flesh and bone that happened to have a heartbeat.

Kirk pulled me to my feet then shoved me through the open door to his apartment. I landed on my hands and knees, adding another set of carpet burns to my list of injuries. Then, a stinging impact came across my ass. I bit my bottom lip to keep in the scream and scurried farther into the apartment.

After a second, the door slammed behind me and an arm came around my stomach lifting me up and carrying me under his arm into the bathroom. "I don't have time for this shit. If you want to live, don't be an idiot and we'll get along fine."

He turned on the shower then dropped me to my feet and with the sudden impact, my stomach decided that it had enough.

"I'm gonna puke." I slapped my hand over my mouth and rushed to the toilet, heaving a few times before my nerves calmed enough for my stomach to settle. My body shook as I lay back against the cold porcelain tile.

Kirk handed me a small paper cup full of water, and I took a few sips, hoping it didn't set off the same reaction again.

After a few moments—as long as I dared to take, I climbed to my feet and Kirk gestured for me to get in the shower.

I stepped over the tub wall into the hot water that beat down on my head and chest. I closed my eyes, emerging myself in the cleansing stream. Kirk handed in a wash cloth and a white bar of soap, so I scrubbed everywhere, concentrating on every inch of flesh the men had touched.

"What am I supposed to call you?" I finally got up the nerve to ask over the sound of the falling water.

"Master," he answered without a hint of emotion. "Everyone else calls me Kirk—that bit of information might be useful if you don't want everyone thinking you're a total idiot."

I peeked around the edge of the curtain to see him emptying the contents of the black bag and setting them out on the counter. Two butt plugs, lube, what appeared to be two wrist cuffs and a collar, and a few items I didn't recognize.

Ducking my face under the stream to hide the tears I feared would finally break, I wished the water was hotter. That it might sear away everything or at least distract my mind from the train wreck happening in my neurons.

After I washed out my hair, and rinsed all the soap from my body, Kirk reached in and turned off the shower, handing me a towel.

"Get dried off then lean against the counter."

Oh god, what now? I rubbed the towel against my skin, weighing my fear of having him snap at me against my fear of whatever he had in mind next.

He stood, arms crossed, leaning against the counter. For someone who wanted me as a sex slave, he didn't actually seem the least bit interested in me standing naked in front of him.

I tried to convince myself that was a good thing. If he had no interest in me, then…. Then, it was more likely he'd pass me off to someone else. Why couldn't one thing lead to a positive scenario?

I dropped the towel and moved slowly toward the counter.

"Lean forward, rest your forearms on the counter," he said, pressing his hand against my back between my shoulder blades. I stiffened, trying to stay straight, but he slammed me forward, and pinned my legs with his knee.

With his hands on me, it all sank in. Sex slave. My insides coiled and then stretched out again. The heat of embarrassment twisted in my stomach and burned my face. Kirk pressed my butt cheeks apart and I dropped my forehead to the counter to absorb its coolness, as I watched him pick up a bottle of lube.

"You're staying here while I take care of a few things before dinner. Don't cause trouble unless you want me to recruit a babysitter for you." As he spoke, he casually slipped a lubed finger inside of me and I shoved my head into my hands. He was gentle, and the fact that it didn't hurt made it all the more humiliating.

"Understand?" he asked while pushing his finger as deep as it would go.

I heard his words, and understood the question clearly, but my mind was elsewhere. Flashes of the people I'd never see again—if I survived this and made it out, I wondered if I'd ever want to see them again. How long could I stay here and still face reality?

"Answer," Kirk growled, pulling my wet hair down my back until my back arched and I had to face him in the mirror.

"I understand."

His finger slipped out of my ass and was replaced with something cold, smooth, and much larger. He pressed and the deeper it went, the larger it became, stretching me until my body rebelled. I jerked—as if there was anywhere I could retreat. My scalp ached as he pulled my hair keeping me in place, and my ass burned, stretched, and throbbed, refusing to yield.

I knew he was going to have his way, but my body had yet to get the memo.

"Relax," he instructed, as if the tip would help.

Oh, yeah, sure. Inside my head, the snarky reactions wouldn't stop, but I attempted to catch them before they slipped out of my mouth and doomed me to another burst of Kirk's temper.

Master's temper. I tried the title out in my head and it sounded just as ridiculous as when he'd said it.

He released my hair, and I slumped forward until my forehead touched the marble counter top. *One breath... two...* I kept counting, concentrating on numbers and breaths, trying to push the pain and tension to another place.

He pressed the plug deeper again, until I involuntarily tightened. My hands fisted, digging my nails into my palms. My hips dug against the edge of the counter and I barely managed to keep myself from squeaking in pain. I wished he would just get it over with, but he waited again.

Five breaths before he moved again.

He pulled the plug out then, pressed a bit more and the stretching was replaced with more pain. The newest jolt stayed with me, even after he drew back the plug. Throbbing, aching, I wished the counter top was soft so I could dig my fingers into it.

Kirk's other hand slipped between my legs and my knees buckled against the cabinet as he found my clit. I gasped, pressing my forehead harder into the counter.

I needed some kind of escape—an impossible escape. Anywhere to hide.

One, two, I started counting again. I had no idea where my last count had left off. I had to get away, to find somewhere safe where my body wasn't being used and I wasn't being humiliated.

The pressure in my ass grew then suddenly eased, and my eyes popped open.

I could still feel it, the uncomfortable pressure. The sensation wreaked havoc on my nervous system. It wasn't pleasant, but it wasn't entirely painful anymore either.

"Stand up," he said, washing his hands from touching me.

I watched him in the mirror, not daring to look at him directly, but he barely looked at me. I felt like nothing to him—a dirty toy that he didn't really want but felt obliged to care for anyway.

He picked up the silver set of cuffs that he'd laid out on the counter, each wrapped in bands of gold like elegant bracelets. He secured one around each of my wrists with a silver lock. Next, he secured the matching collar around my neck. They were cold and unforgiving, but loose and skinny enough to be tolerable.

"There's a tracker inside each one. So even if you managed to get past everyone in the building, an alarm would sound as soon as you hit the perimeter, and the guards would track you down before you made it much farther than that."

I stared down at the silver shackles. Slowly, my hope was fading.

"Come on," he said, pulling me along and slipping his index finger into a hook on the collar as he grabbed the black bag.

He led me out of the bathroom and through the next door into his bedroom. A large oak bed frame—at least a king size bed, possibly larger—dominated the room. He dropped the bag on the foot of the bed and pulled out a long length of chain.

My stomach twisted, and I went weak, slamming into his chest as I fell.

Kirk laid me on the bed and rolled a blanket up to raise my feet. I was moderately aware as events passed but it seemed more like a waking dream where only bits of reality filtered in around the foggy and warped edges. The effects weren't as extreme as what I had experienced in the infirmary, but I still felt lightheaded and disconnected.

"You get these spells often?"

I shook my head.

"How do you feel now?"

"What do you care?" I scoffed, rubbing my hands over my face.

Kirk picked up my wrist and felt for my pulse. "I can't have any fun with you fainting all the time."

Well, then, I thought, *maybe I should have said that it happens all the time*. But even if he didn't want an unconscious woman, something told me the others would have no qualms with taking advantage.

Kirk took a deep breath. Although he was acting concerned, his lips sat firm in that straight line they'd been in all along. He knelt next to the bed, then rose and attached the end of the chain to my wrist.

"Was lunch yesterday the last time you remember eating?"

I almost smarted off again—*that's what I said earlier*. At least I was fairly positive that we'd already had a conversation about what I remembered. "Aside from what you've fed me, yes, that's all I remember."

"Are you allergic to anything other than latex?"

"Rabbits and ragweed."

He pressed his lips together, obviously not impressed with answers that meant nothing in his world. Without another word, he disappeared through the door.

"What if I have to use the bathroom?"

"Hold it until I get back," he yelled back.

I tried to sit up to take a small drink, but the butt plug shifted with every small motion, filling me with sensations that balanced on the border between pain and pleasure.

Kirk stopped at the doorway and looked back. "Don't even consider taking out the plug, or the next one will be much bigger, and I'll make sure you can't move at all."

I nodded but Kirk remained in the doorway like a statue

while I pulled the blanket around myself and laid out the food beside me. Then, he closed his eyes, exhaled, and pushed away from the doorway, approaching the bed again. I stiffened, pressing my head into the headboard.

Kirk touched my skin, directing my gaze to meet his. "Yes, Master. Thank you, Master."

"Yes, Master." I had to swallow my pride to force it out, reminding myself he'd saved me from a worse fate. "Thank you, Master."

———

AFTER HE LEFT, I had nothing better to do than stare at the ceiling. My joints were swollen from the abuse. My ribs and stomach ached, and every time I moved to relieve them, the plug shifted and pressed against a new set of nerves.

It gave me a firsthand understanding of why uptight, condescending people were described as having sticks up their asses—it was fucking miserable and they needed someone to take it out on.

I rubbed my hands over my face. Even after the shower, I felt dirty and violated. If I could have scrubbed off my first layer of skin, I would have, and the plug only served as a constant reminder of how far a person could fall in a single day.

"I'm never apologizing to her. It's not my fault she can't keep her damn pants on." The last words I had uttered to my mother two weeks earlier ran through my head.

"Do you two even remember why you're fighting?" she'd replied.

I did. Even eight months after she packed up and moved out, I remembered exactly why we were fighting—because after she squandered half of her rent money to go out and get drunk with her ex, I told her to grow up and stop acting like an idiot teenager or move out.

I needed to find something to keep my mind occupied. To keep myself from ripping my hair out at the thought of never going home to them.

I rolled to my side, trying desperately to find a way to relieve some of the pressure, but every movement excited nerves I had never felt before.

I wondered if I could take it out, and replace it before Kirk came home, just to get some momentary relief. But there were two major problems. The first was that it took him a good deal of work to get it in and I didn't think I was capable of repeating it on myself. And the second was that he could walk back in the door at any minute.

Or he could be gone for hours, but I doubted that, since it was already half past seven and we'd have to go to dinner sometime.

Find a way out, I reminded myself. I needed something besides the pressure in my ass to worry about. I pulled at both cuffs, attempting to slide my hand out, but they were too small to slide past the base of my thumb. I yanked at them, then the chain, looking for some kind of weakness. Even if I couldn't exploit it now and get out of the room, I thought I could find something that might be of use later, but everything was solid. The cuffs although small, were strong, which left the lock, and I had the lock-picking skills of a tortoise.

I flopped onto my back and looked around the bare room. One vague picture hung on the wall, more like something that would be found in a hotel room rather than a man's bedroom. The table nearest me held a lamp and alarm clock, the most interesting features to the room.

I slid the drawer open and found a stash of condoms. I

45

rolled my eyes, given what I'd already seen, it wasn't very surprising. Below the condoms was a black notebook with a plain cover. As tempting as it was, he probably had the condoms laid on top so he'd know if anyone was nosing around.

Sneaky bastards are like that, I thought.

Every way I rolled was just as uncomfortable as the last, so I rolled off the bed to my feet. The plug pressed uncomfortably in me and my stomach clenched. Ignoring the discomfort, I dragged my chain over the nightstand to look out the window.

Trees and grass. When I looked straight down, the height made me dizzy for a moment. I hated tall buildings. When I was on the ground, they always felt like they were crouching over me, trying to crush me with their massive presence. Being inside the large building wasn't much different.

I concentrated on the rest of the view, but there wasn't a single identifying characteristic I could find to narrow down my location. I rested my face against the warm glass. The sun was just beginning to set, and I could see the purple prequel to twilight creeping over the horizon. Kirk's bedroom seemed to face Northeast, I knew that much, but it wasn't enough to be helpful.

I stumbled back to the bed grateful that no one was around to see my bow-legged struggle. Lying down on my stomach, I hoped to alleviate the sensations. I let my arm hang off the bed, following the chain down to where it connected—not with the bed—with a large hook fastened to the wall. I pulled and twisted at the hook but couldn't budge it barehanded.

It was becoming more and more apparent that every

struggle and half-formulated plan was a waste of time and energy.

Chapter Four

EXPOSED

THE BEDROOM DOOR SLOWLY OPENED, and I peeked over the blanket. I simultaneously wanted to lurch across the room to punch him in the face and hide under the bed.

"Want me to remove the plug now or after dinner," he asked.

I stared back wondering what the hell I was supposed to say. *Please, Master, I love it so much, let me keep it?* I couldn't believe people got off on this shit, although the ones who did were probably in very different situations.

Instead of being smart about the situation, my brain hopped to the crudest thing that popped up first. "I have to piss."

Kirk rubbed a hand over his short hair. Then, he lowered his eyes to me in a dead stare. "Try again."

My mouth refused to open. It was stupid and childish to push him, but I was too frustrated to be compliant.

"Fine." He turned away. "I'm going to have my shower. If you piss my bed, I'll take payment out of your ass when I get back."

"Please," I called after him. Thanks to detoxing from whatever Gabe and his gang had slipped me, I'd had so much water I couldn't possibly hold it. Especially if he was on the other side of the wall with the shower running. My voice wavered. "Please, let me go to the bathroom."

I hoped that would be enough, but he leaned against the door frame and waited.

So, I closed my eyes and added in a whisper, "Master." As simple as the concession seemed, I felt something inside me whither a bit more.

He nodded and came back to me. "I guess that'll do for now." Pulling a key from his pocket, he freed my wrist. Then he helped me up and released my arm. I took a step, knowing it had to be too good to be true that he was letting me walk through the apartment on my own.

"Crawl," he instructed.

I swallowed and turned back. His face was still stoic, eyebrows raised and daring me to argue. I was still seething from forcing the word "Master" out of my mouth just to be able to use the bathroom, but that was in no way going to be the end of the downgrading humiliation. "Is this how you get your jollies?"

"You're going to become very familiar with how I get my jollies." He stepped toward me and I dropped my gaze to the burgundy carpet—as if it could offer a solution.

It didn't and neither did my screaming brain, so I dropped to my knees. I closed my eyes and put my hands on the floor, then crawled all the way to the toilet and stared it down. The last time I'd been eye-level with one, I'd caught swine flu from a co-worker. And much like then, all I wanted to do was curl up next to it and rock myself into a peaceful oblivion.

When I reached the living room again, I felt the

emotion surge up from my gut. Frozen in the middle of the living room floor, the anger and uncertainty choked me. I managed to keep quiet, hoping I was quiet enough that Kirk didn't notice anything. After a few long shaky breaths, I calmed myself enough to sit back and rub away the tears. I blinked up at the light a few times, forcing back the remaining tears until I was composed enough to face my captor again. When I crawled back into the bedroom, Kirk was laying on the bed, his ankles crossed as he toyed with the chain.

All the things he could do with that chain flashed through my mind—beating me with it stood out the most. I knew Gabe wouldn't hesitate, but I still wasn't sure about Kirk.

I hesitated near his feet and he dropped the chain. "Come up here."

The only way to get onto the bed was over him, unless I took the small path of empty mattress below his feet, but that would have left me vulnerable to getting kicked, if he wasn't particularly amused with my attempt to avoid him. So I moved closer, to where he patted the bed.

I stood, and he caught my leg as I lifted it onto the bed, positioning me so that I straddled his lap, my bare pussy against his jeans. The position pushed the butt plug up at a new angle and I bit the inside of my cheek to keep from making a noise.

He put one hand on each of my thighs as he looked me over. "They did a number on you this morning," he said with a sigh. My tired muscles absorbed the heat from his soft touches as he examined each injury, but when he reached for my face, I jerked back.

"Hate me all you want, Sugar," he said. "I'm the only ally you have."

"Ally...?" I whispered. "You're going to hurt me." I challenged him, hoping he'd argue. Even a small attempt at correcting me or proving me wrong.

"I am," he replied, so quickly that it smashed what was left of my hope. He lifted me off his lap and pushed me across the bed as he moved to stand behind me. "Ass up."

I clutched the bed sheets as he pushed my face down into the mattress and manipulated me until I sat back on my heels. He pulled at the plug and I tensed. It was bad enough inside, but if coming out was as bad as going in, I'd rather it just stay where it was.

"Don't tense. It doesn't matter how you feel, the only thing you have control over is your body. Learn to make things easier—and less painful—on yourself."

The plug gave with a sudden plop and he pulled it free, leaving me feeling awkward, used, and empty. What might have been a second of relief inspired new trepidation—no plug meant he was free to insert other things. Instead, he smacked my ass cheek and told me to roll over, chaining my wrist again.

"I'll be back in a few minutes then we'll get ready to go up to the Outlook. I trust that you can say quiet and obedient through dinner?"

"Yes, Master." My stomach grumbled in response to the mention of dinner.

TEN MINUTES LATER, Kirk returned to the room with his hair still wet from the shower, and a towel draped around his waist. He opened the closet door and tossed the towel into the corner. I lowered my head, whether it was embarrassment or just stubbornness, I didn't want to see his naked form.

At least that's what I told myself.

Curiosity got the better of me and my gaze wandered up his body. Another snake tattoo decorated his leg, running from his ankle up to his knee. The tribal tattoo on his left shoulder extended around, touching his shoulder blade. Not a bit of him wasn't sculpted and toned. His back muscles contracted as he slid into a black short-sleeve button down shirt, then I got a full-frontal view as he threw a pair of black jeans onto the bed.

"You're blushing, Sugar," he teased as he slid on a pair of boxers then yanked on the jeans. "What am I going to do with a slave as red as a beet?"

I looked down at my hands, keeping my jaw clenched shut.

Kirk huffed and walked out to the living room, returning a few seconds later with a bundle of red material. He unlocked my wrist cuff and pulled me to my feet. "I assume you can dress yourself."

I grabbed the pile of red fabric and turned my back to him. Nothing more than lingerie—a lacy bandeau top with a matching skirt. It barely came to the bottom of my butt cheeks, and it did nothing to hide any of my bruises. A mesh overlay hung to the front of the skirt, designed to be pulled up and laced around my neck with a choker of silk ribbon. I pulled my hair and twisted it, so it stayed on my shoulder while Kirk tied the choker.

Kirk studied me for a second—looking at me more like he was examining some specimen in a zoo, than a girl in lingerie—then jerked his head to the door. "Bathroom."

I took a step, and he cleared his throat. My stomach twisted as I looked over my shoulder.

"Until further notice, you crawl."

I wasn't sure how long I could tolerate the feeling that I meant absolutely nothing.

I dropped to my hands and knees and shuffled to the bathroom. I was going to have a bitch case of carpet burn soon, and that wouldn't be the worst of it—my clothing wouldn't cover much of anything if I had to crawl through the hallways.

At the bathroom counter, he pulled me to my feet by my silver collar and handed me a comb and a bag of cosmetics.

"We'll probably have to round up some stuff that matches your skin tone, but this will do for tonight."

I glanced wide eyed at the bag of makeup. I could barely apply eyeliner on a good day without looking like I had drunk five too many cups of coffee. And that was the pinnacle of my makeup skills.

I dragged the comb through my hair then applied a light foundation and red lipstick that almost matched my dress. I sorted through the eye shadows and eye liners.

"Look, I really have no idea what I'm doing here," I sighed.

Kirk handed me the black eyeliner, and I traced my eyes as best I could. It was still jagged and uneven.

He lifted my chin. "You're going to have to work on that, but you're lucky the room will be dark. Let's go."

With a leash attached to my collar and me crawling like an animal on my hands and knees, he led me to the elevator and up to the twelfth floor. As soon as the doors opened, it looked like we were in the middle of a millionaire's night-club. There was glass all around, even in the floors and ceiling. Men and women dotted the room—many of the women kneeling on the floor or serving food and drinks to others.

There was no violence, no commotion. The slaves tended to follow their men around, and either sit at their feet or crawl into their laps—generally looking *content*.

Their contentment nauseated me. I wanted to run up to all of them and shake them until they saw what was happening.

Kirk jerked my leash, and I realized that I'd stopped in the center of the room. I pushed myself forward, following him to a center room that was encased in glass. Above, the moonlight shined through the glass ceiling, and below, sections of the floor had been replaced with glass, over-looking the sex scenes below.

My stomach clenched, and I must have jerked the chain, because Kirk pulled it up and glared at me. He took a seat and pointed to a spot near his feet. "Sit."

I did, keeping my head down so he wouldn't see my glare while he unfastened the leash and draped it over the back of his chair.

"I'm surprised you've made such fast progress, Kirk." Suit said, as he took a seat at the head of the table with a trio of women around his feet.

I clenched my teeth—the anger flowing through my nerves created the sensation that I could rip out of my own skin at any moment.

Two more men entered and sat across from Kirk, followed by the same dark-skinned man who'd joined forces with Kirk in the hallway and a blond-haired slave at his feet. When he sat, the girl immediately sat on her heels before him.

Another wave of nausea rolled my stomach, almost choking me. I felt off balance and disconnected from myself, like my body had been taken over by some distant instinct. Only survival mattered, not the revenge or escape that swirled in my brain.

Kirk tapped my temple and pointed to the floor in front of me, reminding me that I was supposed to keep my gaze on the floor in front of me. Now I was reduced to something only worthy of crude hand gesture.

I am not a damn object to just sit at your feet and obey! But, instead of speaking my thoughts, I dropped my gaze, knowing that if I screwed up in front of all those people, I was done.

"Finally found a girl worthy of your feet?" A brassy tenor voice said from behind me.

"She was unintentionally acquired."

I couldn't believe how many times I could be reminded of that in a single day. I had a "Master" who didn't even want me, and I couldn't help but wonder why he even bothered. It would have been easier for him to shove me off and let me be someone else's responsibility.

Except that wouldn't be as effective in pissing off Gabe, and I suspected that was his main goal.

I heard the men behind me snicker. "Do you think Ross just keeps him around because he talks like a damned professor?"

I peeked up and saw Suit smile, I assumed he was Ross. He touched the heads of two of the slaves at his feet and pointed to the two lone men behind me.

I tried to take in as much as I could without being obvious, hoping to find some clue or weakness that would help me escape, but all it did was serve to show me that there were even more people around than I had imagined—and every one of the men would probably bring me right back if I dared to run. And, they'd eagerly stand in line to beat me if I messed up.

Kirk nudged me with his foot and I stilled, returning my gaze to the floor. Even that wasn't helpful since there was a glass square a few feet away overlooking a room where two men shared a curvy redhead.

I couldn't do that—I couldn't do this.

Hard as I tried to fight it, my pulse spiked, and my body shook with equal parts anger and fear.

Above me, a conversation continued between the men, as casual as a family getting together over pork chops. My chest clenched as I wondered what they'd do when they noticed my anxiety. Then came another flash of anger at their disinterest in any of us. We were there to do their bidding—whether it was kneeling at their feet and being completely ignored or putting on a show. Like a toy set up with limited functions. Perform on cue but wait on the shelf until someone tells you to do otherwise.

Two women in black leather bikinis served platters of food to each of the men at the table. I felt my stomach rumble in response to their neglect. As if it wasn't bad enough that none of the men cared, not even the other slaves seemed to acknowledge each other's existence. Above, the men began cutting into something that smelled like steak—apparently Kirk had been correct—and my mouth watered.

"Is the new girl going to perform for her dinner?" One of the men behind me asked.

I lowered my head even more, so that my hair fell around my head and hid my glower. And, I hoped, my fear.

"Not tonight," Kirk said. "It's her first day, and she's still working on the basics."

I had half a mind to show him basics. If he wanted to treat me like a dog, I could growl and bite his finger off.

Instead, I dug my nails into my palms, momentarily taking my mind off everyone else.

"Yes," Ross drawled. "First day and already causing a fair share of trouble, no less. You better train her to be worth it."

As I tried to calm the ball of tension in my gut, the conversation turned to business. I tried to latch on to what they were saying, hoping for a small nugget to help me figure out exactly where I had ended up, but it was either too vague or specific for an outsider to understand much of anything.

I learned that the men across from Kirk were brothers, Taylor and Demetri, and the dark-skinned man—the damn oaf who had helped Kirk torment me in the hallway—was Miles. He was also apparently second in command. Kirk seemed to be more of a PR intelligence man—the brains behind the twisted boss and his grimy brawn.

Lucky me. I'd been claimed by the voice of reason within their fucked-up world.

From what I could tell, the operation really was close to the self-sustaining hive as I'd guessed, but like all criminals, there was more power and money to be gained, and that required making deals. They probably had hands in the pocket of every politician, big business, and otherwise influential person in the area, which explained why the authorities weren't rolling down on the operation yet.

Just as I began to tune out, Kirk touched my cheek. I jumped and sat up to look at him. He held a piece of steak for me. Not only was I being ordered around like a dog, I had to eat like one, too. My stomach grumbled, and I decided against protest, scarfing down the food before the offer was rescinded—bits of fries, broccoli, and more steak followed.

Despite the circumstances, it was the best steak I'd ever eaten.

I snuck a peek at the other girls—all being fed the same way and apparently basking in the attention, rubbing against their master's legs and smiling as their masters patted them on the head.

I had to get out before I was that far gone.

Goals, I thought, trying to focus my thought. Kirk, well, to be honest, he could be worse. I could bide my time by being a good girl and hopefully he'd focus more on other things.

But there was still the sex…. I hoped not to be around that long, but I convinced myself that I could play along—if necessary—until I found a way out.

Then again, I couldn't play along too well. Kirk was smart enough that he'd realize something was up, or get the idea to, as one of the brothers suggested, make me "perform for my dinner." I could only imagine what that would entail, and what my mind conjured was bad enough. I didn't want to know what could be conjured by the dark minds surrounding me.

With a partial survival plan set, I felt a little more confident until Miles moved to stretch out his legs and positioned his slave between them. She unzipped his pants and took him in her mouth as if he was the most delicious desert she'd ever tasted.

There went my confidence.

I felt queasy just thinking about what they'd make me do, and now that I had food on my stomach, the nausea seemed like a more troubling problem.

Kirk touched my chin, and I shook my head as much as I dared. I kept my head down, feeling the tears threaten to brim over. At the edge of my vision, I saw him glance over at Miles as if he hadn't even noticed what was going on, then he looked back at me. His finger traced my jaw line, lowered a glass of wine, and put it to my lips.

I hated wine, but it smelled bright and fruity and I didn't delay in swallowing it down. It tasted like I had licked the inside of a barrel filled with stagnant fruit and burned my throat.

Wine for the pet. It didn't seem like anyone was surprised by the gesture and I figured there were things they were willing to concede to have a compliant pet.

His fingers slid through my hair and I stiffened. One drink wasn't going to make me that tipsy. I heard a low grunt behind me, but despite whatever was going on below the table, the men kept talking. I heard scratching as they moved things across the table above me, then the table groaned and shifted slightly.

I looked up before I could stop myself as Kirk slid his chair away from the table. I dropped my head as soon as I saw his blue-grey eyes connect with mine.

Please, I squeezed my eyes closed.

"You're not leaving already?" One of the men behind me asked.

"I've been kept from my business most of the day," Kirk said.

I heard the chain of the leash in his hand, and as he fastened it to my collar, I realized how much I was shaking in comparison to his steady hands.

He touched my jaw and I raised my gaze expecting anger, or the same straight emotionless face he always had, but there was something else there, a softness creeping out around the edges.

He looked exhausted.

My insides clenched as another chair scraped across the

floor and Miles drew the blond girl into his lap. "You work too much."

Kirk scoffed as he stood. He nodded to the men behind me and pulled me toward the door. As I crawled along behind him, I stole a glance back, noticing that the two girls who Ross had brought for the guests were now on their knees on top of the table, fondling one another.

The leash jerked, and I crawled faster—it wasn't possible to get out of that room fast enough.

———

A BUNDLE SAT outside the door to Kirk's apartment and, after he opened the door, he kicked it inside, apparently unconcerned with its contents. After locking the door behind us, he unhooked the leash then pointed to the bundle. "Take it to the bedroom and spread it out on the floor against the wall next to the closet."

"Do I have to crawl while I'm carrying it?"

"Push the damn if you want to." He draped the leash over the door knob and rubbed his hand over his short hair. "Don't act like it will be that hard."

The rolled-up bundle was taller than I was on my hands and knees, but didn't have much weight, so I rose to my knees pushed what I assumed was my new bed toward the bedroom door.

I laid it out near the closet. Even though it was nothing more than a rolled-up cushion—like a pet bed big enough for an adult human—it was soft at least, and it came with a blanket and a pillow.

It also meant that I didn't have to share Kirk's bed, so I counted that as a double win.

I spread everything out, neatly arranging the only little thing I could reasonably call my own.

My mind wandered, going over how much everything had changed over the last several hours: waking up in horror surrounded by a sex-obsessed brute squad, and being thrown into life with Kirk.

All I wanted to do was go back to normal, but it seemed so far away that I wasn't sure that would ever be possible. I had to find a way back while there was still hope—before I became a complacent slave with no hope. Until then, I'd find benefits where possible and hope that Kirk wasn't feeling frisky after watching the sex fest.

I turned to see him watching me, no doubt wondering what was going on in my head. "Satisfied?" I asked.

"I could ask that of you."

My mouth dropped open. "How would I be?"

"You're alive." He tilted his head. "And I presume, no longer hungry."

"There's that," I conceded. But if we balanced that with being forced to give up my own life and live in this nightmare, satisfied wasn't exactly how I would define it.

"How's your pain?"

I turned away and fidgeted with the edge of the bed. I couldn't figure out why it bothered me more when he seemed concerned.

"Silver, I just want an honest answer."

"I got beat up this morning. I hurt, okay. You weren't concerned with that when you shoved that plug up my ass, or when I had to kneel through dinner, or crawl through the hallways."

Kirk shook his head and disappeared. He returned and handed me two more red capsules and the rest of the water from the nightstand. Instead of just dropping them off and leaving me in peace, he crouched beside me. "I can be reasonable, but you need to stop considering the impossible. You can't go home, you can't escape, and I can't let you go. It is what it is."

It is what it is. I hated the fucking bastard. Anger tightened my muscles and tendons and clouded my brain— sending it into overdrive. "Go to hell. You don't really give a damn about me."

"Don't press your luck, Silver. I don't have time for this, but I won't stand by and watch you get beaten to death for no reason."

"But if there's a reason, it's okay?"

Kirk shrugged, I could tell he was trying to look nonchalant, but his muscles were just as tense as mine. "Your choice. Do as I say; I'll protect you and we'll get along just fine."

"I don't know whether to be offended or amused that you don't really want me here. I'm not a damned whore."

"Never said you were, but things change, and sometimes you don't have a choice in the matter."

"So, my new role in life is to stay chained to your bed all day until you decide you're horny or you want me to kneel at your feet during dinner?" My body was shaking so hard that my voice quivered with each syllable.

"I'm trying to be patient but you're cascading down my bad side. You'll do what I tell you to do," he yelled, yanking me off the cushion and slamming me into the closet door. "Beyond that, stop berating me and stop looking for a way out unless you want to learn your place the hard way."

I stood on my toes to keep him from ripping all my hair out of the top of my head. This was supposed to be the easy way to learn my place?

He pulled harder until it felt like part of my scalp would tear away.

"Okay." I squeaked. "Master. I understand, please."

He released me, and I slumped against the door, sliding to the floor as he walked away. I tried to push my hair away from my face, but as impossible as it was, it seemed like the strands themselves hurt.

"You have anything else to say?" he asked, partially concealed by the doorway.

I shook my head, and after he disappeared, I curled up on my bed, pulled the blanket over my head and tried to ignore the screaming thoughts that would only get me into more trouble.

Chapter Five

GROOMED

THE SUN PEEKING around the curtains woke me the next morning and I looked around the empty bedroom. I wouldn't have even known that someone else had slept in the room if I hadn't stirred the night before when Kirk locked my wrist to a chain connected to a hook in the floorboard before crawling into bed. There was no doubt that these rooms were set up for the men and their slaves.

And, as if things weren't fucked up enough, I was living with a criminal who made his bed.

I sat and felt the heavy movement of the chain. It clattered across the floor as I dropped my arm and flopped back. I wouldn't have guessed that tedium would have been one of the worst parts of the experience.

"You're up."

I heard Kirk's voice but didn't look up.

"I figured you were already gone," I mumbled.

He made a sound in his throat and I heard his shoes moving across the floor toward me. I wanted to roll toward the wall, to keep as much distance between us as possible, but I didn't have anywhere to go.

"I figured I should at least feed you first. Hungry?"

I was but asking him for anything made me feel even more hopeless. "I could eat."

His knee popped when he knelt beside me to unlock my cuff. He was already in a new pair of jeans—dark blue, and a V-neck shirt that clung to every rippling muscle. As he hovered next to me, I chewed on the inside of my cheek to keep all the questions churning in my mind from spilling out.

He rested his forearms on his knees, balancing on the balls of his feet. "What is it?"

"I'm keeping my mouth shut and staying out of trouble." I tried not to look at him. I didn't want to remember the things I'd seen the night before or think about all the things that were yet to come. If I looked at him, all my hate and anger would rise to the surface again.

He touched a finger to my chin, and I almost thought I could see a smile. "We both know that's not going to last long, so you may as well say what it is while I'm offering to listen."

I rolled over, trying to push myself up as my sore muscles and bones objected. *Don't do it.* My heart pounded in my throat, anticipating my mouth's inevitable betrayal of my better judgment. "Why can't you just let me go home?"

Kirk stood, towering above me. I wanted to shrink into a ball, shrivel away where he couldn't hurt me. But he was going to hurt me. It didn't matter what I did or didn't do. I at least deserved a reason why.

He grabbed my hair, and I pushed myself to my feet as quickly as possible. My scalp was already sore and at this rate, I'd be bald by the end of the week.

"Look I don't even know where we are, who you are… And I don't care. I just want to go back to my life. To my home."

"That's not an option. And you and I both know that you wouldn't keep your mouth shut for anything. There's only one way you get out of here, and it wouldn't involve going back to your life afterward."

My body went numb as I struggled for words. "I can't do this." My chest shook with every syllable, leaving my words chopped off and mangled, just like my optimism. "What I saw last night—I can't do that."

"You don't have a choice." His jaw was tight, but his voice displayed the same lack of emotion he had when he sealed my fate in the basement.

"Why'd you bring me up here?" My armor cracked, leaving me with nothing but seething agony. My skin felt tight and foreign, like it was squeezing to keep me together. "You don't give a fuck what happens to me," I yelled with every bit of strength I had left.

His hands went to his belt. My eyes widened, and I tried to duck away, but he grabbed my arm and swung me against the bed, pinning my knees against the footboard and pushing me over against the mattress. I heard his belt slip free of his pants, but the impact I braced for didn't come. Instead, he twisted my arms behind my back and looped the belt around them, tightening it then using it to pull me off the bed.

He kept my arms raised behind me, right on the threshold of pain. Every movement felt like it'd rip a shoulder out of socket. Pulling me away from the bed, he turned me to stand in front of him and nudged my chin around to face him. "Still haven't learned your lesson, huh?"

"I learned running is useless. You asked what was on my mind and I told you."

With a twist of the belt, I yelped and lowered my upper body, trying to change the angle that my arms were rotated.

"Please." My voice squeaked at the top of its range.

"Stop questioning the things that don't matter and stop begging for the impossible. When you're given the chance to talk, use it wisely." He dragged me into the bathroom and turned on the tub faucet, letting the tub fill half way.

"Decision?" he asked, knocking my legs out from under me so landed on my knees next to the tub.

I screamed as my bones crashed against the floor. Luckily the bathmat kept them from hitting solid tile, but it still shot pain through my bones and up my back. "Please, stop." My voice echoed off the tile walls and floor.

"That's not a decision." He pushed me over the tub wall leaving my face millimeters above the water. He left me there for a few seconds, and then pushed my face lower until the water danced at my nose. I had to breathe through my mouth to avoid inhaling it.

"No." I gasped, taking in a mouthful of water and choking on it. He gave me just enough time to catch my breath before shoving me down again.

I tried to kick out my legs to dislodge him, and finally, he jerked me back.

"You're fighting pretty hard, so which is it? Choose to die or fight to live."

"You don't want me to fight." The water ran down my face and neck, and tiny droplets got caught on my breath as I tried to breathe or talk.

"I don't want you to fight and continuously question *me* —the person who's trying to keep you alive."

Trying to keep me alive while forcing me to give up my

life and turn over my body and soul to his sick fantasies. "You're the person trying to turn me into a sex slave. If I shouldn't fight you, who should I fight."

"If you want to live, it's all a matter of perspective. I'm not asking you to be okay with it. You can choose to live, but beyond that the choices are mine. You simply do as you're told." He eased up and let me straighten then he pulled my hair until I had to face him. "It might not be so bad."

I gritted my teeth together, feeling the sour bile rising up in my throat. "You're sick."

His lip twitched. "Years spent in the wrong profession will do that to a person. I can always give you back to the others."

"No," I answered immediately. Given the choices available, the idea of ever having any of them lay a hand on me was the most repugnant.

"I won't deliberately hurt you unless you give me a reason. I can't say that about your other options." He wiped the mixture of water and tears from my face.

"I hate you," I spat.

"I wouldn't expect otherwise. All I want is for you to do as I say. Can you do that?"

My chest didn't want to expand to take a breath. My mind screamed, *No*, so many no's I couldn't keep up. I didn't want to be offered up to the motley crew. I didn't want to die. And I didn't want to listen to this jackass so he could take his perverted pleasures from my body.

Unfortunately, those were my only three options at the moment. And of them, Kirk was the least offensive. There was nowhere else to hide. I knew he could rip me apart—he could certainly do more than ripping out my hair and pinning me against the bath tub. But he hadn't yet. It was hard to ignore the fact that within our context he was probably downright gentle.

I nodded.

Kirk pulled me to my knees and up off the floor, slipping the belt off my wrists before releasing the plug to drain the tub. "Go to the kitchen and sit down at the table. Do not move, and do not touch anything."

I looked down at my nakedness but didn't think it was a great time to mention clothes. I didn't dare push him any further, so with a defeated sigh, I dropped to my already bright red knees, and crawled quietly out to the kitchen. I fidgeted in the seat, twisting my hands in my lap as I wrestled with my decision. When I heard footsteps behind me, I froze.

Kirk walked past me and opened up one of the cupboards, setting out a bowl and slamming the wooden door closed. He poured out a portion of cereal, covered it in milk and dropped a spoon in the bowl, then slid it across the table to me.

He sat down across from me and took a deep breath. "Ask your questions."

I choked on the first bite, the milk attempting to try a new route through my nose. "Do you want me to shut up or open up?"

"Do as I say. Let's get it over with." He leaned across the table. "No asking about getting out."

"What do the—" the word slaves echoed through my mind, but I couldn't get it out "—girls do all day?"

He smirked. "You saw what the *slaves* do last night"—he emphasized the word as if he knew I struggled to say it—"during the day, some of them stay with their masters. There are also some who stay in a common room when they're not with guests. A lot of them are thankful for their situation. They've been in worse places. We keep them fed, give them a place to live, and medical attention."

"So, in your fucked-up mind, you're a hero?" I bit my lip then shoved a mouthful of cereal in my mouth, just to keep myself busy.

"Why don't you tell me otherwise?" He stood, and I nearly slid out of my seat to the floor. "Tell me where you'd be if not for me."

"I…." I didn't want to admit it. "I don't know."

"You do know." Resting both palms on the table, he leaned toward me. "What would Gabe and his friends have done to you?"

"I don't know," I yelled louder as if that would make it truer.

Kirk didn't move.

I fisted my hands and dropped them into my lap, leaning back in my chair. "They would have beaten me."

Kirk raised his eyebrows.

My voice dropped to a whisper. I didn't want to think about the details. They'd crossed my mind, but I didn't want to allow them the validity of passing through my lips. "And raped me. And probably killed me."

As the first tear trailed down my cheek, the anger rose again. "But tell me, how is their raping me any different from what you're doing? What you're going to do? You're not beating me, but—"

"It's not," he admitted, sliding back into his seat. "But there's a big difference in the final result."

I took a slow breath, unable to believe that he'd just admitted that. The world slowed to a frightening pace while my brain raced around with images and thoughts I didn't want to consider. I took another bite of cereal, barely managing to swallow it as the emotions tightened in my throat—but at least eating gave me something else to concentrate on. I glanced up to see Kirk paying more attention to something on his phone than me.

An infuriating relief. A reminder that he wanted nothing to do with me, even though my future depended entirely on him.

I choked down the rest of the cereal and slid the empty bowl across the table. Kirk put it in the sink and rinsed it out. "I'll be here for another hour and then I have a meeting. I suggest you take care of business"—he nodded toward the bathroom—"before then."

"Can I take a shower?" I asked, hoping to wash away the filth that had coated me since yesterday. Even though I realized that most of the filth was in my head and the water wouldn't help.

Kirk nodded. "Door stays open—I don't care what you need to do, don't argue this time."

"Got it," I mumbled I started to drop out of my seat, back to my sore knees, but Kirk caught my arm.

"Sorry, Master." I hoped correcting myself before he did would earn me a smidgen of karma in his book. "I'll leave the door open, Master."

"Next time work on conviction." He released my arm. "If you can follow orders, you don't have to crawl through the apartment."

Close enough to good karma. I walked away, still cursing the fact that my lack of clothes didn't even matter. I had nothing left to hide and nowhere left to do it.

———

AS I STOOD under the hot stream of the shower, I took a

mouth full of the hot water then let the stream fall over my face before spitting the water into the drain.

Fucked and tied with no way out. Kirk knew everything about this place, yet he claimed he was only keeping me because there was no way out.

I was convinced there had to be a way; I just had to find some kind of weakness. And some way to remove the damn collar and cuffs. All I managed to do was think myself around in a circle.

I pressed my back against the shower wall as my mind ran through a futile cycle of the things I could be asked to do before I figured a way out. Taking a deep breath, I splashed a pool of water over my face, wanting nothing more than to break apart and sink into a pool of flesh and bone.

But I was too damn stubborn for that. No easy way out. No escape. And yet, I couldn't even do what I was told in order to survive.

One day at a time—hell, one hour at a time, I told myself.

I turned off the shower and pushed back the curtain, glaring at my reflection in the mirror, my body marred by black and blue marks. I wrapped a towel around myself and crept toward the open doorway.

As I entered the living room, Kirk glanced up—a quick glance as if he didn't plan on actually paying any attention to me, but then his gaze stuck, and he arched an eyebrow.

"You want me to put the same clothes on again or…?" *Do I just run around naked all day?* My brain filled in where my mouth had stopped.

"No," he sighed. "I guess you could use something else."

He stood and nodded toward the bedroom. Such a simple gesture, but every time he stood, I felt a new lump of dread. At least the towel provided more coverage than

I'd had in a while, but knowing that he was walking behind me, just out of my sight—no amount of covering would matter.

He opened a drawer and then tossed me one of his black tank tops. I stared down at it and blinked. *Bright side*, I told myself, *at least it isn't pleather or see-through.*

When I didn't move, he reached to my chest and yanked off the towel. "Let me help you with that." His voice sounded like a Mack truck driving over a patch of gravel.

Before he decided to "help" further, I stretched the tank over my head. The straps came down to my nipples, barely widening enough to hide them. The bottom hem rested halfway down my thigh. At least, it was longer than the outfit I'd traded it for, and it was soft.

"Now what?" I asked.

Kirk shrugged. "I can put in another butt plug."

I clenched at the thought. "Do I get a choice?"

His chest rose and fell, as his gaze drifted down to my chest. With a nod, he directed me to the living room. He returned to his seat at the desk near the rear wall then pointed to the floor at his feet.

"I'm not a fucking dog." This time the thought slipped out, and my eyes widened. At this rate, I knew there was no way I wasn't going to end up getting myself killed.

He barely had to move, just a flash of his eyes, and I took my position next to him, dropping to my knees. I cursed him silently as my shoulders slumped and my head dropped.

"Smart girl," he whispered.

"I don't want to die." The quiet words slipped out.

Kirk leaned forward and tilted up my face. "Don't. No more crying."

"Why? You have a soft spot for crying girls or does it just

piss you off?" Once again, my rogue tongue was getting the best of me.

"Neither, but Ross does get a kick out of it. He loves making girls cry, so if you don't learn to control it now...." He trailed off. "I'm not giving you a reason to cry at the moment, so don't."

"It's not that easy."

"Follow orders and stop thinking." He slammed something down on the desk above me. "And for fuck's sake, stop talking."

I opened my mouth but caught the words before they spilled out. *Stop thinking?* It wasn't the words that I *thought* about that got me in trouble. It was the ones that slipped out without consideration. I sighed and put my head down.

———

I LOST track of how long I sat there motionless—not daring to even adjust to re-establish circulation to my feet. By the time Kirk allowed me to stand again, my legs would barely move. Sharp pain shot from my knees to my toes as I tried to shake off the numbness.

He packed up some papers and slid his phone into his pocket. I already missed real clothes so bad that I felt a pang of envy that he even had pockets.

"I have a lot of stuff to take care of today, so I'll be gone for a while and I can't leave you tied to the bed all day."

My heart thumped, but I didn't think I should latch on to the glimmer of hope. There was no way he was going to leave me in the apartment, even if I didn't have a key to unlock the front door.

He grabbed the leash from the door knob where he'd

left it the night before and my mouth dropped open. I was bombarded with the scenarios and questions that clattered through my mind.

Kirk crooked his finger at me. "You'll be safe."

Everything down to my core shuddered. "Kirk—"

With that, his calm gaze clouded. He flipped me around, pressing me into the wall. His wide blue eyes bore into mine. I blinked and struggled to against the reluctance of my tongue. "Sorry... Master." I forced the word out of my mouth just to appease him, even if only for a moment, but his glare didn't melt.

"Just because I've tolerated your voice this morning doesn't mean you can pop off whenever you want." He leaned in, crushing me against the wall. "You're going to get yourself killed."

"It's been one day," I whispered, terrified of setting him off again. "I don't want to die, but I can't change everything about myself overnight. *Please.*"

"That's not my problem. I don't care how you do it, or how you feel. Shut up and do what you're told."

I took a deep breath, habit wanted me to argue, but I nodded. It wasn't easy to hold my tongue and behave when I was uncertain of my future. I wanted to know that by complying I'd be safe. That I'd be taken care of, but all I got is that I wouldn't be dead. It wasn't the most comforting reassurance.

He clicked the chain to my collar and I started to drop to my knees, but he kept a hold of my elbow.

"You can walk," he growled. "Stay behind me and keep your head down."

I wanted to cry again. Not because I was scared— because I felt overwhelmed and confused. I didn't know what to do and it felt like every time I tried to do something right, it just made him angrier. All my emotions wanted to pour out all at once and I didn't know how to pull it back.

Kirk tugged at the chain and opened the door. I fisted my hands at my sides and followed him down the hall to the elevator. My knees shook under me. I was afraid of screwing up, afraid of Gabe or one of his men seeing me. I wanted to wrap my arms around myself but figured that wouldn't go well. At the edge of my vision, I saw Kirk look back as we stood in the elevator.

"No one will touch you," he promised. "Gabe and his crew aren't in this part of the building."

I had to give it to the asshole, he was intuitive.

We only went down one floor, and when we stepped off the elevator, it looked exactly like the floor we'd just left. He led me to the third door and knocked.

I ducked behind him as soon as the door opened. *Miles*—I wanted to fall to my knees and beg Kirk not to leave me. It was almost like the first day of kindergarten, except at least this time I had a reason to be petrified.

Please, don't be leaving me here.

Just beyond Miles, I saw the blonde girl who had accompanied him to dinner. She was wearing a cropped T-shirt and short track shorts, and had her legs propped up on the arm of the couch as she painted her toenails.

"Sure you're up for this?" Kirk asked. Unfortunately, he wasn't talking to me—and even if he were, my honest response wouldn't have been acceptable.

Miles was all legs and muscle. He stood at least six inches taller than Kirk, his chestnut skin stretched tight over muscles that made almost every other man here look scrawny by comparison. "I can handle her for a few hours."

My throat felt like it would swell shut when Kirk dropped the end of my leash and pressed me toward the door. I took one reluctant step after another, waiting for Miles to reach out and grab me like a Venus flytrap.

Instead, he stepped out of the way, and let me enter without moving to touch me. I glanced back at Kirk before the door closed, hoping he'd offer some kind of comfort, advice, acknowledgment—anything.

His chest filled slowly, and he held his breath for a second. "Sorry she's not exactly housebroken, yet. Take it easy on her."

"She'll be fine. I'll turn Alley lose on her and they can talk all the girly stuff I don't want to hear."

Kirk smirked. "You really sure you want to do that?"

"I'll lock them in the bedroom. Go on, get to your meeting. I *can* handle two little slaves."

I wrapped my arms around myself as the door closed. I suddenly wanted to run after Kirk and beg him not to leave me. The blonde was now leaning over the back of the couch, and Miles petted her head as he passed. Much like I'd seen Ross do with the girl in his office.

The memory churned my stomach.

"Both of you, come here." The blonde jumped up and walked to the back of the couch to kneel in front of Miles, so I followed suit.

"Either of you causes trouble, you both suffer the punishment." He gave each of us a long look, but he paused on me noticeably longer. Now I really felt like I was back in kindergarten or being chastised by my best friend's mother the first time she let us play unsupervised after we'd let a frog loose in the bathroom.

"Yes, Master," the blonde said.

"Yes, uh—" I assumed that Kirk was the only one I was to refer to as Master, but then I wasn't exactly given a handbook, or a list of titles.

"Sir works fine for you," Miles said. Between his deep voice and intimidating physique, I was terrified of simply looking at him the wrong way. I'd already experienced his strength firsthand, but now he seemed laid back and slightly amused at my awkwardness.

"Yes, Sir."

I held my breath as he unclasped the chain that hung from my collar. "Kirk didn't tell you where he was bringing you, did he?"

"No, Sir." *Luckily.* If he had, I probably would have gotten into a lot more trouble along the way.

Miles laughed then flicked his hand at us. "Go on, Alley, try to keep our guest entertained and out of trouble."

She jumped to her feet, but I was much more cautious in my movements, trying to watch both her and Miles as she towed me into the bedroom. My feet felt heavier with each step. Nothing in this place ever made sense. The man who'd slammed me into a wall and felt me up the day before was now... civil. More than civil, he was jovial and almost pleasant.

In the bedroom, a mahogany dressing table and a matching dresser sat in one corner of the room.

"Silver, right?" Alley asked, pulling out the bench.

I nodded as she grabbed my shoulders and directed me to the bench.

"I'm Alley—spelled like the road, not the nickname. Where are you from?" she patted the bench, for me to sit down, then pulled over a chest from in front of the bed and took a seat herself.

Small talk. I hated small talk in every situation, but this just made it weirder. "Why does it matter?"

"Just curious." She shrugged. "Didn't they give you any clothes?"

I looked down and pulled at the fabric of the tank top. "You're looking at them."

"You're not going to keep anyone's interest looking like that."

I grimaced, more offended that she suggested I wanted anyone's attention than her remark about how I looked. "Why would I want interest? I'd be perfectly happy with fading into the background."

"Interest usually means favor, darlin'. If you want things, if you want to be comfortable, there's only one way to get it around here." She ran a hand through her hair, pulling it all over one shoulder. "You really are fresh, aren't you?"

"I figured they already told you all about me."

"They said you were just brought in yesterday, which is why I wondered from where?"

"From my house, I reckon," I snapped. "Thanks to whatever Gabe dosed me with, I don't really remember much."

Alley looked me over for a few seconds, her eyes wide.

I angled myself away from her; I was tired of being looked at like a fresh specimen.

"When Miles said Kirk was bringing you down here and asked me to explain some of the rules, I just assumed that you'd been working at one of the other retreats."

"Retreat?"

"That's what we call them. Milo owns several of them. I used to work at one near St. Louis, but I came here about two years ago. It's better than anywhere else I've been in a long time."

All I could manage to do was stare back at her blankly.

"Kirk's a good guy, darlin'. Everyone wants him, but no one can get him. Not for long at least."

I propped my elbows on my knees and leaned my chin against my fists. "He's not all he's cracked up to be."

"First rule of survival, don't talk bad about the men, especially your Master. He's taking care of you, so appreciate it. Kirk doesn't let himself get wrapped up in all the superfluous like the others. That's why he's good at his job. But he's good to us. And he's fucking gorgeous."

I laughed in spite of myself. "Have you tried to get with him?"

She smirked and shrugged in a mischievous way. "I have enjoyed his company, but I have my own Master to attend to most of the time."

She talked about it like it was the most ordinary thing in the world. I wondered if I would get to that point. If meaningless sex would just become some mundane part of my life.

"He particularly likes—"

"No." I stiffened, smacking my hands against my knees. "Not ready for this."

Alley giggled then her face became serious. "At this stage I guess you'll think I'm crazy for calling you lucky, but you are."

"Lucky to be locked up and told to have sex with people I have no feelings for?" I let my mouth go. It was the safest place I had to vent, and I just had to hope that Alley would take pity rather than running to tell Miles.

She touched my shoulder. "I have sex with whomever I'm told, but since Miles claimed me, that doesn't happen that often. I like serving him."

"I noticed," I mumbled, then slapped my hand over my mouth.

She laughed and shrugged. "I wouldn't have expected you not to."

Chapter Six

THE MAIN COURSE

KIRK MUST HAVE FIGURED that where his threats and violence failed, Alley's light-hearted charm and apparent love of her Master would show me to appreciate my new lot in life. I wasn't sure I'd go that far, but an afternoon without almost having my hair violently ripped out was a nice break.

"Can I ask how you got here?" I asked. She'd wanted to know my history, so it was only fair that I could ask about hers.

She sighed and rose to her feet, opening one of the drawers on the dressing table to pull out a comb. "Turn around," she said, waiting next to the stool for me to move.

I hesitated, not entirely ready for anyone to be touching my tender scalp, but cooperating was the best way to get information, so I swung my legs over to the other side and faced the mirror. As soon as I saw my reflection, I glanced away. I didn't need a constant reminder.

Alley carefully dragged the comb through my hair, loosening the tangles and smoothing it down. "I came from a good home," she said. "I got decent grades, played sports.

When I was sixteen, I started seeing this guy. He was eighteen, and I thought he was the coolest and greatest guy in the world."

She laid the comb down and started a braid at the side of my hair, weaving it to the back of my neck as she slowly relayed her story. "He gave me everything I wanted, and then he convinced me to entertain him and some of his friends. I passed out at the end of the night. I woke up to find that he'd sold me."

I closed my eyes, feeling sick to my stomach. Alley and I weren't so different, and after everything I'd said—or worse, everything I thought—I wasn't sure I could face her again. Even though she hadn't heard the things I thought, it didn't make me feel any less guilty for thinking that she must've been weak or pathetic for letting herself end up here and finding a way to enjoy the situation.

As she started a braid on the other side of my head, she continued. "Most of us have good lives here, we came from much worse. Even St. Louis was an improvement over being beaten and starved every day. We have food, a comfortable place to live, regular medical care. I've seen plenty of girls come in broken, and others come in fighting and swearing that they'll never give in."

"But you recommend I just give up?"

"It's not giving up. It's accepting your current circumstances. I rebelled once, but I realized that there's nothing that I want that I can't get here."

"Love? A real relationship? A family?" I finally met her gaze in the mirror, searching for signs that she wanted more.

Her mouth cocked up in a half smile. "I wanted those things once. I also thought I had the man of my dreams once." She shrugged. "Now I just think it's overrated. I'd rather have a guy who keeps me safe than a guy who offers me the stars."

"And you're fine with the sex and violence."

"We don't really see that much violence. Ross has some warped tendencies, but he doesn't just go around beating anyone." She tucked the braids around in a bun at the side and secured it with a few bobby pins. "Sometimes things get out of hand, but the guards usually squash it pretty quickly. I've never seen one of the girls get seriously hurt."

"I almost did."

"But Kirk stopped it, and he'd stop it again. Give him a chance." Alley pleaded, as if she'd known him his entire life and he was just some guy hitting on me in a bar.

This was completely normal to her and yet I couldn't wrap my brain around the fucked-up-ness of it all. "I don't want to be here."

"Sweetie." She sat down next to me and took my hands.

I refused to meet her eyes. "I know it could be worse and I know I don't have a choice in the matter and I should look at the bright side, but I'm pissed. I'm not a sex toy to be passed around."

"Then convince Kirk to keep you."

I pulled away and stood up needing to move, to pace until the anger dissipated from my system. "I'd like to choose my own partners, thanks."

"Then, convince him to give you up. Which, with your current attitude, you could easily do."

"That would put me at the mercy of the masses." I waved my hands in the air then collapsed back down on the stool.

"Yep." She shrugged slapping her hands against her thighs. "You're busy concentrating on the choices you don't have. If you want to keep doing that, no one can stop you."

"What are my chances of getting out of here?"

She stared at me and slowly shook her head. "Even if you somehow managed to get off the grounds—"

"The tracking device." I rolled my eyes, and shook the cuffs on my wrists. "So, I have to get rid of these damn things first."

"Short of chopping off your hands and head…."

Still feeling restless, I started to slide off the bench again, but she grabbed my arm. "You have to face this."

"Is that what they told you when you were sold?"

"No, they beat the message into me. If you think you're in pain now, with the bruises and scratches Gabe and his gang inflicted." She grimaced. "That's nothing. If you feel like fighting and digging in your heels, you'll learn that real quickly. Even these guys will get sick of your disdain and rebellion."

"I've slept with three guys in my entire life. I was nineteen when I lost my virginity and I haven't exactly been adventurous. But now, I'm supposed to put out for every guy who comes in here and tells me to."

She pursed her lips. "Not if you get Kirk to take a liking to you."

I groaned and buried my face in my hands. It was always back to that. "Even then…."

"It doesn't have to be that bad. Kirk doesn't pay that much attention to us, so while you have his attention, keep it."

"He doesn't really want me. All he does most of the time is scowl at me or ignore me entirely."

"But he does want to protect you. That's a good place to start."

"Fine." I exhaled and rubbed my sweaty palms against

the shirt. I couldn't convince myself to accept it, but she had a point. "Tell me what I have to do."

"Lose the attitude."

"Yeah, I keep getting that."

She put her finger over my lips and raised her eyebrows. "And you're not doing so well at it. Maybe we should start with something easier."

Trapping me back at her vanity, she pulled out a makeup case and began simultaneously teaching me all about makeup and all the rules I needed to know to survive as Kirk's "pet."

Never make eye contact—well, I'd shot that one to hell at least half a dozen times.

Keep your hands folded in your lap.

Everyone who isn't Kirk and Ross should be addressed as "Sir." The hardest part to swallow would be addressing Ross as "Master" as well, since apparently his rank negated all other claims when he was present.

The most important rule was to do whatever Kirk said.

I wasn't even any good at doing that at work or school. I had a habit of challenging even the smallest things someone *told* me to do. Ask me, and I consider it. Dictate, and I rebel.

By the time she finished, I could only remember half of what she'd told me about the makeup... or the rules.

My brain had decided to go into standby mode until things made sense again.

"What do you think?" Alley asked, stepping away so I could look in the mirror.

"Um—" I blinked not sure what to say. I half expected to look ready to walk the streets; but instead, I had more of a formal date look. Soft and not at all over the top.

"You hate it?"

"No." I shook my head, finally tearing my eyes away

from the reflection. "It looks great. I've never quite seen myself look like this."

"You'll probably have to talk Kirk into ordering you some stuff."

"You make that sound easy."

"After tonight…." She winked.

Tonight. I wasn't ready.

"Come on, I think I have something you can wear."

"Wear? But… Miles… won't he—" I didn't know why I was objecting, I knew it was Kirk and Miles who put her up to all of this to begin with.

"You're still not getting the whole 'go with the flow' thing, are you?"

I raised my eyebrows and stared at her. So now I was being ordered about by the men and fellow "slaves".

Welcome to the very bottom of the totem pole.

She handed me a black mini-dress with cut-out shoulders, and little gold clasps that attached the straps in front.

I glanced around for the best place to change then told myself to stop being an idiot. I pulled Kirk's tank over my head and draped it across the bench. Alley handed me the new dress and I squirmed until I had arranged the tight fabric over my chest and hips. It had ruching up the sides and I had to admit, it wasn't a bad look—although still too short.

I turned to the side; the hem of the dress barely caressed the bottom of my butt cheeks.

"I bet Kirk will love it."

I blew out a slow breath. "And if he doesn't?"

"Blame me. I have Miles to protect me."

I narrowed my eyes at her, but she smiled and hooked her arm around my shoulder. "You look saucy, girl."

Trying to get the guy. Not trying to get the guy. Trying to get away from the guy by getting the guy.

One day and I was already confused.

My only hope was that my full test results hadn't come back yet, and Kirk would at least be keeping his distance for one more night.

————

WHEN IT CAME time for Kirk to return, I worried he wouldn't like my new look, that he wouldn't appreciate my changing out of the tank top he'd given me. I tried to calm my worries, but after Alley and I moved out to the living room, all I could do was fidget and hope that Miles wasn't sitting behind me watching every twitch.

Finally, there were three knocks on the door, before Kirk opened it and let himself in. His eyes widened as he watched me stand and straighten the black dress, but he didn't say anything, nodding to Miles as they exchanged my leash. Kirk kept his eyes on me the entire time, not even bothering to fasten the leash to my collar before he took my arm and led me out of the room.

Once the elevator doors closed, he turned to me. "What got into you?"

"Alley," I whispered, keeping my gaze down as my cheeks flamed.

"At least you look ready for dinner. Saves me the trouble."

Of course, that's all he could say. I don't know what I expected. Recognition for Alley's work. Acknowledgement that I was at least trying. A hint that he cared about more than just saving himself the trouble of getting me ready. "Are we…? The same place?"

"Yes."

"Will I have to…?"

"Do you want me to write you out an agenda?" he snapped.

Pulling away slightly, I shook my head, but I doubted that he saw it since he'd turned his back to me again.

We went back to his rooms and he ordered me to the bathroom, and ushered me to the counter, pulling down a butt plug and lube. "You know the drill."

"You're going to make me—through dinner?" I squeaked.

He nodded to the counter. I took a deep breath and leaned over, pressing my forearms into the cold countertop and pushing out my ass as he wanted.

He slid the bottom of the dress up over my hips, then snapped open the bottle of lube.

"Silver," he whispered, pressing a lubed finger into my ass.

I wanted to ask—beg—if there was any way I could get out of this part, but I didn't dare.

He pumped his finger inside me then rubbed some of the lube over my clit. I gasped, burying my face against my forearms.

"You're tensing up," he said calmly.

"Will you just get whatever you're doing over with?"

"That wouldn't be any fun."

I bit my lip, unable to stop my hips from rocking against him. His finger slipped out and something else pressed against my hole. I braced myself for pain while trying not to tense. With a little work, he slid the entire plug into place—a lot easier than I had anticipated.

After washing his hands, he squeezed each of my butt

cheeks before pulling my dress back down. "I have to get ready. Follow me."

I assumed that he only wanted me to follow him, because he knew I'd be in misery walking with the plug shoved up my ass. It was almost worse than crawling; every step took extra attention as it moved around inside me and made my regular gait feel strange.

In the bedroom, he pointed to the bed. "Have a seat, Sugar."

My mouth dropped open, and he smirked, crossing his arms and waiting for me to sit before moving on to getting himself ready. Biting the inside of my lip, lowered myself on to the foot of the bed, as the plug shifted upward.

He stripped off his clothes in front of the closet, my eyes fell on the sizable lump in his boxers and refused to move until he turned his back to me and pulled on another pair of pants. Then he slipped on a grey t-shirt and picked up something small off the dresser.

"There's a little surprise to this plug," he said, fiddling with the small object. It clicked, and the plug started vibrating.

My back straightened, and I grabbed the foot board. The slow and steady vibrating turned into a series of pulses before it settled into a rhythmic pattern. I cried out as my insides squeezed around the plug. My nerves relayed the impulses through my gut and straight to my brain.

"Please." I shook my head. "Not in front of everyone."

"Then," he whispered in my ear. "Behave and do as you're told."

"Yes, Master."

The vibrations stopped, and I wanted to collapse back onto the bed. Instead, I had to follow him, on hands and knees, through the hallways and back up to the same dining room we'd visited the night before.

"How is your little trainee?" Ross asked.

"Improving. Slowly." Kirk directed me to, again, sit at his feet.

"Slowly, but well enough to join us again." Ross stepped around Kirk and tightened his fingers in my hair. "I think we should have some fun with her."

I concentrated on breathing and managed to keep my expression as calm as possible.

"Doc hasn't cleared her yet. And she's allergic to latex."

"Then we'll limit our interaction to eyes and toys." Ross pulled me to my feet. "The sooner they learn their place the better."

I risked a glance at Kirk, hoping that he'd say something else to protect me for one more night. Ross tightened his grip on my hair and jerked my head back. "He's your boss, but I outrank him. Lay across the table, with your feet toward my seat."

My breath came out in a huff as my chest tightened, but I forced my shaking body to do as he ordered. He spread my legs so that my feet pointed toward the corners of the table. The same men from the previous night filtered into the room, surrounding me, and then two women in cat suits served dinner, placing Ross' plate between my legs, and two plates at my sides.

I wouldn't be eating.

"Nice decoration," one of the brothers said, slipping his fingers down the top of my dress to squeeze my breast. I remembered their names, but since they were behind me, I wasn't certain which was which.

My chest shook with nerves as I inhaled, and I heard them chuckle at my jiggling breasts. Another hand slid up my leg pushing up my dress. Kirk squeezed my leg, and I stared into his eyes, trying to find another place to hide.

"Where's the remote?" Suit asked, and my heart jumped into double time.

I watched Kirk swallow a bite of food then he fished the small device from his shirt pocket.

I stared through the window above me to the sparkling stars above as Ross began scrolling through the settings, leaving it on a steady intense buzz. For the first few minutes, I tried to separate myself from the sensation, but my body started to respond. My hips tried to rock, and my muscles clamped around the plug, forcing me toward arousal.

I caught Kirk's eye, his heated glare indicating that he noticed my arousal—probably like every other man in the room, but they all went on with their dinner, leaving me on the table to swallow my agony.

While eating, Ross seemed to forget about the remote, and I pushed myself ahead of the waves of stimulation, letting my mind slip farther away, concentrating on nothing more than the stars above unless I had to. Unfortunately, my mental escape did nothing to alleviate my physical arousal.

By the time they all finished eating, I felt like I'd erupt with the next touch, but by then most of the men were paying more attention to their own slaves than me. As the sounds of sex rose around me, I wanted to squirm out of my position, find something to give me relief.

Ross pulled on my ankles, dragging me down the table toward him. I tried to keep my gaze on him, but my eyes flew to Kirk as I moved.

Ross slapped the inside of my thigh. "I said I'm in charge. You keep your eyes on me."

He positioned my heels on the edge of the table, leaving me wide open and exposed. He slid two fingers inside of me and I gasped and bucked. I was already slick and wet with arousal, and to make the experience even more horrifying, I moaned as he touched a vibrator to my clit.

As he pushed me closer to the edge, I tuned out the feeling of the vibrations, but soon his rough motions and the pulses from the vibrators seemed to cancel out my arousal until I felt numb. My slower, muted reaction only spurred him on to push harder until they became more painful.

But at least the pain I could handle. I wanted to feel the pain. It was more appropriate and less humiliating than the knowledge that every person in the room might see me get off with the bastard.

Through the valley created by my legs I saw him rub his engorged cock through his pants.

Kirk rose, distracting me for a second and I winced. From Ross' smile I couldn't tell if he mistook that for a pleasurable response or if he was enjoying my misery.

"She's mine," Kirk said. "I want first honors to have some fun with her."

I wanted to shake my head, but Ross stepped back, and Kirk took his place, sliding two fingers inside of me and hooking them up to massage my insides. One simple move trashed all my barriers.

I cried out and thrust my hips forward. His thumb circled my clit in delicate circles—a sharp contrast to Ross' motions—and as the numbness from the vibrator wore off, his ministrations set off my arousal again.

His touch abandoned me for a moment, then I heard his pants unzip. My helpless cry came out as a moan as his heated head pressed at my entrance. I wanted to scream. Arousal tore through my nerves, but frustrated anger thickened my blood. I grabbed the edges of the table as he pressed into me.

So much for not being cleared by the doctor.

His first thrust was long and slow, and I felt myself quiver around his large shaft. Why couldn't he be furious? Pound into me? Fuel the hate? Why did he have to turn it into pleasure?

The vibrations from the plug changed into a pulse, and I involuntarily pushed against him, taking him deeper and shaking in physical pleasure. I tried to pull back, anchor myself against the table, but that just drove the plug in deeper, and I cried out, grinding against him again.

Squeezing my eyes closed, I felt the tears coming. I couldn't control my body.

He nudged my clit and the next thrust pushed me over the edge. I plummeted over the other side crying out and convulsing into the table as his thrusts became stronger and erratic until he emptied himself inside of me.

The buzzing stopped, and he slipped out the plug, dropping it in a plastic bag that Ross handed him, and placing it on the floor next to his chair. Then he pulled me into a seated position.

Do not cry. Do not cry. I repeated over and over in my head. I saw lips moving around me, but the mantra in my head was all I could hear.

My body no longer belonged to me.

Every muscle in my body twitched as Kirk helped me into a seated position at his feet. Kirk moved his leg and the smooth material of his pants brushed against my arm. I wanted to jerk away when his fingers found my hair, but I told myself to be good for the show. I followed the pull of his hand and pressed my cheek against his thigh. On some level, I was thankful for the bit of support.

The rest of the evening passed in a blur with people around us groping and having all forms of sex. Ross brought in a few new girls, but Kirk excused himself and by default, me.

I could barely hold myself up by the time we reached the apartment.

"I need a shower," I said, still trying to hide my emotions.

"I'll fix you a sandwich since you couldn't eat."

"I'm not hungry." I started for the bathroom, but he lifted me to face him. The last thing I wanted to do was look at his face.

"Silver," he said calmly.

"I hate you." I forced through my clenched jaw.

"I know."

I know? The fury burned out of my chest, singeing my throat, and I stormed away.

"Would you have preferred that I let Ross continue?"

Fists clenched, I spun back to face him, the five feet between us spurring my confidence. "You could have stopped him before it all got started," I yelled.

"He gets his way." Kirk's forehead was creased with anger, but he didn't attempt to close in on me. "I have to pick my battles, too. He wouldn't have stopped. And you were fighting him, pushing yourself farther away and into misery."

"I was fighting what I didn't want. I could have suffered through until he was done. You humiliated me."

I grabbed a cushion from the couch and chucked it across the room, knocking a painting off the wall. The glass and frame shattered when it hit the floor. Kirk moved toward me and grabbed my arm, and I felt the sting of impact as my hand met his face. When I realized what I'd done, I jumped away and fell to my knees.

"Oh, god," I whispered.

Kirk cocked his head, closed his eyes and took a deep breath. Veins popped out along his wrists and neck and I waited for the impact to come.

"Next time I'll let Ross continue until he gets tired of you." He grabbed my jaw and twisted my neck to face him. "He wouldn't have stopped with some little game. It was either him or me."

"I thought my tests haven't come back yet."

"Then we better hope you didn't lie. Ross wouldn't have taken that chance—and I knew the look on his face. If I had let him continue, he wouldn't have left you alone. And he wouldn't have given a shit whether or not you're allergic to latex."

As I caught on to what he was saying, my chest shook making it hard to inhale. My stomach fell and twisted around. "Please."

Kirk released me, speaking slowly and enunciating every syllable. "Go take a shower, Silver."

I stared back, I wanted my body to move because I didn't want to face the rest of his anger, but my body felt paralyzed and disconnected from my will.

"You want to beg me for the impossible. I don't need a pain-in-the-ass responsibility who won't listen to anything."

My gaze fell to the floor. My stomach would have revolted if it had any contents to throw up. I dragged myself to my feet, walked past him to the bathroom, and turned on the hot water, letting it heat before stepping under its abrasive stream. I had fucked up the only person who had stepped up to protect me.

I curled up in the back of the tub, letting the water beat

down on my back, until the sound and feeling of the water was the only thing that existed.

————

THE SHOWER WENT OFF, but I didn't lift my head. Kirk pushed the shower curtain back and knelt beside the tub, draping a towel over my back.

"I wasn't done," I said.

"Quiet," he warned in a whisper. "Your skin is red, and you've been in here for over half an hour."

"I hate you." The tears started falling, and I tried to rub them away.

Kirk lifted me out of the tub, and to my surprise, he sat back and held me in the middle of the bathroom floor. I wanted to fight, to push him away, but even stronger was my desire to stay right where I was.

Safe.

I needed him. No matter what he did to me, or what he would make me do. "Please, don't let them…." I trailed off. "I'll listen. I'll do whatever you want."

"No, you won't."

I straightened.

"But." He tucked me back against his chest and kissed my forehead. "I'll keep you."

"So, you're not going to beat the crap out of me for hitting you and attempting to trash your living room?"

He groaned, shaking his head. "You really want to remind me of all of that?"

"I hadn't wagered that you'd forgotten already."

"Get dried off," he said, dropping the subject and helping me to my feet. "There's a sandwich waiting for you on the coffee table."

As I rubbed the towel over my body and squeezed the water out of my hair, he stripped off his now wet clothes. My heart pounded—I was exhausted, but when I tried to look away from him undressing, I just caught him again in the mirror.

"Trying to avoid me?" he smirked.

"Why do you have to notice everything?"

"That's why I'm good at my job."

My insides were already at war. I wanted to scoff at him and his "job". He was a fucking criminal. Rapist. My temporary solace faded, and my chest collapsed, so I locked those thoughts away.

"Come on," he said, taking me by the waist and walking me to the living room. "Clean up the mess, then eat your sandwich, and go to bed."

"Can I...?" I looked down at my naked body, but Kirk pinched the bridge of his nose and I decided against bringing up clothes.

"There's a broom and dustpan in the kitchen."

I dusted off the cushion and put it back on the couch next to Kirk. Then I walked past him to pick up the broom and dustpan to clean up all the broken glass. I carefully stuffed everything except the painting into the trash can and sat down on the floor at his feet to eat the sandwich.

Chapter Seven

DANGEROUS GAME

THE SMELL and crackle of bacon filtered through the empty bedroom and pulled at my stomach as I rolled over on my makeshift bed. Kirk had already unlocked my chain before I woke up, but I still debated whether or not to get up and face him. When I'd gone to bed his anger seemed cool and contained. Now that he'd slept on it, it could either be worse—since he wouldn't be exhausted—or better if he wasn't the kind to hold grudges.

Somehow, I doubted he was big on forgiveness.

But what did I know? He was brilliant at reading me, but he was the most confusing person I could imagine. If I could predict his reaction just once, I'd feel less anxious about every move I made.

I rolled off the cushion, wrapped the blanket around myself, and walked out quietly to peek into the kitchen.

Kirk glanced back at me then sat a plate down on the table. "You going to wear a blanket to eat in?"

I shrugged even though he wasn't looking at me.

He turned back and glared. "Put the blanket away. There's a robe for you on the back of the couch."

I scowled and did as I was told. I expected the robe to be something short and sexy that barely qualified as covering, but I got another shock when I picked it up and slipped it over my arms. It almost came to my knees and was made of a thick but soft terrycloth. I pulled it tight around myself then returned to the table to take my seat.

"Thank you, Master."

A robe wasn't what I had expected after last night's outburst, but since I was certain he hadn't left anytime while I was asleep, I assumed he must have ordered it before my minor attempt at trashing his living room.

I sat and stared at my food until he also took his seat and began eating. For once, I was glad for the silence—and delighted that my mouth wasn't currently running faster than my brain.

After breakfast, Kirk took me to the living room. "I have a meeting in a few hours, but you're stuck with me until then." He handed me a bag and I pulled out an e-reader, a blank journal, and a book of crossword puzzles.

"Is this your way of apologizing?"

"I'm not sorry." He sat down on the other end of the couch and flipped on the television to the news. "It's my way of giving you something to do so you don't trash the place. The e-reader doesn't connect to wi-fi, so don't get any ideas. I'll upload a few to it, but after that, you earn the rest."

I could only imagine how I was expected to do that. "So, I have sex with you, and you buy me books?"

"No, you keep your mouth shut and do as you're told, and I buy you books," he said dryly. He really was determined to shut me up. "You'll be surprised how often that may not include sex."

He watched the TV screen for a few minutes, then slumped down and put his feet up on the coffee table. "There are a few bags of clothes behind the couch, too. Alley will take you down to the laundry room tomorrow, and you can beef with her about whatever you hate."

I stared at him for a minute, but he wasn't even paying attention to me. *Down to the laundry room*? "Just the two of us? Like wandering around the building alone."

"Planning an escape?" He cocked an eyebrow but didn't look away from the television.

"I'm just surprised, and…." *Gabe*. He had to be around the building somewhere.

"You're allowed on floors seven through nine. Ten only if you have to go to the infirmary. You're not allowed unsupervised on any of the floors guests can access. And *you*"— he pointed for emphasis—"aren't allowed anywhere alone unless I say so. If you get into trouble tomorrow, Alley is taking half of the blame."

"Yes, Master." I fiddled with the e-reader in my lap, then moved my new acquisitions to the coffee table and curled up on the edge of the couch, letting my mind find a distraction in the news, even though I half expected my name or picture to flash across the screen at any moment. I knew my boss must have noticed I was gone, since I had already missed a day and a half. But I hadn't talked to my family in over a week, and I couldn't remember whether or not I had met my friends on Friday night like we had planned. My friends… Charlene and Becca were supposed to meet me at the restaurant at seven for dinner and drinks. If I had made it there…

I shook my head and buried it into the couch. I didn't

even know if my friends were safe and I had no way to find out.

Kirk tapped his phone, then tossed it on the end table and stood. "Any books you want me to download before I leave?"

As if books made things better. I shrugged, keeping my eyes on the television. "Are we going back to the outlook tonight?"

He towered over me, reaching toward the ceiling and stretching his back. "What does that have to do with my question?"

"I don't know what books I want. I was just wondering."

"No." He pressed his lips together. "Taylor and Demetri left this morning."

"If I ask two more questions, will you rip my hair out?"

He seethed for a moment then relaxed. "Not unless you give me a reason."

"Can I pick out the books tonight, and do I get a pen or pencil?" I held up the crossword book.

He frowned at me, apparently not convinced that I wouldn't use a writing utensil to off myself or dig through the wall, even though I couldn't imagine it'd be an effective tool for either. Even if I was desperate.

He grabbed a pen from the desk and tossed it to me over the back of the couch. "Try not to make any mistakes."

I had a feeling that was meant as a double entendre, but I chose to ignore it. "How long will you be gone?"

"That's an extra question." He slid his phone into his pocket, and clipped keys to his belt. "Only a couple of hours at most."

KIRK LED me to the bedroom, and I headed for my own bed, but he grabbed me by the waist and pushed me toward his bed.

"I don't want to stay on your bed. There's a chain right over there."

"The bed is softer."

"Thanks for caring—it smells like you—" I didn't mean for the last bit to be my audible argument. I still hadn't gotten over everything he'd done to me, I wasn't sure if his smell made me feel aroused, safe, afraid, or angry. It did for damn sure make me frustrated and I didn't feel like laying in it even if it was for a couple of hours.

"When"—he jerked me around and brought me up to his face—"will you learn to stop being stubborn?"

"I—" I didn't have an answer. Being stubborn made me feel like I was fighting to protect some part of myself and my sanity.

He jerked the book and pen out of my hand and tossed them onto the bed, along with the bottle of water he'd grabbed for me. "On the bed."

He pushed me to the bed, so I rolled over to the other side, landed on my feet and grabbed my blanket.

"Silver," he growled and started around the bed post.

I figured I shouldn't press it any farther, so I threw my blanket on his bed and jumped on top of it. He grabbed my wrist and hooked it to the chain.

"Ass in the air. I'll be right back."

Fuck. My stomach dropped. But at least I had thoroughly earned this one. And I suspected that meant it was going to hurt. I rolled over, sitting back on my heels and then laying my head down on the bed, leaving my ass stuck up in the air.

I knew pushing him any harder would only result in things I really wanted to avoid.

I heard footsteps, the only warning I got before a lubed finger pierced my ass. I grunted then pushed the feelings down, keeping them silently hidden below my gut.

He pumped into me a couple of times, before he inserted another finger. I fought to keep the moan silent, but fingers found my clit and rubbed.

I dug my hands into the blanket. "Why do you have to make me—" I whispered.

"It'll hurt less."

"It's humiliating."

"Humiliating implies that you care what anyone watching thinks about your reaction. Have you paid attention to anything happening in the outlook? Your body's reactions don't make you stand out, unless you fight it."

And not standing out was a good thing, I reasoned. I gritted my teeth but let him continue. As if I had a choice anyway.

Another set of fingers slipped inside my pussy as his thumb continued rubbing circles around my clit, while his other fingers pounded into my ass.

I felt his phone shake and he pulled away from me long enough to check it. I didn't know whether to be relieved or frustrated. He'd put me in this damn mess, pushed me closer. Made me wet. And now it was all gone as he stepped across the room to answer his phone.

"Yeah, two minutes."

"Your reprieve," he said, pulling me to my knees by my hair. "Kiss me. Make me believe it, and you get the night off."

I ran my teeth over my lower lip. I wasn't sure I made my last boyfriend believe it when we kissed and now, I had to impress this man. I closed my eyes and sealed my lips to his. The heat from his body radiated into mine as I teased his mouth open with my tongue.

I expected—wanted—him to taste fowl. A hint of cigarettes—even though I'd never smelled it on him or seen him leave to smoke. Morning breath from a man who hadn't brushed. I hoped for some vile reprehensible taste to fill my mouth and remind me why I was fighting him.

But I got none of that. What I got was resolve-twistingly fresh. Our tongues battled for superiority as his hand fell to my breast—gently coaxing my nipple until it stood erect.

He broke away first, breathless. Lust relaxed the features of his face as he backed away. "I guess that'll do."

From the lump visible in his pants as he walked away, it did more than that. I collapsed to the bed and squeezed my legs together. My clit was swollen, and my pussy wet for the taking.

What the hell was this man doing to me?

And how the hell was I going to make it stop?

———

I LAY on my stomach across Kirk's bed, working on my fourth puzzle of the afternoon when the front door slammed. Kirk had already been gone for over three hours, and the ruckus he made only confirmed that something was up.

He walked into the bedroom and jerked his shirt over his head. "Ross has summoned us to the Outlook."

"You promised me the night off."

Kirk stripped off his T-shirt and tossed it in the corner. "It's no longer my choice. We have twenty minutes."

I didn't move, but it wasn't like I could do anything while chained to the wall anyway.

With most of his clothes in a pile on the floor, Kirk leaned over the bed to unlock my wrist.

"Why?" I asked, jerking away from him. "Why the big change in plans?"

"Are we really going to do this again? Ask Ross if you really want to know. I'm not exactly keen on worrying about you during another business dinner either."

He yanked me to the edge of my bed by my ankle—the same ankle that one of the buffoons had slammed into the table. I bit back the pain and squirmed away.

I had a feeling it wasn't me that had him worked up, but no matter what, I was going to get the brunt of it.

"Go to the bathroom and fix your makeup and do your hair. I'll pick out your clothes."

At least he didn't make me crawl; in fact, he barely paid attention to me as I left the room. I took a deep breath and stared into the bathroom mirror. There was no way I could get anything to look like what Alley had done, but I tried to imitate the makeup as well as I could. By the time I got to my eyeliner, I realized that I still needed a lot more practice.

Kirk returned and placed a short skirt and halter top on the table. He examined my makeup in the mirror then leaned against the wall next to me.

I could smell him again and feeling his gaze on my naked skin made me squirm.

"I don't know what to do with my hair." I hated that my voice sounded choked and anxious.

"Just leave it down. It'll be fine."

I zipped on the skirt, and Kirk tied the halter behind my neck while I threw everything back into the little makeup bag. "Should I be worried?"

"Not if you do what you're told."

In other words, yes.

———

WHEN WE GOT up to the main room, a hulk of a man stopped us from going to the center room where we normally ate.

"Boss said to send you down to the clear room."

Kirk nodded then led me toward the stairs. He pulled me to my feet.

"What's wrong?" I whispered.

"Nothing." He said, but he was tense, straighter, and even more distant than normal. "I just don't think you awkwardly crawling down the stairs is going to be a sexy sight for anyone."

He yanked my chain and led me down the stairs, and then through a maze of black walls until he found the one he was looking for. Through the glass tiles in the ceiling, I realized we were going into the room just below our usual one.

"K—M…. Master." I stuttered out managing to not let his name slip out.

He opened the door and revealed a room equipped with a medical-looking bed and implements from whips and chains to shelves full of butt plugs and dildos covered every wall.

"No," I whispered.

"Once again, you missed the lecture about choice."

"Fine, but you don't want this either." Anxiety took over. Anything was better than this. Better than the things he was going to make me feel when my body betrayed my mind. "You don't want me."

"Does that hurt your feelings?"

I despised that he was only playing my master because of some duty—and because of that he had to force himself to touch me. A criminal who lived in a sex den had to force himself to touch me. And even worse, he got me off while doing it.

I glanced to the window above. "Can they hear us?"

"Doubt it." He lifted me to the bed and removed the chain from my collar. "The rooms are soundproofed, but there's a mic. It doesn't look like it's turned on." His jaw was clenched as he moved away to drop the leash on a nearby counter.

"Am I infuriating you?"

"Yes." He glared at me, but kept his body relaxed, as if he didn't want anyone to notice our argument. "Take off your top."

If I pushed him hard enough, I hoped I could avoid the whole, enjoyment part of the issue. As stupid as the idea sounded, I preferred when he acted like the asshole criminal. He was easier to hate, and easier to understand. "No."

"Damn it, Silver," he growled. "Do you think you're safer if you disobey down here than if you disobey up there? You're not. Do as I fucking say, or they're going to have a damn good time watching me beat your ass. And then, I'll ask them to get in line for their turn."

He ripped my top open and pressed me down on the bed with one hand wrapped around my neck. The move was intimidating, but not enough to cut away my air.

"Why is everyone afraid of you?"

The pressure increased. "What is it? You figure if you piss me off. I'll get it over with? Want nothing to do with you? Or maybe you enjoy the brutality?"

"Fuck you," I hissed back.

He held me to the table by my throat then reached underneath to pull up a chain with some kind of contraption on the end. Without warning, he took my nipple in his mouth, rolled it with his tongue then pinched it with his teeth.

The pain radiated out, this time there wasn't an ounce of pleasure behind it. As he moved his head away, he clamped the end of the chain on my nipple and pulled it tight, fastening it over my arm and under the bed. I gritted my teeth to keep from moving, unsure if I could go through with the piss him off and get it over with plan.

He wasn't intent on getting anything over with.

As he stepped back, I reached to move but he held me there with his glare.

"Not as much fight now," he taunted with a low voice. "You don't want to fight a losing battle with me like you did with Gabe?"

"You ass, you know I want to fight."

"So, now you're smart enough not to. Yet you continue trying to piss me off. Which means you'd rather it hurt."

I looked away as he repeated the process on my other nipple. With each breath, they pulled sensitive flesh and I was afraid to move a millimeter in any direction. I looked up trying to see into the room above, wondering how intently they were watching, but the lighting in our room made it hard to see through the glass, and all I got was my own reflection.

Chained. Disheveled.

I didn't want pain, but somewhere I wanted a reminder of how much I didn't want to be here. How much I hated them for this. How much I hated myself for this.

"You went quiet for once," Kirk said.

"And now you're complaining. Maybe you want me to egg you on to give you an excuse to hurt me."

"Maybe if I make it painful enough for both of us, you'll stop." He smacked my stomach. The impact wasn't hard enough to hurt, but it made me jump and pull against the nipple clamps. "They're going to wonder why we're doing so much talking."

Kirk stepped back and looked around the room. Probably wondering how best to torture me in my current position. Suit liked humiliation—and as far as I understood it, I was being trained to please his clients. Unless they were all into torture and doing all the work, that currently left Kirk in an awkward position unless he wanted to show off how utterly useless I was.

And there I was, met with a brick wall again—the source of my overactive mouth. Every time I ran into it.

I could repeat over and over that I wanted Kirk to protect me—and I did. But then I gave him no reason to. Neither he nor I had anything to work with but my stubbornness and ego.

"I get it," I whispered. My limbs began to shake. "Tell me what to do and I'll do it. No more lip and stupid remarks."

He barely looked at me. "You're not ready. I don't know if you can be."

He walked around the room, grabbing a few things, then returned and dropped them between my legs.

I jerked as he forced my legs apart and the clamps bit into my nipples. He placed something cold in my crotch and it squeezed around my clit. Another part slid inside. It wasn't too deep, but I had a bad feeling as he secured the device with a strap around each of my hips.

"Pull your legs up."

I pulled them up to my chest and a lubed finger slid into my ass.

This time I bit back the noise and stared back. I knew what was coming next, and bit the inside of my cheek, trying to keep my expression hard. That was probably a bad idea, since I tensed the rest of my body in the process, making the insertion of the plug hurt even more.

I grunted as it finally slipped past the ring of muscle and settled in place. He pulled my legs straight again and strapped them to the edge of the bed, pushing everything up tight inside of me. Then he pressed a button. I expected vibrations between my legs but instead, a buzz engulfed each nipple traveling over my skin like an army of tiny spiders.

I clenched my fists and he laid another strap over my forearms and stomach. "The current will stay at skin level, so you aren't in any danger, but…" he turned it up and I jerked. "It may not be so pleasant—then again, it may."

He flipped another button and the device on my clit flittered to life, hitting both my clit and g-spot with intermittent waves of vibration.

I squeezed my eyes closed but felt him lean over me. "Best part," he whispered. "The remotes work through the glass, so I can go have dinner and enjoy the view."

"No."

He raised an eyebrow.

Why the hell did I object? What difference did it make whether he left or stayed?

"No one else will come in."

"Please." My body bucked with the sensations. "Don't leave."

His gaze traveled over my body, and I felt my skin turn

to goosebumps, making the shocks on my nipples hurt more.

"If I stay, you'll piss me off more, and I'll do something stupid."

"No. I promise."

He slid the remotes into his pocket and didn't even look back at me as he left me locked in the room.

I squirmed, pressing my legs together, then trying to pull them apart—anything to get a break, but anytime I started getting used to the sensations he changed a setting to throw me off again until I couldn't fight it anymore. My stomach contracted, hips rocked forward, and I screamed as the first orgasm claimed my body. I spasmed against the restraints; the clamps pulled at my nipples, drawing out my agony.

Then for a moment, it felt like everything lessened. I hoped he'd achieved his goal, but the assault started again—this time joined by the butt plug. Each pushing me closer in a different rhythm. My brain couldn't compute it.

The next orgasm slammed into me and by the time it was over, I wanted to cry. My muscles continued to quiver long after the wave of pseudo-pleasure wore off.

I wanted out. How long could he keep this up?

I could see shadowed movements above me, but not enough to decipher what was going on. The vibrations against my sensitive clit resumed and I whimpered. There was nothing I could do. There was nowhere to hide.

My focus went blurry and for a while I became nothing except for the convulsions that traveled through me at varying intervals. It seemed like it had been hours when the door opened. I blinked at Kirk's figure, not sure if he was real.

"Nothing sarcastic or stupid to say now?" he asked.

I shook my head.

He removed the equipment, dried between my legs, and sat me up. Then, he pressed a glass of water to my lips, only giving me a few sips at a time, so I couldn't drink too fast.

He tilted his head, taking in the sight of me. I felt disheveled and slightly vacant, and imagined I couldn't look any better.

"Think you can walk?"

My legs shook with exhaustion and I shook my head. "I'll crawl."

He wrapped a small blanket around me and lifted me up. I opened my mouth, but he glared, so I thought better than to object.

In his rooms, he ran me a bath and helped me into the tub. After relaxing and scrubbing myself, I pulled a towel around my shoulders and hobbled to the living room.

Kirk shook his head and pulled off the towel, replacing it with my robe then he wrapped the towel around my hair and squeezed out the extra water.

"Your food is on the table. Sit on the couch before you collapse."

I did as he said; staring at the sandwich for a few moments and hoping that by some miracle it would appear in my lap.

That hope was answered by Kirk, as he sat down next to me and placed it in my hands.

Chapter Eight

NO HONOR AMONGST SLAVES

I WOKE up the next morning in Kirk's bed. I didn't remember how I got there, or even finishing my sandwich.

My muscles ached and refused to move, but I sat up and dropped my legs over the side of the bed. My robe was hung over the foot board, so I pulled it around me and tested my shaky legs.

For the first time, I had woken up to an apartment that wasn't filled with the smell of food and my stomach gurgled in protest when I walked into the living room and saw Kirk stretched out on the couch with his phone.

From the look he gave me, I gathered that he'd heard my stomach. "Food should be up in a bit."

I nodded, but didn't move from my spot until he turned, taking his feet off the couch and patting the cushion beside him. I curled up in the seat next to him and picked at my nails. The tips were rough; most of them had broken off.

There was a knock on the door and Kirk rose to answer it. My stomach growled again, expecting food, but I looked up to see Ross.

He walked right into the room and glared down at me. "I assume from last night you haven't made much progress."

"It's barely been three days." Kirk leaned over the back of the couch, and I felt like a wild animal suddenly trapped between two hunters.

"You're going easy on her." Ross stepped back, cocked a finger at me, and pointed to the floor at his feet. I jumped from the couch and sank to my knees in front of him, folding my hands in my lap like Alley had instructed. I stared at Ross' shiny black shoes, waiting for one of them to shoot off the floor and connect with my skin.

"I believe the point of you having your own girl is for her to finish you off so you don't have to borrow one."

Kirk made a sound in his throat. "Since when are you possessive. By your logic all of the girls are open to anyone upon request."

"It's the principal of it." Ross leaned over me, wrapping his fingers around my neck and pulling me up to stand on my knees. I twitched when his breath hit my ear and knew there was no way he didn't feel it. He chuckled then moved his mouth even closer. "I'm going to enjoy you."

His hand left my neck and he ripped open the front of the robe and pinched one of my nipples.

I winced, and he squeezed harder, whispering in my ear again. "Don't move or make a sound."

I clenched my teeth as he stood over me, wrenching my nipple as he continued his conversation with Kirk. "I'm leaving for a few days. You and Miles keep an eye on things and stay away from Gabe."

Ross let go and I held back the gasp of relief as he patted my cheek and walked to the door. My eyes stung I watched it close behind him. I stayed frozen in my place while Kirk knelt in front of me and pulled the robe closed.

His thumb rubbed my cheek and I realized the tears had fallen over.

I climbed to my feet. "You—after you tied me up down there... you went upstairs to get your rocks off with another girl."

"She had more effective ways of using her mouth. Why the hell do you care?" Kirk rubbed the bridge of his nose. "Beyond that, why the hell am I arguing with you? Sit down and shut up if you want to eat today."

Why did I care?

Because if I was useless to him, someone else would make use of me. There was another knock on the door and Kirk swung it open, taking the paper bag and muttering something I couldn't understand. He returned to the couch and set out the food on the coffee table.

I wanted to say something so badly, but I bit my lip. I couldn't understand the feelings of betrayal. I didn't want him to touch me, and I'd done nothing but ask him for help, then tell him off. Nothing I could say or do would make things better.

Or even tolerable.

———

KIRK DIDN'T TALK to me for the rest of the morning. He went from being semi-amicable when I got up to a silent boil after Ross' visit.

"Put on some clothes," Kirk said, snapping his computer closed. "I'm going to drop you off with Miles."

"Great, at least he's not moody."

The slap to my face came so quickly I had to brace myself against the wall. When I righted myself, I didn't dare say anything or even look at him. I ducked my head and went into the bedroom to pull something out of one of the bags of clothes. I found a crop top and pair of hot shorts and pulled them on. My cheek smarted, but it was as much the action as the pain that affected me.

He'd pulled my hair, slammed me into walls, and threatened to drown me, but there was something different about the direct hit.

I knelt near my bed and pulled the comb out of the black makeup bag, quickly ran it through my hair, and stood.

"I'm not kidding when I say your attitude is going to get you killed."

I jumped at the sound of Kirk's voice. I hadn't noticed that he was standing in the doorway behind me.

Swallowing the lump in my throat, I lowered my head. "Yes, Master."

"Let's see how long that lasts."

I cocked my head. It wasn't fair that he wanted me to bite my tongue but continually egged me on. Kirk held out his hand, and I reluctantly crossed the expanse between us and dropped my hand into his.

He lifted my chin to look at my stinging cheek. He took a deep breath and blew it out slowly. "I have to get going, so let's go."

"Yes, Master."

He picked up a large laundry bag from beside the dresser and handed it to me. I struggled to hold it up, let alone to drag it down the hallway while keeping up with Kirk.

***

MILES OPENED the door and ushered me inside, closing the door to leave me and Alley alone in the apartment. I dropped the laundry bag and stared at the closed door.

"You okay?" Alley asked, touching my arm.

I leaned my back to the wall next to the door to face her. "I'm sore, and... beyond that I'm not sure." I thought to ask her who Kirk had "borrowed," but that would have simply reaffirmed my desire to care. "Miles doesn't seem happy."

"He doesn't think you're ready."

That sounded familiar.

I blinked, squeezing my arms around myself. My nipple still hurt from Ross' not-so-subtle reminder that he could do what he wanted, and I had nothing to say about it. I slid down the wall and dragged my fingers through my hair. Alley crouched next to me, putting her arm around my shoulders. "Why does everyone seem to think it's so easy? After twenty-three years, being me isn't an easy habit to break."

Alley drew up her shoulders and shook her head. I felt like I was quickly burning the only bridges I had in this world, but she blew out her breath and sat down next to me. "I get it, darlin'. It's overwhelming."

"And confusing. I don't want to lose myself. That's exactly what will happen if I give in and do what they want."

"Or maybe you'll find a part of you that you didn't know existed."

"The part that enjoys this?" I asked dryly.

"The part that proves you're stronger and more flexible than you think you are."

My head thudded against the wall as I dropped it back. I wasn't done holding onto freedom, which meant I was going to keep pissing people off.

Eventually, it'd be the wrong person.

If I latched on to Alley's idea, I had to admit defeat. I could either try to be what Kirk wanted, and take orders, or hold on to the hope that I'd get out of this place. As long as I was torn between the two, the confusion would never end.

"I can't just turn it off."

"You're just afraid of what will happen when you do. There's already no going back."

The door opened, and Miles waved his hand for us to come out of the apartment. Alley and I each grabbed our bags of laundry and followed the men to the elevator.

Neither of them said a word to us. Kirk pressed "7", but as soon as the elevator stopped again, he grabbed my arm and nodded for Alley to leave first.

"Remember what I told you? You get in trouble and she shares the responsibility."

"Yes, Master." I glanced past him to Miles. I definitely didn't want to piss them both off at the same time. Having already experienced the two of them working together to torment me in the hallway, I couldn't imagine what they'd do for a serious punishment. I wasn't sure that would be survivable.

Miles held the elevator door open until Kirk was satisfied—patting my ass as he nudged me off the elevator.

Alley and I were standing in what looked like a large lounge. Mostly girls filled the room, except for the two men standing next to the elevator. Presumably guards assigned to make sure none of the slaves were up to anything questionable.

"Everyone has an assigned laundry day," she whispered, leading me to a door on the opposite side of the room.

The other girls were scattered across the room, most wearing lingerie and none of them were more modestly covered than I was. They gathered in groups of various sizes, some lounging on the floor and whispering, while others had gathered around tables covered in clothes and shoes.

Although they appeared to be going on with their business, the sideways glares were unmistakable. I felt like the new girl who just walked into a classroom a few months before graduation. Being left chained to the bed was far less demeaning.

Alley pushed open the laundry room door, and held it open with her foot, so I could pass.

"Does everyone just come down here to hang out?"

"Sometimes. There can be lots of fun to be had down here. It's a lot more fun than staying around the apartment all day with nothing to do except clean or watch TV."

The laundry room was three times the size of Kirk's apartment. Many of the washers and dryers were already full, but Alley and I walked to the back of the room and started loading up washers with the contents of our bags.

I picked at the clothes in the bag. Not only was it filled with some of my new clothes, most of it was Kirk's dirty laundry.

"So, in addition to sex, laundry, and cleaning…. What do you normally do?"

"You mean responsibilities or fun? Although I'd categorize sex as both of those things."

"Responsibilities. I'm more concerned with the things that could get me in trouble."

Alley snorted. "Then do whatever Kirk tells you. And stop talking back."

"Does everyone know every detail of last night?"

"Everyone knows Kirk wouldn't have done what he did

without a damn good reason. But you had him worked up in more than one way."

I wanted to dunk my head in one of the washers, not only to hide but to wash away the imagery. I dropped the last pair of underwear in a washer and closed the lid. "He'll barely look at me most of the time."

"Well, earn it, sweetie. Ever think it's because he gets a hard-on when he does, and he doesn't feel like wrestling you to take care of it?" She put her hand on her hip, and popped it out, giving me a straight-mouthed stare.

"It's like being in the Twilight Zone."

Before I could close the lid on the last washer, another girl stepped into the room and cleared her throat. The same girl who had been crouched behind Ross' desk giving him a blow job on my first day. At least today she was wearing clothes, sort of. Since Kirk had given me a pair of shorts and a T-shirt today, I wondered if everyone intentionally dressed in lingerie or if it was the only thing they were ever given.

"Don't start, Kat." Alley said, rolling her eyes. She pressed the start button on all three of the washers she'd filled and jumped on top of the third to sit down.

"I just wanted to see the princess in person."

Princess? I wasn't sure what the hell she was talking about, so I kept my head down, trying to figure out the controls on the washer.

Alley scoffed and jumped off the washer, setting the dial on each of my washers and pressing the start button. Then, she looped her arm through mine. "Come on; let's go find a deck of cards."

As we tried to leave, Kat stepped in front of us.

"You obviously don't do anything for him," She smirked, reaching up to touch my hair, and then scowling.

I figured it out then begged for it not to be true. She'd been the one that Kirk had used while I was tied and tortured in the room below.

"So, why does he waste his time on you, instead of a girl who can actually get him off?" She smacked her tongue inside of her mouth and leaned against the large counter in the center of the room.

"I guess you're not *that* good." It was bad enough taking the inferiority shit from Kirk and Ross; I certainly wasn't taking it from the blow girl.

Alley pulled on my arm and shook her head. She started for the door, but Kat grabbed my other arm, and I found myself to be the human rope in a game of tug o' war.

"You think you're special now," Kat whispered through clenched teeth. "But he'll throw you away and you'll be down here with the rest of us. Be careful where you step."

She released my arm and I stumbled backward into Alley. Kat spun around and slammed through the door.

I rubbed my hands over my face and pressed against my temples. *Please let me wake up, even if it's on the floor in Kirk's room.*

"Just stay away from her," Alley said. "Rummy?"

I blinked. "Cards. Right." *That'll fix everything.* I sat down at one of the small tables in the corner near the laundry room, while Alley went off to find a deck of card. At least, I could keep an eye on everyone from here.

She sat down and began to deal, while I picked up my cards one at a time and organized them by suit.

"Have you ever pissed one of the men off?"

"Ross. Don't even ask about that. But it was shortly after that Miles sort of claimed me. Which also pissed off Ross, so he'd use me or give me away just to push Miles' buttons

121

for a while. His attentions turned to other girls though. I think he gets bored fairly easily."

"Not reassuring for the new girl."

"Sorry." She gave me a half smile, and sat down the deck, turning one card over and putting it in the discard pile. "Miles and Kirk have managed to change a lot since then. They're well respected, and between the two of them, have nearly as much power as Ross, simply because of their rapport with business partners. All you have to do is make it through initiation and—"

"Initiation?"

"That's what we started calling it. Milo moves around the girls every few months, so every once in a while, we get new girls—they've usually already been trained, but Ross likes to do a little extra breaking in before he deems that they're allowed to stay. Kirk didn't tell you about any of this?"

"I shook my head."

"Just…" She looked away. "Follow orders and you'll be fine."

"Comforting," I mumbled. "I'm horrible at that."

"Kirk and Miles are a lot alike," she whispered. "At least they realize we're still people."

I chewed on the inside of my cheek, adding "initiation" to my list of worries, as Alley took her turn.

The elevator door opened, and a group of men stepped off. One of the guards pointed to a few of the tables in the middle of the room and then a string of men came in carrying boxes. My gaze locked on one of the men, as green eyes turned on me.

Gabe.

I panicked and lowered my head, hoping that he hadn't actually noticed me among other girls. All the girls started gathering around the boxes and the men, including the main guard struggled to keep them under control. It was like the first rush of Black Friday.

"It's a flippin' free-for-all when they bring new clothes in here." Alley shook her head and laid down a card. When I didn't move, she glanced over her shoulder again. "Just stay away from him and you'll be fine. He's not going to try anything with everyone around."

I drew a card, but I was still paying more attention to keeping track of Gabe than a stupid card game.

Three girls broke from the crowd and came our way- each had an armful of clothes.

"Come on, Alley," one of them said. "I know Miles buys you everything you want, but a game cannot be more interesting than free clothes."

Two girls grabbed her arms, and ushered her over to the group, while the third—a tall redhead, grabbed my hand and tugged me out of my chair.

The tiny woman was stronger than she looked, and I eventually rose to my feet. "I really don't—"

"You need it, new girl." I couldn't figure out why they'd care. Less competition seemed like a good thing, and I already had piles of clothes that I hadn't even looked at.

My eyes scanned the room for Gabe as she dragged me closer to the mob. She pulled me to the front of the group then disappeared. With everyone touching me and pushing past me to get to the clothes, my airway tightened.

I couldn't see Gabe anymore, and no one had gotten onto the elevator, so he still had to be in the room.

My heart pounded, and I fought to get away from the girls, backing across the room until I was clear of the stray hands.

I looked around again and saw Gabe standing next to

the elevator, green eyes focused on me. His mouth twisted to the side, and I slowly stepped backward.

I had no idea where Alley had gone and most of the other men were paying more attention to the girls fighting over clothes or slipping off their clothes to try on their new acquisitions.

I felt a door behind me and shoved it open.

A stairwell.

Oh, god, I thought, *I'm dead one way or another*. I couldn't go back or they'd know, and I knew that almost anything moving forward would get me caught. But I ran anyway. Putting as much distance between me and Gabe as possible

Flight after flight, my heart beat out a tense chorus as I waited for either a door above or below me to open.

And then, it happened. As soon as I neared the third-floor landing, the door opened. I pressed myself against the wall and attempted to creep back up without being noticed, but my breath came in loud huffs and I knew I was anything but discrete.

Footsteps came from above, and I froze. My palms grew slick as I held tight to the railing behind me. A tanned figure rounded the staircase below me.

Miles.

He crossed his arms and stared up at me. He didn't even seem startled to see me, which meant he was probably looking for me.

He also didn't seem eager to grab me. I stepped away from him and looked up. A tattooed forearm appeared just above the railing.

Kirk slowed his pace as he descended the last flight. He knew I was pinned. I looked from one man to the other, then dropped my head, and sank to the floor. Surrender was the only choice that might keep me alive long enough to explain.

"I'll meet you in the basement," Kirk said to Miles.

Miles nodded, looked us over once again, and disappeared the way he came.

Kirk lifted me to my feet. His tight jaw moved, but he didn't say anything. Silence was more terrifying than threats or violence.

"Please, don't kill me," I whispered, on the verge of letting the tears break free. "I—god, I didn't mean to—I freaked."

"You didn't mean to run. Seems like quite a feat to happen by accident."

"I saw Gabe. I panicked." *Please understand*, I silently begged.

Chapter Nine

NEVER GO BACK

KIRK TOOK me by the forearm and dragged me down the last two flights of stairs and through the door to the first floor.

He'd told Miles that he'd be in the basement, so I assumed that meant he'd be doing something with me first.

Then, I saw the door we were approaching. He shoved the door open and pulled me out on the catwalk.

Miles and Ross were waiting at the bottom of the stairs and my guts turned to stone. "Please," I mouthed.

At the bottom of the stairs, Kirk shoved me forward. "On your knees."

I fell to my knees in front of them. Trying to hold back the flood of tears—all the while wondering if they'd do me any good. At least crying would show my remorse.

"She said she saw Gabe and panicked," Kirk said.

"Where's Alley?" Miles asked.

Oh no, I shook my head. "They brought in clothes, two girls dragged her off and I lost track of her. Gabe saw me and… I didn't know the door led to the stairwell."

"But you thought once you got there you may as well run for it."

Ross shoved his hands in his pockets and turned away. "You really think she's worth the trouble."

Kirk groaned.

Please. Please, say yes. At least say maybe.

"She will be worth it."

"You've yet to show any evidence of that."

Ross grabbed my hair and jerked me back—straining my neck to an unnatural angle. "Are you worth it?"

"No, but I want to be."

"Prove it." He leaned forward putting his face in mine. "Show your Master you can do something productive with your mouth. Keep your hands laced behind your back and stay on your knees."

I shuffled over to Kirk lacing my fingers beyond my back. Staring at the crotch of his pants, I wasn't sure what I was supposed to do. I glanced up at him, but he didn't make a move to unbutton or unzip his pants.

I took a deep breath and went for the button with my teeth. I was glad he wasn't wearing a belt.

Finally, I got it to pop open and I managed to get the zipper with my teeth and slide it down. By the time I was done his bulge was pressing against the thin material of his underwear making it slightly easier to free.

I took his head in my mouth, flicking my tongue over it then rubbing my tongue against the base. Swallowing, I took him slightly deeper. Then, I moved my mouth up and down the shaft licking and sucking as he grew harder in my mouth.

I tasted the first drips of pre-cum on the back of my tongue and picked up the pace. Bobbing frantically against him. Lick, suck, swallow.

A hand grabbed the back of my head, nails digging into my scalp and forcing me to take Kirk's cock deeper. His hair tickled at my nose and his tip pressed down my throat cutting off my airway. I clenched my hands together behind me and concentrated on keeping them there and not biting down. I glanced up, silently pleading for air, but it wasn't Kirk holding me there.

My body jerked, and Ross jerked me back, then pushed me forward again, forcing me to take Kirk's cock down my throat repeatedly before he got bored and released me. I coughed, wanting to curl up on the floor, but I took his cock again, knowing that if I didn't put on a good show this time, I wouldn't get another chance.

Kirk took the sides of my head, holding me steady as he took control of the thrusts. He pushed deep, but his motions weren't as violent. Leaving me room to breathe and calm my aching chest.

His hands dropped away, but I continued.

Lick. Suck. Swallow.

Taking him as deep as I could without gagging, I looked up, his hands were fisted at his sides and after looking down at me for a brief second, he closed his eyes and put his head back.

Kirk grunted, I could feel his orgasm begin in the tightening of his muscles. Then suddenly hot cum shot against the back of my mouth. I concentrated on trying to swallow, breathe, and milk him dry.

I licked up the rest and sat back, keeping my gaze on the ground. I hoped that no one expected me to put it back and zip up his pants with my mouth, but soon that fear was quelled as Kirk stuffed his cock back in his pants and zipped them up.

"That's quite a show from someone who nearly refused

to strip a few days ago. But she still has to pay for running. Twenty lashes, then throw her in lock-up until you're sure she's learned her lesson. I'd love to stay and watch the rest of the show, but I have a plane to catch." Ross brushed passed us.

"Stand up," Kirk said.

I pushed myself to my feet but kept my head down. Then, he spun me around.

"Take off your shirt and shorts."

My back was toward them, but I felt my skin burn as I stripped then Kirk pushed me over, so that I was at a ninety-degree angle. "Hold the pole."

I wrapped my fingers around the iron pole of the stairs. Digging my teeth into my bottom lip, I braced for whatever was going to come.

"Here." I heard Miles voice behind me, and then the sound of him removing his belt. For an instant, I thought that would be what Kirk would use on me, but he folded it up then lifted my chin.

"Open your mouth."

When I did, he shoved the thick leather between my teeth. I dug my fingers into the pole as tight as possible.

As soon as the whip came down on my back I screamed into the belt, struggling to fill my lungs as the next lash connected. After two, I was ready to collapse. I had eighteen more to go.

I squeezed the pole as hard as I could, fearing that my hands would snap under their own strain as the next three lashes came.

My muffled screams turned into steady sobs as I felt the tears dripping off my face and forming little puddles beneath me.

Six. Seven. Eight.

My chest shook with each breath, and I fell to my knees. The crack of kneecap against concrete was nothing compared to the fire eating my back.

"On your feet," Miles said. He lifted me up and braced me there for a second while I locked my knees.

The next two strikes came in rapid succession. Halfway there.

I thought I was going to pass out. Or throw up.

Kirk gave me a few seconds to catch my breath, but the radiating burn didn't let up. Snot and saliva clogged my throat and nose, making it hard to breath.

I wished he'd just get it over with.

I braced myself again, and five more streaks were added. I heard a hoarse scream with the fifth, and it took a second to realize that it came from my own throat.

My knees landed against the concrete again and my vision clouded. I cried out again, just knowing that there were five more to come.

Miles lifted my head, but it was only to shove the belt back in between my teeth. I shook my head, silently pleading where words failed me.

"You're almost done," he whispered, helping me to my feet again.

Almost done, but I wasn't really. Five more strokes and Kirk would be done. The pain wasn't going to end just because the strikes had stopped.

I dropped my head, my legs quaking beneath me.

"Silver."

I felt like every structure in my body shattered into a thousand pieces at the sound of Kirk's voice.

"Stand up."

They both lifted me to my feet, but my legs were useless under my weight. Miles held me up, while Kirk's fingers slid through the hair at the top of my neck. I waited for him to jerk my head back, but he leaned down and whispered in my ear.

"Don't break, Sugar. Push it away. Focus on something else."

I locked my knees and braced my head on my arm. *One, two,* I counted my breaths, *three, four....*

Crack.

Just keep standing.

Crack.

Air in. Air out.

Crack.

The darkness began closing in.

Crack.

I could still feel the intolerable burn, but it didn't seem connected to my consciousness.

Crack.

Kirk and Miles each took an arm, pulling me upright. Lava poured down my back. And I shuddered as my hair fell over my shoulder brushing one of the welts, every movement, even the touch of air, adding to the fire.

Kirk twisted my hair and pulled it in front of my shoulder, then he and Miles guided me back a few steps, so I could sit against the table. I didn't want to remember the table. There wasn't any more room in my head for torture, even if it was just a memory.

The door at the top of the stairs opened, but I kept my eyes on the floor in front of me until I heard a female gasp.

Alley.

"Please, Master," I whispered, looking from him to Miles and back again. My voice was hoarse, and it was painful to talk, but I needed them to understand. "It wasn't her fault. She didn't have anything to do with it. Please, don't punish her too. *Please.*"

Miles shot up the stairs taking them two at a time.

"Please don't hurt her," I breathed. My voice was almost gone.

Kirk wiped the tears from my cheeks but didn't say anything. It broke my heart to think that Alley might get the same punishment because she'd been assigned to keep an eye on me today. The guard who had walked in with Alley walked down to us, followed by Miles and a tearful Alley. The guard moved to take my arm, but I jerked away without thinking.

I didn't want anyone else touching me. I'd had enough of people touching me. Every subtle sensation rolled through my body superheating the burn on my back.

"Take Alley to my apartment," Miles said, handing the guard a key. "Let her in then wait outside of the door until I get back."

The guard nodded, taking Alley up the stairs, while Miles and Kirk took my arms to support me. They pulled me up the stairs and through the side door at one edge of the catwalk. It led through a back hallway to the elevator. They took me up to the tenth floor.

My only sense of relief came from the fact that Ross had probably already left for his plane. We walked down the hallway, past the two rooms I knew until we reached a large silver door. Miles pressed his thumb to a keypad and the metal door opened. Inside, there were four identical metal doors.

Using his thumbprint again, Miles opened one of the doors and they led me into the small room. It was empty except for a small cot in the corner, and a small toilet and sink.

They laid me down on the bed, on my stomach.

"I'll bring her some water," Miles said.

Kirk nodded and crouched in front of me. As Miles left, Kirk lifted my chin, forcing me to at least look in the direction of his face, even if I couldn't focus on it. He rubbed his thumb over my lips.

I waited for the next chastisement. His reminder of why I was in pain. Anything but silence, but as soon as Miles returned and sat the bottle next to me then they both left me, locking the door behind them.

I was lost in my own mind, running from the pain.

———

AS THE PAIN began to recede, it made room for the panic to set in. What if Gabe found out where I was? Would anyone try to stop him here?

The door clicked, and I jumped. My body tensed, preparing for the worst.

Then, I saw Kirk's face. He leaned against the wall across from me and let the door shut.

"What do you want, Silver?"

"To live. To not hurt this badly. I'm scared." I breathed, and it was like blowing oxygen into the fire on my back. "I panicked."

"I know. We watched the surveillance video," he pushed away from the wall, and caressed the back of my arm. "Let's go upstairs."

My eyes lifted. I wondered for a second if I was imagining the whole thing, but he carefully lifted me from the bed, and put another hand on my hip trying to brace me.

"I'd carry you, but I don't think you want me to touch your back."

I shook my head. I forced myself to stay upright, but by the time we reached the apartment, all I wanted to do was collapse. Kirk led me to the couch and let me sit down. He walked away and returned a few seconds later piling pillows on the far end of the couch then taking a seat next to me.

"Lay on your stomach across my lap."

I crawled across him, feeling like a thousand snakes were biting my back at once. Kirk pulled my hair up, tucking it to one side as I settled. My muscles twitched, adjusting to the new position.

"I'm going to put some ointment on your back. It'll sting at first, but then it should ease the pain."

"Why are you being nice to me?"

"I think you've been punished enough under the circumstances."

He started brushing the ointment on my back with tender strokes. I buried my face in the pillows, trying not to scream at the initial touches. Once my body grew used to it, the initial sting wasn't as bad. I blocked out the pain and went to my own little grey world.

I noticed that he had stopped moving, but he didn't ask me to move, so I didn't argue. He rested a hand on my upper thigh and dragged his other through my hair.

"Bend, don't break, Silver."

———

The skin-crawling sensation on my back roused me, and I glanced around the empty room. No longer was I laid across Kirk's lap.

I didn't even see him around.

Something on my back moved, and I jerked to get it off. Then, I felt the skin ripping sensation of something biting. Pain radiated out from it, spreading through my entire body.

I twisted, trying to see it.

Still feeling rough skin move across my back, I finally caught a glimpse of the snake.

It struck again at my lower back and I jumped off the couch trying to get away.

My limbs went numb as I watched the snake slither off the couch, its large triangular head ready to strike again. It coiled back baring its fangs and I jumped away.

Fingers grabbed my arms and I looked over my shoulder. Ross glared at me, his fingertips digging into my muscle.

"You're supposed to be in lock up. Take your punishment."

The burning in my back spread. Every pulse of my heart sent the venom coursing through my veins, until my vision blackened.

"THANKS." I heard Kirk whisper as the dream faded.

"I saw the same thing you did." I recognized the second voice as Miles. "But are you sure bringing her back up here was the best thing?"

"Yeah." I felt Kirk's fingers brush my neck. "I need her to trust me."

"Ross wouldn't agree with that."

"So, I won't tell him. You understand. She's not like the other girls."

"Careful, you're sounding like a heartsick teenager."

"Not what I mean. She came from a normal life, so she didn't come in wanting to win our acceptance."

"She came in wanting to fight for her freedom—that's a tough thing to break."

"I don't want to break her."

They both went quiet. I heard something rustle then the smell of pizza hit my nose. Hot and slightly acidic with the smell of tomatoes.

"Don't tell me you expect me to serve you, too," Miles said.

"No, but you can help me sit her up." He rubbed my arm. "How much can you move on your own?"

I wondered if he knew I was awake the entire time. I moaned into the cushions. Then, I felt them both lift me, and help me back so that I was sitting sideways on the couch. My hair fell down over the welts again.

"We really need to take care of that," Kirk said. He stood, leaving Miles to brace me and returned, handing Miles one of my hair ties. Kirk sat in front of me, while Miles twisted my hair up into a messy bun.

"This is irony," I mumbled, turning to Miles as he moved from behind me. "Alley?"

"She's fine. She'll have double laundry duty for a while, but since you begged for her reprieve and we watched the tapes, we did as you asked."

"Thank you."

Miles squeezed my arm then I heard his footsteps retreat toward the door.

I leaned my head against the back of the couch, trying to keep myself upright, careful not to let anything touch any of the welts that stained my back. I imagined that it was red and oozing hot lava.

Kirk rubbed my cheek as he rose again. "Just for a little while, Sweetie."

The combination of words tugged at my chest. I didn't want him calling me "Sweetie." And yet, my emotions battled over it. It either meant he felt sorry for me, or possibly that he didn't hate me as much as I thought. "Does that mean you'll let me sleep on your lap again when we finish eating?"

"Is that what you want?" He handed me a paper plate

then flung open the pizza box lid. He dropped two steaming slices of pepperoni pizza on my plate and I settled with my side against the back of the sofa.

I shrugged and winced as I bit off the tip of a slice.

"Here." Kirk picked up a bottle of pills and handed me two capsules. He dropped my water bottle on the couch between us. "It'll help with the swelling and pain.

The pain you caused.

There wouldn't have to be any pain, but Kirk was following orders.

I was the one who broke the rules. I'd slowly break apart every shred of my own sanity if something didn't give.

Kirk had warned me that he was my only ally. He admitted that he'd hurt me. Rape me. And he was the truthful one.

I promised that I'd do what he said if he protected me. I begged him to keep me and not turn me over to the others. He'd kept his end of the deal.

The criminal was better at keeping his word than I was.

I wondered what that said about me.

I also wondered what it meant that I was thinking about giving in.

"How much did you overhear?" Kirk asked, watching me out of the corner of his eye as he ate.

He knew that I had been awake. If I lied and said I only heard the final bit, I'd be screwed if he already knew otherwise.

"I woke up when you told Miles 'thanks.'" I glared down at the snake on his arm—no doubt the inspiration for my nightmare. "I'm sorry," I whispered.

"Your back is going to need a while to heal. Then, we'll start over. You get a clean slate."

"And if I screw up again?"

"When you do…." He sighed. There was something different about him. He looked exhausted. Sounded exhausted. "We'll go from there."

We finished eating in silence, and I'd scarfed down so much, I felt like my stomach would explode, not such a good idea since all I wanted to do was lay down and go back to sleep and I certainly couldn't do that on my back.

I laid against the back of the couch while Kirk cleaned up the mess. When he was done, he sat next to me again, rubbing a thumb against my jawline. "I know you're a strong girl. I know that everything inside of you is telling you to fight. I'm not telling you to ignore it, just to be smart about it."

"How? How am I supposed to use the urge to fight?"

"To stay alive. Sometimes that means not saying what you're thinking, and just doing what you're told."

"That's not fighting."

"You're wrong. Sometimes the only way to win is to stay alive and not break. If you keep fighting like you have been, you'll break."

"Maybe I have already."

Kirk shook his head and put a pillow next to his legs. "You haven't." He motioned for me to lay across his lap.

"I don't need you to take care of me."

"You don't want me to take care of you. Believe it or not, that's what I've been doing since you got here. If I weren't—"

"Don't say it. I'll…" I sighed. "I'll keep my mouth shut."

I crawled across his lap and dropped my head to the pillows he'd laid out. As my body relaxed, stretching out my back again, I flinched in pain.

"I can't put any more pain ointment, yet."

"I'm oka—" I grunted, then took a slow breath. "I'll be okay when it settles."

He pulled the blanket up to cover me up to my waist.

"Don't you have stuff to work on?"

"Yep, that's exactly what I'm doing." He rubbed my back under the lowest of the welts, massaging down my hips and legs.

I took a deep breath and relaxed. At least in this position, I stood no danger of rolling onto a welt. It also felt childish. Waiting on him to take care of me and soothe my wounds.

I didn't fall asleep, but I lay there silently until the sun set and the room darkened. I was at war with my own mind and body. I felt completely alone with no one to talk to about my feelings, to ask if I was really doing the right thing. I had to look inside myself for those answers, and it terrified me.

Kirk sat quietly with me, rubbing my leg or patting my head when I got particularly squirmy until the pain dulled again. But otherwise he didn't move, allowing me the use of his body for my comfort.

"Thank you, Master," I whispered.

His fingers tightened on the back of my thigh.

"Thank you for bringing me back up here and sitting with me." I hated the words as I spoke them, not because they weren't true. I truly appreciated it. I hated them because of what they did to me. They made me his, attached me to him in ways nothing else had.

My mind and soul were ready to admit that I needed him, that on some level, I craved his attention, because it was all that I had. It's all that I would have.

I desperately needed to stop thinking. "How bad do you think a shower would hurt?"

"How bad does moving hurt?"

"Too much."

"Then, multiply that by ten." He massaged just above my tail bone and I moaned into the pillow. His hand continued in circular motions down my ass, then each of my legs.

My body wanted his tenderness so badly that it was willing to do anything he wanted to get it and my brain latched on to every pleasurable sensation—no matter how small—just to get away from the pain. His hand got to the end of my thigh and stopped.

I whimpered.

"You want a distraction?"

"No more pain."

"I'll be gentle."

Gentle would ruin me. Crush up my insides like a used piece of paper and toss me in the garbage ruin me. "Yes."

He pushed down the blanket, allowing his fingers to graze the inside of my naked thigh.

"Remember the kiss you gave me yesterday?"

"Yes." *No, please don't pollute my mind, too.* I locked in on the memory, the feeling of him leaving me needy, wanting.

Wanting. I repeated to myself.

I could taste his tongue on mine.

What the hell was my mind trying to do to me?

I tried to push it back, but his hand parted my legs, moving up toward my hot core. I felt the cool air. His light touch.

I wanted to spur him on as much as I wanted to damn him.

A finger found my clit and rubbed it gently. Not enough. I pressed against him—instantly embarrassed at my need. And at the rate that my body tried to overthrow me.

My back burned as it arched, and Kirk took advantage of the increased access to my folds. He pressed his fingers inside me, pressing down against my tender flesh. He added another finger, stretching and filling me. My hips rocked, wanting more. Wanting him on my clit.

He moved me slightly and slid his leg farther down my stomach until his knee rested close to my pelvis.

So close.

I moaned. Moving my hips, wishing his knee was a little closer.

"Good girl," he said, dragging his fingers through my hair, caressing and tickling my neck.

I inched up until his knee was close enough for me to rock my hips and press my clit against it.

I moaned, using his body to push me closer to my pleasure. The stinging pain in my back faded, replaced by pulsing in my veins, and tingling nerves.

His fingers increased their pace and I inched closer.

My insides squeezed around his fingers, and he slowed, leaving me momentarily balancing on the painful pinnacle. Just a little farther before I fell. I rubbed into him but needed more.

He rubbed his fingers through my juices then inched closer to my ass.

I moaned a protest, but a finger slipped back inside my pussy and the sensations pushed me toward compliance. His thumb pressed at my tight hole slowly moving inward.

The knot inside me wound tightly and burst as I tensed around his thumb and fingers, still grinding against his knee as I spasmed and moaned.

Kirk pulled the blanket up to my waist again as I panted and came down from the orgasm. He readjusted his legs under me so that my stomach was lying across his lap and I could relax my head on the pillows.

"How's the pain?" he whispered.

I hummed into the pillow, exhaustion overcoming me. "I'm good."

"Ready to go to bed?"

"Do I get more distractions?"

"I think you're high on endorphins."

I pushed myself up and managed to sit with a little help. I didn't want to look him in the face, to face my carnal desires, but I lifted my gaze. His blue-grey eyes met mine in the dusky room.

"You're sleeping in my bed."

"I'm not sure if you want me to argue or comply."

He moved, his face stopping inches from mine, until I could feel his breath on my skin. "What do you want?"

"I want to be stubborn and say that I want my own bed, just to irk you. But all I really want is sleep in a soft bed."

"You're all trouble, Silver. For both of us." His lips brushed against mine, and I kissed him back with everything I had.

Chapter Ten

SERPENTINE

My eyes opened in the quiet dark room.

It was eerily quiet, and I pushed myself up, feeling a strange weight on my gut. The weight shifted with my movements and I pulled down the blanket.

A long, coiled snake stared back at me.

"Not again," I whispered. I froze, and the snake lay back down, relaxing against my skin.

I squeezed my eyes closed and wished for the serpent to disappear. The door opened, light filling the room.

I lifted my head.

Kirk.

He walked toward me, whip in hand.

"Please," I whispered.

"Quiet, Silver."

"No." I was terrified to move. Terrified of what would happen if he startled the snake. "You don't understand."

"I said quiet," he growled. He knelt next to me, his fingers tangling in my hair. "I thought humans learned long ago to never trust a serpent."

He flipped my covers back; the snake was gone.

His hand slipped between my legs and rubbed my mound. I was already wet and wanting for him.

Ruin.

I pushed him back and my back erupted in splintering pain.

Kirk pulled me off the floor and dropped me to his bed.

"Remember," he whispered, rubbing his hips against me. He kissed my neck, nipping and sucking at my skin all the way down to my collar bone.

I moaned and pushed against him.

He palmed my breast. Pinching and twisting at my nipple until all my nerves betrayed me, joining in his bitter and swirling symphony.

My body was his, under his command.

He traced a finger down to my belly button, leaving a trail of goosebumps and tingles in its wake.

Testing the connection, I pushed his hand away, and screamed again in agony as the pain returned.

It's a dream, *I told myself. Even my mind was turning against me. Training me to be his. Pulling me into his dark fantasy.*

My resistance only gave him the opportunity to break me open and douse me with his venom. It burned through my veins, clouded my mind, and twisted all my nerves until my body screamed for him. His cock rubbed at my entrance, and I fisted the sheets under me, arching my back.

Fighting meant pain. Giving in meant exquisite release.

I needed his touch. I needed him to fill me.

Nothing else mattered anymore.

Then the world shattered, and I woke in my old home. Under the window, the sunlight danced off the small collection of snow globes.

Home. I pulled open the curtains, taking in the light of freedom until a cloud moved over the sun, and the scenery darkened. A man in a suit stood about a hundred feet away then turned toward the window.

Ross.

I retreated into the bathroom to escape his view, but that window was also wide open.

I could feel the eyes on me even if I couldn't see them. I covered the window and slammed the door shut, trying to lock it, but the door was slightly too small for the frame, and the lock wouldn't catch.

I heard footsteps, then Kirk calling for me. I sat in front of the door, trying to keep it closed, but he pushed it open a few inches. Enough for a snake to slither inside.

"No," I screamed, jumping away from the door and into the bath tub.

The door swung open, but there was no one there. It was just me and the snake.

"Kirk," I yelled. "Please, Kirk, help."

Wake up; it's a dream, why can't I wake up.

If it's a dream, just face the snake.

My heart pounded so hard, I started to feel dizzy.

No escape. I dropped to my knees. The snake slithered closer, only a few inches from the side of the tub. So, I took a deep breath and picked it up. It was calm for an instant, but fear took over again, and as if it smelled it, the snake whipped around in my hands.

I tried to wrestle its long body, holding just behind its head, so it couldn't bite me.

I remembered the pain of the snake biting my back.

No more pain. Please, no more pain.

Arms surrounded me, pulling the snake free from my hands. The snake stilled, wrapping around his arm.

"Kirk."

His lips took mine, lifting me, and pressing me into the shower wall. I let my pain and fear flow out through the kiss, immediately replaced by arousal and lust.

"I need you." I rubbed against him and he lifted my legs. I twisted them behind his back.

His hard cock pressed at my entrance, a slow taunting promise of what was to come.

I WOKE from the dream with a gasp. The room was still dark, so I buried my face in the pillow and tried to slow my breath. I was still so hyped up on the dream; I could feel the moisture between my legs.

"Silver."

I held my breath when Kirk whispered my name and felt him roll toward me. I'd been sleeping in his bed for the last three nights, three long nights of intermittent sleep thanks to the pain in my back and crazy dreams. He hadn't touched me except for the first night when I'd rolled onto my sore back and woke up crying in pain.

"Crazy dream," I whispered and rolled to face away from him.

Even during the day, he had been giving me room to heal, but it wasn't the same remote distance as before. Now, even when he sat across the room, I could feel him watching like he was trying to absorb every move and draw the pain away.

"You need anything?"

For the pull in my stomach to go away. I pressed my legs together, yearning for a release I couldn't have.

Unless I could find a few minutes alone to scrub it away.

"Silver," he repeated when I didn't answer. His hand felt my hair, making the feeling unbearable.

"I'm fine."

He grunted but didn't roll away as I had hoped.

The thought of giving in and letting him take care of

the problem crossed my mind. He'd done it before and obviously had no problem with it.

I squeezed my eyes closed.

Sleep. I needed sleep.

I was just tripping on the effects of the dream and letting it play with my emotions.

Of course, returning to the source of the problem could also make it worse, I realized, but that was my last thought before waking again to the smell of food.

For the last two mornings, I hadn't woken until after he'd already eaten and decided to bring my breakfast into the bedroom so I could eat as comfortably as possible.

The skin on my back still felt tight, but the worst of the burning pain was gone, leaving only the deep soreness from the bruising. I'd gone from one crashing change to yet again having everything I expected flipped upside down. I'd seen his dark side and survived—even though he didn't seem to enjoy the punishment any more than I did.

He had it in him to make sure I did as he wanted, but while I was in pain, he was gentle and attentive. It was still nearly impossible to understand anything that might be going through his mind, but he'd softened. I accepted that it might only last until he was sure touching me wouldn't send me into a fit of agony.

I rolled over and Kirk's smell caught in my nose, reawakening the imagery from the dream. I couldn't go on like this. Teetering on insanity. Holding on to one life and a distant set of convictions while living here.

I had yet to accept never being free again. But there would be a certain level of freedom in submitting to Kirk.

I either had to do that or get back the brooding and remote Kirk. I wasn't sure which situation was worse, but every time he did something nice another piece of my willpower slipped away.

Before long, I wouldn't have a choice in the matter.

I had to take control of something while I still could.

I looked at the clock, it was still early, and Kirk had probably just sat down to his own breakfast.

If I waited in bed long enough, he'd bring my plate in and let me eat in bed again, but after the dream, I felt restless. I wasn't too sure that I wanted to see Kirk, but I definitely didn't want to lie in bed and think about him either.

I crept out of the bedroom and found Kirk sitting at the table eating. "You're up early," he said, sitting back in his chair.

I kept my eyes lowered as I walked toward him and dropped to my knees at his side. He made a pleased sound in his throat and cupped my cheek as he handed me a piece of bacon. I carefully took it from his fingers then laid my head against his thigh as he stroked my hair.

"Come up here," he said, patting his leg. I slowly crawled up, my back aching and burning with every move.

He proceeded to feed me, bite by bite, the rest of the food on his plate. As I tried to take a bite of the scrambled eggs, before they rolled off the fork, he chuckled. It was a tense chuckle, but at least he wasn't still completely pissed at me.

"You're enjoying this."

"Shouldn't I?

I nudged his neck with my nose and ran my fingers down his chest. He caught my hand and lifted me to my feet.

I shook my head—emotionally and physically thrown off balance. "I'm trying to be what you want me to be."

"Why?" he whispered, sitting back.

"Because it's the only thing I can do. I need you to protect me, and…." And, I still wasn't being completely honest. My body still wanted him.

"And you'll trade your body and will for that?"

"Isn't that what you've wanted all along?"

He watched me through narrowed eyes. "You're a schemer."

"We both have reasons not to trust each other, but every time I try, you shut me down and I don't know what I'm supposed to do." I stepped back, pulling my robe tighter. "If you really don't want me, just give me to someone else."

"No." He growled, knocking his chair backward as he stood. He ran a hand through my hair and stepped forward until his body was against me. "You're mine and you're not going anywhere."

"Fine, then introduce me to your other personalities. Maybe then, I'll know how to deal with them all."

He pushed me into the refrigerator. The cold surface stung the healing welts on my back. He paused for a second when I winced then his lips smashed against mine.

He pulled back when we were both breathless. "You're really willing for me to pass you off?"

"Despite all claims otherwise, you care. You don't want me to be killed, so even if you did, I figure you wouldn't give me to anyone horribly nasty."

Kirk cocked an eyebrow. "You don't really want to do this."

"I want…" I took a breath, his woodsy scent claiming my rationale and words. "I don't want to hurt anymore. If sex can prevent that, I'll do what you want."

"How bad does your back hurt?"

I shrugged. "I hurt. All of me hurts and it's not just from the beating."

"You're lonely."

"So are you," I countered, matching his conviction.

"This isn't about a relationship."

I scoffed. "I wasn't ignorant of that memo." I bit my lip and looked down. "I have to do something. You told me to stop considering impossible situations, so I'm taking advantage of the current one."

"You're taking advantage?" he drawled. "And when I hand you off to the others? To Ross?"

My conviction wavered. "I'll do what you want—"

"If I give you what you need," he finished.

He pressed me into the refrigerator again and pulled away my robe sash, slipping his hands inside. His fingers brushed against my sides then pulled my hips against him while his knee slid between my legs.

I giggled, and he pulled back.

"What are you laughing about?"

"I think I just figured part of you out."

His face darkened, and I hoped I hadn't just busted my chance at avoiding his temper.

"The only time I really get a rise out of you is when I stand my ground."

The way he pressed his lips together I couldn't tell if he was hiding a smile, or if I had just hit a raw nerve. "Standing your ground is dangerous."

"You're the only person here, and it seems like the only thing I'm in danger of at the moment is—"

He kissed me so hard the words whirled around in my head and shattered. "Quiet, Silver."

He held me against himself, pulled me away from the refrigerator and walked me backward to the couch. He pushed the robe off my shoulders, his hot hips brushing against my cool, freshly-exposed skin.

"You're strong," he whispered into my neck. He nipped my skin and I arched against him. "Hold onto it but be careful about who you let see it."

The back of my calf bumped the couch and Kirk let the robe fall away. He removed his shirt then pushed me across the couch. After dropping his pants, he rested his knee between my legs and leaned over me, taking a nipple in his mouth and rolling it with his tongue.

Then, he captured my mouth—his tongue pressing against mine. He sucked and nipped until I had to gasp for air.

I was still worked up from the dream, and he didn't have to do much work to have me yearning to go. His fingers slid through my folds and he raised an eyebrow but didn't say anything.

He adjusted and lifted my hips as he slid inside me, pressing his thumb to my clit as he slowly filled me.

It shouldn't be like this, I thought. I felt guiltier for enjoying it than agreeing to it. I matched his thrusts, pushing upward so that each stroke pushed me deeper into pleasure.

Someone knocked on the front door and Kirk dropped against me, panting in my ear. He pressed himself up with a grunt. "Can it wait?"

"No," a deep voice answered.

Kirk sat back and rubbed a hand over his face. He wouldn't look at me as he shoved his legs into his pants and stalked across the room.

I heard whispered voices and then approaching footsteps. "Get dressed," Kirk said.

I sat up and looked over to see Miles. His eyes raked over my nudity and I froze for a second.

Dressed, I repeated to myself, resolved not do disappoint

Kirk again. But I had no idea what he expected me to put on. I stood and nodded, ducking into the bedroom.

I looked at the pile of clothes I had near my bed and rubbed my hands over my face, the full impact of what I'd just been doing fell on my gut. I felt physically off balance as my emotions engaged in a hopeless battle.

There was no winning. No way out. No way back to who I used to be.

Kirk stepped in and put a hand on the small of my back and directed me toward the dresser. He pulled out a pair of jeans and a tank top—both my size, at least, the size I'd been when I arrived.

I frowned at him. Somehow excess clothes seemed especially suspicious. Sitting against the dresser, I stared at the clothes in my hands. "I'm horny, frustrated, and confused. Can you go back to being distant and horrible?"

His eyes drifted over me, as if he wanted to help me but had no idea how. "I thought you didn't want to be miserable anymore."

"No matter what, I keep sinking. I can either take a final gulp of water and drown, or sprout gills and never go back. I'm not good at letting go."

"Then, what was that out there?" Kirk's forehead crinkled, and he leaned against me, placing a hand on the dresser on either side of me, and I drew back.

"I—" I knew there was a risk of pissing him off if I told him the truth, but I let it roll out anyway. "I wanted the choice to be mine. You could force me to change, this place could force me to change, but I don't want to lose every part of my autonomy."

He stared at me, the look in his eyes unchanging, and I waited for his anger or at least annoyance, but he leaned back, and his face softened.

"You're not mad?"

He shook his head and waved at the clothes. "Get dressed, I have to tend to some things and you're coming along."

I pulled on the clothes and flipped my hair over my shoulders. Kirk grabbed a belt loop and tugged me closer. "I can respect that you still want control, but if you do anything to test me or a reason not to trust you, you'll regret it."

The pacing footsteps in the living room indicated Miles was getting restless waiting on us. "I know you want to finish your fuck, Kirk," he yelled. "But can we get this over with? Alan is waiting in the security room."

Kirk grabbed my hand and led me to the living room. After so long, it felt strange to be so covered, I wondered what kind of business a crime leader would take his sex slave to.

But wondering about his intentions would get me nowhere except trouble, so I didn't dare ask about it.

"You sure you want to bring her," Miles asked, pointing to me as if I wasn't there.

"Yes, as if you haven't toted Alley around a hundred times."

"Alley didn't just try to run."

"Not recently, but Alley caused her own fair share of trouble once," Kirk said. "I've heard plenty of stories about her first few weeks here."

Miles shook his head. "That's the very reason I don't take to the new ones." He gave me a glare then headed out the door.

Kirk gave my arm a tug and I followed the two of them down the hallway to the elevator and down to the lobby of the building. They led me down a hallway until, I recognized where we were. Kirk pushed open the door and we stood on the catwalk above the room where I had woken up.

The room I had been dragged to for my punishment after running.

My stomach clenched, and I grabbed the railing, hoping this wasn't a cruel joke or worse.

Kirk glanced back, squeezing my hand, but he didn't slow down or give me time to pause.

I swallowed the emotions, fighting the clog in my throat, and keeping my eyes on the floor. We continued across the catwalk past the stairs leading downward, to a door on the other side.

The room was hot and heavy, and filled with the buzz of electronics. The blond man sitting in front of the computer panel swiveled in his chair as we entered and nodded.

Past him, monitors covered a wall, showing hallways, a pool, the overlook, a grassy area outside, guest rooms....

Kirk wasn't kidding when he said everything in the place was being monitored. I figured he'd dragged me here to teach me a lesson about how hopeless it was to try to get away.

I continued studying the monitors while the men next to me whispered about a "guest" who had been in a restricted area with one of the "girls". The man at the desk rewound some of the footage and showed it to Kirk.

"He was probably trying to get privacy," Kirk said.

"People don't really expect that here," the blond replied. "And Kat went right along with him."

Kirk cleared his throat and glanced at me. "Well, we don't exactly encourage them to correct customers or go against their wishes."

"What I mean is, she doesn't look even the least bit startled. Usually, I'd expect to see one of the girls to look antsy at least, as they're being led into a place, they know is off limits. She looks completely calm."

"Morton is new," Miles added. "Which is either an excuse or a reason to be more suspicious. There was no harm this time, but I think we should keep an eye on him."

The blond nodded. "I'll make a note for everyone to keep track of him. He's registered here until tomorrow afternoon."

"I'll have someone chat with Kat later," Miles said.

Kirk chuckled. "By someone, I presume you mean Alley. I assume nothing came up in his initial background check, but I'll see if I can dig a little deeper."

Miles nodded then glanced at me.

"She won't say anything." Kirk lifted my chin and stared into my eyes. "Understand?"

"Yes, Master."

"Why don't you bring her down to dinner with Alley and me?"

I twitched, and Kirk must've felt it because he squeezed my hand. "I'll let you know later. Text me if anything else comes up."

"I'll take that as a hint not to come knocking on your door again."

"Yes." The edge of Kirk's lip tipped up, but his eyes were dead serious.

Miles chuckled, and smacked Kirk on the back of the shoulder as he left. Then, Kirk nodded to the blond. "Take a ten-minute break."

The man smirked. "Planning a quickie in the security office?"

"No less chance of being interrupted here than in my

own room. I'll keep an eye on him, but I also have a lesson in mind for my errant slave."

"Don't make a mess; I'm on shift for another hour, so I can't exactly get away with leaving it for the next guy."

"You have my word." Kirk chuckled, placing his hand on the back of my neck. My body stiffened, and I tried to read his body language out of the corner of my eye.

His eyes were soft, even after the blond man left us alone.

"I take it this is a lesson in why I shouldn't try to run?"

"Partially." He pulled me to him, smiling as my body reacted to his nearness. "What are you afraid of?"

"Gabe...." Among other things, but nothing in this room could address those fears.

"I said I'd protect you from him," he whispered—it was more of a promise than an admonishment. With his arm around my waist, he nudged me closer to the monitors. Holding my back to his chest, he clicked a few keys then pointed to the desktop monitor. It was the common room where Alley and I had been waiting on the laundry....

I saw myself standing alone, arms wrapped around my stomach as the girls crowded around the table. I remembered the fear that swirled through my veins as I watched Gabe across the room. The video continued, and I watched myself run out of the room. Kirk switched the video to the stairwell—where I stood and debated what to do.

"Someone knew from the moment I headed toward the door. That's how you found me so quickly."

"Yes. They paged me as soon as they saw you move away from the group. Although they didn't recognize it as panic, until we realized who you had seen. He wasn't supposed to be there."

"Do you think he was looking for me?"

"Maybe, no one has mentioned it to him. If he didn't realize you were there, it'd confirm his suspicions."

I felt his breath on my neck as he explained, and I shivered. "He knew I was there. I saw it on his face."

"If he tries anything, we'll catch him as quickly as we caught you, as long as you stay where you belong, you'll be fine."

I relaxed, letting my body sink into his. "Are there cameras in your room?"

"No, only guest rooms and public rooms."

"So isn't it possible that—"

"Don't, Silver. Do you know how much trouble he'd have to go through just to get you to a room without a camera?"

"Is this how you knew I was here?"

Kirk shook his head. "One of the men with Gabe was supposed to be on duty here, and the guard at the other station was in on it, too. They've all been taken off security duty, plus Miles and I can access the feed from our computers. We're keeping an eye on all of them."

They'd actually done some in depth investigation into a single girl being dragged on premises. It proved they wanted to know how and when anyone and anything came and went on the property.

My eyes scanned the monitors again. "This place is huge."

"We manage."

The breath on my neck turned to kisses, and I wanted to pull away as it sent waves of tension down to my core. I'd only lasted a week, and now, beyond all rational thought I felt like I'd become obsessed with sex.

I wanted the few minutes of pleasure to numb my brain

to the pain. His acceptance and protection— they were the promise that the pain would go away.

Kirk stiffened, then leaned around me and tapped a few keys to bring up a different image.

"Damn it." Kirk spun toward the door and typed something into his phone. "Stay close to me."

Better than getting left behind. He slid his phone back into his pocket and reached back to grab my wrist.

"Lesson learned, I'm staying with you," I promised.

He glanced back with a half-smile and squeezed my arm, then loosened his grip, moving it down to my hand and pulling me into a jog as we crossed the catwalk and re-entered the hallway on the other side.

I was relieved to get away from that damn basement room as quickly as possible, but Kirk didn't slow down. Instead of the elevator he led me to the stairs, I managed to keep up with him as he jogged to the third floor, but my lungs felt like they'd caught fire.

The third floor looked like a hotel, and it wasn't hard to conclude that these were the guest rooms. But I hadn't gotten a good look at the monitor he was concerned with, so I had no idea where we were going or what the hurry was. The door at the end of the hallway was wide open, with Miles standing just inside.

I lingered in the hallway as Miles and Kirk confronted the patron, and the slave—Kat. I almost wanted to gloat. Three more men came up behind me, and Kirk pushed me against the wall, keeping me right behind him.

"We weren't doing anything against the rules," the patron said, crossing his arms over his chest. Kat crouched down next to him, keeping her eyes on the floor.

Miles motioned to the other men. "Take him to the security office and search him for drugs."

My head jerked up in interest. All this commotion over some guy with drugs. What kind of criminals were they?

"I got it on site," he hissed as two of the men wrestled him toward the door.

"If so," Miles said. "We'll find out."

The guy kept hollering as they pulled him down the hallway, then I heard a crack and he went silent.

"Stand up, Kat," Kirk said, holding out his hand. I thought for a moment he was offering to help her up, but she rose and kept her hands to her sides.

"I don't have anything; you can search me if you want." She grinned and held up her arms.

"You were with him when he passed off the drugs in the hallway."

"Didn't see a thing. He never seemed intoxicated."

"You do," Miles said. "You know the rules."

Kat scoffed and took a step back. "I haven't taken anything." She glared past them to me.

"You know what happens if we find out that you're lying."

"If I'm lying... I've never been in trouble. I don't know what you saw, but I guess you need someone to take things out of when the favorites can't pay for their own transgressions."

"What are you talking about?" Miles asked, giving Kirk and me a sideways glance.

"You're all in here interrogating me, but no one interrogates *her*."

I lifted my eyes and found everyone staring at me.

"She tries to get out, and—"

"She got her punishment," Kirk said.

"And yet she's wondering around—"

Miles growled and grabbed her forearm, pulling her

toward the door. "It's not your place to make empty accusations, Kat."

"We're supposed to tell you everything we know, but not make accusations?"

Miles swung her around and pinned her to the wall by her throat. I winced at the soft crack of her body, followed by a hiss, as she hit the wall. "Do not get smart."

I crept closer to Kirk.

"If you have something to say, keep it simple and make it good." Miles growled.

"She's plotting something. I overheard her talking about a meeting, then she slipped out while we—"

"Get her out of here, Miles," Kirk yelled.

Miles pushed Kat out the door to the third man who had been waiting in the hallway. "Take her up for a blood test then lock her up." Then, his attention came back to me. "You're quickly making a lot of enemies."

Kirk squeezed my hand. "Kat was looking for a convenient scapegoat. Silver has only been out of my sight a few times and she's—"

"I agree, but we should find out who is involved *before* Ross gets back. I'm not sure he'll see it our way," Miles said, rubbing his thumb over his lips. "I'm going up to have a chat with Alley. Pull up what you can on Morton and get the records of every girl he's requested."

Chapter Eleven

SCAPEGOAT

KIRK and I took a detour back to the security room so he could download the data he wanted, while Miles headed back to his apartment. I leaned against his shoulder as the elevator set off to return us to the ninth floor. We slowed to a stop on the fourth floor and I straightened, moving to my position just behind him and lowering my head.

I saw two sets of feet enter.

"Well, if it isn't Kirk and his feisty whore."

I recognized Gabe's voice and my stomach dropped. Kirk didn't speak as the men flanked him and the doors closed, but he widened his stance and his body tensed.

Gabe reached around to touch me, and Kirk knocked away his hand and punched the button for the seventh floor. The other man grabbed Kirk by the throat. The elevator shook then the doors opened. Kirk broke free and kicked Gabe, then shoved me out of the elevator. I twisted around trying to keep my eyes on them and landed on my ass in the middle of the seventh-floor hallway. Before I could get to my feet, the elevator doors closed.

I ran to the stairs and up to the next floor. Miles' door opened just as I entered the hallway.

"I got the call," he said, still holding a phone to his ear. He pointed inside. "Wait with Alley."

I didn't move, looking back at the elevator.

"One of them pushed the emergency stop." He grabbed me and dragged me to the door. "They're in the control room putting in the override. Wait here."

He shoved me through the doorway and tossed a key to Alley. "Keep it locked unless it's me or Kirk."

The door slammed in my face, and Alley slid the key into the double cylinder deadbolt. "They'll be fine," she said, but I could see the lack of conviction in her eyes.

I paced around the room, rubbing my hands over my face then wringing my fingers in frustration. I needed something to do other than standing helplessly in someone's apartment. My chest tightened, and I leaned against the back of the couch then bent over, pressing my hands into my knees.

"Here," Alley said, handing me a glass of water. I hadn't even noticed that she'd gone into the kitchen.

"I'm fine," I said, brushing her away.

"You're panicking, just take a few sips and calm down."

"Why? Did you drug it?" I regretted the words as soon as I saw Alley's face. I knew she hadn't, but—

"Damn the alcohol is strong tonight," I said, pushing away the glass of reddish liquid.

"You're just overly sensitive since you never drink." Charlene pushed my glass back in my direction. "We're barely two drinks in, don't be a pussy during your early birthday celebration. We're having fun tonight."

"And if I drink much more, I'm not going to remember any of it. I think something is off." I rubbed my forehead and laid my head back.

Two men came over and sat down next to us. "Evenin' ladies," the one who sat next to me said.

"We have friends coming," I said, but my tongue felt useless and all my words were slow. "Oh, god, you drugged us."

I slide down the back of the couch to the floor, pressing my forehead against my knees.

"Silver," Alley called, shaking my shoulder. "Are you okay?"

"Yeah, sorry. What I said wasn't really meant for you. I just remembered something."

"You were drugged? Gabe?"

Rubbing my forehead, I shook my head. "I don't remember seeing him. And the two guys I do remember, I haven't seen here."

There was a thud at the door, and I jumped. Alley peeked through the peephole and unlocked the door. Kirk walked in behind Miles, but his face was red, and his cheek-bone and knuckles bloodied.

I climbed up and ran over to them.

Miles stepped out of the way, collecting Alley in a hug. He looked like he had the beginnings of a black eye, and his right fist was also bloodied. "Security took Gabe and Drew up to lockup. Go get your Master cleaned up."

Kirk leaned against the wall for a moment, closing his eyes.

"What's going to happen to them?" I asked.

"They wanted revenge, they got it." Miles said. "They'll stay in lockup until Ross gets back, but he'll probably release them."

"So what can't they get away with?"

"Silver," Kirk snapped, and I pulled back into slave mode.

"Sorry, Master."

Regardless of Kirk's admonishment, Miles answered my question. "Like everyone here, they stay as long as their value is more than their trouble."

I took that as a jab at me as well and nodded. Kirk put his arm over my shoulder and I helped him back to his apartment. He locked the door behind us and pulled off his torn shirt.

"Shit," I breathed. "You look worse than I did."

"They wanted to play with you."

"Well, I at least hope they look equally bad." I left him on the couch and went to the kitchen, grabbing a few bags of frozen vegetables and wrapping them in dishtowels. Then I filled a bowl with warm water and grabbed a small roll of paper towels.

I put the icepacks on his chest where the injuries seemed to be the worst then I used a wet paper towel to wipe away the dried blood on his cheek.

Kirk caught my hand and brought my palm to his mouth and kissed it. "This is quite a switch. And, yes, they look at least as bad as I do."

"Good." I finished cleaning his cheekbone, and put one of the smaller icepacks against it, cleaning the rest of the blood from his knuckles while he held it there. "Anything else I can do?"

"Ibuprofen is in the cabinet above the refrigerator. Bring me that and a glass of water."

I had to climb onto the counter next to the fridge to reach the bottle of pills then I jumped down and filled a glass with water. I stared down at it for a second. It hadn't been that long since he hadn't even trusted me with a glass, now I was waiting on him.

He took the pill bottle and sat the glass down on the end table while he dumped three capsules into his palm. He tossed them back and took a swig of water. Placing one of the cushions on the edge of the couch, he moved around to lie across it, and brought me down to sit between his outstretched legs.

"I should get to work," he groaned.

"You just got beat up in an elevator."

"And that doesn't help me figure out who is responsible for the drugs."

He kissed my neck and I scooted away so he could get up. "Can I help?"

"No."

I opened my mouth, about to let everything spill that I had remembered while I was in Miles' apartment, but I thought he had more important things to tend to at the moment.

Kirk brushed his thumb over my bottom lip then kissed me. "What were you going to say?"

"It's not important right now. Go do your job."

"Then why are you thinking about it?"

"I remembered something, right before you and Miles came back—about the night I was brought here."

Kirk sat back. "Tell me."

"I told you that I was supposed to meet some friends for dinner, but that I didn't remember going. I must've gone, because I remembered being there with one of my friends, we were having drinks and I felt strange—especially since we were only on our second drink. Then two men sat down at our table, and that's all I have right now."

"What restaurant?"

"The Pufferbelly. It's always a quiet restaurant."

He nodded. "I know the place. And your friend's name?"

I bit my lip, debating on whether to give it to him.

"Silver, I'm trying to find out what happened and if your friend is okay."

"Charlene Wilson."

Brushing his hands through my hair, he kissed me again, slower this time. "I'll find out what they did to you."

"Thank you."

He blew out a long breath then stood, holding his side as he moved to the desk. I picked up the ice packs and returned them to the freezer then I laid across the couch.

I HEARD something thud against the desk and sat up to look over the back of the couch.

"Ross is arranging a flight back to deal with everything," Kirk explained.

And if Miles was right, I was in trouble. "He's fond of Kat, isn't he?"

Kirk shrugged. "Kat thinks everyone is fond of her."

"Yeah, I got that."

He frowned at me.

"She told me that she was the one… with you the other night."

"Of course she did." He rolled his chair over to the couch and put his hand around the back of my neck. "You don't have anything to worry about. Not from her or Ross."

"Then why is he coming back? And why can Gabe get away with everything?"

Kirk sat back in the chair and crossed his arms over his chest. I sucked my lower lip in and gnawed on it, realizing I'd probably overstepped my bounds again.

"Ross is suspicious of new people, especially when they don't listen and cause a fuss. It can get bad for business fast.

Kat throwing you under the bus won't help your cause, but Gabe attacking me may help, since it adds credibility to you running because you were scared. Honestly, I knew it was coming, but I was hoping you wouldn't be with me. He has a vengeful streak, but usually once he gets it out, everything goes back to normal."

"Why put up with it in the first place? You said he's always causing trouble."

"He's paid his dues. He's been with Ross a long time, a lot longer than I have. He knows the right people, and he knows enough about them, that they know better than to cross him."

"And you're sure he's not the weasel?"

"No, but if he is, he needs to screw up big enough for there to be no doubt about it."

"You've been watching him." I realized. "That's how you found me."

Kirk nodded. "And now you know too much."

"That mean you're going to kill me?"

He smirked and shook his head. "Keep it up, Silver. You almost went too far in front of Miles."

"I was distraught." I sat back on my heels, still facing the back of the couch. "I don't want to piss you off or get in trouble, I just need an outlet, and you're kinda the only person I talk to. When you don't have your scary face on, you're not horrible company."

"I have a scary face?"

"At the moment, it's more like pathetically bruised face."

He raised an eyebrow into something that more closely resembled scary face and I backed down.

"I should be putting you in your place, but as long as you're obeying and not causing trouble, I can deal with you talking. It's far better than trying to figure out what you're quietly plotting." He cocked a finger at me. "Come here."

I leaned over the back of the couch. He stood, and before I could duck back, he dragged me over the back of the couch to stand in front of him. Then he sat down and pulled me on top of his lap, straddling his thighs in the computer chair.

"The chair is going to break." I said as it creaked under us.

"I doubt it, but even if it did, I'd take most of the impact. You'd probably have a good laugh."

"You're already half-broken." I poked near one of the bruises and he grimaced, grabbing my finger and twisting both of my hands behind my back.

"I'm not half-broken." He took both of my wrists into one hand, pulling them backward so my back arched, and my breasts thrust outward into his face. Then, he pushed my shirt up and rolled my nipple between his fingers.

The same one Ross had tried to twist off, but his erotic movements overrode the pain, and even though I still wanted to wrestle myself away, I was afraid of the chair giving out, so I held my statue-like pose.

Faster than I could think, Kirk lifted me up and sat me on my feet. I grabbed the couch to keep my balance and stared at him wide eyed.

He looked away dismissively. "How about being a good pet and making dinner. Alley and Miles are coming up in an hour."

At least pet was better than slave, I thought, but— "You're doing it again."

Someone knocked on the door, and I balled my hands at my sides. It was probably a good thing I couldn't say my peace, but it didn't make it any less frustrating. The office chair spun around, knocking into the desk as Kirk went to answer the door. I crossed my arms over my chest and sat against the back of the couch.

Hot, cold, fucked, ignored, friendly, distant. I wanted away from the mood swings.

And half of them were my own.

A scrawny black-haired man stood in the doorway, I thought I'd noticed him in passing, but I had no idea who he was or what his role might be.

"Don't punch the messenger, but I was sent down to let you know that Ross threw down the order to release Gabe and Darian. Ross will be back tonight, and he wants everyone in his office—including your slave—when he arrives. You may want to stay here until—"

"Unless that's an order from Ross, I'll damn well do as I please," Kirk said.

The other man nodded and made a clicking sound with his mouth. "Okay, I was just—"

"Anything else?"

Black hair looked past Kirk to me, and I turned my gaze away, dropping my hands to the back of the couch. I probably shouldn't have been standing there, let alone listening, but too little too late.

I heard the door click and the deadbolt slide into place. Kirk had started leaving the key in the inner lock while he was here. Apparently, he really did trust me not to run, not that I'd make it to the front door without him noticing.

"Dinner," he reminded me, waving toward the kitchen.

That was the last thing I wanted to think about, but since everyone knew about Gabe, I figured they'd all be watching for another attack. "What am I supposed to make?"

"It's a full kitchen. Make something good."

"I didn't notice any frozen pizzas or fish sticks."

"Now's not the time to be a smart ass."

"I'm being fucking serious. I was never a—" I waved toward the kitchen. "Whatever they call people who are good in the kitchen. You want me to build a table or cabinet and I'm good, around glass and cooking things I'm a disaster. I have burned Ramen."

Kirk covered his face with both hands. "I don't even know what to say to that."

"I always wanted to be at the shop with Dad, not in the kitchen…" I almost fell to my knees at the thought of never seeing them again. "Can we forget I said that?"

Kirk tucked me against his chest. I avoided looking at him, as I swallowed the tears and emotions.

"I can't believe you all even cook anyway." I shrugged him off. "Can't we just order food?"

"That won't be half as amusing."

"Right, watching me set fire to your kitchen is going to be fabulous. Maybe we should ask Miles and Alley to come up now and enjoy the show."

Kirk stepped toward me and I dodged his grasp, darting into the kitchen. He caught my wrist and pinned me to the counter, so I took the opportunity to rub against him.

"You're tempting fate," he warned. "I put some pork chops in the fridge last night, get them out and put them on a cutting board. I'll be right back."

Cutting board? That was dangerously close to giving me a knife. I laid them out and threw away the packaging. Then, I saw what Kirk returned with.

"I'm sorry," I squeaked.

"Wash your hands, pull down your pants, and lean over the counter."

I watched him lube up the plug as I slowly ran my hands

under the hot water. I couldn't tell if it was the vibrating one or not, and I shuddered at the thought of trying to cook with that thing having a fiesta in my ass.

"I'm the boss," he said as I pulled down my pants and got into position. "Even if you're trying to be cute, no trying to passive-aggressively top me."

There was no foreplay with this one, but I had been worked up all day, so it didn't much matter. He pressed the cold tip to my hole and slid it in slowly. It was one of the larger ones, so by the time he had it nearly in, I wanted to climb up the wall. It fell into place with one more push then he rubbed against it with the palm of his hand. "Put your pants back on."

He was going to kill me.

I pulled the pants up and buttoned them, the tight material pressing firmly against the base of the plug. You took control by giving up your control, I reminded myself, dragging my hair away from my face.

Kirk heated up a pan and poured in some olive oil and sprinkled seasonings over the two pieces of meat. I wasn't sure if it was the pressure in my ass and the combination of everything else but watching him stand over the stove shirtless and cooking wasn't doing a damn thing to help me reign in my gung-ho sex drive.

"Grab a baking sheet." He pointed to a tall cupboard next to the fridge. "And make some fries. You can handle that, right?"

We'll see. I nodded. Walking with the plug in made me want to drop to my knees. Crawling might have even been easier.

Hold it together.

The fries pinged against the metal of the pan as I poured out a layer and spread them out.

"What has gotten into you anyway?"

"I don't know," I admitted. "I prefer the pleasure to the pain, and—"

"And for some reason the pleasure's the only thing on your mind today?"

I nodded, pushing the baking sheet across the counter to the stove. "Tomorrow is my birthday," I whispered. "The more I hold on, the more miserable I feel. I just want to let go and feel something else for a while."

The oven beeped, and Kirk slid the fries onto the bottom rack. Then, he took my hand and pulled me closer. I felt the heat of the stove against my side as he pinned me between himself and the counter. "Let's get through tonight, and I promise, I'll give you a good day."

"You sure you can promise that? What if Ross—"

He silenced me with a finger. "I've been dealing with Ross and Gabe, and everything else in this building long enough to know it'll blow over."

Kirk placed the pork chops in the hot oil and seared each side, then turned down the heat, pulling me back against his chest.

A criminal with a soft side—a very thorny soft side, but it was there.

"Even if this blows over, Alley said." I swallowed, my mouth felt like it was flooding from trying to hold down my emotions. "She mentioned initiation."

Kirk grunted and tilted his head back.

"Why didn't you tell me?"

"Because I didn't think you were ready to know yet."

I struggled out of his grasp, knowing that it was a mistake, but Kirk let me go. "When would I have been ready to know?"

"When you can listen; when I tell you to calm down and come back over here."

My gut tightened, hands fisted at my sides. I wanted to disobey just to show that I could. Choices. I took a deep breath and took the two steps to close the distance between us.

Kirk wiped away the tear that escaped.

"What's he going to do to me?"

"Hard to tell. I think he just comes up with it on the spot. It's not worth worrying about tonight."

I bit my cheek, and as if he knew, Kirk lifted my chin. I released the pinched skin and nodded. Even though I was still worrying.

"What if it is tonight?"

"He likes to do it during the weekend, when there's a big crowd, so you have at least a few days. Worry about it when I tell you to worry about it."

I scoffed. "You won't tell me to."

"Then, give me that." He flipped over the meat and checked the fries. "I just got into an elevator brawl over you. Don't question everything that I do or tell you to do." He kissed my neck then patted me on the ass, intentionally hitting the plug.

"Keep an eye on the food while I grab a shirt."

I pulled the fries out of the oven when the timer went off and put the sheet on top of the stove. Then I peeked through the cupboards until I found the plates. I sat out two and divided the fries between them.

Kirk popped some pills into his mouth as he rounded the corner and took a swig of water, leaving his glass on the corner of the counter. "The pork chops should be done," he said, removing the lid. He poked one with a knife then turned off the burner, leaving me to plate them.

"They're on their way down. Set the table and put out a beer for Miles." He disappeared into the living room again. Since he didn't give me a drink preference, I filled up his glass with water, and sat out the food and silverware, finishing just as I heard voices in the next room.

Miles stepped around the corner and smirked at the table. "What the hell'd you do to the girl?"

Kirk rubbed the base of the plug and a breathy moaned slipped through my throat. "Simmering misery looks good on you."

I had to bite my lip as I knelt as his feet when we sat down to eat. The position pulled my jeans even tighter against the butt plug. The only comforting thing was that Miles could no longer see me from where he sat. I leaned my forehead against Kirk's leg. He pressed his hand against my neck and traced my jawline with his thumb, winking when I looked up at him.

He really was enjoying every moment of my discomfort.

Chapter Twelve

WHO'S YOUR MASTER

AFTER DINNER, I finally got my reprieve from the butt plug. Even though being sprawled over the kitchen table in full view of Miles and Alley wasn't my preferred method, at least it was done. And with little time to spare, since he and Miles got a message from Ross to be in his office ten minutes later.

Alley gave me a quick hug and half smile before following Miles out of the room, so he could get her back to his apartment before the meeting.

I wished she was going up with us. I was fairly certain I wouldn't have much to worry about with Kirk and Miles in the room, but around here, being the only girl in a room of men never seemed like a good scenario.

Kirk skipped the leash, probably to show Ross that he trusted me, although we'd been over half of the building today without it. Before he opened the door to the apartment, he lifted my chin.

"Keep your eyes down and do exactly as you're told. No

pauses, no second guessing. Walk behind me. In his office, stand just behind me. Ignore Gabe."

"Yes, Master." I tried to lock my fear in some quiet place in my mind, but I could feel my entire body quivering with adrenaline.

Kirk pushed me into the wall, capturing my mouth. Wrestling to control my emotions, knowing I couldn't, I opened my lips and his tongue plunged inside, leaving me with the taste of him.

He led me to the elevator, not even taking my arm to keep me behind him. It was up to me to prove my worth.

To prove that he owned me.

I wanted to grab his hand when the elevator opened on the tenth floor.

"Breathe," he whispered without looking back. We stood in the hallway, and he glanced at his phone. A few seconds later, the elevator dinged again.

Oh, god, what are we waiting on, my brain screamed. I imagined Gabe stepping off the elevator and beginning the entire confrontation again, but Kirk was calm, and as the elevator doors opened, I saw Miles.

He walked past me, and he and Kirk walked side by side in front of me until we reached Ross' office door. They stayed close, flanking me slightly as we joined the group already in the room—Ross, Gabe, Darian, the one who'd aided in the elevator attack, and Alan, the blond from the security room.

Beyond accounting for the bodies in the room, I resisted looking around, not only to stay out of trouble, but because I knew that I'd just get flustered if I saw their faces again.

"Tell me," Ross began. "Why the hell I had to fly back here when you are supposed to be in charge."

"We had it under control," Miles said.

"I can tell that from all of the bruised faces. We have a breach, someone selling drugs, and all you can do is fight amongst yourselves." Ross knocked his chair backward as he stood. "You argued to keep her, Kirk. Was it simply to piss Gabe off or put her to use? Because frankly I'm tired of the shenanigans."

"I find her to be far more fun alive, and I didn't feel like having to clean up a murder, or deal with the mess they would have made even if they left her alive."

"And you still believe that after this morning's altercation?"

"Yes."

Ross groaned. "Why is she even wandering around after she tried to run?"

"She was punished, she learned her lesson, and she hasn't caused any problems since."

"You don't consider this morning a problem?"

"She wasn't directly responsible."

"I think you're smitten. You don't spend enough time with the other slaves; you don't understand the mindset or how to make them behave."

"With all due respect," Miles said. "I think he does. I think he made better work than most of us would in training a strong-willed girl."

"And look who's talking." Ross waved off Miles. "I suddenly feel like I'm surrounded by humanitarians."

I heard Gabe snicker, and Ross' head jerked in his direction. "And you, fighting over a damn slave girl. You shouldn't have brought her here in the first place. If you want to have your fun, do it elsewhere and make sure it doesn't get tracked back here."

Ross righted his chair then sat down. "Silver."

Concentrate. "Yes, Master."

"Come here."

I walked past Kirk, hoping that no one could see my body shaking. Hell, I hoped they couldn't feel it as I walked up to the desk.

Ross turned to the side, motioning for me to stand in front of him. "Take off your shirt."

No hesitating. I pulled it over my head and held it in my hand, unsure of what he wanted me to do with it.

"Turn around and kneel."

As if being this close wasn't bad enough, he had to be where I couldn't see him. I turned and dropped to my knees in front of him, gathering my shirt in my lap.

He brushed my hair off my back, tucking it around my shoulder, then he traced every single mark left from the beating he'd ordered Kirk to give me.

I struggled to keep my breath even as he pressed the still-sensitive skin hard enough to aggravate the deep bruises.

He was counting them, I'd realized. Making sure that Kirk hadn't gone easy on me. Making sure that every single one was exactly what he expected.

"Turn around," he ordered when he was finished.

I stayed on my knees but shuffled around to face him.

"You've learned your lesson?"

"Yes, Master."

"And what is it?"

"To do as I'm told, Master."

"And if I told you to crawl across the room and suck Gabe's dick?"

"Then, I would do as you ordered, Master." *Breathe. It's just a test. Please let it be just a test.*

Ross grabbed the shirt out of my hands. "Crawl over to Gabe and undo his pants."

My stomach turned into a ball of ice. I moved to hands and knees and dragged myself across the room, keeping gaze glued to the floor. I didn't want to see anyone else's face. I didn't want to seek Kirk's neutral expression, or Gabe's smirk, or Ross' scowl.

When I reached Gabe, I sat back on my feet. His belt buckle clanged as I released it. I popped the button free and slid the zipper down.

I already wanted a shower, a scalding shower to rinse away the feeling of having to touch him. Even his clothes reeked of cigarettes.

A bulge grew just behind the blue fabric of his under-wear. But I dropped my hands to my lap. I'd done exactly as Ross had said.

Gabe grabbed my hair, but I wasn't taking orders from him. I waited for Ross' next command. Seconds ticked by, and Gabe grew impatient as his erection grew.

Ross chuckled. I heard his footsteps behind me.

He was going to force me to take Gabe's cock, just like he'd done with Kirk.

Instead, he dropped my shirt in my lap and patted the back of my head, pushing Gabe's hand away from me.

"You think I should reward you for everything? Kirk was right to take her from you. To keep us all out of trouble and what could have become news."

Ross jerked my head back. "Put your shirt on and go back to your Master. And you..." He grabbed Gabe through his underwear. "Stop thinking with your damn cock."

I pulled my shirt over my head and scurried over to stand behind Kirk.

Gabe grunted loudly then stumbled backward. Served him right, I thought, but then Ross approached Kirk.

"Now that we've taken care of the nonsense. Where do we stand on the drug investigation?"

"He sold them to at least two girls. Caught him on video passing a dime bag and we recovered the drugs."

"How were the girls paying for it?"

"I doubt they were," Gabe groaned. "Freebies get them hooked then they'll do anything for more."

Ross nodded and sat back against his desk, I felt his gaze on me again. "Unless the slave wants to service us all while we talk, her presence is no longer needed. Gabe—"

My heart shot into my throat.

"—do Kirk a favor and escort her back to his apartment."

Kirk's back straightened, but as he'd told me before, he had to pick his fights with Ross, and I suspected this wouldn't be one of them. He unhooked his key ring from his belt loop. Gabe held out his hand, but Kirk handed them to me, holding up one in particular. "Lock the door behind you, take a shower, and go to bed."

"Yes, Master."

I held onto the key he'd held up, thankful they at least gave me something to claw Gabe's face with if worse came to worst.

"Gabe," Ross added. "Be back here in five minutes."

Gabe grunted and pushed open the door, he didn't wait for me to even catch up. There I was, sprinting after the man who'd kidnapped and nearly raped me. The last thing I wanted to do was climb onto the elevator with him, but there was no choice for me. I kept as much distance between us as possible—still careful to stay close enough that he wouldn't have an excuse to say anything.

On the ninth floor, he led me to Kirk's door and leaned against the wall while I unlocked it.

"Don't worry," he said.

I made the mistake of looking up in confusion, and he winked.

"I'll have you yet, Princess."

I jumped inside the apartment, slammed the door shut, and locked it as fast as I could.

———

I SAT ON THE COUCH, checking the time every few minutes while I waited for Kirk to get back. I turned on the TV trying to drown out my own brain, but after Gabe's threat I didn't dare step in the shower where I wouldn't be able to hear if anyone came in.

Gabe was upstairs with the rest of them, so I reasoned he wouldn't be coming down to get me.

But reason doesn't always win in a completely unreasonable situation.

Around one in the morning, I heard the deadbolt snap, and I shot up from the couch, looking for something to grab.

"Easy, Silver." Kirk slid in and locked the door behind him. "I thought you'd be asleep."

"Oh, sure after today, I'm going to sleep like a baby. Besides, I thought I'd have to let you in."

"I told you to go to bed. I picked up a spare key from security. You haven't even showered."

I looked down at my clothes. It was lucky only he knew that I hadn't listened.

"Did Gabe do anything?"

I shook my head. "Do, no. He said he'd have me though."

"What?"

"Don't worry." I mocked Gabe's voice. "I'll have you yet, Princess."

"Princess?"

I rolled my eyes.

"Time for a shower." Kirk wrapped an arm around my back and lifted me off the floor. He winced with the motion but didn't let me go until we reached the shower.

"You going to wash my hair?" I teased as we stripped, waiting for the water to warm.

"Don't press your luck," he said, picking me up again and dropping me in the still cool stream.

I squealed and moved to the back of the tub. "If you didn't look like an invalid…."

"You're really asking for it tonight, aren't you?" He stepped in the front of the shower and I charted the injuries, the largest bruise was on his left side, paired with a smaller one near the bottom of his ribs on the right. There was another just above his left hip, the outside of his right thigh.

I was afraid he'd turn around and I'd see even more.

"I'm still walking and breathing, Silver. I haven't left you to the wolves yet."

I leaned against the wall, sleep threatening to claim me right there in the shower. Apparently now that he was back, my body no longer felt the need to stay on high alert. Kirk pulled me against him and lathered up my back.

"Why do you care what happens to me?" I whispered into his chest.

He didn't stop his movements, and I wondered if he

even heard me. I pulled away, even though my body felt weary and no longer willing to stand under its own volition.

"Why?" I asked again. "Why did you save me? Why do you hold me when I'm freaking out or hurting? Why do you let me get away with running my mouth to you?"

"Because I want you."

"As a slave."

"Yes." He pressed me into the wall, but didn't take his motions any further. "As my slave. The other girls aren't like you, Silver. If they fight, it's for a very different reason. You're alive—every bit of you. You fight for that. You're a torrid of emotions." He kissed me, pulling the rest of the energy out of my exhausted body. "I want to keep you that way, but that kind of attitude is dangerous here."

He rubbed the soap between his hands then caressed it over my breasts and ass. "And, I like having you as a distraction too much."

"I want that good day you promised me. I need a distraction, too."

"Right now, you need sleep."

I shook my head and covered my eyes as the tears came up from nowhere. "I didn't—I was terrified he'd make me keep going. Hell, I'm terrified of what you do to me. Everyone else instills a level far beyond terror."

He pulled my hands down and twisted them behind my back. "Do what I say, and you have no reason to be afraid of me."

"You even control me in my dreams now. You and your damn snake."

I wasn't even sure I was making sense anymore, so I kept my mouth closed. Leaning against the back of the stall and watching while Kirk scrubbed his own skin then turned off the water.

"Come on, Sugar."

I stepped out of the tub and wrapped a towel around my body, drying off as quickly as possible so I could crawl into bed and pass out.

Unceremoniously, Kirk and I both climbed into bed, and I pulled the covers up to my neck. Every day I ended up more confused, and I needed a reprieve. Not that I was any more likely to get that in my sleep.

Chapter Thirteen

THE SNAKE AND THE SCHEMER

I MANAGED A DREAMLESS NIGHT—OR at least I didn't remember any fucked up delusions the next morning. Kirk and I were both quiet during breakfast. I figured he had work to take care of, and for once, I was thankful for it. After the past twenty-four hours, I wasn't sure what I'd do if given the opportunity with him alone.

I stayed in the kitchen, trying to at least stay on his good side by doing the dishes and cleaning up, but it didn't take long to run out of things to do that wouldn't involve being in the same room.

He glanced up at me when I entered the living room, but continued working, his attention divided between his phone and computer.

"You ever decide what books you wanted?" he asked.

I pulled the notebook he'd given me from the home I'd given it under the couch and tore out the first sheet of paper. I put it on top of the e-reader.

"There are more than three books here."

"You said I could earn more," I said, leaning over the back of the couch. "Is everything okay?"

Kirk nodded. "I just thought you wanted some space, so I've been giving it to you."

"Do you really have to read me so easily?"

"Makes life easier," he said, hooking the e-reader to his computer. "Am I going in order?"

"Sure."

"I do have to go upstairs for a while."

I bit the inside of my cheek, I didn't want him to leave me alone or take him with me.

"You'll be fine" he handed back the e-reader. "You have two books; I'll do a couple more tonight."

He patted my cheek as he stood, and I jerked away.

"What's that about?" He twisted his fingers in my hair and pulled me to his face. "Sugar, you will be fine. No one is going to come in here to get you."

"You didn't see the look on Gabe's face last night."

"I already made sure that Gabe isn't even on site today. I'll be right upstairs, five minutes away, and I'll be back soon." He kissed me, and I parted my lips, giving him what —as far as anyone here was concerned—was his. "It's going to be a good day. I promised you that, and I'll give it to you, but I have to take care of things first."

"You're the boss."

Kirk scoffed. "Be ready to leave for lunch when I get back."

"Leave?" My heart pounded. "Where exactly are you taking me?"

"You'll see. Be ready in an hour. The clothes I want you to wear are in the top drawer."

As soon as the deadbolt clicked, I ran into the bedroom to see what clothes he'd left, hoping it'd give me some clue to what he was planning. The only thing in the top drawer was a cropped tank top and a pair of jean shorts.

The last time I'd stepped out of this room wearing regular clothes, the day had gone to hell fairly quickly.

———

THE DOOR OPENED, and I dropped the e-reader into the couch to look at the clock.

"You don't look ready," Kirk said.

"Um, you're fifteen minutes early," I said, but I wasn't entirely convinced of the argument myself. I held up the e-reader and waved it. "I was enjoying not being here for a while."

"Stop making excuses and get dressed." He crossed his arms and leaned against the wall, but what really caught my attention was his smile. I didn't recognize it. It wasn't the one he wore when he was being conniving to make me miserable or reassuring me even though he was worried. It was light and reflected a spark of mischief.

I was torn between running for my sanity and embracing it.

I slid the e-reader under the couch and sprinted into the bedroom, pulling on the clothes that he'd left in the drawer for me. Then, I met him at the front door.

"Swear you're on your best behavior." He said, putting his arm over my shoulders.

"Yes, Master."

As we stepped off the elevator on the ground floor, I could see freedom right through the front door—only 100 yards away, but before I could take a second step a young boy tackled Kirk's leg.

Kids? I couldn't imagine why on earth kids would be in this place.

An older girl followed behind and took the boy's hand. Kirk went down on one knee and ruffled her hair.

"Who is she?" the girl pointed to me.

"Silver."

A woman shouted from across the room. "Greg. Mindy."

Both kids jumped and retreated to a bench near the wall. The way the woman scowled, I guessed that she wasn't particularly happy with the kids talking to us. Either that, or she wasn't happy to be here. Ross stepped from around the corner and glanced in our direction. I dropped my eyes to the floor, watching everyone from the edge of my vision.

Ross and the woman turned their attention to each other.

"Ross's family," Kirk whispered. My eyes widened as I jerked back to look him in the face to confirm he wasn't kidding. I forced my mouth to stay closed.

Across the room, Ross silently summoned Kirk.

"Do. Not. Move."

I took a deep breath and pressed my back to the wall. "Yes, Master."

I stared out the window, but noticed the woman approaching in my periphery. I glanced passed her, but neither Ross nor Kirk were paying attention, so I assumed she was just tending to the children. She whispered something to them and pointed to Ross, then continued in my direction.

The kids scampered off to stand with their father—I still couldn't believe that Ross could serve in such a role.

I couldn't imagine what she'd have to say to me. Maybe she didn't know who... what I was. Maybe—

She stopped in front of me, without saying a word. Her mouth pressed in a line then she swung, hitting my cheek with the back of her hand.

I stumbled, sliding against the wall as Kirk and Ross ran toward us.

I wiped the blood from my lip while Ross' wife walked away as calmly as she'd approached. Ross intercepted her, and they exchanged a few heated whispers before she stormed out with the kids.

"What was that for?" I whispered to Kirk as he examined my face.

"Wrong place, wrong time."

"Story of my life lately." I knew I should have stayed in the apartment.

Ross handed Kirk a handkerchief, his gaze raking over me. Then, without a word, he walked around us and boarded the elevator.

Once Kirk had dabbed away the visible blood, he led me into a back room, stopping at an industrial sized kitchen sink to wet the handkerchief. "Are you okay?"

I nodded, even though the tinge of blood still polluted my mouth. "Maybe you should put me back in lock down."

"Emilyn gets pissy at least a few times a month. She wants him to get out of the business—mostly to get rid of the slaves. They've threatened divorce half a dozen times in the last year." Kirk tilted his head and snorted. "Like I said, you're trouble for the both of us. Need some ice?"

I shook my head. "She didn't hit that hard—just enough to startle me. I think I bit my lip."

Once he was satisfied that the bleeding had stopped, and nothing was swelling too much, he took my hand and led me into a walk-in refrigerator, handing me a bottle of water then strapping a cooler over his shoulder.

In another nearby storage room, he picked up a blanket and handed it to me.

My eyes widened. "You're taking me on a picnic?"

He nodded.

"Outside," I breathed. All the nerves in my body tingled at the thought of being outside. The grass, the sun. All I wanted was outside of these walls. It would be close enough to freedom for now.

"You run—"

I shook my head. "No running. I got the message."

As soon as we got outside, I wanted to drop the blanket and bask in the sun. Two steps were all it took, and I didn't care whether we went farther or not. My body felt lighter than it had in weeks, and the air smelled sweet, carrying the scent of spring flowers.

A long drive wound down the hill next to us, with a large gated fence at the end. But Kirk led me in the opposite direction of the drive, toward a large area of grass dotted with trees.

"To the outside world we're a large and very exclusive retreat. It hasn't been a difficult image to maintain since we screen anyone that we let in. They all know to keep their mouths shut. If they might be a danger to our cover, they don't get out."

I looked around. The grounds were beautifully maintained, but I didn't see a single other person around. "Why are you telling me this?"

"Because I figured if I entertain your incessant curiosity with information, you might manage to keep your mouth shut and keep yourself out of trouble."

"I find trouble even when I don't say a word. I feel bad for Ross' wife."

Kirk made a sour face. "Don't. She knew what he was when they got together. She saw money and power."

I wondered what Kirk saw, why he got into all of this when he seemed so different from the others, but I didn't think that'd be a great question to lead with.

"Do you want a family?"

"No," he answered quicker and with more certainty than I had anticipated. "I never considered sharing my life with anyone, definitely not kids."

We stopped in a slightly wooded area overlooking a small lake and I spread the blanket out while he opened the cooler, pulling out wine, potato salad, cole slaw, and chicken club wraps.

Kirk entertained my questions while we ate, even though his attention seemed to be directed at watching the area around us.

"Thank you," I said, unsure if it was the wine talking or the comforting feeling of the sun. I stretched out on my stomach across the blanket and let the sun warm my back. Kirk stretched out next to me, resting on his side.

"I'm not completely heartless and unreasonable."

I smiled then rolled to my back. I leaned up and kissed his lips.

His eyes widened, and he jerked back slightly. "You don't have—"

"I know, but every time you try to protect me, I make things harder."

"I manage."

"I know, but—I just—Can you make me forget where we are? Just for a little while?"

He looked like he was going to argue, but he pressed his lips to mine, and slid one hand up under my shirt. His fingers left tingling coolness in their wake as they traveled up to caress the underside of my breast.

"What are you up to, Silver?"

"We discussed this already. Then we got interrupted and the day went to shit. Can we just skip all of that today?"

His thumb traced the outside of my nipple and I felt it stiffen. Seeing his muscle, watching him use it, and being the victim of its use, it seemed contradictory that he could touch me with such delicacy.

He was probably quite experienced in getting women right where he wanted them with as few steps as necessary. I arched toward his touch, and his soft caresses turned into pinches, and rougher massaging motions. He pulled my leg up and slid his finger up the leg of my shorts and into my underwear while he kissed down my jawline and nipped at my earlobe.

"Unbutton your shorts," he whispered directly into my ear. "Take them off."

I did, lifting my hips to slide them down and then, kicking them off. He flipped me over to straddle his hips, and lifted my shirt over my head, before taking my breasts into his hands and capturing each of my nipples between two fingers.

My hips rocked, rubbing against his. I nearly fell forward when he released my breasts and trailed his fingers down my sides. He sat up, and I slid against his hips, into his lap. He took his shirt off and threw it on the blanket behind me, pulling my bare chest against his as he explored my neck and chest with his mouth—and intermittently his teeth. I felt his erection growing under me with each subtle movement I made.

I dragged my fingers through his short hair then pulled

back, tracing my fingers over the curves of the tattoo from his shoulder down to his elbow.

"You really like snakes."

"You want to talk about tattoos right now?" He bit my lip, and then laid me back on the blanket, to unzip his pants and free his erect cock.

I shook my head, lifting my hips to meet him as he slid inside me. As much as I wanted to forget where I was, and why I was doing this, it continued echoing in my head. I wanted to know if this was what it was usually like. And I wanted to gut myself for not only giving in but inciting him.

But I also wanted to enjoy the moment, the electrifying sensation as he filled me, and stimulated the nerves inside of me. The most intimate of acts, with someone who didn't even know my real name.

Kirk paused. "You're pulling away."

"Please, no lectures about how I need to—"

"No." He kissed my nose then traced my jawline.

"Sometimes you can border on sweet."

"Don't." He closed his pained eyes. "Don't expect sweet."

"But I can enjoy it now?"

He brushed his lips across mine, down my neck to my collarbone. "It is your fantasy today. Happy birthday."

I giggled and pushed against him. "Deal and you can tell me not to get attached to it tomorrow."

———

I CURLED UP AGAINST KIRK; we were both still naked in the middle of the field. "You seem different today."

"Re-evaluating my tactics," he replied, running his

fingers over the stray strands of hair that dangled over my shoulder.

"And discovering that a little honey works better than ignoring and barking at me."

"I never barked at you."

"You did a lot of growling." The wind shifted, drawing the sweet smell of nearby daffodils toward us. I thought it might be best to change the subject instead of egging him on. "Why do you have so many snake tattoos?"

"I like them."

"Snakes, or snake tattoos?"

Kirk dragged his fingers through my hair and pulled my knee up to hook it over his hip. "Both. I was a country boy. I loved finding snakes, but the tattoos just seemed fitting."

But? The way he phrased it made it seem strange—he didn't have the tattoos because he liked snakes. There was another reason. A reason I'd probably find myself in trouble for digging for. I waited, giving him a few moments to continue his thought and clarify if he wanted, but he traced his fingers down my arm to my thigh and down to my knee, leaving a tingling trail that lit up my nerves again.

"If you don't want me to get used to this, you should really stop doing that."

"I like watching your reaction."

I rolled against him, so I could stare into his face. "What do—what am I going to be expected to do to be a good slave?"

"I thought you wanted to forget about that today?"

"I figured I'd rather ask you while you're in a good mood."

He took a breath and pushed me off him, retrieving his shirt from the edge of the blanket. I had definitely ruined the serene mood. "What's expected depends on who you're with. Just do as you're told."

"But am I supposed to instigate, to…interact?"

"Most of them will expect you to at least act into it, yes. A blow-up doll would be cheaper and more effective if they didn't want interaction." He handed me my shirt. "Beyond that, they'll tell you what they want."

I slipped it on and rubbed the back of my neck, pulling my knees up to my chest and dropping my chin against them. Kirk smiled and twisted around, putting one leg behind me and one in front and holding me to his chest.

"I don't plan on sharing you more than I have to," he whispered, kissing my temple. "I've never been great at sharing."

"Is that why none of the other slaves can get your attention?"

"One reason among many."

I rested my head against his shoulder and watched the breeze lift up little ripples across the lake, creating a skewed image of the sky and surrounding plants. I felt like that water, trying to reflect back what everyone was projecting on me, only to have it distorted and unclear.

Kirk gathered my hair away from my neck, so he had access to kiss it, and I drifted back into that place of lust that he'd created for me. He moved the leg that was behind me.

"Lay back."

I silenced the arguments and questions, rolling back onto the blanket.

"What were you thinking about?" he asked, as if it wasn't bad enough that I had to give up every part of myself, now he wanted my thoughts, too.

"I don't want to piss you off."

His eyebrow raised, and the faint smile faded from his lips.

"Nothing that bad," I said. "I'm not contemplating my next breakout attempt or anything. I'm just afraid of losing myself."

"Sometimes that's the only way to survive. You shed the old life and move on. Cling to it and it'll suffocate you until you die."

"Shed," I repeated. "Like a snake."

He squinted down at me, as if he hadn't made the connection—or he hadn't expected me to make it. I wondered what he had shed off. How he came to be a leader—a young one at that—in a sex retreat, yet he'd never show much interest in the slaves.

"How did you end up here?" I asked before I could put a damper on my curiosity.

"You have to earn that answer." He crouched over me, slipping a hand up my stomach. I wanted to be pissed that he could put me in a place of complacence so easily, but on the other hand, it was a blessing. It made things less painful.

"You have to trust me," he said. Sitting back on his heels and spreading my legs.

Full trust wasn't an easy request.

His fingers caressed my folds, and I nodded. I had to trust him, the only tether I had to safety, to human contact. I heard faint voices and looked up to see a small group of people about a hundred yards away. They had stopped to watch us, and instead of feeling embarrassed, I felt... uninhibited.

I locked my gaze on Kirk, feeling myself slip away.

"I'm scared," I whispered. I hadn't even been able to hold off the change for a few weeks. I was becoming like the other girls, making excuses for the abuse, letting myself slide into the pleasure to escape. There was freedom in letting everything else go—not worrying about school, car payments... rent. I wondered what happened to my things, but it didn't matter. I wondered if my family had noticed that I was gone. I moved away to get my space, and even though Mom demanded that I call regularly, I stretched as much time as I could in "regularly," ignoring their calls for weeks at time, and sending little texts in between just to tide them over.

"I'm going to get you to stop thinking," he smirked.

"You know brain surgery?" I whispered, afraid the onlookers would notice my rebellion.

Kirk laughed quietly. "No, you'll have to keep your body relaxed."

That didn't encourage my confidence in either of us, but I nodded and let him spread my legs further. He pulled out a rubber glove and a pack of lube that had been hidden in the side of the cooler.

"And you called me a schemer."

"Latex free," he said, slipping the glove over his left hand. Then he coated the fingers with lube. Two fingers pressed inside of me first. His thumb rubbed my clit while his fingers searched for my g-spot. I jerked, raising my hips off the blanket when he found it and he slid a finger inside of me. The way he concentrated on the two spots, I thought he was going to take me right to the edge, but then he slipped another finger inside of me, stretching and fill-ing me.

I moaned and fisted the blanket, when he stretched his large fingers out stretching me nearly as much as having his cock in me, but not nearly as deep.

"It's going to hurt," he warned. "But as long as you don't tense up too much, it won't last long."

My eyes widened, but I nodded, relaxing so he could slip his last finger inside of me.

What the hell did I just agree to?

The stretching was on the verge of burning, but it turned to pleasure as he continued massaging inside of me. I heard the lube bottle click open again, and felt it run down my skin as it rolled off his hand.

"Lift up your shirt," he said. "Pinch your nipples, and roll them between your fingers."

I had to arch my back to get my shirt up high enough to reveal my breasts to him, then I began fondling myself as instructed, the sensations adding to the buzz of my over-whelmed nerves.

My hips pressed down, my body wanting his hand deeper. The sensations at my clit stopped for a moment, before he pinched it between the thumb and forefinger of his other hand. I gasped and jerked in pleasure, but that forced his hand deeper, causing a new burn.

"Ah." I tightened in pain for just a second then reminded myself to relax. He folded his thumb in with his hand and pressed inside of me. I squeezed my breasts harder, teetering on the precipice of pleasure and pain as he pushed inside of me. I focused all my tension in my hands, kneading and abusing my own breasts and forcing the rest of my body to be as relaxed as possible.

Just as I thought I couldn't take any more, his hand stilled, buried up to his lower forearm inside of me.

"Holy shit," I said as we both paused.

Kirk ran his free hand across my stomach, then the hand inside of me twisted, moving slowly, but every motion stimulated new nerves. I tightened around him, unable to stop the convulsions as they raced out from my core.

My breath came in sharp pants, each enunciated with a sigh of pleasure.

"Keep playing," he reminded me—a gentle correction.

I squeezed my sensitive nipples again. The sensation paired with his hand still buried deep inside of me was close to sending me over the edge again. Kirk rubbed his thumb over my clit again, spreading some of the lube over it, then flicking and pinching it gently.

I screamed, feeling the pressure building inside of me. I bucked once, then again. Kirk pushed my hips to the ground, keeping me still, but my stomach clenched, and I jerked and spasmed on the ground. I cried out again, pinching my nipples as hard as I could. Finally he moved the hand inside of me, and everything exploded.

A commotion erupted above me as my body shuddered on the blanket. By the time I'd come back down from the orgasm, Kirk was lying next to me with a suspiciously satisfied grin on his face. I looked up, and the onlookers had already moved on.

"You win," I whispered, closing my eyes, and drawing my body toward the sound of his chuckle. With my cheek against his chest, I expected him to tense or find some way to push me away, but he carefully tucked me against his chest.

———

I FELT KIRK NUDGE ME, and I opened my eyes.

"If we don't get up, we're both going to have some strange suntans tomorrow."

I blinked and sat up, unsure of how much time had passed since I'd dozed off. Still half-naked, I sat up and reached for my shorts. "I'm going to be sore tomorrow."

"Good." Kirk scoffed, fishing through the cooler again. He handed me a bottle of water and then a small piece of chocolate brownie.

"Oh my god, you've been possessed, haven't you?"

He moved to snatch it away, but I jerked it to my chest, and he leaned back next to me, relining against one arm. I unwrapped the morsel and took a bite, the moist chocolate filling my mouth. I chewed slowly, trying to savor every second of the taste before swallowing.

"I should probably thank you for today."

"Probably."

I offered him a bite of the brownie, and he took a small chunk.

As I watched him chew, his eyes trained on the lake, I realized that the beating had changed him as much as me. My pain had come at his hand, and in the moments since, I convinced myself that this…whatever I made of it wasn't as bad as having my back set on fire with a leather strap.

I wasn't sure if that made me insanely weak for giving in early, or smart for knowing when to admit defeat. I wanted to lean toward smart, but some small part of me couldn't get over the weakness. That part told me that I was a coward and a fool, but hell, I was alive for it to tell me that, so I couldn't be doing that badly.

I wanted to survive. I wanted to fight. But what was I going to fight against? The most intense orgasm I'd ever had or the last few bites of brownie left in my hand?

Certainly not against the man who'd given them to me.

I was fucked in every way possible. I shoved the last of the brownie in my mouth then took a drink of water to wash it down.

"We can take a walk around the lake before we head back."

"Do we have to head back? I like being outside."

"We can make it a slow walk." He stood and then glared down at me. "Why the hell am I negotiating with you?"

"Because it's my birthday." I smiled.

He laughed and shook his head, offering his hand to help me up. I started to fold up the blanket, but he dropped the cooler in the center of it and told me to leave it.

"One of the grounds keepers will pick it up."

"Handy."

Kirk raised his eyebrows and hummed, leading me toward a small worn path that circled the lake.

"Did I earn my answer?" I asked.

"Actually, I had hoped that you forgot about the question." A twig snapped under his foot as he lifted a branch for me to pass underneath. "I came here because I didn't have anywhere else to go. I was working on the street—"

I gasped.

"Not that kind of working on the street. Moving drugs, dabbling in gambling—whatever I could to earn a roof over my head and a meal. I lost a bet and ended up owing a lot of money, so I went into hiding and came to this town. Someone mistook me for someone else, and I got in on a deal, and the strange thing is, once Miles found out my con, he asked me to work for him."

"You don't talk or act like someone who grew up on the streets."

"I'm a quick learner," he said.

"Yeah, but—"

"I started college when I was sixteen," he said with a groan. "Pre-law."

"Shit." I dropped my bottle of water and it rolled into the bushes. I scurried to pick it up but was startled when something moved under the leaves next to it. I jumped back, and Kirk caught me before I stumbled and fell into the lake.

"Not a country girl," he said with a smirk.

"I visited my uncle's farm… once. He had a bull and it followed me around everywhere I went. Pretty freaky, if you ask me."

He reached into the bush and plucked up the bottle, dusting it off before handing it back to me.

"Thank you," I said as he took me by the waist and led me down the path. I leaned into him, resting my head against his shoulder. "Do you think I'm pathetic?"

"Uh." His pace slowed. "One, why would you care what I think? And two, why would I think you're pathetic?"

"Because you're the only person I can ask who might give me an honest answer, and I…." I shook my head.

"I think you're stubborn and motivated by wanting to survive and eventually find a way past this."

I shivered in the cool shade as the breeze fluttered by, picking up twigs and dead leaves left over from the previous year. "But…." I couldn't manage to find the right words—the ones that would help me focus on how I was feeling without pissing Kirk off. "I feel like I shouldn't be enjoying it or enjoying you. By doing that I'm…."

"You're surviving. We want human interaction; we seek pleasure—if we didn't, this place wouldn't exist."

"I'd be okay with that." The soreness between my legs hinted otherwise. I may not have wanted to be a slave—on any level—but that orgasm made me want more.

"So, you enjoy sex."

I scoffed and shook my head.

"You don't enjoy sex?" he asked slowly, tipping his head to watch my face as I considered my answer.

"Well …" My tongue tripped awkwardly against my

teeth. "It's never exactly felt like that before. Never even remotely close."

I rubbed my face and started walking faster, hoping he'd just drop the conversation, and knowing that there was no way in hell that he would.

"You've had an orgasm before?"

"Yes," I said forcefully. Although, since the two experiences couldn't compare—sex with my exes and out-of-my-mind sex with Kirk, I began to doubt myself. And I certainly didn't want to admit that to Kirk. Then, I really would be pathetic. I somehow convinced myself that keeping that to myself made me less pathetic and needy. "Why don't you like playing with the other slaves?"

Kirk growled. "I've already told you, I don't like sharing."

"But you could have found one of the others and claimed her so you wouldn't have to."

"Honestly, they all want attention, but very few of them want attention from only one person."

"More people to buy them things?"

He nodded and laced his fingers through mine as we rounded the back side of the lake.

"It's more than that, though," I said, knowing that I bordered on pushing him again. "You don't like being forceful with the girls."

"You think I'd have to be forceful to get any one of them in my bed?"

"Well, no, but maybe to keep them there and to keep them from getting out of hand."

"Believe me, Silver, you're the most out of hand girl in here—aside from Kat, but she's never been a problem before."

"Maybe that's because she's been a problem all along."

Kirk gave me a sideways glance, and I chose to bite my tongue before pushing the issue any further.

"You think she's the head of the drug ring?"

"You think there's a drug ring? I thought it was just one guy selling to a few of the girls."

Kirk stopped, crossed his arms, and glared down at me.

I scraped my thumbnail against the rivets of the bottle cap in my hand. One minute, his eyes could make me want to jump him, and the next they made me want to run away and find a snake hole to hide in.

Finally, he shook his head and took my hand again. "I'd tell you not to say anything to anyone else, but—"

"You're the only one who gets the brunt of my verbal diarrhea."

Kirk snorted. "Why do I have the feeling you're going to get us both in trouble?"

"If you really thought that, you'd kill me now." I knew I had to stop making snide remarks at everything he said, but as long as he wasn't completely blowing up about it, it was cathartic.

And for whatever reason—and whatever result—I was relieved that he had loosened up and wasn't threatening to beat or get rid of me at every opportunity.

Chapter Fourteen

GOOD DAY TO DIE

THE SORENESS between my legs had doubled overnight, and I thought about staying in bed. I heard the roar of the shower running on the other side of the wall, which meant that it wasn't quite time for breakfast.

I laughed to myself and buried my face in the pillow. I was the slave, yet, aside from last night, Kirk was always the one waiting on me. I rolled onto my back, stretching all my muscles, and finding the soreness to be surprisingly satisfying.

Trying to get back to sleep would be pointless, since my mind would just continue to race as it always did, especially when I thought too much about my circumstances. The more I let that happen, the more I wanted to complain even though, I rationalized, in the big scheme of things I didn't have much to complain about.

I was taking on all the traits in Alley that I swore I never would. I was finding reasons to enjoy my time here, to rationalize, and accept Kirk's actions.

I decided I could accept how things were, or risk doing something to set him off and get beaten again.

I put on my robe and walked across the living room to grab my e-reader from Kirk's desk, hoping that he remembered to download some new reading material after I had gone to bed. A small card under the computer caught my eye.

I told myself to leave it alone. There was nothing to be gained from snooping on Kirk that would be worth the punishment I'd get if he found out.

But the shower was still running.

I turned on the e-reader, hoping to distract myself long enough for the curiosity to fade, but my gaze wandered back to the small card. I slid it out from under the laptop and flipped it over.

"Oh my god," I whispered, dropping the driver's license to the floor.

My driver's license.

The bastard not only knew who I was, but where I lived and probably much more, since he was usually the one digging into the background of clients to find out all their darkest secrets.

I stormed into the bathroom and pulled back the curtain.

"How long have you known who I am?"

Kirk shut off the water and stared down at me, water dripping, and gleaming on his body. A scene that a few minutes ago would have sent me into a lust-fueled frenzy, now didn't move me at all.

"You were snooping?"

"I picked up my e-reader off your desk. My driver's license was laying there."

He rubbed the water off his face and ran his fingers through his hair, squeezing out the excess water. His jaw twitched under the tension, and I thought I'd collapse from his snarled gaze alone before he spoke. "It was under my computer."

"Not entirely." My anger remained, by my conviction at confronting him was quickly fading. "How long have you known?"

"Since the beginning," he said. "Hand me a towel."

I huffed, grabbed a towel off the rack, and chucked it at his crotch. He caught it before it managed to hit anything, but that didn't mean he was any less pissed.

I was momentarily glad for the tub wall between us, even though it was a minor obstacle.

"Silver." He called my name as I stormed out of the room. I paced the living room until he emerged, mostly dry, from the bathroom, wearing the towel around his waist.

"Why?" I screamed.

"I had to make sure no one would come here looking for you."

"You've been spying on me so you could make sure and crush any efforts to rescue me."

"You're not getting out alive. We already discussed that, Silver."

"Silver? You fucking—" I shook my head, looking for something else to throw at him, but he caught my arms and pinned them to my sides.

"Want me to call you by your real name?"

"No. You have no place in that life. I became Silver. I became what you wanted. But they're separate, you're not supposed to know anything about her. You said you didn't even care what my name was."

"Because I didn't want to know." His hands slowly slid away from my wrists, allowing me to step back. "Miles got your license from Gabe. He told me to check you out and make sure you wouldn't be a danger to the organization."

"What kind of danger would I be to this fortress? I'm just a regular girl."

Kirk folded his arms over his chest and I backed up, but he caught my arm and pulled me closer. "I had to make sure you weren't somehow involved with everything going on. Then, I had to make sure that Gabe hadn't screwed up and left a trail for someone to find you here."

"So, all along you knew my birthday was yesterday. And what, were you planning that all along? Just trying to play me? Find out more information?"

"No. Yesterday was exactly what you thought it was then. I wanted you to have a nice day. I wanted to get to know you because I want to trust you."

"Don't worry; I'm not here to bring down your fucking retreat."

"I know. If I had any doubts about that I sure as hell wouldn't have been giving you information yesterday. I wouldn't have taken you to the security room. I wouldn't be standing up for you."

His grasp on my arms tightened as he drew me closer. I could smell his body wash, the soft woodsy scent that tugged at my gut. My body loosened, and he held me tighter, locking his arms around my back.

"Are people looking for me?"

"Silver, don't. You'll drive yourself crazy. You'll get yourself into trouble."

I sucked back the tears, and let my body fall against his. He combed his fingers through my hair and kissed my temple. "I'm sorry," he whispered. "I had to do my job."

"And doing me is doing your job."

"No, doing you is my new pastime. It's much more enjoyable than the job."

I smiled. The jackass had a way of lightening my mood, and whether I liked it or not, it made me hate him and the situation less.

"I have a meeting," he said.

I started to push away, but he pulled me back, squeezing my chest against his.

"It's off site and I'll be gone for a few hours."

"So you're sending me downstairs?"

"Up to you."

"You can't leave me chained to a bed all day."

His lip twitched. "I didn't plan to, but that was before. You were here alone the other night."

He took my face between his hands and pulled me to meet him.

"You'd leave me in the apartment for hours while you're not even in the building? Free to walk around and everything? What if Gabe comes back?"

Kirk nodded. He squeezed my face between his palms and pushed my hair away from my face. "That's why there's a lock on the door."

"There's an extra key." I pointed out. "Everything he's already done, I don't think it would be above him to go get it."

"I'll make sure he can't. Are you okay staying here, or not?"

"I'm pissed, but I'm not going anywhere or doing anything. It's not even like I could go back home now if I did escape. You probably know everything about me and my family." I grabbed his forearms. "And don't explain about how you had to do it. Can we just bury it so I don't have to think about it again?"

"How about some breakfast and post-breakfast sex to take your mind off of it?"

"I don't really get a choice in the matter, do I?"

"No," he whispered with a smile that did all the wrong things to me. Ironically, the more I fought, the easier it was for him to break me and make me his.

———

I HAD Kirk's apartment all to myself, and yet I chose to do the boring thing and curl up on the couch with a book. Just as I had sunk into a new chapter, someone knocked on the door. The e-reader fell into my lap, and I slumped into the couch, unsure of whether I should answer or just let whoever it was go away. I didn't want anyone else to know I was up here alone.

The knock sounded again. "I know you're in there, Silver."

Recognizing the deep voice as Miles', I let out the breath I'd been holding and pulled on my robe.

"Yes, Sir." I called, not sure what the appropriate protocol for a slave answering the door.

"Why the delay?" he asked as I opened the door.

"I was afraid you were Gabe, Sir." The awkwardness of the terms had vanished, and they now rolled off my tongue as habit, especially when anyone aside from Kirk was around.

"Kirk asked me to stop in on you before I started my shift downstairs."

I bit my lip, wondering if he wanted more than to just see if I was okay. Was I supposed to let him in, so he could see I wasn't trying to burrow through a ninth story wall?

He brushed my cheek and I smiled at the soft gesture—further confirming that I'd lost my rational mind. "Good to see you staying out of trouble."

"No kidding," I mumbled, then clenched my teeth together.

"Maybe we should have kept you away from Alley." He smirked and turned away. "Be good, Silver."

I closed and locked the door and returned to the couch. Sometime in the midst of reading a slow chapter, I fell asleep, and woke to another knock. This time, I jumped off the couch, hoping it was Kirk, but considering that it might also be Miles again.

I glanced at the clock; I couldn't have been asleep for more than ten minutes, since it wasn't even noon yet. I reached for the key, checking through the peep hole just to confirm who it was.

It was the same lanky black-haired man who had come to the door to let Kirk know that Ross was coming back early. I'd also seen him around, usually whispering with Ross and then disappearing, but I had no idea what his name was.

"Y-yes, Sir?" I said through the door. I didn't know him well enough to simply open the door, and I wasn't sure if Kirk would send him to check on me as well.

"Ross wants to see you."

"About what, Sir?"

He banged on the door again and I jumped back. "You don't ask questions."

I had no idea what his true role was in the organization, but it wouldn't be the first time Ross had sent this guy to deliver a message. My heart raced with apprehension as I considered the possibilities. I had never seen him with Gabe, or any of his goons. But if Ross wanted to see me, I didn't anticipate a positive outcome either way. "My Master told me to stay here."

"And your Master's boss told me otherwise. Ross sent me to get you—we need to talk about the drugs, and *Kirk*."

What the hell? My hand shook over the key in the dead-bolt. I wished there was someone I at least half-trusted that I could ask. A way I could call Kirk, or even Miles.

"I can tell Ross to come get you himself."

Fucking hell. Ross wanted me dead in the first place, or at the very least miserable. Pissing him off, or even miffing him in the slightest, wasn't a viable option. The scrawny man pulled out his cell phone and a set of keys.

Fucker had the master keys. It stood to reason that Ross would have his own set. That threw any possibility of holding up here until Kirk came back.

My wrist flicked, releasing the dead bolt, hoping I could avoid pissing him off any more. I pulled the key out and opened the door. He nodded toward the elevator, so I locked the door and followed. Inside the elevator, he pressed "7" and my stomach churned.

I opened my mouth—knowing that if it was legitimate and I argued I'd just get myself in more trouble, but I had a bad feeling. Before I could say anything, a hand came over my mouth, blocking it and my nose. I struggled, trying to get him to break away just long enough to catch a breath, but for a scrawny man he was damn strong and limber. By the time the elevator halted, I was already feeling dizzy. The doors slid open, and I stared into Gabe's eyes once again.

I tried to scream, but there wasn't enough air in my lungs, and what did escape further weakened me. He grabbed me, and helped Black Hair pull me into the first door where two other men waited to join the fray. The hand over my mouth gave me enough room to inhale then blocked my airway again.

The cameras, what about the cameras? Surely someone saw them grab me and pull me in here. When they'd attacked Kirk, everyone was on the move within a few minutes. What did they hope to accomplish?

I clawed and kicked, but between the four of them, they deflected most of my attacks and managed to render my limbs useless.

I already knew the rooms were fairly sound-proof, if they weren't, all anyone would hear would be their neighbors having sex all day and night, but I was sure a scream would carry, even if I only had a second.

Gabe flicked open a knife and pressed it to my throat. My vision was already dimming. I needed air.

"We'll let you breathe, but if you scream, I cut."

I nodded, anything was worth air, and I figured someone had to be on the way. The man behind me released my mouth and I sucked in a breath, almost coughing. I drew in breath after breath, as my body replenished its supply of oxygen and my vision slowly returned.

"They'll come get me," I said. As my mouth opened to say more, Gabe shoved a wet cloth into my mouth and another put a piece of tape over it. Whatever the cloth was coated in had a slightly soapy taste.

One man pushed me toward the bedroom. I tried to resist, but I felt sluggish, tripping over my own feet as I walked over the carpet. *No,* they had drugged me again. Scrawny kept one arm, while Gabe took the other and they dragged me to the bed.

Gabe ripped off the tape and pulled the cloth out of my mouth, tossing it aside.

"Feeling better?"

"You fucking b—bastard." I tripped over my own words. I waited for unconsciousness to come—hell, I longed for it since I wouldn't have to be awake for their assault.

He put a fresh piece of tape over my mouth, while the others pulled my arms and legs toward the corners of the bed to tie me down.

I jerked as hard as I could, but it was a feeble attempt at best and only caused the ropes to cut into my skin and dig under the silver cuffs.

I moaned through the tape again, hoping I could make just enough noise for someone to hear, but a heavy hand busted across my face leaving the taste of blood in my mouth.

I sobbed, trying to swallow the liquids in my mouth before I choked. Gabe pulled off his belt and folded it over in his hand. I shook my head and sobbed, but he raised his hand and it came down with a *thwap* against my ribs. I screamed in pain and another strike followed.

One of the men fisted my hair and put his finger over his lips to tell me to be quiet. Gabe moved the strikes down to my legs, while the other men grabbed and twisted at my breasts.

Please, I hoped the drug would knock me out. Maybe even if I was awake I wouldn't remember it afterward. Where the hell was the security team?

The black-haired man's gaze caught mine, and he hissed in my ear. "Pity they got the wrong mole."

My eyes widened, and I screamed against the tape. The belt came down against my crotch and my scream turned into a cry and then sobs.

I couldn't breathe. My chest tightened and shook, tears rolled down my face, and gunk clogged my nose and throat.

Gabe grabbed my chin. "Every sound you make will

make everything hurt more," he whispered with a rough, low voice.

The belt came down on my thigh, a strike to my hip, and one across my breast. The room blurred as I sobbed into the piece of tape that held back my pleas and screams.

One of the men jerked off his pants and climbed on top of me.

I shook my head, mentally screaming for him to stop and shrieking into the thick tape. Another strike came down on my chest. The man on top of me took Gabe's belt and pressed it against my neck, cutting off my air supply.

What if no one comes to stop them, this time?

I felt an excruciating slam of pain as he pressed inside me, but then the room went mercifully dark.

Water splashed on my face and I roused. It was down to three men now; the scrawny man who'd dragged me down here was gone. My throat burned from my useless screams, and my body shook with a mixture of pain, anger, and adrenaline.

I didn't want to be awake for this.

Another stepped forward, but Gabe shoved him back. "No way. It's my turn." He punched me in the gut and the ropes cut into my skin when I curled up in response. "Help me turn her over."

Oh, no, god no. I thought. But I didn't have the strength to fight all of them off as they flipped me over and retied the restraints. Apparently, they weren't taking any chances this time. I felt something wet slide down my crack and then a finger pushed inside. I screamed into the pillow and the belt came down on my shoulder blades. Ten more strikes crossed my back until I felt like I could neither scream nor cry anymore without suffocating.

My consciousness flickered. I thought I was going to

pass out again—sweet oblivion, to pull me away from the assault, but I only half left. I could still hear the men around me. Now they took turns with various implements smacking them across my ass. I felt some kind of stick, then a whip that left multiple bites with each stroke.

Someone lifted my hips, and I waited for another dick to stretch me open. Instead, something fluttered against my clit.

No, even worse. I bucked, trying to get free, but a finger slid into my ass again. Every time I jerked away from the vibrations, the finger went deeper.

The room twisted again, and I was the in backseat of a vehicle.

Fuck, I passed out long enough for them to get me out of the building.

But there hadn't been an escape, my body was still in the room.

I was crammed into the small backseat of an extended cab pickup. A hand pressed over my mouth. "She's awake."

"Give her the sedative." A blond man handed something over the back of the pickup seat.

Alan. The mole in the security team is Alan.

I bucked and kicked at the door, but a pinching pain pierced through my arm, and I lost control of my limbs. I rocked in the seat as the truck accelerated quickly. The drug numbed my body, but for some reason I was still conscious.

I looked up at the man holding me. "What-do-you-want?" It all came out sounding as one long word. "Where's Charlene?"

"Shut up bitch."

A hand struck my face and I jerked awake. Gabe grunted; he was kneeling over me with his hand still between my legs. "It's not nice to zone out when I'm working for your pleasure, Princess."

The vibrator still hummed against my clit, and as Gabe slid another finger into my vagina, I realized I was wet. My damn body was giving in and turning against me.

I screamed against the tape again, and his hand came down on my ass. The motion caused my hips to rock harder against the vibrator, and I felt the tingling ball of tension growing inside of me.

No, no, please don't let it happen. I tried to force the sensations away, like I had done with Ross in the Outlook, but they pounded into my nerves too quickly. I had lost control of my mind and body.

Tears soaked the pillow. Despite my best efforts to keep my hips still, they bucked with Gabe's movements. More hands joined the frenzy, rubbing against the fresh welts on my back. The welts weren't as painful as whatever Kirk had used, but the touches sent my nerves into overdrive—somehow amplifying everything Gabe was doing.

I screamed again into the tape then buried my head in the pillows. My body rocked then jerked. The possessive orgasm wrung through my muscles, and all I could do was sob.

I took deep breaths, trying to find air, but then I felt something large pressing between my ass cheeks.

I moaned, and twisted, even though I knew it was impossible to buck him off. Everything convulsed as he forced his erection inside my tight hole.

"Kirk hasn't trained his slave very well." Gabe jeered, pulling my head up by my hair. "Guess we'll have to fix that."

He slammed my head back down then rammed his cock into me. Lying down over my back, I felt his lips at my ear. "My man wasn't the only mole, there's a far worse one, and you've been sleeping in his bed," he whispered the message for me alone and my insides turned to rock. "Do as we say, or your protector will be dead within the hour."

I thought that everything inside of me had died when I gave myself over to Kirk, but I was wrong. I felt it withering and rotting as Gabe pumped into me. Thrust after excruciating thrust.

He shoved in deep, leaning over my back to untie my wrists.

"You sure you want—" One man began, but Gabe growled, and the blond shut up.

Gabe pulled me up to my hands and knees, allowing him better access, while another climbed onto the bed in front of me. He twisted my head up to look at him. "You scream or bite and I'll take out your teeth."

I heard a crash from the room behind us, before he could even peel away the tape.

"Go on," Gabe yelled—I assumed he was talking to the other men. I heard a scuffle, muffled words, and more banging and shouting. Then, Gabe was ripped off me.

I collapsed on the bed, feeling one hand touch the back of my leg while another cut my legs free. I kept my head down, but the hands gently tilted my head up and pulled off the tape.

"Kirk," I mouthed, my larynx too sore to make a sound. He wrapped his shirt around me and lifted me into his arms. On the other side of the room Miles held Gabe against the wall.

"We'll get them upstairs and let Ross figure out what to do with them," Miles said.

"She's a slave," Gabe said, trying to shake Miles' hand off his shoulder. "And she has a sweet ass. Guess you just couldn't give her everything she needed."

My eyes fell on the black form on the bed next to me. I

grabbed it—the metal still warm from Kirk's hand—and raised it, pointing the gun to Gabe's head and pulling the trigger before I realized what I was doing.

"Silver." I heard two voices yell as Gabe's body collapsed to the floor.

Kirk grabbed the gun out of my hand.

I heard a commotion outside, but the room started going dusky and I dropped my head to Kirk's shoulder.

I bobbed there semi-conscious as Kirk and Miles exchanged frantic words. Then, Miles patted my cheek, each time becoming rougher until I shook my head and focused on him.

"Kirk fired the gun. Do you understand?"

I stared back and started to space out again, but Miles shook my chin.

I stared into his brown eyes, undecided if I wanted to stay with him and Kirk or let unconsciousness wash over me. "Alan," I said.

Miles frowned at me, and Kirk squeezed me tighter against his chest. I tried again. "Alan—" My throat was too dry and abused to make much noise without cutting out from the slices of pain. "—drove the truck that brought me here. He's the mole."

Miles squeezed my forearm. "How do you know?"

"I remembered. Only a bit." I tried to swallow but it was almost impossible.

"She's drugged," Miles said. "She could have been hallucinating."

"Three men. Alan driving. Extended cab pickup," I gritted out. I wasn't sure how I was still even conscious, let alone talking. "Blue dash lights."

Above me, the men stared at each other. I tried to force out the rest of the information. To tell them about the scrawny black-haired man, too, but the room started to sway and spin.

"I'll kill him," Miles whispered. Then he touched my chin, rubbing his finger gently over my skin. "Silver, I need you to listen to me now. Kirk fired the gun. Say it."

I took a deep breath and whispered. "Kirk fired the gun."

Chapter Fifteen

FIRE INSIDE

I WOKE up again as Kirk opened the door to the infirmary. Everything hurt, and I felt like everything between my legs was on fire. I cried out as the cold table irritated my beaten back.

"Make it stop, Kirk. Please."

He rubbed his hand over my least injured cheek and lowered his lips to my ear. "Stop calling me that before someone hears you." As he straightened, he kissed my temple.

I jumped when Clarence pulled over a tray of instruments. I hadn't even noticed he was already in the room, and I wondered if he'd heard my slip up. As he snapped on a pair of purple gloves, I tried to crawl off the table toward Kirk.

"Be still, Silver," Clarence said.

I wished people would stop telling me to do impossible things. I remembered what he was like. The subtle enjoyment he got out of pressing and poking me to the edge of my pain limits. I wasn't sure I could handle him touching me at all. Kirk rested his palm against my chest, while the other gently brushed at my bangs, trying to keep me lying down and calm.

"Everything hurts," I sobbed. I couldn't hold back, even though crying simply made everything worse. I throbbed in places I didn't know it was possible to hurt in. The skin on my back felt prickly and raw. Not as much pain as the whip Kirk had used, but uncomfortable in other ways.

"I'll take care of the pain first," Clarence whispered, rubbing my arm with an alcohol pad and then injecting a pale, yellow liquid. As the warmth spread under my skin, my body went limp, and my already heavy eye lids almost refused to move. By the time Clarence had prepared the rest of his instruments, the pain had faded to a fuzzy feeling.

"I'm just checking your injuries," Clarence explained. "You shouldn't feel anything too painful, but if you do, let me know."

This time, his touch was delicate and slow. Or at least it seemed to be. Everything seemed slow and distorted.

I nodded my head, unable to do much else. He started with the swollen patch on my face, feeling carefully around it and then laying a cold pack wrapped in towels over it. Kirk took a stool near my head and held the cold pack against my cheek, resting his other hand on my shoulder. My head bobbed to the side, I was face to face with the tribal snake that decorated Kirk's forearm.

I felt Clarence's hands working down my body, applying salve to the red marks across my breasts, stomach, and thighs.

I blinked, and the snake tattoo moved, as if it was uncurling from his arm. My eyes closed, and I gasped, forcing them open again.

"Pain?" Clarence asked.

I shook my head. Kirk leaned over me, his grey-blue eyes seemed almost glittery then his pupils turned to long slits.

"Then what is it?" he asked.

Reaching a hand up, I rubbed his cheek, then dropped my hand down to the tattoo, which had stopped moving again. "I'm either dreaming or hallucinating."

Kirk's head jerked up. "How much morphine did you give her?"

"Enough," Clarence replied. "And stop scowling. It was less than half a dose. I was afraid of it reacting to anything they gave her."

It was enough, the room danced around us, and shimmery figures moved across the ceiling. Much better than pain, something gripped inside my chest, waiting for the images to turn dark and scary. I squeezed Kirk's arm, and he bent forward to kiss my forehead. "I got you," he whispered, and I gave into the warmth.

I lost track of time, floating on the bed, with Clarence slowly working over me. Then, he pressed my legs apart and I snapped out of my calm retreat.

"Easy," Kirk said softly, brushing the back of his fingers against my uninjured cheek. "He needs to check your injuries. Just concentrate on me, okay?"

I nodded but convincing my body to relax again while Clarence worked between my legs wasn't so simple. He moved with care, positioning me so he could do a vaginal exam. Every poke hit a tender spot, but the drugs made it tolerable—physically if not mentally. My mind screamed, trying to crawl away from the violation. I wanted clothes, a blanket, a place to hide. Siding with my brain, my skin broke out in goosebumps.

"I'll grab her a blanket," Kirk said. "She's freezing."

I caught his wrist as he rose, terrified of him leaving me. Under my grasp, the serpent tattoo moved again.

"I'm just walking to that cabinet," he said, kissing my forehead. "I won't be out of sight."

I kept my eyes on him as he walked the five feet to the cabinet, but as soon as his back was turned shadows grew from the corners of the room, slipping out of the cabinets, under the doors. I whimpered, pulling my arms around myself and Clarence stopped his work. "Silver."

Kirk draped it over me and cupped the side of my face. I struggled to inhale as the darkness strangled my lungs.

"It's not real, Silver," Kirk whispered. "Breathe."

My body started to calm again, and he returned to the stool next to my head.

"There doesn't appear to be any vaginal bleeding," Clarence said. I sighed in relief, but given the amount of pain, I couldn't believe it was really possible.

"There is a lot of bruising, and some chafing."

I wrapped my fingers around Kirk's, and he squeezed my hand. The worst of the hallucinations were already starting to diminish. "Your tattoos stopped moving," I mumbled, my throat felt like a gravel pit.

"Were you having any hallucinations before Kirk brought you up here?"

"I wish. Snapped out of it once."

I felt something pressing against my anus again and groaned.

"Shhh," Kirk cooed, caressing my cheek and wiping away the tears.

"No rectal tears. She's going to be sore for a while, though. I'll give you some Vicodin to hold her over. You should probably keep a close eye on her for the next few days."

Clarence stood and lifted my legs from the stirrups pulling the foot of the bed back out and laying my legs gently across it. "I need to have a look at her back now." He touched my arm. "Can you roll on your side? Toward the door."

They both helped me roll over just as the door to the infirmary opened. As the cool draft drifted in, followed by the smell of Ross' cologne, I was thankful for the blanket.

"Can I talk to you, Kirk?"

"Please," I begged. I didn't want him to leave. I feared what Ross would do to him. To us.

"I won't leave the room," he whispered.

I shook my head. "The shadows will get me."

"Are you still seeing things?" Kirk asked.

Ross approached and grabbed his arm pulling him toward the door, but Kirk held his ground. A black hooded cloak rose up, enveloping Ross. Death had come to claim my Master.

My body clenched, and I kicked to get off the bed. A hand grabbed me from behind.

The cloaked hand dropped away, and Kirk crouched in front of me, putting his hand to my face. "Breathe, Sugar. What do you see?"

I shook my head, digging my fingers into his wrist. I blinked, feeling once again like I had just come out of a dream, but just as quickly reality slipped into darkness.

Clarence roused me, but I didn't want to leave my stupor. "I need you to answer some questions, can you do that?"

I shook my head.

"It's important, Silver."

I opened my eyes enough to see Kirk and Ross across

the room. Kirk leaned against a wall, his arms folded over his chest, his gaze never leaving me as Ross spoke.

"Silver." Clarence repeated my name.

I didn't want to speak, but I nodded.

"What'd they hit you with?"

I definitely did not want to go there. Why the hell did it matter enough to make me conjure up the memory. "Belt," I replied quickly.

"Anything else?"

Fucking hell. I fought, trying not to slip back into the memory. "A stick or something. Didn't see."

"Did they rub anything on your back?"

Rub? What? My back, prickly, hot, pain. I remembered their hands on me. "Maybe."

Kirk broke away from Ross and came back to my side.

"Does your back itch?" Clarence asked.

I moaned, trying to decipher the rush of messages I was getting from almost every inch of skin and muscle. "I guess."

"What's going on?" Kirk asked. Ross stood behind him, grimacing. I had a feeling he wasn't through saying everything he wanted to say, but Clarence continued his own inquisition.

"How does your throat feel?"

I wasn't sure where the line of questioning was going or how he was jumping from my back to my throat. "Sore. Itchy. Dry."

"Clarence?" Kirk growled.

"She looks like she's having an allergic reaction. I'll have to wash the site and make sure all of the allergens are gone then I'll put on an antihistamine cream."

I blinked, and it was like watching a movie that kept skipping. Kirk and Ross were once again huddled in a corner. Something warm and wet rubbed across my back and I jumped.

"Easy, Silver," Clarence whispered. "I know it's sore, but I'm almost done."

"Will I forget?" This time I wanted to forget. I'd been searching so long to get back the memories of how I got here, but now I wondered if I wanted those either. "They gave me something, tasted soapy."

"GHB. It'll clear from your system pretty quickly."

"And I'll forget?"

"I don't think they gave you enough."

"I forgot last time. Forgot how I got here—" My voice caught in the back of my throat and I coughed.

"I'm sorry, Silver. I wouldn't get your hopes up."

"Can I have water?"

"Sure." He nodded. For a moment, I felt completely alone even though Clarence was only a few feet away, and Kirk was still in the room. I was exposed. My soul carved open and left on the table. The morphine felt like a blanket under my skin, but it also made me feel even weaker. I hugged my arms around myself, wishing Kirk and Ross would get their conversation over with.

Clarence returned with a small cup and helped me roll to my back. Then, he raised the head of the bed up, so I could drink.

The voices across the room grew louder, and for the first time I could make out their words.

"It wasn't your call," Ross said. "You need to get it in your head that she's a damn slave."

"It was me," I said, my voice quivering.

They both looked my way, and I saw Kirk's head shake slightly.

"Let your Master handle this," Clarence whispered,

patting my shoulder. He looked up and shook his head. "She's on pain killers, she's been rambling."

I have not, my brain shouted, but I managed to silence it. I had been hallucinating, and to be honest I couldn't be sure whether I had been rambling or not. Ross crossed the room and looked to Clarence. "How bad are her injuries?"

"You know, I don't mind taking care of the girls, but stuff like this. It shouldn't happen."

Ross nodded. "Can you tell me what happened, Silver?"

I wanted to shake my head, but I knew he wouldn't be as patient and forgiving as Kirk or Clarence. "He said you wanted to see me. Had the master keys. They... they, beat me... and... and..."

"It's okay," Kirk said.

"They saved me. Miles and Kirk."

Ross raised an eyebrow and looked at Kirk, it took my mind a few seconds, but I finally realized my error. *Master. Master, damn it.* No wonder Kirk always yelled at me for using his name.

"Then what?" Ross asked.

Concentrate, Silver. I glanced over slightly to see Kirk, but my eyelids were getting so heavy that every time I blinked, I could barely get them open again.

"Gabe started shouting, tried to get away from Miles. Master shot him. Master kept me safe."

A half grin spread on Kirk's face, and I closed my eyes. I wanted sleep to reclaim me with that image in my mind, one tiny moment of satisfaction within the storm of chaos and pain. Through the haze of drugs, I told the story I was given.

But my body shook, a hand patted my cheek.

"She's hurt and high on pain killers, Ross," Kirk yelled.

"Best time to get an honest story." Ross leaned over me,

until I could smell the coffee on his breath. "Anything else I should know."

"Alan took me."

"From your room?" He scoffed. "He's not even here today."

I shook my head. "Brought me here. Drove the truck."

Ross looked to Kirk, and Kirk nodded at me. "You wanted her information."

Ross made a growling sound in his throat. "She's still hallucinating."

"I'm not." Well, maybe I was, but not about what I remembered. "Extended cab pickup. Blue lights inside. I remember."

"What color was the truck?"

"Isn't the blue light enough. Alan had the lighting installed two months ago."

Ross ignored him, staring down at me. His hand moved, and I twitched away.

"I don't remember anything else about the truck. There were two other men. One with black hair held me, another in the front seat. I never saw his face." I pushed out the information as fast as possible, unsure I could fight unconsciousness any longer and fearful of what Ross would do if I fell asleep without permission. I bit my lip then looked to Kirk wondering if I should bring up the dark-haired man.

"I need to finish her back," Clarence said. I could have hugged him for the interruption. "We're not going to get anywhere right now. She needs rest."

Ross scowled at the doctor, then shoved his pants in his pockets and backed away. "We'll talk later then."

"Thank you, Sir." My eyes closed, and I felt the bed flatten under me again, so they could roll me back to my side.

———

I WOKE up stretched out on the couch back in Kirk's apartment; I was half propped up against his chest, nestled between his legs.

"Hey, Sugar," Kirk whispered when I readjusted myself.

I looked up, managing a small smile despite my swollen face. A pain poured deeper into my chest that the pain meds couldn't touch, but I wasn't ready to voice it. I didn't even want to think it.

There was a thud on the door and I froze.

"It's Miles," the voice outside announced.

"Come in," Kirk yelled.

I glanced back at Kirk as the lock snapped.

"He's holding on to all of the master keys until we get things sorted." He kissed my forehead, putting my current concerns at ease.

Miles entered with a case of beer and a small black box.

"For you." He handed the box to me. I squinted at first then opened it, discovering chocolate mousse cake. "According to what Alley tells me numerous times a month, chocolate fixes everything."

I felt Kirk's chest shake as he chuckled. His fingers drifted through my hair.

Then, Miles slid the case of beer across the table. "That's for you. I figure she has pain pills, so you'll need something."

"Thanks, Miles." Kirk said.

I dipped my finger in the mousse and licked it off. "Yes, thank you, Sir."

Miles shook his head and disappeared into the kitchen, while Kirk lifted forward so that I sat leaning half-sideways against the back of the couch. When Miles came back, he slid a spoon into the black container and dropped a bottle of water on the coffee table before taking a seat next to it. "Everything is taken care of—for now. Alan is with the others in lock up, but no one is really talking. He hacked into our system today and forced through an old feed, so they wouldn't be caught on camera dragging her into the room downstairs. It's also curious that he was the one on duty when Morton was passing drugs to the girls."

"A diversion," Kirk said. "Just how deep does it go?"

Miles cocked his head. "I wouldn't count on being able to trust anyone outside of this room right now."

He leaned toward me and I closed my eyes, savoring a bite of the rich chocolate cake. "I don't know anything but chocolate, Sir."

Miles chuckled and ripped open the beer case, handing one to Kirk, and taking one for himself.

But I did know something else. I stabbed the cake with my spoon and twisted to face Kirk. I opened my mouth, then chickened out, biting my lip, but both men were already watching and waiting.

"The black-haired guy who came down to tell you that Ross was coming back...."

Kirk raised an eyebrow and nodded slowly.

"He's in on it, too." I shuddered, pulling my knees closer to my chest. Every single movement hurt, especially my attempt at curling up into an unbreakable ball. Behind me, Kirk sat, pressing his body against me, holding me together before I had the opportunity to fall apart. "I don't think I was supposed to be alive to tell you that."

Miles jumped up. "And what the hell were they planning on doing with a missing slave and her dead body?"

"They'd already set her up," Kirk growled. "Alan called

us down and alerted us about the suspicious patron, who then gets caught with Kat. She tries to link Silver with it—"

"And Silver had already tried to run." Miles ran his hand over his short hair and paced around the couch. "If she disappeared it would have confirmed the suspicions that she was involved with the breech. And if you weren't paranoid enough to have installed a damn alarm on your door… we wouldn't have known until it was too late."

I looked back to Kirk and nearly dropped the cake onto the floor. Paranoid. I was thankful for his paranoia but if he was a mole like Gabe said, he was paranoid for good reason.

Kirk raised his eyebrows briefly and rubbed my side. "We'll have to round up Mitch, but with Gabe gone, and so many of the group getting busted, I think our best hope is that anyone else involved either gets wise enough to fall back in line or stupid enough to get caught."

Taking another bite of cake, I hoped to lose myself again.

Miles shook his head and stood. "Ever wonder why we do all of this?"

Kirk made a sound in his throat but didn't really answer. "Are you thinking about getting out?"

"Thinking like that would get me killed. Don't get me wrong. I love playing with the girls, but I don't like seeing them hurt."

I lifted my head, giving him a half-hearted smile.

"I better get back downstairs and find out where our last little rat has run off to." Miles took a swig of beer and squeezed my shoulder lightly before he left.

After the door closed and locked, I twisted to see Kirk.

"Enjoying your cake?" he asked.

I nodded, taking another decadent bite. I wanted to ask

him about what Gabe had said, but I was afraid I didn't want to know the answer. I didn't want to know the whole story. If he was a mole, who was he working for?

There was already too much going on.

Instead, I finished the last bit of cake and snuggled against his chest again. Fuck the rest of the world and everyone else in the building. I didn't care who he was working for or why as long as I didn't have to leave the couch.

Chapter Sixteen

THE WALL BEHIND THE TRUTH

I felt the heavy metal of the gun in my hand, so heavy I couldn't lift it.

I couldn't remember why I even needed the gun then I heard footsteps behind me and spun around.

"Gabe." I shook my head. "You can't be here."

"Why is that?"

"Because, I…" I looked down at the gun in my hand and raised it to his head.

"You've already shot me," he said, closing the gap between us.

I took a step backward, the gun shaking in my hand. I felt a wall at my back, leaving me nowhere else to go.

Silver, a voice in my head shouted, and I shook it off.

"You're just a piece of meat. Only difference between me and your snake of a Master is that I don't muddle your role in the world."

The gun clattered to the floor and I pushed off the wall attempting to get past him. He grabbed my arm and I spun to the floor.

Silver. *I heard the voice again but couldn't find anyone else in the room.*

I dragged myself across the floor on my back, as Gabe dived at me. Pulling my body under him and pinning me down with his knee. His hands ripped off my shirt, and warm drops of blood landed on my skin.

Gabe's forehead opened up, until blood poured onto my body. I screamed, trying to push him away. I covered my face with my hands trying to block the flow of blood, but I tasted it in my mouth and felt it in my eyes and nose. Rolling down into my ears.

I was going to drown in his blood.

"ROSE"

I sat up, gasping for breath on the couch in Kirk's apartment. He sat behind me, his arm braced around me. He touched my face as I calmed.

"Don't call me that." My voice cracked with emotion and abuse.

"I'm sorry," Kirk whispered. "You wouldn't wake up."

"I know." I tried to lean back or find a more comfortable position, but the slightest movement set everything ablaze again. "I'm pretty sure I could hear you." I took a deep breath and let it all fall out—tears broke free, and I buried myself in Kirk's chest and cried.

"I'm sorry," he repeated. I heard it over and over through my sobs.

"I shot him."

"No—"

I jerked away and looked into his eyes. "I can tell your story, but I shot him. He was just standing there, and I shot him."

"He deserved it." Kirk brushed my hair back and

leaned his forehead against mine, but whether or not he believed that, the ramifications of what I had done would be up to Ross.

"Is that what everyone else thinks?"

"Close enough."

"Why is Miles covering for me?"

"Because he saw what happened. He saw what I saw when we busted in, and he understands. He said if it had been Alley, he'd have done the same thing."

Adrenaline and a wash of emotions shook my body, and I twisted to lean sideways against the back of the couch and face Kirk. "What are they going to do to you?"

"Nothing." He shook his head. "I'll probably get the ass end of the stick for a while, but that's it."

Even then, I didn't like the thought of him taking the blame for something I had done. I had caused him enough trouble. "What if they knew it was me?"

"If they did, you'd already be dead."

He handed me a glass of water and an oval white pill.

"I get glass now?" I said, forcing a smile and hoping it'd lighten his mood a bit.

The corner of his mouth lifted. "You've had the whole apartment twice. That included the glasses and knives, and everything else in the room."

In the moment we both started trusting one another, everything fell apart again. "I want a bath."

"It's probably going to sting."

"I don't care. I need it."

He nodded and slid his leg around me, so he could stand. "Sit here while I run it."

Kirk returned a few minutes later and gently lifted me from the couch.

I wrapped my arms around his neck and inhaled his scent. Safe again.

"I'm sorry, Silver" he said again.

"Stop apologizing. You saved me…" I paused. "You and your damn alarm. Still afraid I'd run?"

"I didn't put it on today." He slowly lowered me into the tub. "But I'm glad I had it on today. Miles texted me right after he talked to you, so I could account for the first time the door opened. I called him the second time, but there was nothing on the monitors and you had already disappeared."

He guided me as I sank down into the warm water. The welts burned as they hit the water, but it soon receded to a tolerable level. "We got lucky," he whispered. "By the time I got back, Miles had managed to narrow it down to the seventh floor since there's a record of elevator stops."

"I promised to protect you," he whispered. "I showed you the cameras; I said he couldn't get to you."

My eyes became heavy again. "It's not your fault. You still managed to find me."

"You did pretty well with your story to Ross," he said, changing the subject.

"Especially while drugged out on pain killers, eh?" My eyes fluttered closed and I struggled to open them again.

"No sleeping in the tub," Kirk said, but I felt him adjust me to make sure I couldn't slip under the water.

I took a breath and held it for a second, as the drugs encouraged my curiosity and wore away at my worries. "What's your real name?"

Kirk stared back for a moment. "Why would you ask that?"

"Just a feeling. You know, 'which of these things doesn't

fit in?' And since you didn't just deny it, there must be something to it."

I heard him swallow then he took a long, slow breath. "James."

It was true. The room may as well have dropped to the ground floor. "I think I like James more than Kirk."

"Me, too." His voice was low, but thick with emotion. "Although sometimes, I don't think I can remember who he is."

"You don't have to remember, he's just who you are when you're not trying to be someone else."

"Apparently I'm not trying hard enough." He brushed his fingers against my neck. "Since you picked me out in a couple of weeks. You're going to make me paranoid that everyone expects something."

"I live with you." I took a deep breath and my chest shook. I didn't want to tell him, but I had to. "Gabe knew."

His soft grasp on my body turned to stone.

I swallowed, trying to find my voice and enough energy to explain. "He whispered it so only I could hear it. Said I was sleeping with the biggest mole, and if I didn't do what he said, you'd be dead within an hour."

Kirk's eyes narrowed. "Is that why you shot him?"

I nodded. "Not that he didn't deserve it for a lot of reasons." I wondered when the true reality of what I had done was going to kick in. I watched the bullet go through his head over and over in my mind, but I couldn't find an ounce of sadness or regret.

Survival. I needed Kirk to survive, and I needed Gabe to be gone. We both needed the rat to be gone.

I tried to take a deep breath, but my chest decided not to cooperate, sending me into a coughing fit instead. I jerked forward, leaning against my knees as I tried to catch my breath.

"That wasn't just a lucky shot," Kirk said.

"I went to the shooting range with my dad a couple of times a month from the time I was eleven." I sat there, curled up for a moment longer after I caught my breath. "Is anything you told me yesterday true?"

"Most of it, in one way or another. I just rearranged and exaggerated my own life—easier to remember that way."

"How long have you been here?" I muttered, the weight of leaning my jaw against my knee muffling my words.

"Too long," he said.

I lay back in the warm water again. I wanted more information, but my brain settled into a numb stupor and left me with nothing to ask, so neither of us talked. All I could hear was the sound of my own heart and our breathing.

I startled as Kirk lifted me out of the tub.

"Not done." I protested.

"The water is getting cold and you're turning into a prune," he said, propping me against the counter so he could dry me off.

He was right about the water temperature, but it didn't seem like I had even been in the tub that long. "I think these pain pills are heavy duty."

Kirk scoffed as he somehow managed to keep me propped up while running a towel through my hair and dried me off. "I think you're a light weight."

"Can I sleep in your bed?" My head bobbed forward.

"Sleeping in the tub wasn't good enough?"

I laughed, and despite the fact that it hurt, it was the best feeling in the world. For that brief moment, I felt free.

"Of course you can sleep in my bed, but I'm sleeping right next to you."

"I'm game for that." It wasn't as if that wasn't how we had been sleeping for more than a week, but for some reason, I needed his affirmation.

Kirk carried me back to the bedroom and tucked me into the bed before stripping off his wet clothes and crawling in next to me.

"Do you still want me?"

"Yes. Why would you ask that?"

"I… you… no sharing."

He kissed my temple and tucked me against his chest. "You're mine, Sugar. As long as you're here, you are mine."

I still wanted more, why he was here, what he was doing, but my grasp on consciousness was becoming tenuous at best.

———

I opened my eyes and Gabe stood over the foot of the bed. Bastard was harder to get rid of now that he was dead than he had been when he was alive. He just stood there, staring at me with the same look he'd had when I woke on the table in the basement.

I reached for Kirk, but the bed was empty.

"Make him go away." I tried to scream, forcing the words out as hard as I could, but it barely came out as a whisper. "Kirk." I tried again, but no sound.

Gabe laughed. "You're pathetic. And weak. You thought you could fight us off, but all along you were like a baby squirrel in a cage of tigers."

"You're not a fucking tiger." I whispered. "You're a sick asshat who has to prey on women because he's too weak for anything else."

He grabbed me, and pain shot through my chest. I couldn't breathe. I couldn't scream.

Something touched my neck, rough but light. It wasn't like the other men. It moved around my neck. I thought I was going to be strangled.

Gabe's eyes widened. "You're pathetic."

The thing around my neck started down my chest. And I saw it, the head of a snake moving between my breasts, toward Gabe's arms.

Gabe let up and I drew in a deep breath. Oh god, I couldn't make a sound. I didn't know much about snakes, but I remembered one lesson—stay away if they have a triangular head. The snake coiled back, preparing to strike, but Gabe laughed—the same laugh I remembered just before the bang of the gun.

The snake struck, nailing him right in the neck. Gabe grabbed the wound and jumped away, stumbling off the bed and into the wall.

The snake slithered down my body, inch after terrifying inch.

Gabe slumped and fell to a mass on the floor, while the snake settled on my stomach.

I AWOKE with a gasp but didn't move.

"Silver," a voice whispered in my ear. I relaxed and fell into the calm place the voice offered. I tilted my head toward it. Then I glanced down and, seeing the snake-tattooed arm wrapped around my waist, I laughed.

"You okay?"

"Just a dream and a new appreciation for snakes."

I heard him grunt, but he didn't question me. He simply kissed my temple and pulled me tighter into him. "How's the pain?"

"Tolerable." My eyes drifted closed again, and I begged for the dreams to stay away.

_____

KIRK NUDGED ME, and I opened my eyes. The way the sunlight streamed in the window, brightening the room, I assumed it was late morning. I'd never seen Kirk still in bed this late.

"You okay if I go cook breakfast?"

"Can I come out to the couch?"

"Yeah," he said, sitting up and wrapping the blanket around me so he could carry me out to the living room. He laid me out on the couch, put a pillow behind my head and straightened the covers—making sure I was warm and didn't need another pain pill before he left.

I dozed again, until he brought me a plate full of eggs, toast, and bacon. "You're a handy guy," I mumbled.

"I'm sure you'd think so." He sat the food on the coffee table and helped me sit up to eat.

"I have to leave after breakfast."

Mid-bite, I dropped the piece of bacon back on my plate. "Kirk...."

He grunted. "You nearly got busted using my name yesterday."

"Yeah, I noticed."

I didn't want to be alone. He couldn't leave me alone.

"The alarm on the door will be set, and I'll be in the building."

"So, you're leaving me here again?" I shook my head. I didn't want to even think about it, so I jumped to another subject before I lost my ability to eat. "Why are you here?"

I saw his jaw tense, and he turned on the TV. I thought he was going to just ignore my question. "Don't you think you know enough? Knowing more will just put you in more danger."

"I think I've got that covered. I'm stuck here with you either way."

"And knowing how I got here is going to make a difference, how?"

"You were so pissed when I showed up…."

"I knew I couldn't get you out. I knew I couldn't keep you completely safe, but I thought it was your best chance."

"And now you're questioning it—and everything else you did."

He tossed the remote onto the coffee table, and it clattered across the wooden surface until it dropped to the floor. "Do we have to do this now?"

Curiosity was getting the better of me. I wanted to know what kind of shit storm I had really landed in. "Yes. I want to understand."

Kirk shook his head and then leaned forward, rubbing his hands over his face just before the flood of words came rolling out. "Since the moment you arrived, I've never been closer to having my cover blown. Every day, you've held it in your hand. I had to play my role and hope to god you could play yours without knowing what was going on."

He paused for a moment, and I could see him trying to gather his thoughts, while at the same time trying to hold it back. I realized that was my effect on him—the struggle between being open and trying to save me, while maintaining his cover as a dark felon. I brought out his humanity, and that was a dangerous trait to rely on here.

I heard him swallow, then he lifted a hand and reached across the couch to gently stroke my cheek. "After a while, this place bleeds into you, and to a certain extent you have to let it to keep from standing out. I've been tempted to lose myself with you. To thoroughly claim you and make you mine just like they all expect."

"But you changed, after I tried to escape."

"After I had to beat you. I may be a twisted-up mess, but that—watching you cry and beg and then throwing you into lockup. Watching you go through everything and take it. Both of us walking the fine line between bending your will and breaking it. I wanted to keep you at a distance, but suddenly I wanted in. I wanted to let you in—despite how much I knew it would hurt you in the long run."

"Fuck the long run."

"I'm pretty sure we did." He smirked, but the amusement didn't touch the rest of his face. "Milo has his hands in a lot of dirty business, and no one has even come close to taking him down. If they take down one operation, he just starts a new one up. The network is massive, but no one will roll on him. Hell, no one even knows his *real* name; he's been nearly impossible to trace."

"You're here to bring the whole thing down?"

"Yeah. I uh… I got inside accidentally while working undercover in a gambling sting, but when Miles asked me to come work with him, I was the first to ever get inside the organization with any cred, so the FBI conspired with my superiors to keep me inside. Sometimes, it doesn't feel like I'll ever get out." Dark wrinkles and shadows clouded his face, and he looked like a completely different person. "It's not exactly a by-the-book operation. Everything is off the table. It's all about bringing Milo in, and I'm just a damn mole they sent in to wait and watch until I can sound the alarm."

"What makes you think anything will stop with him gone? There will be a second; someone will fill in where he leaves."

"But we're hoping there will be enough chaos to give us an in. He's guilty of far more than sex trafficking."

We shared a smile and went back to eating, but as soon as Kirk sat down his empty plate, I started to lose it.

"I don't want you to leave."

"I won't be gone long, less than an hour, and I can be back down here in a few minutes if anything happens. It'll pass in no time if you sleep it off."

I shook my head. "Every time I go to sleep it gets taken over by freaky dreams. What happens to me now?"

"No one will expect much until you're healed. And when you are, I'm going to find a way to get you out of here."

"It's not going to happen. Not without insane ramifications. Even if you could manage it successfully, they'll get suspicious and you'll end up outing yourself."

"I can't keep you here, Silver. I couldn't keep you safe. And I can't ask you to—"

"You don't have to ask me." I finished my plate and put it on the table. I pulled the covers away and although every movement ached, I crossed the couch to straddle his lap. "I can play my part, and with you… I can enjoy some of it. But even if you get me out, it'll all be for nothing. I want them all to pay for what they've done, and if I stay, you can make sure that happens."

"Silver, I—"

"Promise me, Kirk. Let me have back this one piece of my free will."

"Revenge isn't all it's cracked up to be. I don't want to see you—"

"I already killed a guy." I whispered. "I think the darkness has already claimed me."

"Exactly why we shouldn't—"

"Kirk, please. I'm not asking you to let me take them down myself. I never want to kill anyone, even if it's in self-defence. But I want to make sure you can do your job. We both have to play our roles."

Kirk took a deep breath and traced my collarbone with his lips. "I'll think about it. For right now, I have to go." He gently lifted me off his lap and tucked me back under the covers. Then he disappeared into the bedroom to change and returned, handing me another white pill.

"Can it wait?"

"You tell me. The last one should be wearing off."

"It makes me too sleepy and I have weird dreams." I just wanted to stay awake while he was gone. The time wouldn't pass as quickly, but at least I'd be alert and not lost in the dreams where Gabe could torment me.

"I'll leave it here in case you change your mind." He placed it on the table near my glass of water. "I'll be back as soon as I can."

I nodded and curled up against the pillow. It and the blankets smelled like Kirk, and that was enough to ease my worries for the moment. I heard the lock snap behind him and it set my mind racing.

I tried everything I could imagine to keep my mind occupied so it wouldn't drive me insane or get me into more trouble. Finally, I settled on a shower, hoping that the heat would ease the ache in my muscles. I smothered myself in Kirk's body wash, hoping to wash away the feeling of Gabe and his men pawing at me. Groping me. Hitting me.

The pounding of the water didn't help with the latter since it stung at each of my bruises and welts. Once I felt reasonably clean again, I shut off the water, and carefully dried my skin. Then I picked up a comb and went back to the living room, resting for a while before I regained enough strength to tackle my nest of hair.

I started with the ends, trying to pull out each painful

tangle, but my scalp was already sore, and my arms refused to hold themselves up for long. I had barely made a dent in the mess when I heard the lock click. I froze, my eyes dancing around the room for something I could use as a weapon. My bruised legs even prepared to pounce or run.

Kirk stepped through and my entire body instantly relaxed. He grinned slightly when he saw me and dropped his things on the desk. "What are you doing?"

"Trying to make my hair look like something that didn't roll out of the forest."

He sat beside me and, damn it all, he pulled off his shirt.

"How long have you been at it?"

"Uh—" I looked at the clock. "About forty minutes. You're late."

"At least you kept yourself occupied."

"My arms refuse to work much."

"Turn around. I'll help." he said, snatching the comb from my hand.

"You'll help comb my hair?"

"Unless you want me to let you sit here and suffer while you do it yourself."

I turned my back toward him, and he adjusted so I could lean against his leg while he worked.

I grimaced as soon as he grabbed a clump of hair, waiting for the pull and the pain. I could barely sit still as a kid when my mom tried to detangle my hair, and back then my scalp hadn't been abused beforehand.

He tugged and gently pulled at each section, very few times did it ever verge on pain.

"Are you actually doing anything, or just trying to appease me?"

He kissed my shoulder. "It's going to take a while, but

yes, I can manage to comb hair. I thought you'd like me to inflict as little pain as possible."

"Well then, you're surprisingly good at this."

"I had a little sister."

Had. I wasn't sure if he referred to her in the past tense because she was gone, or because he was separating himself from his own life. "I didn't think that was a brother's thing —brushing his sister's hair."

"She was sick a lot. Couldn't always do it herself, and she refused to let Mom cut it."

"At least she had a good brother." I wanted to know more but was afraid to pry. One more glimpse into who he really was. "Is she—did—um…." I couldn't think of a good way to phrase anything.

"She died when she was fourteen. She had cystic fibrosis, and despite everything the doctors could do, she had trouble with lung infections—for a while it seemed constant. My parents didn't even know they were carriers, and they took it pretty hard when she died."

"I am sorry." I wanted to say more, to somehow find a way to ease the pain in his voice, but I didn't have the slightest idea how. My side spasmed, and I flinched, sending waves of pain through the rest of my body. "I think I need the pain pill now."

Barely moving me, Kirk reached around me to hand me the water and the pill. "Hello oblivion." I whispered as I popped it in my mouth and swallowed.

As my eyelids grew heavy, my defenses fell again. "I had a big fight with my sister, and we've barely talked since."

"You'll work it out." he said, tugging at a difficult knot.

"Will we? It wasn't even our first big fight. She got everything she ever wanted and as soon as something didn't go her way, she went running to someone for a pity party—

our parents, an ex… It became a never-ending cycle. She moved in with me, and things got serious between her and my best friend, Peter. That's when everything started to go to hell."

He smoothed out a section of hair and laid it over my shoulder. "What happened?"

I shook my head, starting to feel too sleepy to hold myself up. I wasn't supposed to be talking about my family, about life before this. "That's not this life."

"Come on, Sugar, you brought it up." Kirk laid down the comb and wrapped his arms around me.

I closed my eyes and drifted into his warmth. "I always had a thing for Peter, but they were good together. I don't know what happened, but she started hanging out with an ex. She and Peter got into a fight then Chey and her ex went out and blew half of her rent money on booze. We got into it and she moved back with Mom and Dad. She wanted an apology. I wanted an apology. We were at a standstill."

"I imagine she's at least half as stubborn as you."

"She found out she was pregnant after our big fight…. I didn't handle that too well either." The surge of guilt churned my stomach, and I couldn't take it anymore. I didn't want to be thinking about things I couldn't fix—especially the ones I might not get the chance to fix. I moaned and used the back of the couch to pull myself up. "Are you going to leave my hair half done?"

I managed to stay conscious as Kirk spent the next half hour working though all the knots in my hair, until it fell around my shoulders again in smooth strait strands.

"You're good." I mumbled, curling up against his chest.

"Try to sleep." He kissed the top of my head and tucked a blanket around me.

"Keep the nightmares away."

I woke up with my head in Kirk's lap, staring up into his sparkling blue eyes.

"What are you grinning about?" he asked.

"No dreams that time." I lied.

The corner of his mouth lifted, and I suspected he saw right through my lie. He saved me, and he protected me. It wasn't a stretch to say that the more I learned about him, the more I adored him.

That also frightened me.

He said that letting me in would only make things harder in the long run, because for us, he never expected a long run. I'd be his until he finished the job, and then I'd be on my own again. On my own to deal with the memories and the nightmares.

"Come back to me." Kirk said, brushing his thumb over my lips.

"I'm here."

"Your mind isn't."

I didn't want it to be. He broke down my defenses too easily now, but I pressed a smile to my sore face. "So, what's next, boss?"

"You heal."

"You're not in trouble for—"

"I told you I wouldn't be. The meeting was about the others. We have to deal with everyone who can't be trusted. Soon." He breathed. "Milo is coming in two weeks. Ross said he held it off so we could finish getting everything cleaned up. I think he's worried about keeping his job after all of this."

That was the most terrifying good news I'd ever heard. "That means you'll have your chance. We just have to play it off for a couple of weeks."

A couple weeks—more torment—and then I'd lose him.

I told myself to stop getting attached, to remember that what we had wasn't real. It was a product of the circumstances. There was no evidence that the two of us would ever work outside of this environment. Hell, there was no way we'd be together any other way. If the two of us had passed in a bar a month ago, I wouldn't have turned my head, and I doubted that he would have either.

Whatever connection we had wasn't real.

It wasn't meant to last.

Chapter Seventeen

INITIATION

AFTER A PEACEFUL WEEK, I know it was wishful thinking that we'd make it through the weekend without anyone bothering us, and the early-evening knock on the door confirmed it. I pulled the blanket over myself and flattened out on the couch where no one could see me. Covered in swollen bruises, being violated by Gabe and his crew had made me even more anti-social than normal.

Kirk understood, but I doubted anyone else would—especially not Ross. He was the one person I couldn't bear to see. Except a resurrected Gabe, but he was a frequent visitor to my dreams.

I briefly heard muffled voices then the door closed.

"It's for you." Kirk said, holding out a box.

"Unless it's chocolate, send it back." I sat up just long enough for Kirk to reclaim his seat at the end of the couch, and then I laid my head on his lap.

"It's from Ross." He laid it on my stomach, but I drew my hands away from it.

"Definitely send it back." I was sure Ross didn't like me

much and Kirk was now on his bad side, too. Probably more so than he was willing to admit.

I wanted to know the details so I'd know what to expect, but even more, I didn't want to know anything anymore. I didn't want to know who Kirk really was, to wrestle with the things both of us had to do to survive.

It was bad enough when I was only concerned with myself. Now, I was terrified of doing something that might give him away.

"Just open it, Silver. It really can't be as bad as you're currently imagining."

"How do you know?" I lifted the box and pressed it to his chest. "You want to know, you open it."

Shaking his head, he jerked the box away and popped off the top. He laid the box on the arm of the couch and pulled out a snakeskin tube dress with huge cut outs running down each side.

"Swanky," I mused.

"There's a matching thong."

I stifled a laugh at his exaggerated enthusiasm and it hurt like hell, but humor was more valuable than pain. "Lookie there, our rat-skinned Master thinks of everything."

Kirk chuckled, dropping the lingerie back into the box. It was rare to see him with a genuine smile, the kind that tightened the skin around his eyes and brought out his dimples. "Just wait."

I heard something else move in the box and he pulled out a pair of stiletto heels with silver snakes coiled around the spike.

"I'd kill myself," I said, instantly losing the humor. "That's like a six-inch heel."

Kirk flicked his eyebrow up then ran his hand over his mouth.

"There's more?" I asked.

"You're to wear them to the Outlook tonight."

"Tonight?" I pulled myself up into a seated position. "I have more dark spots than an over ripe banana."

The corner of his mouth turned up as he dropped everything into the box and tossed it under the coffee table.

The hardest part about knowing his secret and actually understanding him, was that I cared about how he felt. Distant and brooding meant he was going to have to do something he didn't want to do.

I swung my leg over his lap, straddling him in an attempt to distract him and at least avoid the brunt of his sullen side for a moment.

"Silver." He exhaled, putting his hands on my hips. "Don't."

"Don't what? We still have a whole hour before we have to worry about anything that happens at the Outlook."

"I need to go talk to Ross." Kirk began to lift me up, but I shifted my weight to delay him.

"Why? I mean, I get that you want to protect me from whatever he has planned, but we should just do what he says."

Kirk grimaced and leaned his head back. "Since when are you gung-ho to do anything anyone says?"

"I don't want to die here—"

"You won't."

"Not if we both keep playing our parts. You get too soft on me. He already sees it, so just...." I shook my head. I couldn't believe the words that were about to come out of my mouth. "Let him do what he wants to do."

———

I DIDN'T THINK Ross had asked us to the Outlook out of concern for my condition and recovery. *Initiation.* The word flooded my mind. I knew it was coming. I hadn't even healed from the last attack, part of me hoped that meant he'd take it easy on me, but I doubted it. As we entered the giant twelfth-story club, I wanted to press myself against Kirk, a single whiff of him, the touch of his skin, anything to calm the growing panic inside of me.

One thing I had on my side while I was injured was the pain meds, even though Kirk had taken me down to half a pill at a time. They didn't make walking in stilettos easy, however.

Kirk took a seat at the table, and I knelt next to him, holding back my grunt of pain as my stiff body settled into the uncomfortable position.

"She really is a tough girl," Ross mused.

"She is." Kirk cupped my cheek. "And she's still healing. I guess we all underestimated Gabe's vindictive streak."

Ross scoffed. I glanced around, usually he had at least one slave at his feet, but today there were no other slaves around. Three other men entered the room, but I didn't recognize any of them.

"Ross...." Kirk growled.

My stomach flipped and churned, the sound of his voice validated my fears.

I struggled to catch my breath.

Miles paused at the doorway and scanned the room. So far, he was the only one to enter with a slave.

Looking under the table, I managed to catch a peek at Alley's face as she sat down, but she bit her lip and kept her eyes down.

My heart pounded, and my body started to shake.

Please, I begged an invisible power, biting into my lip.

"She's hurt; she's not ready for this."

"She's out of time," Ross hissed. "One chance to prove herself before Milo gets here."

Six men and two slaves. That was eerily close to the odds I'd faced when I woke up in the basement. *Keep it together, Silver. Only a little longer.*

I could hear their voices over me, but not a single syllable registered as having any meaning. The tendons of Kirk's hand pulsed as he fisted it against his leg. I wasn't the only one struggling to keep up the show.

Ross stood, looking down on me, and I heard my name, just before his hand clamped down on my collar and pulled me to my feet. My feet slid out of the shoes as I stumbled toward him.

I was actually quite thankful to be rid of the shoes. At least I wouldn't be ending the night with a broken ankle—I hoped.

As we passed, Kirk took a deep breath, but didn't otherwise move.

I followed Ross—although it wasn't as if I had a choice since he was dragging me by the metal ring around my neck. He placed me in front of a small table. It was as tall as his waist and just big enough for a person to lay on.

He lifted me on to it and pushed me back. My muscles were tense, but I tried not to resist as he positioned me so that my head rested against what looked like a movable portion.

"I hear you're good with your mouth," Ross said, pressing two fingers to my lips. I opened my mouth and he shoved them inside, straight to the back of my throat. I gagged, pulling in a breath of air through my nose and trying not to clamp down on the invading fingers.

"Good girl," he whispered. "Definitely gaining control of your body. That'll help."

Shit. My brain rambled off every curse word I'd ever heard.

Ross slid his fingers out, then back in. I jerked with my gag reflex then forced myself to breath past it again. "Kirk, strap your lovely slave down."

I saw Kirk shake his head slightly then approach. He picked up a cuff that was chained to the bottom corner of the table, and pulled my leg to the edge, rubbing the inside of my ankle with his thumb as he fastened the buckle. He then repeated the same thing on the other leg.

The next strap went over my chest, just below the still bruised ribs and right on top of where one of Gabe's men had punched me. I winced as Kirk tightened it, but Ross simply turned back toward his guests.

"You okay?" Kirk mouthed.

I shook my head, feeling like I was about to cry.

"Pain?"

I closed my eyes, pushing back the tears, and shook my head again.

The men around the table erupted into laughter and stood. My heart beat so fast I couldn't even think straight. Everything in the room slowed as Kirk lowered the flap on the table under my head then stepped away. The three men I didn't recognize circled me.

I forced myself to keep breathing, long deep breaths for as long as I could manage. I promised Kirk I could do this. I promised I could take anything they put me through just to bring them all down.

Just get through it.

The first man approached, tangling his fingers in my hair and pulling it tight.

"Beautiful girl," he said in a strange accent. Then he undid his pants and pulled out his cock.

Kirk. I cried out in my head. *I lied. I can't do it.*

Stroking it slowly next to my head, the other men, including Ross followed suit. Kirk touched Ross' arm and whispered something in his ear. Ross frowned then nodded, without ever taking his eyes off me.

The first man pulled my head back and pressed his cock to my lips. I opened, and he pressed forward until I gagged. He paused, not withdrawing, just waiting.

As soon as I suppressed my gag reflex, he pushed deeper until it pressed painfully against the back of my throat. I struggled to take a single breath without biting down.

He slowly moved out then thrust back in again. I jerked.

I was strapped down, so the only thing I could do was lay there and take it. I concentrated on breathing and not gagging so hard that I would clench my jaw closed.

He thrust in and out slowly a few times, coating my tongue with his musky salty taste. Then he picked up the pace, slamming into the back of my throat with every thrust. I fisted my hands at my sides, feeling my body shake with the effort to stay in control.

Ironically, I was glad to be tied down. At least then I didn't have to worry about what the rest of my body was doing as well.

He pulled out a final time then stepped back for the next man to take his turn.

A new cock was shoved down my throat, thicker but shorter, so not every thrust hit the back of my throat as forcefully. But when he pressed in completely, it blocked off my windpipe entirely. He held it down, watching me struggle for air and then backed off before repeating the same thing.

The struggle aggravated all my previous injuries and before much longer I was buried in a fog of pain and confusion.

Ross was next with his long slender shaft. Every thrust was fast and powerful, pushing as deep as possible. I started to cough around it, but it only spurred him to move faster.

He pulled out and I choked in a breath of air.

"You look so nice for your Master tonight." He leaned his face closer to mine, rubbing his hand over my neck and down my sternum. "It was a fitting ensemble, don't you think?"

"Yes, Master," I whispered. Involuntary tears slipped out of my eyes from the gagging and the stabbing pain in my lungs.

He smirked, tracing my chin with his fingertips. "It's not really fair that your Master is standing by and not having any fun." He straightened and licked his lips, then pointed to a chair that had been pushed up against the wall. "Kirk, have a seat and whip it out."

Kirk wouldn't meet my gaze as he walked by and took a seat. He unzipped his pants and pulled out his half hard cock.

"Alley," Ross said, waving to Kirk. "Take care of him."

I saw Alley make eye contact with Miles before she dropped to her knees and took Kirk in her mouth.

I wanted to clench my jaw, or look away, but Ross had positioned him perfectly so that even if I didn't look over, I could see the motion in my peripheral vision.

Mother fucker.

"Well, what do you think of that?"

"Whatever pleases him." I had to force it out, but I

hoped that the raspiness caused by my sore throat covered it up enough.

Ross stepped away and the fourth man took my hair, smacking my face before he slipped his cock in my mouth.

I heard Kirk grunt, but I wasn't sure if it was because of Alley or the man smacking me.

This man thrust in slowly, easing his cock down my throat every time. I wasn't sure if I was becoming numb to it, or better at controlling the gagging, but I managed to take him without my entire body convulsing.

The rest of the men gathered at the side of the table, rubbing my skin while they violently tugged at their own shafts waiting for their next turn.

Please, make it end, I begged silently.

The first man came up again. This time, he wrapped both hands in my hair, pulling it with each thrust. I tugged at all the restraints, trying to catch a breath, but he forced himself deeper and I gagged harder with each thrust. My gut clenched, setting my bruises on fire.

I heard Kirk grunt again. And this time there was no doubt in my mind what caused it. The sound was familiar. I could see the way his body tensed just before coming. My hatred for Ross tightened every muscle and thickened my muscle until I felt like my body was hardening to cement. He wanted to torture us both, to fuck with both of our minds. So, instead of falling into his sick game, I let my mind latch on to his sounds even though I resented that they were caused by Alley.

I concentrated on our connection, remembering his tongue on my skin, his lips on mine, the sensations that relaxed my body and quieted my mind. I'd finally found a piece of that place where I could hide from the attacks.

The first man jerked and spasmed then pulled out of my

mouth, spilling his liquid on my face. It dripped into my mouth and nose, making it even harder to breath. I swallowed, and barely got my mouth open in time for Ross shove his cock in my mouth again.

He squeezed my breasts as he pumped into my throat. Three quick pumps, then he'd hold it there, in my throat blocking off my oxygen. I tried to time my breathing accordingly, but every time I adapted, he threw off his rhythm slightly to block off my airway as soon as I exhaled.

My grunts, shaking, and flailing must have pushed him over the edge. He came in the back of my throat and I struggled to swallow it before my chest demanded that I inhale.

It didn't entirely work.

I coughed, and jerked, feeling the liquid in my mouth, and throat. All over my face. The room dimmed as the lack of oxygen set in.

I heard voices around me, laughter.

I faded back into the room with Gabe. I turned my head, focusing on Kirk. Miles now stood next to him, with a hand on Kirks' shoulder as if he was holding him there.

A hand touched my face and I jerked.

"It's okay, sweetie," Alley whispered, wiping the cum off my face and away from my nose. Apparently, they weren't entirely ready for me to pass out, since all the men waited behind her while she finished what she was doing.

I jerked with another wave of coughing and forced myself to swallow it all back down.

Alley stepped away and that was nearly enough to push me over the edge.

What had I agreed to?

Why was I letting this happen?

I knew when I agreed to stay with Kirk, to help him that

I'd be used and degraded, but I still wasn't sure how much of it I could take without breaking.

I sent my mind to another place. I didn't have to be there. Nothing that I could do would change anything they did to me. They enjoyed pushing my body's automatic responses.

But I still had to fight, to keep my teeth from clamping down, to keep my chest from inhaling too much of their vile liquid. That's all I concentrated on, letting the rest of reality fade to the edges.

My only reprieve came when the next two men came quickly, probably from enjoying the show, and I finally felt hands releasing the cuffs on my ankles, and the strap across my chest.

My eyes wouldn't focus on anything.

A form pulled me up and tucked me to his chest. I took a breath of his scent and crashed into unconsciousness.

———

I WOKE up in another coughing fit as Kirk swung open the door to his apartment.

"Bathroom please," I rasped.

He sat me on my feet near the toilet and as the last cough subsided, I heaved, and coughed up more cum.

"I should have found a way to get you out of here."

"I said I wanted to stay. Now I just want to bring them down more than ever."

"Silver—"

I shook my head, putting my fingers to his lips. I knew what he wanted to say. He didn't want me to end up fucked up for the rest of my life. He wanted to remind me that revenge was a slippery slope.

"If I don't help, they'll keep doing this. Maybe it's small in the big scheme of things. There will be other traffickers. Other people who hurt women. But I can at least help make sure some of them get what they deserve."

Kirk huffed then kissed my forehead. "You're a stronger girl than I gave you credit for."

"I am pretty damn amazing, aren't I?" I winked, putting on a show even though my voice was raspy and barely audible. Neither the sight or sound could have been remotely attractive, but it helped lighten the tension.

"I'm not sure I should feed your ego after that."

"After tonight? Yes. Then, you should drag me into the shower and make me forget."

"You need to drink some water first." He kissed my forehead. "Will you be okay for a minute while I grab a glass?"

"Yeah, fill it with vodka."

"You think your throat burns now?" He tousled my hair as he passed. "You haven't even had dinner."

I shrugged. Quicker path to wasted, which is exactly where I wanted to be.

———

KIRK CLIMBED into the shower with me. He stood behind me, rubbing lathery soap over my skin. I could barely keep my eyes open, let alone enjoy his feathery touches over my skin, but I wanted my escape, that momentary release and rush of pleasure to help me escape the nightmare. Even if it was only temporary.

"Please, make me forget." I rubbed my hands over his pecs then up and hooked them behind his neck.

"You're exhausted," he kissed my neck. I rested against his chest as he massaged the shampoo through my hair, then

I leaned back, letting the water fall over my face and rinse the soap down the drain.

I shrugged, dropping my head on his shoulder. He was already taking most of my weight.

He helped me out of the tub then wrapped a towel around my body. I quickly dried myself off, eager to get off my feet and collapse in bed. I opened the medicine cabinet and took a mouthful of mouthwash. I considered swallowing it, just to sanitize the rest of my throat.

I swished it around and spit it out, and a horrible thought occurred to me.

"Those men…. They're clean, right?"

"Yeah, Ross is careful."

"But tonight he seemed pretty vengeful."

"He gets that way especially…." He trailed off for a moment, leaning sideways against the wall near the counter. "We haven't had new girls in a while, so I think he was particularly enjoying himself."

He gently ran his fingers over my shoulder and pulled me a step closer. "One more week," he promised.

I followed him out to the living room and watched him walk into the kitchenette to fix us each something to eat— and hopefully drink. I noticed the pill bottle sitting on his desk and tiptoed around the couch to pick it up.

Vicodin. The reliever of my pain and deliverer of oblivion.

"No, Silver."

"I hurt." I pleaded.

"Then, I'll give you some Aspirin."

"I've been taking this stuff all week."

"For pain, not an escape."

I stared down at the bottle, hearing Kirk put the food

and drinks on the table. Tears broke free in streams down my face.

He grabbed my waist, holding me against his chest until the worst of the sobs passed.

"I shouldn't have let you stay."

"You couldn't have gotten me out. No thinking about the impossible, remember?"

He kissed my cheek, then my neck. "You are pretty fucking awesome."

I breathed a faint laugh, feeling the knot in my stomach unwind.

"I mean it. Now, let's eat so I can help erase it all." He took the drugs out of my hand and tossed the bottle back on his desk, then tugged me to the couch.

I took a long swig of the drink he'd mixed, it burned all the way down, but no more than my emotions.

After we finished eating, Kirk made us each a second drink. By the time we went to bed, I was stumbling and buzzed.

"I can now add taking advantage of a drunk girl to my long list of sins."

"I'm not that drunk, and I asked for this before I started drinking."

He pushed me down onto the bed, kissing from my belly button up my sternum to my neck, but by the time he got to my lips, I could barely keep my eyes open.

"How about we do this in the morning when you can enjoy it?"

I forced a smile and nodded.

He pulled the blankets around us and drew me into his side.

"I forgive you," I breathed.

Chapter Eighteen

REMNANTS OF ME

I WOKE in the middle of the night coughing so hard, I was sure part of my lung was going to break off. Kirk rubbed my back, as I braced myself on hand and knees through the assault.

I leaned over the side of the bed and spit into the trashcan—phlegm mixed with liquids I never wanted to think about again.

"Is it possible to drown on cum?" I croaked.

"I don't think you're currently in danger of that."

"Ross did it on purpose, knowing I'd have to inhale as soon as he got off," I grumbled as I gasped for air, feeling almost as bad as the time I was admitted to the hospital with pneumonia in sixth grade. Kirk sat up next to me, supporting me with one arm and caressing my back with the other.

"I think I'm dying." As I calmed, it became easier to at least draw in a slow shallow breath.

"You're not dying. Your lungs are just irritated, producing extra mucus." He kissed between my shoulder blades and lifted me to face him. "I'm sorry."

"Don't start," I mumbled burying my face into his neck, so I didn't have to see his pained expression. "I said I'd stay; I knew it could get bad."

"Why are you so determined?"

"Because...." I didn't want to talk about my reasons. "I'm already in. Gabe...." It was hard enough saying his name. "He brought me into this. He dragged me down as low as I could get. I want something to come out of this that's bigger than my freedom."

Kirk grimaced, pulling back to run his thumb across my chin. "You feel obligated because you shot an asshole that kidnapped and raped you?"

"He would have done it again. There are others who will." I wrapped my hand around his forearm, my fingertips resting just above the snake tattoo that had infiltrated my dreams and fantasies in so many ways. I hoped that after this was over, I could shed the pain of this life away. "I want this Kirk. I deserve it, and I sure as hell didn't go through everything tonight for you to change your mind."

"I don't want to have to watch anything like that again." He pulled me into his lap. His hot palms spread against my back, keeping me tight against him. "You reminded me of who I really am and what I came here to stop. But you make it very hard to maintain my façade."

Before I could respond, his lips covered mine. He nipped at my lip, but given what I'd just been coughing up, I kept my mouth closed.

I pulled away a fraction, and he grimaced.

"You really don't mind kissing me right now? I'm coughing up other men's cum for Chrissake."

He nipped at my collarbone. "Never say that again."

I chuckled, and it sent me into another fit of coughing. I

hated crawling out of his lap to spit in the trash can again, but my chest finally felt like it was beginning to clear. I emptied my glass of water and sat back against Kirk.

"Anything I can do to make you more comfortable?"

"Can you make it easier to breathe?"

"Lean forward and put your arms under your head to spread out your shoulder blades." He maneuvered me until I was exactly how he wanted me, then he pulled the blanket over my back and began pounding over my lungs.

I closed my eyes, transfixed by the steady rhythm as it broke up the congestion in my chest. I coughed several more times, and spit into the trash can again, before finally being able to take a deep breath.

"You're good," I said, rolling onto my back.

"Of course I am." He lay down at my side, rubbing his hand in delicate motions across my stomach. Even in the dark, I couldn't escape his drooping eyes, and wrinkled forehead.

"Stop looking at me like you just killed my favorite pet." I laced my fingers through his and drew his arm around me. "We are where we are, and I believe a few days ago, it was you trying to convince me of that."

"That was when I thought I could keep you from getting hurt." His voice was low, and I could almost feel the sting of pain that hid behind his words.

"So, what exactly was your long-term plan? Claim me and keep me hidden from everyone else until the person you've been waiting for shows up?"

"Pretty much. He'll be here next week, and I suspect that's why Ross pushed the initiation."

"I get the feeling that tonight was supposed to be a punishment for you, too."

"Perceptive," he dawdled.

"I'm getting this whole criminal thought process down."

Kirk grunted a laugh then rolled onto his back, pulling me with him so that my head rested on his shoulder.

"Thank you," I whispered.

"I haven't done anything worthy—"

"Quiet."

"You keep this up and no one is going to buy your act."

"Why? I'm petrified around the rest of them—enough to keep my head on. I managed to lie through my teeth while high on pain meds, I think I can keep it together." I laid my head on his shoulder. He pulled me closer, his arms wrapped around me.

I took a deep breath, but I still couldn't manage to escape the burning in my soul that clogged my thoughts. I wanted to laugh it off, pretend it was something I could lock away, and forget it had never happened.

"I can feel you thinking," Kirk whispered.

"I'll add mind reading to your list of capabilities."

He hooked his hand behind my knee and pulled me on top of him. His hot chest pressed against mine, and I stared down into his blue-grey eyes.

I wanted to melt into those eyes and hide there until it was all over.

"Do you still want that distraction?"

"Do you still want to give it to me?" My lips twitched. "I feel like I'm the one taking advantage of you now."

"Even if you were, I'm not complaining." He rolled me to my back and pressed his hand to me.

I had to give it to him. No one had ever made me appreciate how good sex could feel before him.

I was supposed to hate it.

I was supposed to hate him.

"What on earth are you thinking about now?"

"I'm not telling you."

He paused, I watched him swallow. I wanted him to move. It was distraction time, and for some reason he was just waiting for something.

"What do you want?" I asked.

"Tell me something about you."

I pushed my lips together and shook my head. He knew all he needed to know—more than he needed to know. "My name is Silver, I woke up here, you know my story."

He closed his eyes. And kissed my sternum. Moving slowly down my body.

"What do you want to know?" I breathed as the arousal twisted with guilt in my gut.

"Nothing."

I slid my fingers through his hair and pulled him against me.

"When I was a kid, my sister and I used dowel rods to 'sword fight' and she nearly broke my hand."

He smiled and kissed my wrist. Every touch of his lips sent a flash of fire through me, touching more than my skin.

"You don't owe me anything," he said. As if he understood my deepest concerns.

"Whether I do or not…." I trailed off and regretted opening my mouth in the first place. Not only could I not put my feelings into words, Kirk paused again as he waited for me to finish what I'd begun.

There was some little part of me that wanted something real with him. Something not based on facades and lies.

A dangerous desire.

Kirk sealed his lips against mine, drawing me out and into his world. The place where it didn't matter that our past was based on misinformation and lies, or that our future was doomed—one way or another.

He moved down my body, latching his mouth onto my breast. Teasing and sucking until I moaned in response. Then he kissed even lower down my stomach, over my bellybutton. His thumb brushed against the back of my knee, as he kissed and gently nipped the inside of my thigh.

His hot mouth settled over my clit—drawing it out with a suckle before pressing his tongue against it. His stubble scratched at my sensitive folds—especially in the places where I had yet to heal completely, but pleasure from his tongue and mouth far outweighed the discomfort, and soon the prickling pain was joined by the pleasure.

He hooked my thighs over his shoulders, his hands gripping the sides of my hips as he buried his face in my flesh.

I moaned, writhing against him as he pushed me closer to orgasm with just his tongue and mouth.

It was almost the simplicity of it that made it even more amazing. His attentiveness to every spot of my body that remained sore and bruised from the attack.

I hadn't been sure that I could take his cock inside of me, even though I wanted it, but he seemed to have come up with a solution without me having even expressed my doubts.

His hand stretched up, rubbing my breast gently. Tweaking the nipple between two fingers.

I bucked and then arched my back. His tongue flickered inside of me, licking up my juices as my insides twisted.

I reached above me, clutching at the headboard as the orgasm built.

Everything down to his hot breath on my skin took my control away.

My hips rocked, and he sucked harder, lips and tongue playing with and exploring every fold.

My toes curled.

My back arched.

And I moaned as my muscles broke free and claimed the orgasmic release.

I bucked, but Kirk kept licking and sucking, drawing out every jerk, quiver, and twitch until I had been drained.

My body simultaneously felt weightless and as heavy as cement—weighted down until it sunk into the bed.

I smelled myself on his lips as they pressed against my own. I tasted it as my tongue flicked out to draw him in.

"And to think I was once a skeptic when people said sex could be that good."

"At least I don't have to ask if you enjoyed it."

"Hell yes."

I had no business holding on to him. Holding onto the pleasure—even the pain.

I took a deep breath and curled against his side as he returned to his place beside me. If the two of us had crossed paths anywhere else, I doubted we would have ever given each other a second look. We were both victims of the circumstances.

We could survive together and feed off each other's strength. But I wondered how much more was possible for us.

If I'd ever see him again when—if—we escaped this torment.

Would we even want to see each other again? Would we want to relive the pain, the things we'd seen and experienced?

Kirk traced my skin in light circles until I shivered.

"You're not supposed to be thinking now."

I sighed. "You make me come apart in ways I don't think I'll ever understand."

"And yet you're still trying? You baffle me sometimes."

I sat up and glared down at him. My chest still felt stiff, and I had a feeling it wouldn't feel better in the morning. Probably much worse, so anything we were about to get out of our system had to be now.

"I'm sorry I can't just shut my brain off at will."

To my surprise, he smiled, rose up, and kissed me. "You baffle me because... here you are. Everything that's happened and against all odds, you're far from broken."

"That's what you were afraid would happen to me in the beginning. Even Ross said it."

I leaned into his hand as he touched the side of my face, moving his hand down my neck to squeeze my shoulder.

"I thought that if I could protect you from them, you might be okay. I didn't know when or if I could get you out of here without bringing down the wrath of the entire operation. You fought me every step of the way until I had to punish you for running."

I stiffened; that was the last thing I wanted to remember. Somehow, the thought of Kirk bringing down the whip on my back overwhelmed my brain even quicker than remembering what the others had done.

Because I knew how hard it was for both of us. Because he was the one that, even then, I trusted to keep me safe. Much safer than the alternative.

"What changed?" he asked.

"I told you. Sex is better than pain."

"It is, but that isn't it."

I scowled back. Who was he to tell me what or wasn't my reasoning behind my change in attitude.

"You changed," I whispered. "Maybe not so obviously, but I saw you differently. Especially after you brought me back up here and took care of me."

"I still forced you to do things against your will."

I clenched my jaw, not wanting to tug on the flimsy thread that held us together. "We're going to do this tonight?"

"Silver, I ..." He squinted at me "I'm not the noble hero. I may have wanted to keep you safe, but there were a lot of other things I wanted to do to you, too. You don't live in this world as long as I have without having the disparity rub off on you."

"Maybe not, but you didn't do them."

"I fucked you in the Outlook in front of everyone, and I got off on it. Even though I knew—"

"Stop," I whispered. I wanted it to sound angry, more forceful.

Less pathetic.

I took a breath and found my voice again. "I got off on it, too, if you don't remember. And you can say that you forced me. In a billion ways you did, but Ross tried that, too. I didn't get anywhere near an orgasm with him. It was you, you and your damn gentle touch. You're never what I expect and that's what always wrecks me."

"I manipulated you." His voice rose, and I felt his muscles harden. "I did it on purpose."

"I know." I rubbed my hand down his chest trying to calm him, but he grabbed my wrist and held it there. "But you kept your promise."

"My promise to keep you safe? Really, I think I fucked that up quite well."

"There wasn't anything you could have done. You still came back for me. You found me. You took responsibility. You can't protect me from every little thing, like some parent who won't even let their kid play in the back yard for fear of him falling down and scraping a knee—"

"It's a little more than a scraped knee. They could have

killed you. Ross isn't going to take it easy on you now, either."

I pushed myself to my knees. The sex was supposed to make everything better, not lead to another argument. "I know, and no matter what you say, I'm not going back on what I said. I'd rather be here until the end. Even if you could get me out—"

Kirk rolled, pinning me under him. He braced his elbows on the outside of my shoulders so that his knuckles just brushed against my cheekbones. "Are you more afraid of what would happen here if you left, or what's going to happen when you go back to your life?"

"Both…" I admitted. I hadn't let myself consider the latter, but I had no idea. I didn't know how to cope with everything that had happened when I got outside of these walls.

Here it was normal. Out there it was debauchery and murder.

"I want to make sure you have the best shot. I'm already bent, so—"

"Silver, the last thing I want to do is add to your nightmares and regrets."

"They're a part of me either way; I'd rather something good come out of it."

"You never actually answered my first question," Kirk whispered, tracing my bottom lip with his thumb. "What made you give in?"

"I did answer." I pressed my palms to his skin and slid them down his hard sides. "You made me change my mind. After I ran, you were different. Before, you kept me at arm's length. I didn't think you wanted me." I bit my cheek, watching the play of emotions on Kirk's face. "I mean, I felt alone. Completely isolated, and the only person who ever looked in on me just thought I was some damn burden."

A burst of air escaped his lungs. "You fought because you were afraid you didn't matter?"

I shook my head and dropped my head against the pillow. "I fought because it was the only thing I had."

Kirk rolled and put his hand on my stomach. "I didn't want you to get close. I could only play the monster up to a point, beyond that... I had to keep you afraid and distant enough that you wouldn't do something stupid. But you just kept doing stupid things."

"I've had a lifetime of practice at that—pushing people to the edge instead of doing what I'm told. I gave in with you, because I figured it was better to have someone fully on my side. And in here, I didn't want that person to be anyone but you." We'd each pushed the other to the point of dangerous vulnerability, and all the little things I hadn't understood before began to take on a new clarity.

"And then the world spiraled out from under both of us. I started letting myself do things to you that I promised myself I wouldn't."

"It wasn't that bad," I muttered. "I know I shouldn't enjoy it, but..." There wasn't really any denying it, he was good. And I wasn't going to tell him that to his face. I was getting attached to a man I barely knew, in an impossible situation.

I knew it.

But I couldn't pull away.

I found my only shred of sanity by indulging in him. By finding pleasure where I could.

"Well, if you don't want to enjoy it, I can stop working so hard," he said with a smug smile.

"Don't even think about it." I poked his side with my finger and closed my eyes.

It wasn't like I was confident that I'd ever have mind blowing sex again. Maybe there was a possibility, but I certainly wasn't good at picking out the mind-blowing sexperts in real life.

Then, I wondered if I'd ever want sex again after getting out of there.

Sex—both good and bad—was intrinsically linked to the experience. "I may as well enjoy it while I can."

I didn't realize that I'd spoken the words out loud until Kirk's eyes hardened.

"I didn't mean that to be as dire as it sounded," I said quickly. "Can we stop talking about all of this now? I'm sleepy."

"You're wide awake. What are you afraid of telling me?"

I pressed my head deeper into the pillow, cursing him for wanting to drag things out of me. Sometimes I missed the days when he didn't want to talk about everything. "If I told you that, it'd defeat the purpose of being afraid." And that was the whole point.

"You're no more fucked up than I am, Silver."

"What happens to us after it's over—and I don't mean us as in couple—I just…."

"We'll probably buy a lot of cats."

I laughed so hard that I started coughing again. "Nice," I grumbled.

Kirk rubbed my back until the fit subsided.

"We'll be okay," he promised, but the conviction didn't quite show in his eyes. "They'll probably lock me in a room with a counselor before setting me lose on society again. I'll make sure they make arrangements for you, too. Whatever you need."

"I'll need people who won't look at me like a freak. What am I going to tell people? It can't be the truth. They'll go all pitiful on me until they find out what I did, and then it'll turn into the blame game. That is, if it doesn't start out at the blame game. 'What the hell were you doing that you don't even remember being abducted?'"

"Gabe drugged you, it knocked out your memory; it wasn't anything you did. It's not your fault. We're programmed to survive. Hell, we're programmed to want contact and connections with people. There's nothing wrong with you."

"Still. I'm looking forward to going back home and getting the short end of the stick whether I tell anyone the truth or not."

Kirk nuzzled my cheek. "You and me both, Sugar."

"First time you called me that, it made my skin crawl. Now I can't get enough." I took a deep breath and watched him for a few minutes.

I couldn't help but wonder what he would be going back to, who he would be going back to, but I didn't dare bring it up. My eyes fluttered closed. Lips pressed against my temple, and the arm on my stomach gripped tighter around me, as Kirk settled next to me and prepared to go back to sleep himself.

Chapter Nineteen

INTERLUDE DISRUPTED

WE EXPECTED THE RUSHED "INITIATION" to mean that Milo had changed his plans and was coming early, but for the next week, everyone, including Ross, left us to our own business, and to wonder why everyone was being suspiciously quiet.

I assumed that everyone had their own way of preparing for the head badass to show up. For Kirk and me, it was gathering around the kitchen table, shoving food into our mouths and hunkered over a crossword puzzle. It was a strange atmosphere—there was no more Master and slave stuff behind closed doors, but we didn't really talk about it either. Instead, we were more interested in the temporary distractions that made us forget where we were and what was coming.

Sometimes we cooked side-by-side in the kitchen, and even once, I attempted making breakfast on my own. But at burnt eggs, Kirk swore to never leave me unattended again.

Not that I could ever get more than ten feet away from

him for more than a few minutes anyway. He almost refused to leave me in the apartment alone, even for brief business.

Kirk's phone jumped, and I drew back, instantly expecting the worst. He put one hand on my knee, and flipped his phone over with the other, drawing his thumb over the screen and typing in his security code.

8-4-7-3. I wasn't sure if he realized that I'd now watched him enter it a few dozen times, or that I'd memorized it, for whatever reason, but he didn't seem to care that I was looking right at the phone.

"Doc wants to see you so he can check your lungs and give you a birth control shot."

"Joy of joys," I muttered. I hated needles, and the only reason I'd gone on the shot in the first place was because I was horrible at remembering to take the pill. One pregnancy scare was enough for me. The checkup seemed particularly redundant since Milo's arrival the next day meant it'd all be over—one way or another.

"Go get dressed," Kirk said, picking up our empty plates. He was usually fully dressed by breakfast, but I preferred my robe. Especially since it covered more than anything else in my current wardrobe and was far more comfortable.

I put on a pouty expression as he turned back to face me.

"My being nice to you apparently isn't serving you well." He crossed his arms, and I watched his muscles move under his tattoos. He took one step toward me, and my body felt heavier in the seat.

I pushed him just as much as ever, somehow finding pleasure in his reactions.

In having his attention focused directly on me—as if it

wasn't usually, there was just something about the intensity of his glare when I pressed his buttons.

He pressed one hand on the table in front of me and leaned into my face. My body tensed, but I managed to hold the daring smirk to my face, even as his breath brushed across my skin.

Hooking a finger under my chin, he pulled me to my feet. "We don't have time for this."

"Lately, time is all we have had."

"All the more reason to get this over with."

I hummed and pressed against him.

"I meant going upstairs to…." He took a deep breath, apparently losing his words. Swallowing audibly, he pressed me against the table. "Why do you have to press your limits now?"

"Because I have a bad feeling about leaving the room," I said.

"So, your plan is to make me walk around with a raging hard on." He grunted, but didn't step away.

"We could remedy that."

Kirk shook his head as he lifted my hips, and I wrapped my legs around him.

"You—" he shook his head. "Sometimes, I seriously question your sanity."

"Why? Because I'd rather be locked up here having sex with you than"—I waved my hand to the door—"out there?"

"And you've decided to use sex to get what you want now?" He captured my mouth in a kiss that ended too soon, and then pulled me away and sat me on my feet. "Get dressed, Silver. I'll make it all worth your while when we get back."

Smirking, he patted my ass and waved me on to the living room.

I stomped away, rolling my eyes when I knew he couldn't see me. So much for that delay.

"You know," he drawled, leaning against the doorway to the kitchen. "You still look pretty sexy when you sulk."

I stopped, looked over my shoulder and stuck out my tongue. If that wouldn't get the fucker's blood boiling, nothing would. He merely raised an eyebrow and turned his back.

I huffed and shook my robe off, hooking it over one of the bedposts and pulling on a tank and a pair of shorts—surely acceptable attire for a trip to the doctor, although I still hadn't been able to decipher the dress code here.

When I came out of the bedroom, Kirk hooked the leash to my collar. He hadn't used it since my first week here. "Seems you're getting a little out of control."

I lowered my head but peeked up at him. "Are you really complaining?"

Making a sound in his throat, he crossed his arms over his chest. "You're worrying me a bit."

I relaxed my shoulders and leaned against the wall. "I really do have a bad feeling."

"Becoming reclusive after an interrupted week?"

"Last time—" my nails dug into my palms as my hands tightened. "I'm—I want control over something. I don't just want to sit around here and have to jump when someone tells me what to do."

Kirk held up his palm, and I unclenched a hand, placing my fingers against his.

"I wish I could give you that," he whispered against my ear. "I'll get it back for you. Just play your part and give me a little more time." He sealed his promise with a nip to my neck, then straightened and gave me a wink.

I nodded, unsure if my voice would be steady enough to talk.

———

THE INFIRMARY WAS COLD. Colder than usual, it seemed, but the last time I had been here, I wasn't conscious of much except pain and crazy hallucinations. The doctor was nowhere to be seen, but Kirk led me to the exam table and I climbed up. He removed the leash and left a peck on my forehead.

I kept my head down, hands loose at my sides, playing the perfect slave—at least as close as I could get.

The doctor came in from the side door, syringe already in hand. I closed my eyes, ignoring the rapid thumps in my chest as cold alcohol touched my arm.

Next to me, Kirk spun the chain leash, curling it around his hand then reversing the direction to uncurl and curl it again. I concentrated on the spinning leash until the needle pierced my skin and muscle. I counted off the seconds as the liquid seeped into my body.

The doctor pulled the stethoscope away from his neck. I sat forward as he listened to my lungs.

"Sounds like she's all clear," Clarence said.

Can we go now?

"Anything else need checked while you're here?" He spoke only to Kirk, as if I wasn't there. Apparently, he only acknowledged my existence if I was in critical condition.

"No, she seems to be healing."

"I'm sure Ross will be happy to hear that."

Even without looking at him, I could feel Kirk stiffen.

"I recommend restricted activity for at least another week," the doctor said. "I'll make sure Ross knows. He let things get out of hand—"

"He pushed things out of hand," Kirk corrected.

"Not really any more than usual. You just don't try to see it."

Kirk was getting pissed, and there was nothing I could rightfully do to ease his temper. The doctor stepped in front of me, closer to Kirk, but that meant his back was not to me. I looked over his shoulder and shook my head.

Kirk sighed audibly and ran a hand through his hair.

"Not so easy when the girl is your responsibility, eh?"

"No," Kirk growled. "Thanks."

Kirk didn't even fasten the leash back on my collar before grabbing my arm and dragging me toward the door. Inside the elevator he released me to answer his buzzing phone. I caught a glimpse of the screen.

The incoming message from Miles simply read. "Incoming."

I didn't dare ask what it meant until we got back to the apartment, but as soon as the door closed, I opened my mouth. "Wha—"

"Get in the shower," he ordered. There was one tone I didn't mess with. I nodded and stripped off my clothes on the way to the tub. As soon as I turned on the water, I heard Kirk's voice.

Apparently, he wanted me in the shower so I couldn't hear what was going on.

A few minutes later, he entered the bathroom, dropped his clothes and stepped into the tub behind me. He put a hand around me, but I shook him away.

"Milo will be here early," he said. "I wasn't hiding from you. If you can be feisty and difficult, so can I."

I elbowed him in the ribs and he pulled my arms back, sucking at my neck.

He may as well have sucked the air out of my lungs. I felt myself go weak as he pressed me against the wall. My nipples hardened against the cold tile. He pulled my hips away from the wall and slid his fingers inside of me.

My back arched, and the tile vibrated against my skin as I moaned.

Kirk pressed his cock to my entrance and thrust into me, barely leaving me time to prepare. He reached around me and put my hands around the bar in the shower. "You might want to hold on."

He rubbed my clit as he pulled me another step away from the wall, leaving me hanging from the bar until I was bent at a nearly ninety-degree angle.

I moaned as he sank into a steady rhythm, and then I felt a finger press at my ass. I tensed, then my body became tied up in the pleasure and I loosened. His fingers slid in slowly, and then matched the rhythm of his cock. He added a second finger. The motions in my ass became a counterpoint to his cock, igniting every nerve.

My knees started to buckle, and I locked them to stay on my feet. The beginning of the orgasm shuddered through me and Kirk picked up his pace. He kept up his assault as I rode the orgasm, then he wrapped both hands against my hips and plunged harder and deeper until he shuddered and moaned behind me.

I used the bar to right myself, but Kirk pulled me against his body, running his hands down my front and pushing my legs apart to rub my still sensitive pussy.

I twitched, and mewled as he washed the area clean before starting on the rest of my body.

By the time he was done, I was so sated, I couldn't even

bring myself to ask what the call was about, but as we left the bathroom, someone knocked on the door, and I didn't have to.

"Look at me, Silver." Kirk whispered, pulling my face as close to his as possible. "Do everything you're told, no hesitation."

Oh, god. The whole reason behind the quickie was to keep me busy so I wouldn't worry about whatever I was going to see behind that door. Kirk shooed me to the couch. "Sit."

Chapter Twenty

END OF THE DREAM

I TIGHTENED my hands in my lap then released them again. There'd be no more distractions, no more avoiding fate. It had come right to our door to collect whether we were ready or not.

After all the days of avoidance, I suddenly wished that I had asked about the plan. If Milo was here, how long would it take forces to move in, and how exactly did they plan on taking a twelve-story building and an entire compound? Then again, it was probably better I hadn't asked, since knowing the truth about Kirk only made me feel more nervous. If I knew about whatever was going to go down next, I probably wouldn't be able to function, even on a base level.

Reminding myself to at least try to look relaxed, I took a breath and tried not to cringe when I heard the door open. A cold droplet of water ran down my chest and over my breast, so I wiped it away and closed my eyes.

"Ross, I didn't expect you," Kirk said smoothly.

If I hadn't already known it was a lie, I would have believed him. I had always been better at speaking my mind and sticking to my guns, but now I admired his talent, the way he wove every reaction into part of his role. I risked a glance over, at least Kirk had slipped his jeans back on, but my robe was in the bedroom, and I hadn't had time to question his order.

Ross stepped into the room. "Milo wanted to have a look around before dinner and he's particularly interested in meeting your slave."

All I wanted to do was disappear from the room. Maybe I wasn't as strong as I wanted to be, as strong as I needed to be to stand until the end.

Footsteps.

I pictured Alley in my head, her cool relaxed features; somehow, she navigated the thin line between looking detached and engaged. She always looked interested, especially if Miles was in the room. I couldn't master that, nor had I really been in situations where I needed to.

Ross always wanted me on the edge of terror and pain. Much as I hated to admit it, that worked to my advantage. It left me nowhere and nothing to hide. No time to think.

Under their quiet observation, I was my own enemy. *Don't fidget. Don't give yourself up.*

Don't give Kirk up.

At least two lives depended on what I needed to do. Two lives and the future of dozens, possibly hundreds of women. Where would they all end up?

"Stand up," said an unfamiliar voice. It was thick and deep. His words were pointed and precise.

I kept my head down but rose from my seat.

A hand shot out and grasped my face. It took every bit of self-control just to keep from flinching, but he didn't hurt me, he simply angled my face toward him. I lowered my eyes, avoiding his face. He was a stockier build than either Kirk or Ross, shorter, too. He wore a blue button-down shirt, tucked into black dress pants and his cologne was spicy and thick.

"Looks like she's been a handful." His accent sounded slightly Russian, but since I was never great at placing accents, I couldn't be entirely sure.

"She was attacked, assaulted," Kirk said.

"Attacked and assaulted," Milo mused. "Hmpf. She's a slave, she served her purpose."

Even without looking over, I knew Kirk was tense with anger. I could almost feel the energy pouring off him—riled and ready to fight.

Milo slid his hand up my back then pulled the tips of my hair down until I had to arch backward. While I was stretched out, his fingers traced down my abdomen, and I waited for their touch to become brutal, or wander between my legs, but he circled my belly button and stopped.

"You're only good for a man's desire, isn't that right, slave?"

"Yes, Master." Too many fucking masters. I hoped I was supposed to call him Master, but he probably preferred Liege or something archaic.

He turned his attention back to Kirk, while I fought the off-balance position to stay on my feet. "And she was worth killing for?"

"Gabe betrayed us; he was a danger to the entire organization."

"And you decided that you should take care of the problem on your own. You expect me to believe it had nothing to do with this little slut?"

Don't grimace. The only chance I had of not jerking away

289

and spitting in his face was to stop listening to anything he said, but then I was afraid I'd miss something I had to hear. I really wished I had played more poker.

Milo let me straighten then ran his hands over my sides, before cupping my cheeks and pulling my face up to his. "I do need a beautiful slave to take the place of my favorite. Do you think you're that slave?"

"If you wish, Master." *Hell no. The cavalry had better damn well be on its way.*

"And I was worried that you wouldn't have learned your place. So fresh." He cupped my ass with both hands, drawing me against him. Then, his lofty voice suddenly turned rough. "So problematic."

"I've learned, Master," I cooed, fighting my body for enough control to keep my voice from shaking. "If you like, I can show you." *I'll show you straight to Hell.*

He chuckled and stepped back. "We've moved dinner up an hour. We'll see both of you soon." He eyed me again, a smirk accentuating his olive face then he and Ross left.

"Where'd that bravado come from?" Kirk mumbled.

I shrugged and collapsed on the couch. Between the sex and the confrontation, I wanted a nap. "One of us had to draw his attention, and since you were about to blow your top, I figured it should be me."

Kirk leaned against the armrest and lifted my chin. "I was not—"

"No point in arguing." I glared back at him. "I thought you wanted me to play the loyal and obedient slave."

He rubbed his hand over his face. "I need to shave."

I scoffed; *score one for the obedient slave*. Reaching up, I took his face between my palms. He'd let his appearance go over the last two weeks, but I liked it when he looked rough, loved feeling it across my skin. Something was happening to me on a much deeper level than I had expected.

He'd captured my mind and body, making me his—giving me his protection. But, the more I saw the controlled bits chip away, the more I wanted to know. The more he captivated me. And scared me.

He would have been better off without me, without the extra burden I brought him in this place, but I wondered how he survived all those months before I came along. How he lived with everything he watched and participated in.

I thought he'd broken me with the whip in the basement, but really, it had shattered him.

"What's going to happen tonight?" I whispered, catching his fingers before he could walk away. Instead of stopping, he tugged me to my feet and pulled me into the bathroom with him.

"Not what Milo expects." His voice was even, but empty. We were at the end of the façade. Soon, we'd have to face everything we'd done in the real world.

"So this is it?" I slid onto the counter, looping my fingers through the top of his jeans as he pulled his shaving supplies out of the cabinet.

Kirk nodded. "Whatever happens, stay with the girls."

"You say that like you expect—"

"Silver, I mean it." I finally heard a crack of emotion in his voice. "I don't want to have to watch you, there's going to be a lot going on. Stay with the girls, you all will be safe. And if we end up separated, find Trent."

"How are they planning on taking this whole place? We'll be on the top fucking floor."

"That's not our problem." He splashed water over his face and started spreading the shaving cream. "We just stay the fuck out of the way."

"It's going to be a blood bath! What about all of the girls?"

"Quiet," he hissed. "Ross has been making arrangements for this. There aren't even any guests on the grounds. He's paranoid about something going wrong."

"Rightfully so, if we're honest. But doesn't that also mean he's going to have increased security?"

Kirk shook his head. "Not too much, he doesn't want Milo to think he's incompetent. Most of the recent problems have revolved around the security team, mainly Alan fucking with our records and security cams. Ross won't have too many hanging out, and they certainly won't be expecting a raid."

———

I SWALLOWED down the bitter taste in my mouth as Kirk and I made what I expected to be our final walk to the Outlook. He'd certainly been right about the lack of guests, and I almost wondered if there was even a point to us all gathering in the swanky den of iniquity if there wasn't going to be anyone around, but as soon as the doors opened on the twelfth floor, I gasped.

There may not have been guests, but every resident of the building had gathered in the lounge. A dysfunctional work dinner—at least more dysfunctional than most. And if everyone was here, trying to make sure that Milo was happy, Kirk was right in assuming that the main defenses would be down.

Seemed like a stupid security policy to me, but that was because I knew what was coming. They had lived in their own untouchable world for so long that they expected any threat to be minor and they definitely didn't expect it to come from the outside.

Indulgence had made them short-sighted, or so I hoped.

The team would still have to get past the guarded perimeter, through the front doors, and up twelve stories to reach us.

And with all of that on my mind, I had to play the detached and obedient slave.

Inside the main room of the Outlook, Alley sat on her knees on the table with her back to the entrance. My shoulders tensed, and I struggled for oxygen when we crossed the threshold.

As soon as Milo saw us, he smiled and reached past Kirk to take my arm and pull me away.

"You'll make a nice addition to tonight's artwork." He cupped my cheek and slid a hand down the top of my dress. Then, he ushered me to the table. "Back to back."

"Yes, Master."

He held my elbow as he lifted me up to sit on the table.

"Closer," Milo yelled, slapping Alley's leg and we both scrambled to arrange our feet so that we could press our backs together.

He pulled my left arm back and twisted it over Alley's right arm, so we were linked at the elbows. Then, he pushed aside the material of my dress to grab my nipple and I grunted. Alley's back pressed against mine, and I guessed she was getting the same treatment. He pulled and pinched then, concentrating on me, he attached a nipple clamp, pulled the chain around my arm and connected the other side to Alley. The chain pulled straight across my arm so anytime either of us moved—even to breathe, it tugged.

I glanced up and saw Kirk sitting in his usual seat at the table. His expression was clouded; both of his hands were below the table. Not only did he have to watch, he had to enjoy. I imagined that wasn't as hard to fake for a man, even if he got to keep his pants on.

Milo moved to the other side of the table, this time linking Alley's arm over mine and smacking us both over the breast a few times. My nipple tightened and hardened from the abuse and he attached another clamp. His hand rubbed over my stomach and legs.

"Spread your legs."

Alley and I tightened our arms together and used the leverage, attempting to spread our knees apart without moving our upper bodies. It wasn't graceful, but it also wasn't as bad as I anticipated.

He pushed the hem of my dress up and his hand dipped between my legs.

Fuck. I knew I was dry, and I silently pleaded for him not to be going there. He pinched my clit then brought up another clamp, and attached it there, tightening until I gasped for air. I pressed against Alley, trying to negate the impact of my heavy breathing on the pull of the chains.

As he drew the chain up, I noticed that it split into a Y and he dropped one part over each of my shoulders then pulled it tight, but I couldn't tell what he'd attached it to.

Hopefully not around Alley's throat. My heart jumped, and he disappeared from my periphery, repeating the process behind me.

When he appeared again, he slipped what resembled a bit for a horse in my mouth and attached a chain on either side. At least it gave me something to bite down on, because every little twitch meant one of us was going to be in even more agony.

Milo took Ross' usual spot at the head of the table— right in front of me, and Ross sat down somewhere behind me. I wanted to glare and sneer at all of them, but I dropped my eyes to the table and concentrated on breathing.

Someone had better buy me a damn good feast when this is over, I thought as three naked women began serving platters of food to the men. Even with the hot dinners surrounding us, it suddenly felt like the air conditioning kicked on, and as the goosebumps took over my body, I struggled not to shiver.

Fucking bustards.

My legs tingled as they started going numb, but I couldn't adjust to get any relief. I counted my breaths, it had gotten me through the butt plug, but it wasn't as effective against the full body assault Milo had planned.

At least it forced me to take slow steady breaths.

Alley suddenly jerked, and I whined as the chains pulled against all my sensitive parts. My breaths turned into sharp gasps, but that only exacerbated the problem. Just as I got my breathing under control, the man sitting across from Kirk reached up and squeezed my breast. I grunted, trying my best not to move, but as his thumb moved over my tender, pinched nipple my head pressed backward, and the chain traveling down my stomach jerked on my clit.

I clamped down on the rod in my mouth, breathing through my clenched teeth.

Kirk sat down his fork and stood, rubbing his hand up my leg and then dipping it and pressing against my opening.

What the hell? I would have shot daggers with my eyes if I let them rise off the table. I was dry. I was in pain and not the least bit aroused, but he kissed my shoulder, glancing over the chain and nipping at my ear. He didn't do anything to force me to move—much—but all his touching meant my breathing increased, yet the pain faded. His hands and lips explored my exposed skin.

I wanted to thank him and curse him in the same breath. The man across the table started to rise, but I saw Kirk's head lifted, and the other man thought again.

Behind me, Alley moaned, and I had to assume she was getting the same treatment from Miles.

Kirk tugged on the chain attacked to my clit, and this time I felt a pang of arousal mixed with the pain. I couldn't tell if he was saving me from misery or making it worse.

He was definitely putting on a show for Milo, though. Playing his dastardly part and showing his claim over my body all at once. He kissed my forehead then returned to his seat and his dinner.

I felt flushed, and slowly the pain overthrew the pleasure again, but the burst of endorphins helped me get through dinner.

After dinner, Kirk and Miles flanked me and Alley. They removed the chains from the bits in our mouths first but left the clamp in place. Then, gently Kirk loosened one of the nipple clamps. The second of numbness wore off and I screamed as blood rushed back to the offended skin. Alley jerked behind me, but since Miles held the other end of my remaining nipple clamp, we were free from worrying whether our movements would hurt the other.

But fuck the removal hurt worse than anything that had happened during dinner.

I drew in a deep breath as Miles prepared to remove my second clamp. The wave of pain pulled at my core. I separated my arms from Alley's and leaned forward against the table.

One more to go. Fucking hell.

My chest jerked with uneven breaths as Kirk sat me

back up and reached for the final clamp between my legs. Behind me Alley screamed, and within a second, my voice joined hers in a deafening chorus. I wanted to flop back on the table, but as the stinging core-twisting pain faded, Kirk pulled me to the edge of the table and righted my clothes, holding me as I stepped down with numb legs. I nearly collapsed at his feet immediately, but he held me upright as the blood rushed through my legs.

I felt his phone vibrate against my hip, and he shifted me to pull it out of his pocket long enough to press a single button.

"Important call?" Ross asked.

"Just an alarm I forgot to turn off."

Alarm. The one on his door, which meant the forces had arrived. I felt my eyes widen, but Kirk pulled my face to his, capturing my lips in a heated kiss. He paused for a minute before letting me go, shaking his head, just a twitch that told me to keep my reactions under control.

When the worst had passed, he sat down, and pulled me into his lap. My head dropped against his shoulder, and I inhaled his scent.

It was all I could do.

My body was already exhausted from the strain.

As I came out of my headspace, Kirk fed me some of the leftover food from his plate, before the girls came to collect the dishes. Around the table, the other men either had slaves between their legs or in their laps. Alley and I seemed to be the only ones not involved in some kind of sexual act. Apparently, we'd earned our brief reprieve.

Until Milo's gaze fell on me. "Silver." He drew out the sound of each letter as he held out his hand.

Fuck. I mentally pleaded for the team to hurry up and get to the twelfth floor. I wondered what was taking them so long, why no one had noticed yet. And worst of all, I feared what would happen once they reached us.

Kirk lifted me to my feet, his silent encouragement to help buy us time, but I was afraid either my heart or brain would explode as soon as Milo touched me. Despite the waves of fear and discomfort, I had to paste an easy smile to my face as I dropped my hand into his warm palm.

As the chorus of groans rose around us, a man rushed into the room and blew past us to the back end of the table.

I heard Ross mutter a curse and my gut tightened again. Something flew across the room and smashed against a window, and I ducked next to the table, afraid the next flying object would be aimed at me.

"Raid," was all Ross could say before the men jumped from their seats, cursing and shouting.

It had begun. All I wanted to do was curl up against Kirk, or in a corner somewhere. Kirk jumped up, pulling me to my feet, and pushing me toward Alley who was gathering all the girls on one side of the room.

"Someone must have tipped them off." Ross said, and my feet slowed.

I couldn't look back, I'd give too much away, but a hand grabbed the back of my dress and threw me onto the table, I slid across it and fell to the other side. My back burned, and my body uselessly refused to move.

"We don't have time for this," Milo hissed, grabbing one of the men and whispering in his ear, before shoving him to the door.

Ross ignored them all and stepped around the table, pointing a gun at me. "Looks like we should have listened to Kat."

"It was me," Kirk yelled. "She's innocent."

A chorus of gasps and murmurs moved through the

room then someone yelled for the rest of the girls to get out of the room.

No. Fucking idiot, I silently screamed.

"Why?" Miles asked his voice barely more than a gasp of air.

"They offered me a deal. I wanted out."

Ross raised the gun, pointing it over the table at Kirk. I lurched, slamming into his gut as the gun went off. When I spun, I saw Kirk on the floor, a puddle of red growing around him. I dove under the table, putting my body over his. Holding my hands over the gaping hole as warm sticky liquid flowed out. I didn't care about anything but stopping the blood. I felt the people moving around me, murmuring, cursing. Someone in the corner crying.

"Don't...Silver—" Kirk whispered.

I looked up to see Miles pointing a gun at us, and I assumed there were others doing the same.

"Let her watch him," Milo chuckled. "A slow death is what he deserves. Knowing he can't do a damn thing to protect her now."

Milo took off out of the room, with a few members of the security team on his tail. No wonder the rat bastard had managed to survive so long, he didn't care about anyone except himself.

"You should go, Ross," Miles said. "Follow him to the chopper and get out of here."

The room went silent. *Please listen*. I hoped I could at least reason with Miles, beg for his understanding.

"No," Ross said, and my heart dropped out of my chest. "They've cost me everything, I'm making sure they're both dead."

A gun went off and I jerked, waiting for the pain, for

more blood. Something thudded against the floor, and I finally dared to open my eyes.

Ross lay next to us, in a puddle of blood that poured out of his head. I raised my head and stared at Miles. Even he looked like he didn't know what had happened. His eyes were glazed over, his mouth flat.

When his gaze settled on me, he shook his head. He dropped the gun onto the floor and rubbed his hands over his face. "It's on you now."

He ran toward the door, leaving me with the two bleeding bodies on the floor. The copper scent burned at my nostrils, but I pressed against Kirk's wound. "Please, don't die, Kirk. Don't die."

Chanting the words over and over, I just wanted him to wake up.

"James, please."

His eyes fluttered for a second then his face went slack.

I could still feel his shallow breaths, the faint pulse as blood seeped around my hand.

Then, I heard more noises, voices. Feet charged into the room. I kept my head down, terrified that it was only more members of Ross's crew. Hands pulled at my shoulders and I yelled out.

"Leave me alone. He's bleeding."

I fought them off, until I heard my name.

"Rose?" I looked up, a blond man stood above me in a SWAT uniform. "We're going to help him."

The blond gently pulled me away from Kirk as two of the others knelt around him, keeping pressure on the wound. I watched, suddenly finding myself seated at the table with no recollection of sitting down. "Please, don't let him die."

"We're going to do everything we can—"

"No," I yelled. "Do more."

"Davis," a man from across the room yelled and the blond next to me nodded in acknowledgement.

Outsiders. I felt them watching me. They saw the girl dressed up like a slut and used as a toy. I wanted to curl up and hide under the table.

"Rose," the blond next to me patted my cheek. "Do you know where they went?"

"Helicopter," I pointed in the direction they'd gone when they left. "That way."

"Do you know how to get to the roof?"

I shook my head, *why would anyone let a slave on the roof?*

"James is going to be okay," he whispered. "He's tough shit; you don't get rid of that so easily."

I pulled my eyes away from the mess on the floor, they'd packed his wound, but he still hadn't moved again. Hadn't made a sound.

"You were his contact?" I whispered. "Trent?"

"Yeah, he wanted to get you out long before now."

"I know." I felt void of all emotion, of all feeling. People shuffled around me. Footsteps. Radios crackling.

The world moved impossibly slow and yet so fast that my mind couldn't keep up.

I was about to lose everything I'd known for the past few weeks. Good or bad. I was about to be thrust into yet another new life. I couldn't go back to who I was before. I'd never see that girl again, no matter how long I looked.

His radio crackled and beeped then I heard the popping of gunfire overhead. They'd found the roof.

My insides twisted, and I threw up. Miles was up there, and I had no idea where Alley was.

"The girls?" I asked, choking on the taste of my vomit.

"We found them downstairs. They're all safe."

301

All? How did they know it was all? I wanted to run away from him, to run down the hall and find Alley.

"There was also a man with them, and he's been taken into custody."

"Miles?" I asked grasping on to the hope.

Davis squinted at me and shook his head. "They didn't give a name or description."

A stretcher came in, and I followed the crew as they loaded up Kirk and carried him to the elevator.

Chapter Twenty-One

RUDE AWAKENING

THE OFFICERS KEPT me separated and away from the eyes of the rest of the group, leaving me to watch through a window as they loaded everyone up into large vans. It was like a morbid parade, they had men sprawled out lying face down on the ground, girls screaming or curled up sobbing. As soon as one van was full, it went on its way and they filled another. I couldn't imagine where they were taking them all. The women alone would fill a couple of floors in a hotel. The men would surely take up more space than offered at the local jail.

Ambulances lined up next to the transport vans. Kirk didn't even get a damn ambulance; they had to life flight him out.

I marched over to the group of men who seemed to be in charge. The ones who had ordered Trent to keep me here. "I want to go to the hospital."

"We'll get everyone checked out," some old man said. I scowled back at him, and another young paramedic tried to grab my arm. I jumped away.

"I'm leaving for the hospital," Trent said. "she can ride with me."

"That's against procedure."

"In these circumstances…" he trailed off and shook his head. "Bluntly, Sir, fuck procedure. I'm going to the hospital, and she's coming with me; you can have my gun and badge if you want."

Davis draped his SWAT jacket over my body and pulled a key from his pocket—Kirk's key.

My gut clenched. He held the link to my final claim of freedom, but as he reached for the collar around my neck, I wanted to pull away.

I wanted my freedom to come from Kirk… James… I wasn't even sure what I was supposed to call him anymore. After removing the collar and cuffs, Trent kept me close to his side as he led me down toward the street where the cars were parked.

"You and K—" Time to stop calling him that. "James, you were close?"

"We trained together. They tried to pass this off to someone with more experience, but we knew each other, and I fought to be his contact." He opened his car door, but instead of climbing in, he leaned over the roof. "You weren't supposed to get caught up in all of this—"

"I know." I slid into the car hoping to avoid future conversation.

As the car pulled away from the retreat, I licked my dry lips and picked at my nails. I was still covered with blood; anyone else who saw me would think I was the one doing all the killing.

My body clenched as soon as we hit city limits and I recognized where we were. Civilization. The real world. People going about their everyday lives.

Not a one of them had any idea what was going on twenty minutes outside of the city.

"Rose," Trent whispered.

I recognized my name, but it felt foreign. I still hadn't let go. I wondered if my name would ever feel like my own again. "I'm fine."

Fine, right. I couldn't even sit still, and I knew Trent saw it. I squeezed my fingers, rubbed them against my leg. Scratched my feet against the carpet. I wanted out of the city so badly I couldn't even see straight.

At the hospital, we waited in the car for a few minutes while Trent checked his phone, and I tried to get myself under control.

"Are you ready for this? There's a private waiting room, so we won't have to be around anyone more than necessary."

I blew out a long breath and nodded. As he led me in, I had to keep reminding myself to keep it together. On some level it felt like a trick. One of Ross' employees was bound to pop out at any second and throw me into lockup. Luckily, no one else boarded the elevator and as soon as we stepped off, we went straight to the nurse's desk.

"They took him into surgery when he got here," he said, waving at one of the nurses and calling her over. "Can you find an extra pair of scrubs?"

The woman looked me over, raised her eyebrows, and walked away, returning a few minutes later with a stack of gaudy green clothes. Trent grabbed them and led me around and through a small private waiting room. I guessed that his business brought him here often. He opened the door to a tiny bathroom and laid the clothes down next to the sink. "I'll let you get washed up."

I handed back his jacket and dropped the straps to my dress.

He cleared his throat and closed the door. In my own little world, I'd forgotten about real world etiquette. Not that his presence really registered anyway. I was on autopilot.

I threw my dress into the trash then pulled a long section of paper towel out of the dispenser and began scrubbing at the blood on my hands and arms. Some had even transferred to my legs when I'd sat down. I tried to clean under my fingernails and wipe up the excess blood, but it seemed like there was no end to the stains.

Finally, I rinsed off and splashed some water over my face before slipping into the oversized scrubs. I looked in the mirror, taking in my rudely disheveled appearance, but the blood was gone. I didn't care about the rest.

Trent was leaned against a chair arm when I opened the door; he stood but waited for me to approach.

"Sorry about that." I waved at the door. "I didn't think."

"It's okay." He kept his distance but didn't look away.

For fuck's sake, I was back to being looked at like a caged animal. I collapsed into a chair, hoping that if he knew I was staying put he'd stop watching my every movement.

"I talked to a nurse," he said. "James is still in surgery so, we can wait in here. I'd like to get you checked out though."

Just saw the doctor this morning, I thought, but no one here would recognize Clarence's opinion on anything. "I'm fine."

"I can have a doctor come in here."

I sighed, rubbing my forehead. "Whatever you want, if you need me to get cleared then do it. Get it over with so I can just be free of all this."

Trent nodded and stepped outside. I almost regretted

what I'd said because now I was alone with no one to protect me—even though I wasn't sure what I needed protection from.

I didn't want anyone else touching me, even if it was a doctor. However, it wasn't just a doctor; it was a doctor, a nurse, and a phlebotomist. My leg bounced off the floor and I stared across the room as they did their work, only giving monosyllabic answers when absolutely necessary. I didn't want to be examined; I wanted to know that Kirk was okay.

That *James* was okay.

As much as I kept telling myself I needed to use his real name now. I was still more connected to life as Silver than life as Rose. After the past few weeks, that was my reality. Just like I couldn't make an overnight change when they had abducted me and tried to turn me into a slave, I couldn't flip the switch and go back to normal now.

Normal was life before Kirk.

Whatever this was, this was life after Kirk.

―――――

IT WAS another two hours before they took James to a regular room and okayed us to visit him. The doctor assured us that although he was still unconscious, he was stable, and should make a complete recovery, but I wasn't ready for what I saw when we entered the room.

He was barely the man I knew, so pale and frail looking with all the tubes and wires. I stopped just inside the door, running my fingers through my tangled hair. I felt the beginning of tears well up and forced myself forward; at least while he was asleep, Kirk wouldn't be able to see my tears.

I slid my hand under his cool fingers.

I heard someone else enter the room, and hushed voices behind me, but I tuned them out, pulling up a stool and leaning over the side of the bed. I was so exhausted, my vision was blurry, but I fought to keep my eyes open, unable to take my gaze off him.

James' hand twitched and I sat up so quickly I almost fell off the stool. I saw a hint of his grey-blue eyes and squeezed his hand, probably to the point of pain for him.

"You don't give up, do you?" he whispered.

"You know better."

Trent leaned over the other side of the bed. "Quite the stubborn girl you found."

The corner of James' mouth quirked up, but his eyelids fluttered closed again.

"They're giving us another fifteen minutes or so," Trent said. "Then, they want to give him time to rest."

I leaned my elbow against the bed railing, using my free hand to rub away the pounding headache in my forehead. "I can't leave. Where would I go, anyway?"

"Home," James whispered.

"Your rent and bills are all taken care of," Trent explained. "We made sure you didn't lose everything."

I glared across the bed at Trent as he spoke. James hadn't only used my driver's license to check my background; he'd at least tried to make sure I could have a halfway normal life when he finally managed to get me out. I couldn't believe it, but part of me drew back at the news, at the thought of going back there. I was afraid of my old life, afraid of facing it again.

"The friends I was supposed to meet for dinner," I said. James hadn't brought it up again since I'd asked about Charlene, and I'd been afraid to mention it myself.

"You only mentioned one," James said, his voice growing fainter every time he spoke.

"Well, I was supposed to meet two, but I only remember being with one. Charlene?" I glanced at James then back at Trent.

"She's fine," Trent said. "She doesn't remember anything happening."

"Why'd they take me and not her?"

Trent shook his head. "She was assaulted and left in her car, but she doesn't know anything. She came into the police station day after day demanding that we find you. Not an easy woman to calm down, I hear."

Feeling lightheaded, I leaned back. It was unfair not to tell her that I was fine, but I wasn't ready to deal with the conversation or the company.

"I heard she went back to Nebraska to stay with her cousin for a while."

I exhaled slowly. "So I just go home and go back to normal?"

"I'll take you to a safe house tonight," Trent said. "We'll give you as many resources as we can to help you get back on your feet."

Resources. The last I checked they didn't make resources that erased the mental images I couldn't escape.

I rubbed my hand over my face. "I'm not leaving." I couldn't. Even for a night, the thought of being alone terrified me. The thought of being away from James terrified me.

My chest tightened, and I leaned over the bed railing trying to compose myself as James squeezed my fingers.

"Rose," Trent began, but before he could say anything else, James cleared his throat. Trent sighed and shrugged. "I'll be right outside."

"You'll be fine," James whispered.

Arguing with him was an unfair scenario—I felt guilty trying to argue with a bedridden man who had just taken a bullet for me. I had my stubbornness and I knew I'd last longer in the argument, but he had the advantage since I didn't want to push him.

"I'm not ready." My chest ached, but I managed to hold back the tears. Either that or I just didn't have any left.

"You are, Rose. Stay with Trent. I trust him, and I know he'll take care of you. We both need rest, Sugar."

A buzzing tingle radiated through my chest. *Sugar.* I didn't even know what that meant anymore. "I can sleep here."

Kirk's pale lips pressed together. We both had to learn how to do this again, how to be people, not-so-normal people pretending to function in the real world.

"Even if I leave, I won't sleep." I said. "I'm not trying to be stubborn about it, I'm just…."

"Terrified?"

All my emotions reflected in his eyes. I leaned over, slipping my fingers through his hair.

The door opened again, and Trent peeked in. "Rose. We have to go."

I kissed James' forehead. "We'll be okay?"

He nodded, and his eyes fluttered closed, but I couldn't pry my hand away from his.

Trent touched my shoulder and I wanted to beg him to let me stay. I'd hide in the closet if I had to.

"I understand," he said. "But they're not budging on the order. We have to go. They'll call me immediately if his condition changes at all."

———

TRENT STAYED the night with me in the safe house but left just before breakfast to head to the station to complete his paperwork on the raid. After an hour of the new crew staring at me as I paced through the living room, I couldn't stand waiting around anymore.

"If you won't take me to the hospital or let me call someone, I'll walk." I stormed toward the door, but one of the officers blocked my way. "I'm not a criminal and you can't keep me here."

"It's for your own safety; Detective Davis will be back—"

"Trent can fucking find me at the hospital." I pushed by him. "The only question is whether or not you're giving me a ride. I'm going to find a way there." They were just doing their job, I supposed, but I was sick of people not letting me make my own decisions.

"Fine." The officer relented and nodded to the other. "Call Davis and give him the update."

I left the officer behind in the lobby, running up the stairs to the room where James had been, but it was empty, so I rushed back to the desk. "James…" I didn't even know his last name, so I pointed to the room.

The nurse shook her head. "We can't give you any information ma'am."

"For fuck's sake, just tell me if he's in the hospital. I'll check every room and find him myself."

Trent rounded the corner. "He's not here," he said dryly. "He's in protective custody. I can't tell you where; I don't even know."

I looked for the nearest thing I could throw through a wall. Trent reached for me, but I backed out of his reach.

"I can't—I need." My body started to shake.

"Is there anyone we can call?" he asked, trying to soothe me from afar. "Family you can stay with?"

I shook my head. Sure there was, but... I couldn't.

"I'll take you back to your place."

I didn't want to go back there either, but it was better than standing in the hospital arguing. And at least then, I hoped I'd get rid of everyone looking over my shoulder and following me. I stalked past him and took the stairs down to the first floor, I was too antsy to wait in one place for the elevator, or to tolerate the elevator ride, but once we got outside, I had to wait for him to catch up, so he could lead me to his car.

The tiny house I rented was only a fifteen-minute drive from the hospital. By the time we got there, the car made me feel claustrophobic, and yet, I didn't want to get out. My hand visibly shook as I reached for the handle, but I forced myself to keep moving.

"Do you want me to come in with you?"

"Sure." I didn't look back at him. I wanted to forget that anyone could see me.

On the way up, he pulled my elbow, and handed me my keys. The exact set I always carried.

I stared down at them for a moment, rolling them around in my hand. "How?"

"We found them in James' room at the retreat. He told me where to look."

"He's okay, right?" I squeezed the keys until they dug painfully into my flesh. I wasn't sure I wanted to know the answer. Was I even alright?

Trent nodded. "They're going to keep a close eye on him for a while."

"He's not going to get in trouble for... for me?"

"No, sweetie. They're just going to make sure he's safe

and recovering. He wasn't exactly trained for what they sent him in to do, and he was there for a long time before you got there."

"Well, he's pretty good at it." I shook my head, staring down at the concrete sidewalk. "Don't know if that's a compliment or not."

"Give him a few weeks, Rose."

A few weeks, that's exactly how long it took to muddle through the horrific mess. It seemed like a lifetime. I didn't want to wait that long, but I nodded and headed up to the door.

The air in the house was stagnant, and it felt completely dead inside. At least we had that in common. I glanced around at the pictures, the throw tossed over the back of the couch, my book on the coffee table. It was all too much.

Even the thought of freedom—though I longed for it— was too much. I rubbed my hands over my face, sank to the floor, and cried.

Trent sat next to me, intuitive enough to stay, but keep his distance.

"Did you find Miles?"

He opened his mouth, and I waited for an answer, but he closed it again.

The silent reaction was killing me. "I just want to know if he's alive."

"Yes. He was the one with the girls like you asked. Do you know why?"

"He and Kirk worked together a lot to protect us— them." I shook my head, realizing I'd said Kirk again. It was all confusing enough to try and muddle through the different names. "He saved us. Miles. He kept Ross from shooting me and Kirk."

"Is he the one who shot Ross?"

"Please." My heart pumped extra hard. "They'll probably kill him if they find out."

"They won't find out."

I numbly answered the rest of his questions, explaining the essentials of what had happened. At least, everything I figured he had any business knowing. I tried my best to skip over the sex, torture, and punishments where I was concerned.

My throat dried out, and I finally pushed myself off the floor. "Want some water?"

"Please."

It was probably a good thing I never cooked, at least my kitchen wasn't a rotting mess, but I intended on putting off opening the refrigerator for as long as possible. I pulled two glasses out of the cabinet, and for a second, I was amazed that they weren't covered in dust and cob webs, but the lifetime I had been gone was only a few weeks to the outside world.

"Do you have a house phone?" Trent asked, taking a sip of the tap water I handed him.

"No, just my cell and I have a feeling it's gone."

"I'll get you a temporary one, you can use it to call me if you need anything, and for anything else you might need."

Calling people. "Have you heard from my family?"

"Yes, they drove up here a few times. Your sister…." His voice trailed off.

All I wanted was for everything to be okay, to go back before our stupid argument, and be there for her. "Is the baby okay?"

"She is, they're both okay. The baby is about three weeks old now. The hospital kept her for a week because she was a bit early, but she's doing fine, last I heard."

I tried to speak but my mouth felt like it had sealed shut.

I dropped against the counter. The world went on while I was gone. "You know her name?"

"Laney Rose." He reached out and touched my shoulder, my mind pulled away at the outside touch; I was too drained to fight it. "They'll be happy to have you back."

I bit the inside of my cheek until I tasted blood. Now that I was ready to put the drama behind me, I wasn't ready for human interaction for a dozen other reasons.

Chapter Twenty-Two

DEMONS

FOR FOUR WEEKS, I barely left the house. I answered calls just to make sure that no one came to visit, even though my family had showed up anyway—more than once. I didn't have anything to say or anything to give that would make things less awkward. The only person I didn't want space from—the only one who understood what I was dealing with had practically dropped off the face of the planet. And then there was Trent, who called to check in at least once a week, and to assure me that James was doing better.

Good for him, I always thought. I wouldn't be impressed until he was man enough to tell me that himself.

Two days a week, I had to go to see my counselor, who basically spent the entire hour telling me that I had to learn to live my life again, and that it would be easier to do that without James. It was all so fucking exhausting.

I closed the front door and latched the deadbolt, dropping my keys onto a hook. Something rattled in the kitchen and I jumped, pressing my back against the door.

"Trapper," I called, hoping it was just the damn cat. Every time I looked at that cat, I thought of Kirk. I hadn't bought her, she just wondered in off the street, and of course, I couldn't help but give her food. So, she decided to call it home.

I took another step and saw her dozing on the couch.

It's just your imagination.

Movement caught my eye, a shadow on the kitchen floor.

Oh, god, not again.

I reached for the door as a familiar blonde figure rounded the corner.

"Alley?" I breathed. Relief washed through me, then panic. What the hell was she doing in my house?

"I saw Miles with your license before he gave it to Kirk," she said. "And, I decided to look you up. Find out what happened to you."

"Alley, I—"

"Shut up," she shouted, pulling a gun from behind her back and aiming it at me. "You did this."

"No—" I whispered, putting my hands up, as if that would help anything.

"Miles—he was the only one who really ever cared about me, ever since I lost my family. He took care of me; I had a safe place. Now he's gone, and I have nothing. It's all because of you." She took a step closer waving the gun. "You stupid fucking whore, why couldn't you and Kirk leave us alone? I thought he cared about us."

"I swear he did. He did what he had to do to make sure that no one else ended up like me."

"The two of you just decided to come in and play us all for fools. Is he dead?"

"Alley, I—" *Dead?* Is that what everyone thought?

"Shut the hell up." She waved the gun, accentuating every word as she moved closer to me.

I backed against the wall, as Trapper jumped from the couch and ran up the stairs.

"I loved him," Alley continued. "You really don't understand. I looked you up. You had a good life. Why the hell did you go in there and ruin everything? It was none of your damn business."

"It wasn't my choice. I didn't lie, Alley. I was taken there, against my will. I wasn't feeding anyone information. I had nothing to do with the raid."

"I don't believe you." Her eyelids were droopy, and her eyes glazed over like she hadn't slept in a week. "Where is Kirk?"

"I don't know." I realized my mistake. If she was supposed to think he was dead, I just gave him away. "I didn't want anything to happen. You were my friend, Alley."

My ears rang from the shot and I landed on the floor. At first, I couldn't see through the shock to understand what happened. Then, I felt the hot liquid pouring from my shoulder.

"Alley, please." I begged again.

"I'd do anything for Miles, anything to get him back."

"I know." I put my hand over the wound. "I know."

I waited for the final shot, but Alley ran out of the house. I crawled to the door, fumbling through my purse to find the cell phone Trent had given me.

My fingers refused to cooperate as I tried to dial 911. My body shook, and I felt frigid in comparison to the hot liquid streaming out of me.

Finally, the call connected, and I heard a woman's voice —a brief wisp of hope.

"I was shot."

"Can you give me your location?"

I couldn't answer, so the operator asked again. "Ma'am, can you give me your location?"

Work, mouth. The phone clattered to the floor.

I drifted in and out of consciousness, a mix of blood loss and pure shock that numbed the pain and ushered me to oblivion.

This is it. After all of that. This is how I die.

I felt hands on my body. Hot hands, so hot against my cold skin.

Too many hands.

My nightmare coming to life all over again. I squirmed, trying to get away, but my body was too weak.

They've come to get me.

"Miss?" a bright light hit my eyes. "Can you hear me?"

I jerked away.

"We're EMTs, Miss. You're going to feel a prick in your arm. Do you hear me?"

I forced my eyes open. Three men stood around me, and two cops stood at the open door to my house.

I nodded, and my eyes fell closed again. I pushed away the hands that pulled at my clothes, poking me, and compressing my painful shoulder.

They forced my hands to my sides, and I screamed.

"How is she still conscious?" One asked.

A hand touched my forehead and I forced my eyes open with a jerk.

"It's okay, Rose," Trent whispered. "Can you tell me who shot you?"

"She shouldn't be trying to talk right now."

I ignored the paramedic's voice and focused on the blond cop kneeling next to my head. "A—A—Alley."

"Did she say anything?"

"Davis," the same paramedic yelled. He seemed to miss the fact that, struggling to speak or not, if I was trying to answer questions, I wasn't fighting them off.

"Do your damn job, Lucas," Trent snapped.

"She's about as stable as we can do. We need to get her loaded up."

They rolled me onto the back board then lifted me to the stretcher.

My eyelids were too heavy to fight any longer. "Trent," I called, managing only a whisper.

"I'll be right behind the ambulance."

———

I OPENED my eyes and saw a stubbly James standing over my bed.

"Am I high?" I whispered, sure he was just the creation of pain killers.

"Probably."

"Good. Getting shot sucks."

He made a sound in his throat and leaned against the railing. "I know."

"Are you real?"

His fingers slid into mine and he squeezed my hand. "Do I feel real?"

"As soon as my arm is healed, I'm going to punch you, then decide."

Every time I opened my eyes, the room seemed slightly different. James was in a different position. I couldn't tell if I was losing time or losing my mind.

"Where have you been?" I asked.

"Around. I wanted to—" he stopped. "My psychologist

and my supervisor warned me to stay away from you. They said you'd heal better if I kept my distance. I wanted to see you, but I wanted them to be right. I wanted... I wanted you to be able to go back to normal."

"There is no normal." I closed my eyes and opened them again. James was stretched out on a small couch next to me. "Am I really fucked, or do I keep falling asleep?"

"Sleep," he said, standing to move closer. "We both know how you fare in your battles against pain meds."

"Hold my hand." I'd momentarily forgotten about being mad at him. I needed contact. An anchor. I felt like I was losing my mind.

His fingers grazed my chin and I pressed toward them. "It's okay, S—Rose."

His almost calling me Silver was enough to bring me out of the stupor a little more. I forced my eyes open.

"You should have talked to me. Given me a choice. Said goodbye. Something. I deserved something."

His head dropped, and he leaned over the railing of the bed. "I'm sorry. I didn't even trust myself to make the right decision."

"But you still decided to make a decision without me. I didn't expect to come back and have everything be fine, but suddenly, I was just on my own."

He lowered his eyes. His thumb dancing over my knuckles. I could see that he felt just as lost as I was, but I still felt abandoned by the one person I'd trusted to take care of me.

The pain in my arm intensified, radiating down into my chest and gut. I wasn't sure what was from the wound, and what was an overblown emotional reaction. "There are things that I'm even afraid to tell my counselor, but she goes on about how finding myself again is important."

"Sounds familiar," he whispered. "I know you wish that

I had given you a choice, and maybe I should have, but what if we both chose the thing that made us most comfortable for the short-term and it didn't work out? Things that work fine in a pressure cooker don't always work well when they have infinite space. I agreed to give it four weeks, but the closer that date came, the more I wondered just what I was supposed to do. Show up on your doorstep and ask how you've been for the last four weeks—"

"At least then I wouldn't have a bullet hole preventing me from smacking you."

He smirked and traced his fingers up my arm.

Another man in a police uniform stepped in and cleared his throat. "We're assigning a protective detail. We'll make sure no unauthorized people enter. Do you have family coming to see you?"

I shook my head.

"Anyone at all?"

"I don't suppose the hospital allows cats?"

The officer squinted at me then glanced to James.

"That would be a no," I clarified.

After the office stepped out, I looked up to catch James' gaze.

"Don't even," I whispered. "She adopted me. Came in when I opened the door, sat down in my damn living room, and refused to move."

He chuckled, and I could almost feel the sound run through my body, like a hot soothing bath, relaxing every muscle.

It was probably mostly the pain meds, though. I wondered if eventually I'd be able to see sound waves. And then I realized I was totally fucked out of my mind.

I watched Kirk for a while longer. He sat on the edge of

the bed, silently holding my hand, and sometimes rubbing the backs of my fingers and up my arm.

I drifted out and woke up in a panic, gasping for breath after a nightmare I couldn't remember, but the confusion was quickly drowned out the shooting pain in my arm that followed. Two sets of hands tried to push me back to bed and I screamed.

Suddenly, the room was alive as two nurses rushed in to join the fray.

I'm fine.

Get away.

My brain was shooting off messages so fast, it didn't seem like they were making it to the rest of my body.

I felt sluggish, and tired.

"Stop touching me," I finally yelled, and everyone backed off long enough for my brain and body to fall back into sync. "It was a dream. I think. I'm fine."

"You're bleeding," Trent said.

One of the nurses pushed him out of the way. "You probably pulled a stitch with all of that—"

James grunted, and the nurse's mouth snapped shut.

"You come in handy," I muttered.

"I need to have a look under the bandage," the nurse said.

Trent stepped back, and the nurse leaned over my bed, glancing up at James as if making sure he wouldn't attack as soon as she pulled down my gown. "You were lucky," she said. I was tired of being in fucked up situations and having people tell me that, but I closed my eyes and let her continue. "The bullet went straight through. There was a lot of bleeding, but they just had to clean the wound and stitch you up. You'll have to give it plenty of time to heal. Without any complications you could go home tomorrow."

I had the feeling she wanted rid of me, and I wondered what the hell I had done to piss her off. I squeezed James' hand, closing my eyes as the bandage was peeled away from my skin.

"I think you got lucky," she said, tossing the bandage away and laying out the materials to apply a new one. "It doesn't look like you ripped anything too badly, but you'll need to stay still. I'll get you some more pain medicine."

"Can I get something else?"

"It's the strongest thing the doctor approved."

"Then, I'll take the third or fourth strongest. I don't like feeling so foggy when I'm awake." It was too much like being back there. Reliving what Gabe had put me through.

"I'll see what the doctor says." She taped my shoulder back up, then pressed a button on the IV machine and walked out.

"What's with her getting all flippy because I want something weaker?"

"She seems flippy in general," Trent said. He eyed me for a moment then looked at James. "We're keeping a couple of people on you until we catch her—"

"I heard, but if she wanted me dead, I would be." I turned to James. "She asked about you. Seemed to think you were dead, but I—"

"It's okay," he whispered.

"They're watching you, too?"

"Currently, by default." He smiled, but I failed to see any humor in it.

"Alley didn't deserve to be put back out on the streets. Why didn't someone make sure she—"

"She refused everything," Trent explained. "Didn't want 'blood money'. The detectives even found her family, but she wouldn't have anything to do with them."

I grimaced, the pain was fading, but the confusion settled in again. That damn nurse had pushed through another round of morphine. I blinked, trying to hang on to whatever conversation we were having. "She said her family was gone."

Trent must've noticed my condition, because he turned and checked the IV machine she'd messed with. "I think it was more like she was afraid to face them after everything."

That sounded too familiar. Not that I hadn't been trying to avoid my family before the abduction, but I had become particularly expert at it since coming back.

"I'm going to grab a doctor," Trent said.

"Silver...." James began as soon as Trent was gone.

"You're going to have to break that habit. Kirk and Silver are gone—"

"They have been for a long time, Sugar."

Hearing that word roll from his lips tickled my nerve endings, a mix of pleasure and pain. Just like every moment with him. My eyes burned, and I squeezed them shut. "You —you're the one that requested this stupid protective detail, aren't you? Does that mean you're planning on leaving me alone?"

"She found you and came into your house to attack you, but it was Trent who ordered it."

"You avoided the second question." The swell of emotions cut off my air. "Maybe the doctors were right. You're the only person I feel connected to. I held on to that for the last four weeks. I couldn't move on, but even with you here. I—" I wanted to erase my life as Silver. That's why I had tried so hard to keep the two identities separate, but now, there was no way to reconcile that with my feelings for James. "I don't think I can do this either."

James stood over me in silence. I couldn't look at him,

I'd end up looking in his eyes and that was something I simply couldn't handle.

"This time I get to make the call. James and Rose don't even know each other."

I struggled to inhale as he nodded and stepped back just as Trent came back in the room.

"Make sure she's safe," James said as he passed.

I dropped my head to the pillow and waited for pain medicine to grant me oblivion.

———

AFTER A FITFUL NIGHT OF SLEEP, I stared out the open window of my hospital room.

"Do you need a ride?" Trent asked, disturbing my peace. He dropped a pair of scrubs on the end of the bed. "Doctor said he'd send in your release papers soon."

"Glad they tell you all of my business." I wondered how many pairs of scrubs I'd end up owing the hospital by the end of all of this. Better yet, I wanted to know if there was an end.

Trent rubbed his hand through his hair. He wasn't leaving whether I said yes or no.

I took a deep breath and rolled to face him.

"You saved his life," he said. "And he's going to kill me for saying anything to you."

"I just returned the favor." I didn't want to think about Kirk lying on the floor bleeding in the Outlook, or the splatter of blood that coated the wall when I shot Gabe. Whatever I'd done to save him was paid off, since I was also alive.

"I don't mean when he was shot, or...." His voice trailed off and I assumed he knew all the details. "I mean.

He was losing it in there. You—gave him something to fight for again."

"What are you trying to do?" My chest burned. This was exactly what I didn't need.

"I know you're not ready, and I know that everyone keeps telling you both to move on separately, but you found something in each other that gave you the ability to fight through things that would have broken most people. And, seeing you both without that...." He shook his head. "I don't think they were right in keeping you two apart. If you're mad at James because—"

"It just hurts." I licked my lips, trying to put the pain into words. "I'm not Silver anymore and he's not Kirk. If not for any of that we wouldn't have met and... how do I let go while hanging on?"

Trent shook his head. "I don't know, but I think you two make each other stronger."

I looked out the window again. I was tired of being an emotional wreck.

"I'll step out so you can get dressed. Want me to send in a nurse to help?"

After yesterday, I wanted nothing to do with the nurses, so I shook my head. I could figure out how to dress myself. Luckily, they somehow seemed to find a top that buttoned up, so I slid it over my injured arm first and then fiddled with the buttons until I was covered. That just left me to pull the pants on without twisting my right arm or extending it.

It was going to be a miracle if I didn't starve to death by the time my arm healed. I wasn't even sure I could take a shower, and I really didn't want to know how I was going to manage to change into most of my shirts since I didn't have a single button up shirt.

Chapter Twenty-Three

LEARNING TO HEAL

I WAS thankful that Trent had a cleaning crew come in, but there was still a partial blood stain down the wall when I got home. At least painting would give me something productive to do. I curled up on the couch, and Trapper decided to take up residence on my feet as I dozed through the afternoon and early evening.

I finally roused myself enough to think about ordering food, but I didn't have the energy to get off the couch and make the call. As I laid there debating, the doorbell rang.

"Trapper, when will you learn to answer the door?" I said. She jumped off my feet and bounded into the kitchen. *Freeloader.*

I wasn't surprised to peek through the window and see Trent, but his usually stern demeanor was hunched, and his face was somber. I jerked open the door, hoping that it didn't have something to do with James.

"Can I come in?"

I couldn't swallow. "James?"

"He's fine, I just talked to him." He waved his hand, silently asking for permission to enter.

I stepped back, my feet moving like iron posts trapped against a magnetic floor. Barely able to hold myself up, I leaned against the door as I closed it.

"Maybe we should sit down and talk," he said, running a hand through his hair. He stepped toward the living room, but I didn't follow.

My thoughts still swirled around James. If he's fine, what else could have possibly happened that could warrant this reaction? Was the rest of Milo's group coming for us? Had Alley told them where to find us? Every time Trent paused—even if only for a few seconds—it gave my mind long enough to speed through a dozen scenarios I didn't want to consider. "Just say it."

Trent lowered his head but kept eye contact. "We found Alley."

My heart jumped. "Can I see her?" She'd just shot me, but there was something off about her. I wanted to help her. I needed to know she was okay.

He pressed his lips together and shook his head.

"What happened?" I grabbed for the door knob as everything spun.

Capturing my arm, Trent steadied me and helped me to the living room where I could sit down.

"She overdosed on heroin. They couldn't—"

"Don't," I yelled. I felt like it was partially my fault. I should have checked on her, made sure everything was okay, but I was wrapped up in my own damn misery.

"Rose." He knelt in front of me, but I pushed him away and climbed over him.

I covered my mouth with my hand, pacing back and forth in the middle of the living room.

"She refused anyone's help, Rose. We tried. You can't blame yourself; you don't know that she would have reacted any differently to you three weeks ago."

"You don't know that." I wanted to rip out my hair. Fall to the floor. Scream and cry. It was like getting shot all over again. My body shut down and refused to do anything to help deflect the emotions coursing through me. "Please leave."

"You shouldn't be alone right now." Trent reached for me and I backed away again.

"I want to be alone right now," I yelled. "And I'm fucking tired of people still telling me what to do. I'm not a slave; I can take care of myself."

I pushed him to the front door, but before I could open it, he dug in his heels.

"I'll leave you alone," he said, and then he pulled out a piece of paper. "It's James' number. If you change your mind, I want you to have it, and if not, he won't know that I gave it to you."

I took it and threw it on the table next to the stairs. He nodded and walked out without another argument. I watched through the window as he went back to his car, but it didn't move. The rat bastard was going to sit out there until he was satisfied. I turned my back and slid down the wall, sitting there and staring into space until Trapper ran up and pawed at my arm.

After pouring the cat a bowl of tuna, I sat down with my phone, dialing a number I knew by heart, but hadn't used in months.

"What the hell, Twig?" Chey said as soon as she answered the phone.

"Don't call me that. I hated it when we were kids, I hate it now." My parents had started the trend; it had nothing to do with my size. It all started when I was four and decided to try and cut my own hair. I don't know what they were thinking, but the damn name stuck, and since Chey was only two years older than me, it ended up getting around to most of my friends and half the school.

I heard her sigh. "You okay? We're worried about you."

I groaned. "I'm fantastic." I took a couple of long breaths before I could continue. "I got shot."

"Shot?" Something thumped in the background. "After—"

"I'm good," I said before she could freak out any more. "I'm home, safe, a cop is watching the house, but they found the person who did it."

"Then, why is the cop still there?"

Ah, fuck. There was no good way to answer that question that wouldn't cause even more worry. *Because I have difficulty dealing with life in the real world.* Even a simple, "because he's worried," wasn't going to go over well. I stared at the ceiling, unable to formulate an answer.

"Rose?" Chey began softly. "You should come home for a while. You can stay here."

I swallowed a laugh. "I'm not good company. How's the baby?" I wanted to talk about anything else.

"She wants to meet you."

I wasn't falling for that. Even the baby wasn't going to make me anymore sociable. "She's seven weeks old; she just wants food and a clean diaper."

"If it was all that simple, I'd sleep a lot more." There was a pause, and I heard muffled voices and pops. "Peter's here. He's worried about you, too."

Perfect. I was considering going to town and having a few dozen cards printed up that said stop fucking worrying about me.

I felt even the smallest laugh in my shoulder, but slowly, as we talked everything unraveled inside of me. "What'd we fight about again?"

"Oh same old, same old. I'm sorry Rose, just come home for a while."

"I'm sorry, too, but I need to do this. I'm not always the greatest at communication and people shit, and I'm going to try, but I'm not ready to be around people all the time." My family knew enough to understand why I hadn't been the same, but that was all I was ready to give up. I needed space. I needed to not have to explain myself and the crazy dreams.

"You have someone to talk to?"

"Yeah, they throw me in with a shrink twice a week. And there's...." *James*. The only person who'd really come close to not needing an explanation. "The cop who's watching the house has been checking in on me."

"Because," she dragged the word out. "He's afraid someone else will come after you or that you'll do something?"

Suddenly, the conversation about our fight seemed like a better alternative. "So, you and Peter are engaged?"

"Rose. Which is it?"

"I don't think he believes I'll call and ask for help if I need it. Nothing to worry about."

"That's quite an obligation from just some cop."

I should have never let that tidbit slip out. "I'm not ready to go into this, Chey. Give me the you and Peter gossip. Give me gossip about Mom and Dad, Uncle Ben, anything, just give me something normal."

"We are engaged and seeing a counselor, once a week. Apparently, I'm not so great with communicating either, but we're doing better. I'm sorry I dragged you into the middle of all of that and then abandoned you."

"And I'm sorry that I get bull-headed and don't want to listen. Let's just put it behind us. It's about damn time, right?"

Chey changed the subject to crazy stories from our childhood, like the time she'd tried going down the slide on a board, and it caught her pants and ripped them off.

By the time we were done with our hour-long conversation, I was too sleepy to even consider dinner, but at least I didn't feel like I was going out of my mind.

———

I GASPED, clawing at the comforter on the bed, tears still rolling down my cheeks. Or maybe they were new tears; it was becoming too hard to tell.

Rolling over, I glanced at the clock, it was three am. I couldn't breathe. My body shook. And the more my mind went over everything, the worse it got. I grabbed my phone and the crumpled-up note that I'd tucked in the drawer, dialing the number before the numbness wore off too much and I talked myself out of it.

"Hello." A barely-there voice answered.

I sobbed at the sound of his voice, unable to even utter a single word.

"Hello?" he repeated, stronger this time. "Are you okay?"

I sucked in a breath. "No."

There was silence, and I hoped he hadn't hung up for some reason.

"Rose?"

"I'm sorry," I cried.

"What can I do for you?"

"Talk…. Say anything… Just… She's dead." I collapsed against the pillow as another fit of sobs tore at the hole in my arm.

"I know," he whispered. "Take a breath, Rose."

I wanted to ask him to come over. Come hold me. Make the fear and sadness go away. "I'm sorry for what I said to you."

"I get it. You needed to speak your mind. I'm glad you did and I'm glad you called."

I bit my lip. I had no idea what else to say. Waves of emotions crashed in my chest, but I had no words that would make sense.

"Are you okay?" James asked after a long silence.

"No." Okay didn't seem to even exist. I felt guilty for not reaching out to Alley. She'd been my friend. She'd played a part in making a horrible situation not so bad, and I never thought to do the same for her. The investigators and doctors told me to stay clear of everyone involved, but she needed someone, and it should have been me.

"Will you be okay long enough for me to get dressed and drive there?"

"I—" *Come on, this is what you wanted.* "I can be." All I had to do was convince myself of that. I went through the house and turned on all the lights, hoping that'd make me feel less alone, then I got paranoid that someone outside could see my shadow through the curtains, so I went back through and turned them all off again.

It had only been ten minutes since I disconnected the phone with James, but it felt like two hours and I had no idea how far away he was. I dragged my fingers through my hair and paced through the hallway until I saw headlights coming up the street. I had the door open before he even made it to the front steps.

"Easy, honey," he said, taking my face between his hands and kissing my forehead. He glanced around then pulled me to the living room.

We curled up on the couch. I enjoyed the simple warmth of his body pressing against my back for a long time before either of us spoke.

"I just have one question," he said. "How'd you get my number?"

"Um…" I bit my lip.

"Trent?"

I nodded. "When he came to tell me about—"

Trapper bounded down the stairs and stopped in the foyer to stretch before continuing on into the kitchen.

"There's my little hobo." I mumbled. "I've been—I wanted to pretend that none of that was me. It was all Silver, and she's gone now." I shook my head and turned to face him. "I was pissed at you for disappearing, but if I cut off Silver and let her die, then nothing exists between you and me."

He pushed back my hair. "It's impossible to make it so black and white. You survived. We survived together. And as much as I'd like to erase some things. It'll always be part of us. We both have a lot of work to do. We can't exactly pick up where we left off and we can't just forget what happened."

His eyes were different. It was far more than being exhausted because I had woken him up in the middle of the night. He'd become distant and detached. "What happened to shedding it all away or smothering?"

"It takes time." He wrapped his arms tightly around me and tucked me against his chest again, kissing the top of my head as I relaxed. "And work. And maybe something to work toward."

A smile tugged at the corners of my mouth. *Something to work toward.* I'd been concentrating on where I had come from, just getting through the day, and hoping it'd finally be the day things would feel normal again. It was time to rewrite my idea of normal. But there was still one thing that stood in the way of what I wanted. "Together?" I asked, hoping that he felt the same way.

"You sure you want to try that?" he asked.

"Yes. But I don't want you to do it for me."

"Good." He rested his cheek on top of my head. "But maybe we should work on becoming friends first."

I grunted and glared up at him. "I assume that means no sex." We used sex to avoid everything else—going back to that would only make it harder to move on. But at the same time, I wanted his hands all over me. I wanted him to ease the pain, to help me remember the good. We had to find a new way to do that. "Anything else?"

He shrugged, dragging his fingers mindlessly through my hair. "We stop apologizing about anything that happened and try to act like it didn't happen."

"Easier said than done. You might have to remind me a time or two, but I can handle that."

James chuckled. "If I only have to remind you a time or two, I'll be worried."

I twisted around just to see the smile on his face. For those four weeks, we'd shared more than an apartment and our bodies. We'd shared the pain, our fears, secrets, trust. Things that I couldn't put into simple words. We came through it, and even though every day was still a struggle, simply having him next to me again made me want to keep fighting. I wasn't ready to let the feeling go again, even if only for a few hours. "Does no sex include sleeping in the same bed?"

"If you want me to stay, I'll sleep down here. We're both tired, and even I can only resist so much." He kissed my neck.

"Yeah, do that again, and I'll make it much harder."

"Go to bed, Rose. You're exhausted and so am I. We'll talk more—" he glanced at the window where the morning light was just beginning to stream in. "We'll talk more this afternoon."

———

SOMEONE KNOCKED on the door and I shot out of bed, pulling a robe over my pajamas. I glanced out the window, but I didn't see any cars that I recognized. The knock sounded again, and I sprinted down the stairs. Through the thin curtains next to the door, I saw a female figure and yanked the door open. "Chey and…." I looked down at the carrier in her hand. "You said, but—you didn't have to drive up here with her."

"No…" she looked past me then raised her eyebrows. "Is *that* your protective detail?"

My face heated, and I followed her gaze. James was standing in the doorway of the living room in his jeans and the white tank he'd worn under his T-shirt.

"Chey, this is K—" *Fuck.* "James. James, my sister Chey and her daughter Laney."

"Nice to meet you," James said with a nod.

"And you," Chey drawled.

I punched her in the arm, and she gently shoved me back.

"I'm holding a baby."

"And I'm swinging with my weak arm." I lowered my voice. "No flirting, you're engaged."

"I still have eyes." She leaned in and whispered as she passed. "Since when do you go for tats?"

I grunted and closed the door, following her into the living room.

James pulled on his T-shirt and shoes.

"You don't have to leave," I said. We weren't even done with our conversation, and I had just gotten him back.

"You should spend time with your family, we can talk anytime." He leaned over to kiss me, but I refused to let him say goodbye.

"At least stay for lunch."

James snickered. "You cooking?"

Of course, he went right for the low blow. "I've gotten damn good at spaghetti."

He raised his eyebrows and made a sound in his throat. "Uh huh. Without burning it?"

"So, this totally wasn't a one-night stand!" Chey said, lifting the baby out of the carrier, and eyeing both me and James.

My jaw dropped, and I covered my face with a hand. "You've got to be kidding me."

"Come on." She giggled. "Just kidding. I'll be good."

James' hands touched my waist pulling me close and as I dropped my hand, he kissed my lips. "How about I go pick up something to eat. You two can do the sister thing and then we'll all have lunch."

I pressed my lips together, he was getting a kick out of my embarrassment, but I nodded and followed him out to the foyer just to smack him in the arm.

"You're violent today," he whispered. "Are you sure you want me here? Or is there a reason—"

"I want to spend time with you. We're supposed to be moving on, right? I just...." *I need you.* I wasn't sure if it was healthy to need a person so much that my chest ached.

"I'll be back," he promised, tracing his thumb over my lips.

I peeked in the living room to see Chey with little Laney tucked over her shoulder.

"I'm going to take something for my shoulder, I'll be back." I pulled myself to the upstairs bathroom and swallowed down two pain pills. I thought about changing out of my pajamas, but I wasn't sure I had it in me to put on anything that didn't involve a drawstring, so I headed back down and curled up on the couch next to Chey, watching her feed Laney a bottle.

"You didn't have to drive two hours to check on me," I said.

"I wanted to see you. Even if most of the trip was driving. Oh, and—" She tried to keep a straight face but cracked a smile that captured her entire face. "I thought I should ask you in person to be the maid-of-honor at my wedding."

My mouth fell awkwardly open for the second time in ten minutes. "When?"

"September, so you have about four months, but you can always come down and help me pick out my wedding dress in the meantime."

Normal. It hadn't been what I was striving for since I got home—it had been what I was running away from. "I'd love it. Just no asking me to babysit while you try them on."

"She's not going to bite," Chey teased.

"You really don't know that." I ran my fingers over Laney's short, soft hair. It was already dark, just like Chey's.

"She looks like you. That's a sure sign that she's a pain in the ass."

"Well…," she drew out the word. "I might have to give you that one."

Chey shifted Laney around and resting her against her shoulder to burp her. "Want to attempt to hold her?"

"Nope," I said, putting my hand up. I could have blamed my shoulder, but even I didn't trust myself with something that fragile.

Chey just laughed and leaned back. She looked so natural with the baby tucked in her arm—I'd never call it easy, but it suited her.

"I'm really surprised you called last night," she said.

I sighed. "Me, too. But nine months of being a stubborn bitch is a bit excessive."

"Sometimes tough love is the only thing that gets through." She half smiled and raised her eyebrows. "You were right, and I didn't want to hear it. I don't want to lose you. Or Peter. And especially not little Laney. You were the only one who straight up told me how stupid I was being."

"Well, at least you know I love you, no matter what." I pulled my feet onto the couch and leaned my head against the back.

"And vice versa. If you ever need someone to talk to, you know I'll be there. Especially if you want to dish about the sexy man you've been keeping in your living room."

I smacked the cushion next to me but couldn't keep a straight face. "I haven't been keeping him anywhere. He's a friend and…."

"And?" her voice almost squeaked.

"He gets it. He got me out of there. Made sure I was safe." I bit my lip, holding everything back before the emotions swelled up behind the flood gates.

―――――

JAMES WAS BACK within half an hour with hamburgers, fries, and shakes from the dairy bar, so Chey put Laney back in the carrier and we moved to the kitchen and everyone chowed down in relative silence. I was thankful since I wasn't entirely sure of the last time, I'd eaten more than a snack-sized meal.

"Bathroom?" Chey asked, dumping her wrappers into the trashcan.

"You're going to leave me alone with the kid?" I asked.

"I'm not going to be that long and you have back up." She waved at James.

But, just like any time I had ever been left with a kid, as soon as Chey stepped out of the room, Laney started to fuss.

"Know anything about babies?" I grimaced.

James squinted at me and grunted. "They like being held."

"I'll get right on that." I pointed to my shoulder.

James shook his head, and lifted Laney out of the carrier, rocking her against his chest. She fussed for a few seconds longer then quieted and took the pacifier.

"Show off." I muttered, clearing off the rest of the table.

Chey stopped in the doorway and snickered. "You really did pass her off to him."

I dropped back into my seat. "Bullet hole in the arm, people. What the heck am *I* going to do?"

"Excuses," Chey teased, picking up her daughter and loading her back into the carrier. "I better get going. Don't forget you promised to go dress shopping with me." She wagged her finger at me.

"Yeah, yeah, although I'm not sure I *promised* anything."
We hugged, and I fluffed up Laney's hair. "Call me."

As soon as Chey and Laney left, James' arm came around my waist and pulled me against him. I twisted, wrapping my uninjured arm behind his neck.

"I told you everything would be fine with you two," he said, he brushed his palms against his pants and stared toward the door. "I should get going too."

I nodded and groaned. I knew I couldn't keep him there, but I wanted him to myself for a little longer. I watched his eyes as his gaze took in my face. His fingers brushed through my hair.

"How are you?" I asked. Seemed a stupid question to ask now, after he'd been at my house all day, but I still didn't know.

He pulled away, shaking his head and pressing his lips together. "I'm here. And I'm alive, thanks to you, but…." Leaning against the counter, he let out a long breath. "Are you really sure you want me around, after everything I did to you?"

So many times, I had tried to imagine what it must have been like for him. "Yes, James. I already forgave you."

"How?" His eyebrows wrinkled, pressing together over his pained eyes. "Every time I get close…." He trailed off shaking his head.

I dropped my shoulders and wrapped my arm around his waist. "It wasn't so hard actually. You told me that my only choice was to give up control or die, but it applied to you, too. And unless you played your part, we both died. Once I started seeing the real you, the emotion and regret you tried to hide, I didn't have it in me to hate you for something you obviously hated, too."

He smiled, but I could tell it was all for show. "You're a strong woman, Sugar."

My lips curled at the nickname. On one hand, I felt like I should run away from it, but I loved the way my insides melted every time it came out of his mouth. "Stronger than I was a few months ago. It still hurts, every day it still hurts, and after the last two days... I just want something good to hold onto."

"It's going to take a lot of work."

"We've already escaped hell, I don't think 'work' is going to stop us." I stretched up to kiss his lips, and he drew me up and against his body. The no sex rule was definitely going to take the most work.

vinci-books.com/skyunbreakable

In a world of shadows, her love is the light that refuses to let me fall.

The bullet should have killed me, but it didn't. I woke up to her tear-streaked face, my body broken but alive.

Turn the page for a preview…

Unbreakable: Chapter One

ALIVE

"HOW MANY WOMEN did you have sex with while you were there?"

This was the third time Dr. Combs had asked me that question. And for the third time, I wanted to avoid it.

I had just gotten out of that hell, and I still had the bullet hole in my chest to prove it, but that didn't stop my boss from pushing the psychiatric evaluation. What he expected it to accomplish right now, I had no clue—I was tired, cranky, and I didn't give a damn about getting my old job back.

Dr. Combs cleared her throat, and I clenched my jaw, still trying to block her out. Some things were left unspoken —better suited to the imagination of nightmares and horror movies than to be discussed openly with any other living person.

I didn't even want to admit the number of women to myself; even though I could see every one of the girls in my mind.

Kat, the red-headed braggart who thought she owned every man who walked into the Retreat.

Gabby, the indignant curly haired brunette.

Raini, a gorgeous but frail girl who was transferred in right after I went undercover. I had feared that one more night in Ross's bed would kill her before her first week was up.

Alley, a blond sweetheart who belonged to Miles, my unconventional friend.

Silver, the girl who simultaneously ruined and saved me.

She was the only reason I was alive, and the only reason I had what was left of my soul—except she wasn't real. Like my undercover alias, Kirk, she was forged from necessity and determination. Now she was gone, and that missing piece was more painful than the hole the bullet had ripped through my side.

That crazy, obstinate woman wouldn't back down. During the raid on the "sex retreat", Ross had turned the gun on me, but she knocked him off balance and I ended up with a graze along my left side rather than a hole through my heart. The bullet splintered two ribs in the process, and left a long and bloody gash, but they'd managed to clean it up in surgery, and so far it was healing without complications.

Now, somewhere out there Rose was learning to live her own life again.

At least that's what I hoped. The day after I was shot, my superiors had me transferred to another hospital and put under protective custody until they were sure I was "safe".

I was fairly positive they were more concerned that any real threat to my life would come from me since there were very few people who knew of my undercover involvement in the operation.

The only company I had been allowed since then was Dr. Combs, my new shrink. I didn't want a shrink. I wanted the woman who saved me—the only person who stood a chance of bringing me any kind of peace.

The woman I could never have.

All I wanted to do was close my eyes and wait for the doctor to leave. But that would put me in a worse situation since she'd just report me for being difficult.

One fucking week.

I still had a hole in my fucking side for Christ sake.

"I want to talk to Trent—this no visitor thing is bull shit."

"It's for your own safety, and we can't do anything until you cooperate."

"Don't preach to me about cooperating." One of the machines next to me screeched and a stabbing pain radiated through my arm, but I'd felt much worse. "I gave up my life to do what was asked of me and I succeeded."

"You need to relax," she warned, reaching a hand toward me.

I shook it off as best as I could in my current condition. I didn't fucking want to relax. I wanted what little I had of my life back.

And, most of all I wanted someone I had no right to want.

"James."

She was just going to stand there and keep yammering.

"With all due respect, Doctor, fuck off."

"I'll have to compile my preliminary evaluation before we can move forward. That'd go much smoother if you'd help me out."

Help. I guess as far as not listening—even for my own supposed good—I could give Silver a run for her money. I waited in silence as a nurse adjusted and silenced the beeping machine. Quiet moments of solitude ticked away—my respite from being expected to answer questions, but it didn't last.

"I don't want to talk about the women," I said when the door closed again. The steady stream of medication weighed down my body and softened my voice, so I didn't sound as menacing as I intended. "I don't much feel like talking about anything, but can we just skip the women and the fucking?"

"All of the women?" Dr. Combs asked, with her usual flat exaggerated calm. "Or is there someone in particular you don't want to discuss?"

I figured pointing out that she was still talking about what I'd asked her not to—regardless of my answer—would be a waste of breath. "You know there is. How about you let me talk to her and I'll answer any damn question you like?"

I didn't even have to glance over to know she was scowling. They wouldn't let me see Trent, my best friend and contact during the investigation, I knew they sure as hell wouldn't let me see Silver… Rose. I didn't even know what the hell I was supposed to call her. She'd made it perfectly clear the few times I'd pressed about her past or used her real name that I had no role in that life.

"She's fine," Dr. Combs assured me. "But I don't think it would be in the best interest of either of you to see each other. You put yourself in a dangerous situation with her."

Put myself? Last I checked I wasn't the one to drag her into the Retreat. "I kept her alive and slightly less broken than she would have otherwise been."

"The two of you adapted to a horrible situation, found comfort in each other—"

I didn't want to hear it.

Stockholm Syndrome.

I wondered if the captor could get it too. Was I even the captor? It seemed like I'd lost control of the situation long ago.

But I'd still been the one to beat her, rape her, bend her will.

Just like she'd bent mine.

I wanted her back so badly I couldn't breathe. The more we talked about it, the worse it got. The harsh reality of it all forced me to face the possibility that I had to walk away if I wanted to do what was in her best interest.

"How long until I can talk to Trent?" I tried again, drawing back a modicum of control by changing the course of the conversation.

Dr. Combs sighed and snapped her portfolio closed. "If it'll get you to talk, I'll make the arrangements on one condition."

I'd already sold my soul, there weren't many more concessions I had left to give.

"I need to know you're not going to try to reach out to Rose—or anyone else."

Did that mean there was a chance she'd see me? Or was Dr. Combs convinced I'd stalk and abduct her anyway? That was quite a laughable possibility, but some sick-as-fuck part of me considered it. "How long are you going to dictate who I can talk to?"

"As long as it's in your best interest. You and Rose need time to heal—being together puts you at a higher risk to continue your relationship based on circumstances that are not ideal. You have to separate yourself from what you became and the things you did in order to survive."

Kirk and Silver no longer exist—she didn't have to outright say it. James and Rose were strangers.

"Four weeks," Dr. Combs said. "Give it at least that long before we discuss the possibility of you two communicating. And even then, you have to face the possibility that it's better for you both to move on separately."

"I know," I growled. It was a tough pill to swallow, but I wasn't going to force myself on her. Again. "And if that's what she wants, I'll give it to her."

"Because you'd give up just about anything to make sure she's safe and happy?"

There was a trap in that question, and even hyped up on whatever the doctors and nurses were feeding me, I wasn't stupid enough to fall for it. There wasn't a right answer. Just like there hadn't been a right answer when I'd found Silver in the basement with Gabe and his group of clods.

"I'll agree to your conditions."

"Are you going to be staying with Trent when you're released?"

"That's a stupid question considering your refusal to let me talk to anyone." I had somewhat of a plan—not one set in stone, but I had given up my apartment, left my belongings in storage and my car with Trent. I knew I'd be coming back to nothing. "I have a cousin nearby."

"Family would be good for you."

"That's only a possibility if no one is coming after me. The last thing I'll do is put my family in danger." Especially since they had a two-year-old living there, too.

"Lucky for you, they all think Kirk is dead. Bled out on the operating table."

"Lucky me," I said drowsily. Kirk *was* dead. He was staying that way.

But Dr. Combs assurance only really told me one thing —they were keeping me isolated because they didn't trust me, not because they were afraid of someone coming after me.

————

AS PROMISED, Trent came in the next morning, and my visitor restrictions were lifted—to an extent. The doctor's new rules still only allowed for Trent and close family members.

I rubbed the exhaustion from my eyes—running a marathon was less tiresome than laying in a bed for days on end, and the meds didn't help. "Fucking hospitable of them to finally let me have visitors the day before I'm supposed to be released."

"I hear you've been quite the agreeable patient, too. It's no wonder they won't let you talk to anyone, they probably want to keep you around." He wheeled over the tall stool from the corner and took a seat next to me. It was nearly eight in the morning, and no surprise, he was already dressed in his suit and tie—all ready for work. I think the thing he liked most about suits was the shocked expression he usually got when people saw below the layers of fabric. He had more tattoos than me, and I wouldn't have been surprised to hear about a few new ones since the last time we'd actually been able to sit down and have a chat in person.

Tattoos weren't what I cared about though, and happy as I was to see my best friend, first I had to address the issue niggling at my mind.

"Have you talked to Rose?"

Trent grunted and sat back in a chair, propping his feet up on the bed frame. "Just jumping right to the point, eh? I'm not playing double operative for either of you."

"I'll interpret that as a yes."

He glared back at me, but he'd given me enough to keep me sated for a while. I assumed that Dr. Combs had already informed him of the agreement.

"I told Evan you're allowed to have visitors," Trent said, "he's coming in as soon as Katie gets off work to stay with Jack."

Jack, my cousin's two-year-old son. I couldn't even imagine how much he'd grown since I'd gone under. "Why do I get the feeling I'm about to become a live-in babysitter."

"You're good with children—dare I even say—"

"Don't." It was difficult, if not impossible, to be intimidating when covered in wires and tubes.

So, of course, he didn't listen. "You like them."

Sure, as long as they belonged to someone else. Living with them was entirely different. But my other possibility was staying with Trent, dealing with his inconsistent work schedule, and sleeping on his couch, which in my current condition didn't sound appealing. Evan at least had a bed, and a quite nice bed as far as I remembered. And since I had a bullet hole in my chest, no one really wanted me staying by myself too long.

Apparently I might fall apart without warning.

I wasn't going to complain yet. Aside from the locked up storage container, I didn't have much of my own left, and time with my cousin—the only close family I had left—was an easy concession. Having his kid also around meant I wouldn't be asked too many questions. Eventually, I figured

I'd get tired of the attention, but for a little while having some things catered couldn't be so bad.

Trent sat forward, his shoes squeaking as his feet landed against the floor. "Was the opportunity to ask about Rose the only reason you wanted to see me?"

"No, I also wanted to see a face that didn't belong to a doctor or nurse, and who, hopefully, wouldn't ask prying questions."

"I think I know as much as I need to at the moment. Until you're able to file all of your reports anyhow."

"No getting out of that?" They already knew what they needed as far as I was concerned, but all of their questions made me wonder if I was now surrounded by sadists.

"Just like there's no getting out of talking to Dr. Combs," he said coolly.

I grunted and dug my head into the pillow. It wasn't enough that she was in my head, now the doctor was recruiting my friends. "How much is she paying you to say that?"

Trent shook his head and shrugged one shoulder. His gaze dropped and he straightened the cuffs on his sleeves. "You've been thinking about not coming back, haven't you?"

That was probably the sanest idea on my mind at the moment. "I'm thinking that I don't have much left to lose and wondering where I should draw the line."

"You have time to figure it out. And—" he blew out a breath. "Don't worry about Rose—I won't play messenger or double agent, but I'm looking in on her."

Much as it pained me that it was him and not me, I couldn't think of anyone else I'd want taking care of her. "Does she also know you're looking in on me?"

"That's only fair, but I gave her the same deal. I'm here

for you because you're my best friend, and I'm there for her because I'm still involved with the case. Never the twain shall meet."

"Now who's the one with dual lives?" I asked with as much of a smirk as I could muster.

He cocked his head. "How long before they clear you for physical activity?"

"I don't know—when I no longer have the possibility of leaking like a sieve out of my chest, I'd assume."

"Good. Heal up. I need my partner and sparring buddy."

Sparring buddy. Trent and I had started Kendo when we were eleven. This was the longest I'd ever gone without practicing. Right before I'd gone under, we'd both been preparing to test for yon-don—my fourth-degree black belt. "It'll be a while."

"Then, I'll test for yon-don without you."

I scoffed. "I'd assumed you already had."

"That wouldn't have been any fun."

"Right, and it'll be so much fun watching my rusty ass fail." Even though he hadn't tested to rank higher than me, he was more in practice than I was, and I had no doubt that it'd take me a long while to catch up.

"At least it'll give you something to do."

Trent's phone sounded, and he peeked down at the display. "I have to head in. Call me if you need anything."

Unbreakable: Chapter Two

WIN, LOSE, OR DOMINATE

DR. COMBS RETURNED in the afternoon for her daily session of torture and spared me no peace by jumping straight to the worst topic possible.

"Tell me about Silver." The statement rolled off her tongue like an innocent "good afternoon," except she didn't wish a *good* anything.

"That's what you're going to lead with?" The one thing she knew I didn't want to talk about. My muscles tensed, but it only sent a radiating pain across my side until I relaxed.

"The first day she showed up, what happened?" She had no idea what she was asking. Her calm voice a drastic contrast to the mental images conjured by every word she spoke.

"Doesn't matter." It was like fighting off a lion that already had a taste for my blood.

"Did you force her to have sex with you?"

My hands clenched at my sides twisting and curling the thin hospital sheets. "Not then."

I tried to think about anything else, but my mind betrayed me and jumped straight to that night. My heart went into overdrive, fueling the anger that already tainted my blood and sending it to the deepest part of my brain.

That first day. It seemed like it had happened years ago, only because so much had changed since the day I'd first seen her in the basement of the Retreat.

"When? Another day—or night," Dr. Combs continued prying.

"Second night—only because it would've been Ross if not me."

"How did she react to that?"

I blew out a puff of air. "I got her off if that's what you'd like to know."

Dr. Combs scowled.

"See there," I said, laying my arm over my eyes. "You don't really want to hear about it anymore than I want to talk about it."

"Be crude all you want. I'm not judging—"

I slammed my hand down on the bed to stop her lie. "Don't fucking give me that. I was there. There is no fucking way in hell anyone hears about the things I did without some kind of opinion. I'm the bastard, the abuser, rapist, villain, liar, thief—and I get away with it all as far as the law and any official judgment are concerned. I'd be utterly convinced that I'm guaranteed a spot in the deepest pit of Hell if I wasn't holding on to the slim hope that the time I've already spent there was enough to burn away my sins—at the very least it might have burned away my soul, in which case it won't matter much once I die because there won't even be anything left."

She smiled—of all the fucking reactions in the world, she smiled at that?

"Finally getting an honest reaction. I do believe that's the most you've said all week."

I scowled, the distasteful sting of bile assaulted my mouth. "You're a gem, you know that?"

"Back to the topic. Tell me what happened."

"When?" I was done fighting, only because the smile told me that she was quite possibly more sadistic than me.

"Pick a night."

Grab your copy...
vinci-books.com/skyunbreakable

About the Author

Skye Callahan is a bestselling author who enjoys writing fiction to explore the darker aspects of human nature and the resiliency needed to survive and overcome difficult situations. She hopes to show that even through the darkest moments and overwhelming circumstances, one can find the inner strength to adapt and eventually heal.

Skye lives in the hills of Appalachia with her husband and their feline overlords: Sassy, Knight, Raith, Dresden, and Crowley, and enjoys hanging out in the yard with all the natural wildlife (except rattlesnakes). When she's not reading or writing, she might be found in the garden, watching horror movies, or playing video games with the hubs. Prior to pursuing writing full-time, Skye earned an M.A. in History and participated in numerous local history projects, including a full-length Civil War documentary for PBS.